Alex Pine was born and raised ... South London and left school at sixtee... ...ong, he embarked on a career in journalism, which took him all over the world – many of the stories he covered were crime-related. Among his favourite hobbies are hiking and water-based activities, so he and his family have spent lots of holidays in the Lake District. He now lives with his wife on a marina close to the New Forest on the South Coast – providing him with the best of both worlds! This is his second novel.

By the same author:

The Christmas Killer

THE
KILLER
IN THE
SNOW

ALEX PINE

avon.

Published by AVON
A division of HarperCollins*Publishers*
1 London Bridge Street
London SE1 9GF

www.harpercollins.co.uk

HarperCollins*Publishers*
1st Floor, Watermarque Building, Ringsend Road
Dublin 4, Ireland

www.harpercollins.co.uk

A Paperback Original 2021

2

First published in Great Britain by HarperCollins*Publishers* 2021

Typeset in Minion Pro by Palimpsest Book Production Ltd, Falkirk, Stirlingshire
Printed and Bound in the UK using 100% Renewable Electricity
at CPI Group (UK) Ltd

MIX
Paper from
responsible sources
FSC
www.fsc.org   FSC® C007454

This one is for Tommy – the latest addition to the family.

Introducing DI Walker and his team...

This is the second book in the DI James Walker series. For those who haven't read the first, *The Christmas Killer*, here is a brief introduction to the man himself and the key members of his team.

DETECTIVE INSPECTOR JAMES WALKER, AGED 40

An officer with the Cumbria Constabulary based in Kendal. He spent 20 years with the Met in London before moving to the quiet village of Kirkby Abbey. He's married to Annie, aged 36, who was born in the village and works as a teacher.

DETECTIVE CHIEF INSPECTOR JEFF TANNER, AGED 46

James's boss and a highly experienced officer who prefers to delegate rather than investigate. He's married with a son.

DETECTIVE SERGEANT PHIL STEVENS, AGED 38

A no-nonsense detective who got off on the wrong foot with James because he was in line for the DI job when the man from London arrived on the scene and took it. Now a loyal colleague, he is married with two children.

DETECTIVE CONSTABLE JESSICA ABBOTT, AGED 33

Youngest member of the team and of Irish and East African descent. She's sassy, as sharp as a razor, and not afraid to speak her mind. She has the closest working relationship with James. Her boyfriend is a paramedic.

PROLOGUE

Sunday December 24th

It was 6.30 p.m. on Christmas Eve and Robert Bateman felt like getting drunk. He accepted that it would have to wait until he got home though, as he didn't dare risk being stopped and breathalysed by the police. That'd be a disastrous end to what had already been a crap day.

He decided instead to polish off what was left in his glass and resist the urge to order another pint at the bar.

Mary had expected him home ages ago. He'd phoned her directly after his meeting in Kendal with the bank manager, telling her he was on his way. But rather than drive straight to the farm – which would have taken him only about thirty minutes – he'd opted to make a pit stop at his favourite pub, The King's Head, in Kirkby Abbey.

He'd hoped it would allow him time to calm down and get his thoughts together before facing his wife and daughter. But after nursing his beer for almost an hour, his insides were still tied up in an anxious knot.

It wouldn't have been so bad if it was just the news from

the bank manager that he had to worry about. But there was also the text he'd received earlier, which had planted a heavy weight in his chest. He tugged his phone from his pocket to read it again and found it just as alarming as he had when he'd first seen it.

I've had enough now and I'm not going to take any more of your shit. You're about to discover that I don't make empty threats, Bateman.

It seemed like the pressure was being ramped up by the hour and there was nothing he could do about it.

It didn't help that he knew he was solely responsible for the fact that they were being forced to sell the farm. He'd failed to rise to the challenge of keeping the business afloat during tough times, and he'd made matters worse by trying to reduce the mountain of debt through gambling, as he'd placed far more bad bets than good ones.

Now he had no choice but to make his wife aware of the true extent of their financial woes. She knew that they were going to have to leave Oaktree Farm, their home for over twenty years, but she had no idea how much money they would still owe even after that. Or just how hard it was going to be to get back on their feet.

They were both in their early fifties and the farm had been their life for two decades. Job prospects for people like them were pretty dire, and it seemed highly unlikely that he'd be able to get another business off the ground at this stage.

It was no wonder, therefore, that he was weighed down by guilt. He'd let his family down. And now he was going to have to face the consequences.

He looked around at the other customers in the bar. They all lived in the village and he'd known most of them for years. He would certainly miss them if he and Mary were forced to move away from the area, something they might have to consider given the mess they were in.

The thought that this could be their last Christmas as part of the community filled him with sadness. He so wished it hadn't come to this.

He issued a heavy sigh before finishing the last of his beer. Then he pushed his chair back, stood and pulled on his padded, waterproof jacket. He was about to head for the door when he paused, deciding to buy some booze to take home.

Martha Grooms, the landlady, was behind the bar. She was a large woman in her sixties with an oval face framed by shapeless grey hair.

When she saw him, she said, 'I'm sorry I haven't had a chance to come over and chat to you, Rob. But as you can see, we're busy this evening.'

'No problem, Martha,' he replied. 'I only popped in for a swift one. I've been into Kendal for a meeting with the bank manager. Now I have to get home to the missus.'

'And how is Mary?'

'Oh, she's grand, thanks.'

'Will we be seeing you over Christmas? We've still got spaces if you want to come for lunch tomorrow, and we're laying on a special Boxing Day buffet.'

Robert shrugged. 'I'll have to speak to Mary. She's got loads in. My daughter Charlotte and her boyfriend Neil are staying with us. But if they're up for it, I am.'

'Well, pass on my best wishes if you all decide to stay at the farm.'

'I will. Now before I go, can you give me two bottles of your house white wine and a bottle of sherry?'

'Coming right up,' she said, and moments later passed them to him in a plastic carrier bag.

He paid her in cash and she handed over the change along with a receipt.

Outside, the temperature had plummeted and the snow that had fallen earlier lay like a blanket across the village. Once Robert was behind the wheel of his Land Rover he switched on the heater.

As he pulled out of the car park, he tried to force his mind away from his mounting problems so that he could concentrate on driving. Home was nine miles from the village and the ice and uncleared snow made the roads treacherous.

The journey along the winding country lanes was slow and thankfully uneventful, and he finally arrived home just before seven.

Oaktree Farm was situated off the beaten track between two of Cumbria's many spectacular fells. It gave off the only light for miles around.

Robert pulled up in the large front yard between the two-storey house and the old barn. He switched off the ignition, then the lights.

He told himself that he wouldn't burden Mary with their money worries until after Boxing Day when their lawyer came to the farm for the meeting he had arranged. Instead, he would try his best to make this an enjoyable family Christmas. After all, the last time he saw Charlotte was when they got together to celebrate Mary's fifty-fifth birthday three weeks ago. Their daughter had moved into Neil's flat in Kendal back in June and since then had only visited the farm a handful of times.

He was looking forward to finding out how the pair were getting on and if Charlotte was enjoying her new job as a shop assistant in the town.

As he stepped out of the Land Rover with the bag of drinks, he glanced up at the brightly lit windows and felt a tremor of anxiety. It suddenly occurred to him just how hard it was going to be to put on a brave face and enter into the spirit of Christmas. In fact, he was pretty sure that he wouldn't be able to make it work without plenty of booze inside him. So, getting tipsy as soon as possible was a priority. The thought actually made him smile as he headed towards the house.

But the smile slipped away when something caught his eye.

There was a set of shoeprints in the otherwise pristine snow, and Robert was sure that they hadn't been there earlier. They were coming from the road and leading over to the steps on the right side of the house, the ones that descended to the cellar door.

And yet there were no prints going in the opposite direction.

It puzzled him because the cellar door was always locked and there was only one set of keys, which hung from a hook in the kitchen. What's more, Mary rarely ventured down there because she'd convinced herself many years ago that it was haunted.

He tightened his grip on the bag and went to investigate. What he saw made him frown further.

The shoeprints went down the steps and stopped in front of the door, which suggested that whoever had gone in there hadn't yet come out.

But who could it be?

He was about to go down and check when the sound of raised voices suddenly came from inside the house. They were loud enough to cause a blast of alarm to shoot through him.

Instinct told him that what was going on in the house had to be more important than what might be happening in the cellar, so he turned sharply on his heels and rushed towards the front door.

Just as he reached it, the shouting was drowned out by a high-pitched scream that sent his pulse racing.

Then, as he pushed the door open, another sound reached him.

The sound of breaking glass.

CHAPTER ONE

Wednesday December 27th

James Walker woke up suddenly, his mind dragged from sleep by the shriek of the alarm telling him it was 07.30.

He stretched his arm out from under the duvet and switched it off.

'Is it time to get up already?' his wife murmured beside him.

He rolled over so that he was facing her, just making out her features in the dark.

'I'm afraid so,' he whispered. 'Work beckons once again.'

Christmas had been and gone and today he was due to return to his job as a detective inspector with the Cumbria Constabulary based in Kendal. He wasn't looking forward to it because he had really enjoyed spending so much alone time with Annie, especially given that this was their last Christmas as a family of two.

Annie was finally expecting and they couldn't be more thrilled.

'I'm going to miss you being here,' she said, snuggling up to him. 'It's been fun with just the two of us.'

He felt a rush of emotion and ran a hand through her thick black hair.

'Well at least *you* don't have to go back to work yet,' he said. 'So, make the most of the next couple of weeks.'

Annie was now employed full time as a teacher at Kirkby Abbey's primary school, which had been given a reprieve from closure for at least a couple of years. The job suited her well and the school was only a short walk from their cottage on the edge of the village.

'There's plenty to keep me occupied,' Annie said. 'For one thing, I want to start thinking seriously about what to do with the baby's room. It's time we stripped off the old wallpaper and put some thought into what it will look like. What colour we paint it will have to wait until we know if it's a boy or girl, but I can order the cot now along with some other stuff.'

James couldn't help but smile. For years they had dreamt of having a baby but for a reason that had never been determined hadn't been able to. Despondency had turned to despair and it even got to the point where they began discussing adoption. But then two months ago, at the age of thirty-six, Annie discovered that she was pregnant at last, and now they were looking forward to welcoming their offspring into the world in the middle of next summer.

'I'd better get a move on,' James said, kissing his wife's forehead. 'Shall I make you a cup of tea after I've showered?'

'No, I'll make you one along with some breakfast. If I stay here, I'll probably fall back to sleep and I don't want to.'

James heaved himself out of bed and stretched, curving his spine as he padded across the room to the window. He pulled back the curtain and looked out on the new day.

It had been another white Christmas in Cumbria, and the snow still covered their short driveway and the road in front of the house, along with the fields he could see beyond the village. Morning light was struggling through murky clouds and trees swayed in the wind and snatched at the sky.

It was a far cry from the view they used to have from their previous home in London, which they were now renting out. There all they could see were brick walls, rooftops and endless queues of traffic.

They'd made the move to Cumbria fourteen months ago, and after spending twenty years as a detective in the Met, it took James a while to adjust to what was a much quieter life. As much as he missed his family – who were scattered across North London – he now wouldn't swap the rolling hills and lakes for anything. And there was no doubt in his mind that the land of Wordsworth and Beatrix Potter was a much better place to raise a child than the crime-infested capital.

He still found it hard to believe that he had already spent two Christmases here.

During the past twelve months he and Annie had carried out renovation work on their four-bedroom cottage, which had been left to Annie by her mother, and they'd made a conscious effort to play an active part in village life.

It had been easier for Annie to settle in because she'd lived in Kirkby Abbey before moving to London. For James it had been much more of a challenge, especially after the terrible events of a year ago when a serial killer went on a rampage in the village.

It took many months for the villagers to get over the shock of it and for life to return to near normal. But thankfully it had, and what had happened back then no longer dominated every conversation.

When James came out of the shower, he saw that Annie had already gone downstairs. He got dressed as quickly as he could, putting on a suit instead of jeans and a jumper for the first time in just over a week, and when he glanced at himself in the wardrobe mirror it made him sigh.

He'd got used to not wearing a shirt, tie and jacket, and he felt uncomfortable. But that was too bad because he didn't have a choice. Coppers were always being reminded that they had to look smart and respectable in order to maintain public confidence.

When he walked into the kitchen a minute later he found Annie standing in front of the oven.

She turned towards him, and said, 'Wow, I'd forgotten how dashing you are when you're going to work.'

'I think it's time you started to wear glasses,' he replied. 'I'm forty years old with a paunch and hair that's going grey.'

She smiled and it lit up her face. 'That's true, but when you're wearing a suit those flaws are not so obvious.'

Teasing each other had always been one of the aspects of their marriage that he treasured. It kept them on their toes and never failed to liven up dull moments.

'I'm making you a bacon sandwich and some coffee,' she said, turning back to the oven. 'Take a seat good sir and I'll serve it up.'

Annie was wearing her thick pink dressing gown with a belt tied around the waist. As James sat at the table, he thought yet again how lucky he was to have her as his wife. As well as being beautiful, with delicate features, bright blue eyes and shiny long black hair, she was also kind, funny and considerate. He knew that if he ever lost her, he wouldn't want to go on living.

She sat across the table from him while he drank his coffee and demolished his bacon sandwich, both of them watching the local news on the wall-mounted television.

It had been a relatively quiet Christmas in Cumbria for the emergency services. Very few serious crimes had been committed and, despite the heavy snowfalls, there hadn't been many road accidents.

'This is what I want to hear,' James said. 'With any luck I won't even have to leave the office today.'

Annie nodded. 'It'd be different if you were still working for the Met. I watched the national news while you were in the shower and they were saying that in London over the past three days there have been no less than six murders, five non-fatal stabbings and two arson attacks on commercial properties.'

James whistled out a breath. 'Well that's one of the good things about living in this part of the country. What happened here last year was a very rare event. I suspect it'll be a long time before we see anything like it again. If we ever do.'

'I hope you're right,' Annie said. 'I'm still so relieved that we actually got through Christmas without another bout of bloodshed.'

James felt the same, although he didn't want to admit it. He'd been worried that some psycho would decide to mark the first anniversary of those murders by embarking on another festive killing spree.

Thankfully, though, that didn't happen.

CHAPTER TWO

Whenever James was reminded of the serial killer who struck in Kirkby Abbey a year ago, he found it hard not to dwell on it. Now, as he left the cottage and drove towards Kendal, the memories came rushing back.

He could still picture those dreadful crime scenes with unwelcome clarity, along with the blizzards that had hindered the investigation.

The media dubbed the perp 'The Christmas Killer' and the damage that was inflicted had left scars in the community that may never fully heal.

It had all started just seven weeks after he'd moved into his new home and his new job, and he was thrust right into the thick of it because the killer had contacted him personally. It had turned out to be one of the biggest and most disturbing cases James had ever worked on, but during the course of the investigation he'd got to know a great deal about Kirkby Abbey and the people who lived there.

The village was typical of many in the sprawling northern

county of Cumbria that encompasses the Lake District and Yorkshire Dales National Parks. It had two pubs, a school, a monthly farmers' market and a population of around seven hundred. And throughout the year it attracted lots of sightseers and fell walkers.

There was also the Catholic church of St John's, which was supposed to have closed at the start of the year because of falling numbers in the congregation. However, just like the primary school, it had secured a reprieve, thanks to a funding boost from a campaign to save it and a government grant, and had been given a fresh lease of life with the appointment of a new priest.

It was a quiet village and, before last year's murderous rampage, had been crime free, save for the occasional act of vandalism committed by bored youths. The county at large also had a low crime rate and was regarded as one of the safest areas to live in the UK.

The Constabulary consisted of over two thousand personnel, most of them active police officers, and operated from fourteen stations, including the one at Kendal where James was now employed.

As a detective inspector, James was one of the most senior officers based in the market town and had a highly professional team working with him.

Though not everyone welcomed him with open arms when he'd started. There were some who viewed him as an outsider and resented the fact that he had been given the job that another long-serving detective had expected to get. Others just couldn't fathom why he would want to move from the busy metropolis to a county where nothing much happened. His stock answer was that he and his wife no longer enjoyed living in London and so had seized the opportunity to move to Kirkby Abbey after Annie inherited the family home from her mother.

He'd not told most people the real reason; only a small number of his superior officers were privy to that information.

The twenty-five-mile drive to Kendal took James through some of Britain's most stunning countryside, and as the sun had made an appearance, the landscape was displayed in all its glory.

Winter had stripped the fells of life and laid down a carpet of snow that was criss-crossed by a web of low dry-stone walls. Wind ruffled the tops of the trees and ice-covered streams glittered like precious gems.

James had never realised just how beautiful the area was until he'd moved here, and he had since come to fully appreciate why it was regarded as one of the 'crown jewels' of England. The stunning landscape contained a treasure trove of spectacular and unusual features – dramatic waterfalls, brooding lakes, deep ravines, awesome cave systems and towering white cliffs. Now a resident, he was determined to make the most of it and in the future planned to visit as many places as possible with his wife and their son or daughter.

He arrived at the station on the dot at nine, and found that most of his colleagues were already in the office. Several had got there just before him and were in the process of unwrapping themselves from winter coats and scarves.

As he approached his desk, someone called his name and he turned to see the smiling face of Detective Constable Jessica Abbott. She was standing on the other side of the room holding a tray and she gestured to it, asking silently if he wanted a coffee from the canteen.

'Yes please,' he said. 'And in case you've forgotten, it's milk and no sugar.'

She laughed. 'I'd not forgotten, guv. You haven't been away for that long.'

He removed his overcoat and hung it up, then sat and turned on his computer.

There was a mound of paperwork on his desk, but he wouldn't go through it until after the morning briefing when those officers who'd been on duty over Christmas would bring the rest of the team up to date. He already knew they hadn't been worked off their feet, and if something serious was going down he was confident he would already have been notified.

His computer screen flickered to life and he was about to check his emails when he felt a hand on his shoulder.

'Morning, boss. Did you have a good break?'

He glanced up to see Detective Sergeant Phil Stevens leaning against the edge of his own desk while chewing on a slice of toast. His shirt was unbuttoned and his tie hung loose at the collar.

'I did, thanks, Phil,' James said. 'What about you?'

Stevens shook his head. 'I couldn't wait to come back in this morning, if I'm honest. It was hard work spending three days and nights with the in-laws.'

It occurred to James that his colleague did look tired. His eyes appeared heavy and sandpaper stubble coated his chin.

'I gather you're in charge today,' Stevens said.

James nodded, but didn't say that he had only just remembered that DCI Tanner wouldn't be in until Friday because he'd spent Christmas in Scotland with his family and was still up north. 'I'll kick things off once everyone is settled.'

Stevens nodded. 'Feel free to offload any crap onto me. I'll need to keep myself busy so I don't doze off.'

James smiled to himself as he thought about how far he and Stevens had come. They'd had a rough start to their working relationship when James first moved to Cumbria, as Stevens had felt ousted by the new arrival. But the longer they worked together, the easier it became, and he was now James's righthand man.

James returned his attention to the computer screen and brought up his emails.

The very latest had dropped into his inbox only ten minutes ago and when he saw who it was from his pulse jumped a notch.

Leo Freeman was one of his former colleagues in the Met and he only ever got in touch to provide updates on a man named Andrew Sullivan, who was the main reason James and Annie had moved out of London.

James opened up the email and learned that Scotland Yard wanted to question Sullivan in connection with a gangland murder that had taken place in the capital a week ago.

'I thought you'd want to know that the bastard has dropped off our radar,' Freeman wrote. 'He's not at home and we haven't been able to trace him. I'll keep you informed of progress. Meanwhile, stay vigilant.'

James felt a ripple of unease; Sullivan was one of London's most vicious gang bosses. He'd served thirteen months of a life sentence for murdering a nightclub owner but was released from prison fifteen months ago after a man who was himself already serving life for another murder confessed to the killing. There was no doubt in James's mind that the confessor was lying. After all, he had nothing to lose since he would almost certainly die in prison given his age and the length of his sentence.

As it was James who secured Sullivan's conviction while working with Scotland Yard's Murder Investigation Team – and because previous to that he'd spent time with the National Crime Agency, where he and his team caused serious disruption to Sullivan's illicit activities – Sullivan had made it known upon his release that he intended to seek revenge.

He blamed James for putting him away and for the fact that whilst he was in prison his wife of five years had left him and took their four-year-old son with her, moving abroad to make sure he wouldn't find her.

In a phone call a year ago, he'd told James, '*You and me have some unfinished business. So sooner or later we'll be meeting up. And it'll be at a time and place of my choosing.*'

During the past year James had come to believe that Sullivan now posed less of a threat because he hadn't been in touch again and his movements in London were being monitored by the Met. Even Annie had stopped worrying about him and he was rarely mentioned these days.

But the fact that he had now vanished from the Met's radar made James wonder if he would seek to settle old scores before the net closed in on him once again.

'Here's your coffee, guv. Milk, no sugar.'

DC Abbott's voice broke into his thoughts and he was glad because he didn't want to spend any more time fretting over Andrew Sullivan. He told himself that there was probably no need, anyway.

'That's kind of you,' he said, taking the Styrofoam cup that she held out for him. 'Did you have a good Christmas?'

She shrugged. 'It was no different to any other year, guv. My boyfriend and I gave each other presents neither of us really wanted and we drank far too much gin and wine, which meant we were nursing hangovers for much of the time.'

James cracked a smile. 'Sounds like your Christmas was no different to most other people's.'

She blew the fringe out of her eyes and smiled back at him.

'That's exactly what my mum told me,' she said, before moving on to hand out more drinks.

James had a lot of time for DC Abbott. She was in her early thirties and one of the youngest members of the team. She was also sharper than a syringe and easy to get on with.

He turned back to the emails and was relieved that they didn't reveal any further nasty surprises.

After that, he convened the morning meeting.

There were eleven people present, including three civilian staff, and they all listened attentively as the list of cases that were being dealt with from the last couple of days were read out, including two burglaries, a public order offence, three acts of vandalism and an attack on a pensioner. The group learned that there were also officers currently attending a domestic dispute in town and a suspected hit and run in Burnside.

Once everyone had been updated on all the active investigations, James handed out various tasks.

'So, it seems we haven't got too much on our plate right now,' he told the group. 'I think it's safe to say that we can look forward to an easy day. It'll give us time to get—'

He was interrupted by one of the civilian staff who thrust his arm in the air and said in a loud, shaky voice, 'You might have spoken too soon there, sir. I've just heard from control. Uniform are responding to a three-nine and it sounds serious.'

'Any details?' James asked.

'The call came from a woman who's at a farm a few miles south of Kirkby Abbey. She claims there are three dead bodies in the farmhouse. And she's described it as a bloodbath.'

CHAPTER THREE

The word bloodbath sent a shudder down the length of James's spine, and for several seconds he was too shocked to react.

And he wasn't the only one. A heavy, palpable silence descended on the room.

The first person to break it was the civilian staff member who had relayed the news from control.

'A scene of crime team is already on its way there,' he said. 'And the pathologist's office has been informed.'

More details quickly followed. The three bodies had been found at Oaktree Farm, which was about nine miles from Kirkby Abbey. It was the home of Robert and Mary Bateman, a couple who had lived there for many years. They had a daughter named Charlotte who was in her early twenties. The person who called the emergency number had identified herself as Laura Sheldon, a solicitor based in Kendal, but it wasn't yet known what she'd been doing at the farm or what her relation – if any – to the victims was.

The name Bateman rang a bell with James and he was sure

he had been introduced to Mr Bateman, probably in one of the village pubs or at a local event. Or perhaps the man had been mentioned in conversation.

As James began to bark orders, the office buzzed with activity and tension. Those detectives who'd been instructed to go with James to the scene were pulling on their coats, while others were bashing phones and tapping frantically at keyboards.

Even though everyone was moving, it was taking time for what they'd been told to sink in. At this stage they weren't sure what to make of it, but the emergency call certainly didn't sound like a hoax. Clearly something awful had happened at Oaktree Farm – something as horrifying as what had taken place in Kirkby Abbey a year ago.

James travelled to the farm in a pool car with DS Stevens and DC Abbott – Stevens driving – and just after they left the station, they were informed that a patrol car was already at the scene and the officers on site had confirmed that there were indeed three bodies in the farmhouse along with a great deal of blood.

It appeared that two of the victims had suffered shotgun wounds. The third had been stabbed. That was all the information they had though as the officers had retreated as soon as they'd determined that there was no sign of life – as was protocol. Gone were the days when first responders trampled over a crime scene and compromised vital evidence.

'And there was me thinking that my first day back was going to be a breeze,' Stevens said. 'This is unbelievable.'

James felt his body stiffen as a thousand questions raced through his head.

Did the corpses belong to the Bateman family? Were they the victims of a gruesome home invasion or a burglary gone wrong?

The more James thought about it, the harder his heart banged in his chest.

Neither Stevens nor Abbott lived near to Kirkby Abbey, so they were curious to know if James was familiar with Oaktree Farm.

'I've never been there, but I've driven past it a few times,' he said. 'It's close to the road, and I'm sure it's been up for sale for a couple of months.'

'What about the Batemans?' Abbott asked. 'Do you know them?'

'I have a feeling I've met Mr Bateman,' James replied. 'But that's about all. Kirkby Abbey is a small village and sooner or later you get to bump into everyone.'

'I really feel for you and all the other villagers, guv,' Stevens said. 'It beggars belief that for the second Christmas running something like this should happen. I wonder how long it'll be before some tabloid hack starts to describe Kirkby Abbey as that village in Cumbria where killers strike whenever it snows.'

It was a bad taste remark, but James let it pass. His mind was already leaping ahead to what horrors awaited them at Oaktree Farm.

Their destination was set in a remote location surrounded by snow-shrouded hills and moors.

A For Sale sign greeted them as they approached the turn off. The stone-built farmhouse and a couple of small outbuildings were set back only about a hundred yards from the road and dread swelled inside James as they drew close enough to see a collection of vehicles parked in the spacious yard in front of the house.

There was a police patrol car, an ambulance, a forensic van, a mud-splattered Land Rover and a smart looking Citroen C3. James hazarded a guess that the Land Rover belonged to the Batemans and the Citroen to the solicitor who had raised the alarm.

One of the uniformed officers who'd been first on the scene saw them arriving and got Stevens to park in a spot alongside a large, wooden barn. As they climbed out, DC Abbott held up her phone, and said, 'Well at least there's a strong mobile signal here. I wasn't sure there would be.'

James had quickly learned that mobile reception was patchy across Cumbria, and it often proved frustrating, but things had thankfully improved since he'd moved up here.

The uniformed officer – Mike Winslow – had been doing the job a long time and James had never seen him looking so rattled. His face was ashen, drained of colour.

'I take it you've been inside, Mike?' he said.

PC Winslow nodded. 'And it shook me up, guv, I can tell you. You probably already know that there are three bodies. My partner and I came straight back out after making sure none of them was alive and we were careful not to touch anything. But it's a real mess in there.'

'Any thoughts on when they might have died?'

'I'd say they've been dead at least a couple of days. The smell is pretty bad and the blood has dried.'

'Do we know who they are?'

'According to the woman who called it in, a Miss Laura

Sheldon, they're the couple who lived here, Robert and Mary Bateman, and their daughter Charlotte.'

'And where is Miss Sheldon now?'

Winslow pointed. 'She's sitting in the patrol car talking to my partner. She says she's the family solicitor and came here this morning for a pre-planned meeting with Mr and Mrs Bateman. When she rang the bell and there was no answer, she looked through a window and saw a body on the floor in the kitchen. Instinct prompted her to check the front door and it was unlocked so she stepped inside and got the shock of her life.'

'I'll talk to her in a bit so keep her here,' James said. 'And you need to station yourself at the entrance to the lane. I noticed there's a gap in the wall on one side that gives access to a field. Direct all other vehicles that arrive to park there. Some more of the team are travelling over from Kendal and will be here any minute.'

'Will do, guv.'

As the detectives headed across the yard towards the house, James noticed that the place was pretty rundown and there were no farm animals in the surrounding fields or buildings. Off to the left there was an empty paddock and the barn door stood open, revealing nothing but a small mound of hay inside.

The scene of crime officers had wasted no time slipping on their pale blue protective overalls and two of them were unloading metal boxes from the forensic van. Others were no doubt already inside the house.

Just to the right of the front door was a box with the protective overalls, along with their accompanying shoe covers, masks and gloves, ready for anyone who entered the house.

'I'll go in by myself to begin with,' James said, turning to Stevens and Abbott. 'You two get suited up and go and check the rest of the farm.'

He gave his name to the officer with the crime scene log and as he stepped into the doorway a SOCO appeared and warned him to tread carefully.

'We've only been here a short while ourselves,' he said. 'So, more needs to be done to protect the integrity of the scene.'

'Not to worry, I know what I'm doing.'

He steeled himself and stepped over the threshold into a short hallway, the baggy forensic overalls rustling with each step.

The rank and pungent smell of death hit him immediately and his stomach rolled. A second later he entered the large open plan living room and kitchen and the sight that greeted him took his breath away and made his insides go cold.

CHAPTER FOUR

James could see all three bodies from where he stood. They were lying close to each other on the grey flagstone floor between a large brown leather sofa and a stand-alone breakfast bar.

Bile rose in his throat as he took tentative steps further into the room. He was aware that two SOCOs had stopped what they were doing to acknowledge his presence, and he nodded in response.

He focused on the older woman first, presumably Mrs Mary Bateman, and the sight of her made him wince. She was thin and grey-haired, and he was sure he had never seen her before. She was stretched out on her back and had a gaping wound in her chest where the shotgun shell had ripped into her. Dried blood covered her white blouse and long, pale green skirt. Her wrinkled grey features were frozen in a grimace, and her dead eyes stared up at the ceiling.

A few feet away from her lay a young woman who James assumed to be the daughter, Charlotte. She was slumped against the side of the breakfast bar with a large kitchen knife lodged in her stomach. Her eyes were closed, her mouth hung open, and her swollen tongue was poking out between thin, blue lips. The blood from the wound had spread across her ripped jeans and beige T-shirt. Despite her current appearance, she struck James as someone who had been pretty in life. She also looked a bit younger than he knew her to be, and the fact that her life had been cut short so brutally made his throat feel tight.

He then turned to the man – Robert Bateman. He too was lying on his back, but James was unable to tell if his face was familiar because there wasn't much left of it. It seemed obvious that it had been blasted with a shotgun from very close range, and the ghastly wound exposed lumps of shapeless, raw flesh and bone. There was a garish spray of blood on the wall behind him and bits of his skull were scattered about the floor.

James felt a sense of unreality consume him and he had to fight down the urge to vomit.

He noticed the shotgun lying across the bottom half of the body, Mr Bateman's right hand resting on the wooden grip and his thumb poking through the trigger guard.

A wretched scenario leapt into James's mind – was this a murder-suicide? Did Bateman, for a reason that might never be established, shoot his wife in the chest before placing the shotgun under his own chin and pulling the trigger? James could see that it was a pump-action weapon and therefore capable of firing off multiple shots before having to be reloaded.

But that left the question of who had stabbed Charlotte. Instinct and experience told him that her stomach wound was not self-inflicted.

He lifted his head and cast his eyes around the room, seeking answers, and what he registered for the first time was that the design of the room was in stark contrast to the bloody mess on the floor.

It was a large but cosy room with exposed stone and brick walls, except beneath the stairs where the plasterboard wall was covered with dark paper that looked like a window covered with shiny raindrops. The kitchen was well-equipped and the granite worktops were cluttered with jars, cereal boxes, tea towels and a plate of mince pies. On the breakfast bar stood a half-empty bottle of wine, along with two glasses and a bowl of crisps.

James could see that the family had been embracing the festive spirit before death descended upon the farmhouse. It would surely have been sudden and unexpected, and he couldn't even imagine what might have triggered it.

He also spotted an acrylic knife block with six slots, one of which was empty. The black handles matched the one jutting out of Charlotte's body.

James turned then to the living room, which was typical of other farmhouses he'd been in. There was an open fireplace, two long, deep sofas with wooden armrests, a glass coffee table, and in the far corner a Christmas tree that almost touched the ceiling. The lights on it were glowing and the decorations matched those that were positioned around the room.

It didn't look as though the room had been ransacked. There were unopened presents on the floor in front of the tree and nothing seemed out of place except for the fragments of glass that were spread over the floor between the bodies.

A key question that would need to be answered by the

pathologist was when the deaths occurred. It was obviously before the family got around to opening their presents on Christmas Day, and from the state of the victims and the awful smell, James wouldn't rule out Christmas Eve as a likely time of death.

'My heart goes out to the woman who stumbled on this,' a familiar voice said behind him. 'It'll haunt her for the rest of her life.'

James turned and immediately recognised Tony Coppell, the chief forensic officer, even though he was wearing a mask and hood.

'I'm sure you're right,' James said. 'I've seen plenty of gory crime scenes over the years, but this one ranks among the worst of them.'

'I haven't seen so much blood since our regular visits to Kirkby Abbey a year ago,' Coppell said. 'We've certainly got our work cut out for us.'

'Have you been upstairs yet?'

Coppell nodded. 'All nice and tidy. Beds are made and some of the lights are switched on, just as they are down here. That suggests the killings took place after dark.'

'Care to estimate how long the bodies have been here?' James asked him.

'You need the pathologist to provide an accurate time of death, but based on their condition I'd say two or three days.'

'That sounds about right to me,' James said, pointing to the shotgun. 'I don't normally draw conclusions this early on, but I reckon this has all the hallmarks of a murder-suicide. This man, who we believe to be Robert Bateman, appears to have tried to blow his own head off. And I'm guessing that was after he killed his wife.'

'That's what I initially thought,' Coppell said. 'And it's a fact that most murder-suicides take place in domestic settings and involve a man and his spouse. But this isn't so straightforward.'

James nodded. 'I agree. For starters who stabbed the girl?'

'Well I think I can help you there, Inspector,' Coppell said. 'You see, there's strong evidence to indicate that there was someone else here.'

James felt a rush of heat burn through his chest. 'What are you talking about?' he asked.

Coppell gestured towards a hallway entrance to the right of the kitchen.

'That leads to a back door which was open when we got here. Now, if you look at the floor there are bloody shoeprints leading from here all along the hallway and out of the house.'

James saw the distinctive markings on the light-coloured tiles and swore to himself.

'Are you sure they weren't left by one of our victims?' he said.

Coppell gave an emphatic nod. 'I'm positive. None of them are wearing shoes.'

CHAPTER FIVE

By the time the bloody shoeprints reached the back door they were barely visible. But the impressions nearer to the kitchen were clear, and revealed a distinctive, rigid sole pattern.

'They look to be a size nine or ten to me,' Coppell said. 'And I've seen enough in my time to be confident that it was a bloke who left them and not a woman.'

James knew that the prints would be a key piece of forensic evidence. The pattern would hopefully reveal a specific shoe type and manufacturer. And the size and make might well help them to build a physical profile of the person they would now be looking for.

'This raises the possibility that the scene back in there was staged,' James said. 'Whoever these prints belong to could have put the shotgun in Mr Bateman's hand to make it look like suicide.'

'If that was the case then wouldn't the perp have taken more care when making off?' Coppell responded. 'Hard to believe he didn't realise he'd left a messy trail of blood.'

'We both know how careless killers can be, Tony. It's why we get to catch so many of them.'

Coppell nodded. 'Good point, Inspector. Let's hope we'll be able to shed more light on what might have happened after we've processed the scene.'

James quickly checked to see what was beyond the back door. There was a small yard containing a weather-beaten shed, an old rusty tractor and several dustbins. It was enclosed by a dry-stone wall with a gate that provided access to a field beyond the lane they'd driven down. Freshly fallen snow covered the ground and obliterated any potential clues that might otherwise have been visible.

James stepped back inside the house where Coppell was waiting to draw his attention to four framed photographs displayed on a sideboard next to the stairs.

'These will probably be of use to you, Inspector,' he said.

James picked up each photo with a gloved hand. The first showed Robert and Mary Bateman on their wedding day. They were standing outside St John's Church in Kirkby Abbey. She was slim and pretty in her white dress, her long brown hair hanging loose about her shoulders. He was a good six inches taller and wearing a smart, grey suit, his dark hair slicked neatly back from his forehead.

The second photo showed Mary sitting up in a hospital bed shortly after giving birth. She looked radiant and happy as she smiled down at their new baby, Charlotte.

The third photo looked as though it had been taken only a few years ago. All three of them were posed together in front of the farmhouse. By then Mary's hair had turned grey and the dress she was wearing looked far too tight for her. Charlotte had blossomed into an attractive young girl with a face that was sharp and thin, and a figure that fit snugly into tight jeans and a skimpy top. Robert was the only one not smiling. He was wearing jeans and a loose-fitting shirt, and holding a hand above his eyes to shield them from the sunlight, the shadow his hand cast making it difficult for James to distinguish his features.

In the fourth photograph Robert Bateman was standing alone in a field wearing a tweed shooting jacket, matching cap and high leather boots – his features clear this time. In one hand he was holding a dead pheasant and in the other a shotgun that appeared to be identical to the one that now lay across his body.

James recognised him immediately and recalled that he had indeed met the man. It was many months ago in one of the village pubs. The topic of conversation between the gathered group was how many Cumbrian farmers were struggling to survive, and how some were being pushed to the emotional and financial brink. A few were even becoming suicidal because of the pressures they faced from plummeting prices, the increasing costs of housing livestock and the damage caused by years of extreme weather. Mr Bateman had made it known that he was among those who might not be able to keep his business afloat for much longer.

James took out his phone and snapped pictures of all four photographs. Then he told the chief forensic officer about his meeting with Bateman.

'That's obviously why the farm is up for sale,' Coppell said. 'The past few years have been really tough for farmers across the north. I know of at least two who've been forced to throw in the towel and do something else.'

'So maybe that was a factor in what led to this,' James said.

'It could well be.'

By now a few more SOCOs were in the house and setting about their tasks with the usual professional detachment.

'I'd better go and talk to the woman who called it in,' James said to Coppell. 'Meanwhile, can you confirm for me that the knife used on Charlotte is from the set on the worktop and also see if you can find any mobile phones?'

'Consider it done, Inspector.'

It was busier in the front yard now, and colder. James felt a stiff breeze pull at his face as he took off his mask and pushed back the hood of his forensic suit.

Two other detectives had arrived from Kendal along with more uniforms and they were all in a group being briefed by DS Stevens and DC Abbott.

Before he approached them, James took a moment to organise his thoughts and take in his surroundings. He tried to picture what the farm would have looked like when it was thriving. He guessed there would have been cattle, chickens, horses and sheep around the place and grazing out on the surrounding moors.

Robert Bateman and his wife would doubtless have been kept busy feeding, shearing and tending to their livestock, while they battled against the extreme elements that were always a challenge for farmers in this part of the country.

James quickly filled the team in on what he had seen inside the house – the bodies, the wounds, the weapons used to kill the family and the bloody shoeprints on the floor.

'This crime scene presents us with a real challenge,' he said. 'Right now, it's impossible to determine who killed who. It could be that Robert Bateman shot himself after shooting his wife. Or maybe that's what we're supposed to believe, and what really happened is that someone else was here and committed three murders. Someone who then left in such a hurry that he made the mistake of leaving his shoeprints behind.'

'What makes you so certain of the gender, guv?' Abbott asked.

'Coppell is confident it was a man based on the impressions left by the soles of the shoes. We'll follow it up though as soon as the SOCOs give us something solid to work with,' he said. 'Let's send photos to the footwear database asap. We also need to get any mobile phones and computers off to the lab and start the process of finding out what all the victims were up to over Christmas. We'll be able to narrow that down once we have a more accurate time of death. And, of course, we need to trace next of kin. I want to inform close relatives before the media gets wind of this.'

'Abbott and I explored the farm like you asked, but nothing struck us as unusual except the absence of animals,' Stevens said. 'There's not much in the barn or the outbuildings. And nothing in the Land Rover to point to what might have happened here.'

'Do we know if the Citroen belongs to the lawyer?' James asked.

'Yes, Laura Sheldon,' Stevens confirmed, and James took this as his cue to go and question her.

The solicitor was standing next to the patrol car smoking a cigarette as James approached. Her hair was covered by a woollen hat, the same dark shade of brown as the overcoat she was wearing, and he judged her to be in her mid-forties.

He introduced himself, and said, 'I'm sorry you've had to hang around, Miss Sheldon. I know you've had an awful shock.'

'You've got that right,' she said, her voice low and hoarse. 'I still can't believe what I saw in there.'

The woman's mouth was pinched and drawn tight, and her eyes were glazed and haunted. James could tell that she was doing her best to suppress her emotions.

'I'll be as quick as I can, Miss Sheldon,' he said. 'And please bear with me because I'll be asking some questions that you've likely already been asked.'

'That's all right. Please just get on with it so that I can go home.'

'Well, firstly I'd like you to tell me what your relationship was to the Batemans.'

'I'm a lawyer and I represent them through my company. I came here this morning because I'd arranged to meet with them both.'

'And when you got no answer you looked through the window and saw one of the bodies. Is that right?'

She nodded. 'I could only see Mrs Bateman's legs and it occurred to me that she might have had an accident. I went to the door to ring the bell again and tried the handle and was surprised to discover that the door wasn't locked. So, I went inside and saw ... well, you know what I saw.'

'And you didn't touch anything?'

'Absolutely not. I came back out as quickly as I could.'

'I see. Could you tell me what you know about the family?'

She dragged heavily on her cigarette before replying.

'I've known the couple and their daughter for a number of years, but have usually just dealt with Robert. Mary didn't have much to do with the business and always stayed in the background. We've met up more frequently in recent months because the farm was racking up big losses and they were being forced to wind down the business and put the place up for sale. That's why there's no longer any livestock. What they had was sold to pay bills, including two much-loved sheepdogs. Robert was about to declare bankruptcy and I was helping him to deal with all the legal ramifications.'

'So how much debt were they in?' James asked.

'It ran into many thousands of pounds. And it didn't help that Robert had developed a gambling habit that only served to add to their financial woes.'

'Did it affect him mentally, or perhaps cause friction between him and his wife?'

'Oh, most definitely. I saw over time that it put a severe strain on their relationship. I came here about three weeks ago and they were having a huge row. I heard Mary accuse Robert of selling something without telling her in order to pay off some of his gambling debts. He was denying it. They were both really embarrassed when they realised I'd overheard them.'

'Do you know if they had any enemies?'

'I very much doubt it. They were a normal couple and they were facing the same problems as several of my other farming clients.'

'What about the daughter, Charlotte? Do you know her well?'

Her swollen eyes were shiny now with unshed tears and her breathing faltered.

'I gathered from what Robert told me that she was a bit of a handful. She mixed with the wrong crowd and there was talk of her getting involved with drugs. She didn't live here with them, though. About six months ago she moved into her boyfriend's flat in Kendal.'

'Do you know who he is?'

'Only that his name is Neil Savage. I've never met him.'

'And do you know if this Neil – or anyone else – spent Christmas here at the farm?'

'I'm afraid I don't. I never got to have that conversation with Robert and Mary.'

James finished off by asking if she had contact details for the family's next of kin.

'They'll be at the office. I know that Robert's parents are both dead, but he has a brother living in Ireland. Mary's father died some years ago and her mother is in a care home suffering from dementia, but she does have a sister who lives in France.'

'We'll need those addresses and phone numbers as soon as possible,' James said. 'And one other thing I need to know is whether the Batemans had wills.'

She nodded. 'They did. It was a very simple document and they left everything to Charlotte.'

He left it there because it was clear that the poor woman was finding it hard to get the words out. He gave her his card and took down her contact details.

'We'll be asking you to make a formal statement for us, Miss Sheldon, and I will almost certainly need to talk to you again,' he told her.

He then arranged for her to be taken home in a patrol car while an officer followed behind in her Citroen.

James spent the next few minutes relaying information back to control and alerting the Constabulary press office that they needed to be aware that this was going to be a big story for the national as well as the local media.

He also made sure the information was passed on to the Chief Constable's office at Carleton Hall in Penrith.

Finally, he called his boss on his mobile to put him in the picture, only to find that DCI Tanner was already in the loop, having been contacted by someone in the Kendal office. He told James he'd be cutting short his break in Scotland and returning to the office tomorrow.

James updated him on the crime scene and the leads they'd found, and Tanner listened in silence. James expected a number of questions to follow, but instead, Tanner dropped a bombshell.

'There's something you need to know about the history of Oaktree Farm, James,' he said. 'As soon as I heard the name it sparked a memory and I just Googled it. It all came back to me as soon as I started reading the old cuttings, and I'm surprised that someone hasn't mentioned it to you already.'

'I'm all ears, guv,' James said, and tried not to show his impatience.

'Twenty-four years ago another dreadful event took place at the farm. The previous owners, a Simon and Amanda Roth, were found dead in the cellar in what was regarded as a murder-suicide. She suffered fatal head injuries from several hammer blows and he killed himself with a shotgun.'

James felt his neck grow hot under his collar.

'Well that's guaranteed to make this an even juicier story for the hacks to get their teeth into,' he said.

'Damn right,' Tanner acknowledged. 'But that's not all. The couple had a three-week-old baby who wasn't in the house when police got there and has been missing ever since, presumed dead. And it gets more intriguing still. Robert Bateman worked for them on the farm at the time, though he wasn't a suspect because he was away on a break with his own family when it happened.'

'Jesus Christ.'

CHAPTER SIX

TWENTY-FOUR YEARS AGO

It's an unseasonably mild evening in late September as Robert Bateman arrives at Oaktree Farm with his wife Mary and their daughter Charlotte.

He was there earlier to work, but this is a rare social visit to mark a special occasion.

His boss, Simon Roth, has just become a father and his wife Amanda has returned home from hospital with the baby.

'Come over and see them this evening,' he said to Robert just before he left the farm to go and pick them up. 'Our girls can meet for the first time and we can drink to their futures.'

Charlotte is already almost a month old and the Roths' daughter, who they've named Megan, was born only four days ago. The two families live just six miles apart and it's already been decided that the children will be encouraged to be play-mates from an early age.

Simon is there to greet them as the jeep pulls to a halt in front of the house. He's wearing a smile as wide as his face and is clearly excited about showing them his offspring.

Robert steps out of the jeep first and then heaves the carrycot from the back seat.

'I'm so glad you were able to make it,' Simon tells them before pecking Mary on the cheek. 'Amanda is really looking forward to seeing you both.'

Baby Megan turns out to be as cute as both Robert and Mary knew she would be. She's still wrinkled and squashed but she already has a healthy set of lungs, and when she cries, she wakes Charlotte from her slumber.

The men share a bottle of champagne and after a while they get bored with baby talk and resort to discussing plans for the farm.

The women stick to soft drinks and share their pregnancy experiences and their concerns about bringing up a child.

Simon hears Amanda tell Mary that she's already finding it harder than she expected and he reacts sharply, saying to his wife, 'Oh for heaven's sake don't be so bloody pathetic. How hard can it be to look after someone that small?'

'Well, you'll find out soon enough when it's your turn to take care of her,' Amanda snaps back.

The couple have a somewhat tetchy relationship and Robert in particular is used to seeing them bicker and hearing Simon being critical of his wife. But thankfully, on this occasion, they choose not to carry it on and the rest of the evening proves to be a delight.

'Take tomorrow morning off,' Simon tells Robert when he and Mary decide to leave just after ten. 'There are various jobs that need doing but they can wait until the afternoon.'

They all agree that they should make meeting up in the evening and at weekends a regular event.

They wave goodnight to each other, not knowing that this is the last time they will all be together.

Eighteen days later, the Batemans are staying at Robert's mother's house in Sunderland when Robert receives a call from a DI Giles Keegan of the Cumbria Constabulary.

The officer informs him that Simon and Amanda Roth have been found dead in the cellar at Oaktree Farm and that baby Megan has disappeared.

CHAPTER SEVEN

James was thrown off balance by what Tanner had told him. He pulled up his overcoat collar and shoved his hands into his pockets. Then he walked over to the big barn and stood in its shadow while taking stock of the situation.

It seemed inconceivable to him that two murder-suicides could have been committed in the same house, albeit twenty-four years apart. Questions whirled inside his head and he tried to ignore his growing sense of unease.

During all of his time as a copper he had never encountered a case with so many intriguing parts to it.

Tanner had told James that he was to be the senior investigating officer, but it was something he found he didn't relish. Tanner had also suggested that James speak to retired detective Giles Keegan, who lived in Kirkby Abbey and was based at the station in Kendal until he left the force six years ago. He had been the lead detective in the investigation into the killings of the Roth couple.

James had first met Keegan during the serial killer case last year, and the ex-police officer had provided useful information about his fellow villagers that had helped the investigation.

James called him on his mobile.

'It's not often that I hear from you, Detective Walker,' Keegan said when he answered. 'Is there something you want my help with?'

'I need to pick your brains, Giles,' James said. 'DCI Tanner suggested I have a word with you. But first I have some bad news to impart about some people you know.'

James told him what had happened at Oaktree Farm, holding back some of the more gory details, and he heard the man catch his breath.

'It's too early to know for sure what we're dealing with, but it could be that someone tried to make it look like a murder-suicide,' James said.

'This is so terrible,' Keegan responded. 'I saw Robert only a few weeks ago in the village. He mentioned that he was selling the farm because it had become more of a struggle as of late, but that he and Mary were hoping to stay in the area – maybe even move into Kirkby Abbey.'

'Did you know him well?'

'Not really, but I liked him. He was always pleasant and sociable.'

'Can you think of anyone who might have wanted to hurt him and his family?'

'Not at all. And if someone did have a serious problem with him, I'm sure I would have heard about it since everyone around here seems to know everyone else's business.'

'What was Mary like?'

'She was quiet and not very communicative. She always seemed on edge.'

'And their daughter, Charlotte?'

'Well I've seen her from time to time, of course, but I've never had a conversation with her. I do know she gave her parents a lot of grief and was once collared for shoplifting and got off with a caution.'

'What about her boyfriend, a guy named Neil Savage? Can you tell me anything about him?'

'No, I've not heard the name and I've never seen Charlotte with anyone but her parents.'

James then raised the subject of the killings at Oaktree Farm back in 1997.

'I was just about to ask you if you knew about those,' Keegan said. 'Tanner told you that I was the senior investigating officer?'

'Yes, so I wanted to ask: do these latest killings strike you as a grisly coincidence or do you think there could possibly be a link between them?'

Keegan was silent for a few seconds as he thought about it, then said, 'For the life of me I can't see how they can possibly be connected since they took place so far apart. But it is flipping weird nonetheless, especially given that Bateman was working on the farm when the Roths were killed.'

'Yes, Tanner mentioned that as well, but didn't specify what Bateman's role was.'

'He was a farmhand and the only employee. He lived with his wife in a fairly isolated cottage between Kirkby Abbey and Oaktree Farm. But they were away on a short break with their daughter at Robert's mother's home in Sunderland when the Roths died. I broke the news to him over the phone and I have to say he was very helpful during the investigation.

We learned some things about the Roths that I hadn't been aware of.'

'Such as?'

'Well, he described Simon as a Jekyll and Hyde character who was good-natured and easy going most of the time, but also a bit controlling and quick to lose his temper, particularly with his wife. They often argued, Bateman said, and it was partly because Simon bullied Amanda and she didn't take kindly to it.'

'And did Robert have a clue as to what happened in the cellar on that day?'

'He shared my view that Simon Roth killed his wife after an argument that got out of hand. She suffered two fatal blows to the head from a hammer that was found on the floor beside her. It had her husband's prints on. We concluded that Simon must have then shot himself.'

'So, what about the couple's baby, Megan?' James said. 'What happened to her?'

'That was the part that really had me stumped, and I've never been able to stop thinking about it. We searched the farm and the hundreds of acres that surround it. We put out appeals and chased down a few false leads, but got nowhere. We never found her body, but we felt fairly certain that something happened to Megan before her parents died – and that was the likely catalyst for the murder-suicide.'

As James listened to Keegan, he noted the arrival of Dr Pam Flint, the forensic pathologist. He was anxious to speak to her before she started to examine the bodies so he told Keegan he had to go but would drop in on him at some point soon to learn more about the Batemans and the Roths.

'I've got one final question, though,' James said. 'Why did

Robert Bateman take over the running of the farm after something so dreadful happened there?'

'The property was originally passed on to Simon Roth's brother because Amanda had no siblings and her parents were dead,' Keegan said. 'The brother didn't want anything to do with it but he did ask Robert to keep it going for a while, which he did for some months while it was up for sale. Robert's mother then died and left him her house in Sunderland but the Batemans didn't want to move there and someone had offered to buy it so they sold it and used the money to purchase Oaktree Farm. Robert felt that Simon and Amanda would have wanted him to save the place along with the animals, so he persuaded his wife that it would be a good idea. Mary had already given up her job as a nurse to become a full-time mum and they both put their hearts and souls into keeping the farm going. Mind you, I learned some years later that it was a move Mary eventually came to regret.'

'Do you know why?' James asked.

'She became convinced that the house is haunted. She mentioned it to a few people in the village and claimed that she often heard noises that seemed to come from behind the walls.'

CHAPTER EIGHT

Dr Flint was escorted towards the house by a uniformed officer. She was already kitted out in full forensic gear, minus the mask.

'I got here as soon as I could,' she said to James as he approached her. 'I was briefed on the phone so I know what to expect.'

Pam Flint was one of the county's most highly rated pathologists and with good reason. She was shrewd, thorough, and she didn't kick off when detectives pestered her for answers.

She had narrow, analytical eyes and smooth unblemished skin. James recalled being surprised when he was told she was in her late forties. He'd thought she was much younger.

'It's a bad one,' he said. 'There's no question the bodies have been there for several days, but I need you to pin down the accurate time of death for me as soon as you can.'

'I'll do my best, James. Have the victims been tampered with?'

'First responders checked to see if they were alive, but that was it.'

'Good. Are you coming back in?'

'Not just yet. I want to brief the team about some new information that's come to light.'

His detectives had dispersed to carry out further checks around the farm and to make more notes but he spotted DC Abbott and called her over.

'Could you go and round everyone up?' he asked. 'I've got some information to share which will need to be actioned.'

While he waited for her to pass on the message, he pulled out his phone and tapped *Oaktree Farm killings* into the search engine.

The results showed a range of stories on various local and national news sites dated twenty-four years ago. Some included photos of the family – Simon and Amanda Roth, and baby Megan.

At the time of his death Simon was thirty-four and he was a bulky, bespectacled man with a hard face and short curly hair. Amanda was the same age, but much shorter than her husband. She had a thin face, pinched features and long, wavy hair.

There was nothing particularly distinctive about Megan. At only a few weeks old she looked to James like any other tiny baby, and the thought that she might have come to harm back then provoked a sudden tightness in his throat. He could well understand why the mystery surrounding her disappearance had played on Giles Keegan's mind ever since. Knowing that he hadn't been able to solve it would have been a hard thing to live with.

Once the team was back together, James told them about

the first Oaktree Farm killings. Not one of them was familiar with the case or its details.

'The surprises are coming thick and fast,' James said. 'I suggest you familiarise yourselves with the events of twenty-four years ago because Robert Bateman worked here as a farmhand at the time and went on to buy the place some months later. His wife Mary is said to have told people in the village that she thought the house was haunted because she often heard noises that appeared to come from behind the walls.'

'That's all we need,' Stevens said. 'If there's a supernatural angle to this story the media will lap it up, even though it'll be total bollocks.'

'That's something we're going to have to live with,' James said. 'Now, according to Laura Sheldon – the lawyer who found the bodies – Charlotte had a boyfriend named Neil Savage and she lived with him in Kendal. If she came to spend Christmas with her parents here then it's possible he did as well, which means it's possible the bloody shoeprints belong to him. So, we need to trace him. I also want us to start probing the family's financial affairs. They were having serious problems, so perhaps that had something to do with what's happened.'

There were no neighbours to interview so James suggested going into the village to make enquiries instead.

'The more we know about the family the easier it will hopefully be to get answers to the questions that will soon be mounting,' he told the group.

Back inside the farmhouse, James found Dr Flint kneeling over the body of Mary Bateman as SOCOs moved around the scene, taking pictures and bagging potential evidence.

The all-pervading sense of death unsettled James and caused his stomach muscles to contract.

He took the opportunity to take a tour of the house and was careful not to get into anyone's way. Downstairs there was a utility room and study. Upstairs there were three bedrooms and a separate bathroom. Most of the furniture had seen better days and the carpets were grubby and well worn.

There was nothing to indicate that the house had been robbed, which suggested to James that the killings weren't the work of a violent and desperate thief or thieves.

He found that Charlotte still had her own room even though she'd moved out. A SOCO who was checking the room showed James a small make-up bag that he'd found in the bedside drawer. Inside was a vape pen kit, a tube of e-liquid, several pre-rolled joints and a jar containing what the SOCO suspected were cannabis capsules. It appeared to confirm what James had been told about the girl dabbling in drugs.

Back downstairs, Tony Coppell was waiting to update him.

'I can confirm that the knife used on Charlotte was from the block on the kitchen worktop,' he said. 'Two mobile phones have been found and bagged. One was in Charlotte's jeans pocket and the other was on the unit next to the Christmas tree. They're both password-protected so will have to be unlocked. The fragments of glass on the floor are from an empty wine bottle that either fell off the worktop or was smashed deliberately.'

Coppell then held up a small slip of paper. 'And this we found in the pocket of Mr Bateman's coat, which was hanging in the hallway. It's a receipt for drinks bought on Christmas

Eve at The King's Head pub in Kirkby Abbey. And it shows that the transaction took place shortly before seven o'clock in the evening.'

'That's one of my local watering holes,' James said. 'Looks like it will be my first port of call after leaving here since it might well be the last place Robert Bateman was seen alive.'

Dr Flint had finished her initial examination of the bodies and was dictating her notes into her phone so James waited until she was finished before asking her what she thought.

'I won't know for sure until we get them back to the mortuary,' she replied. 'But based on the patterns of lividity and the rigor mortis, I would say they died on Christmas Eve or in the early hours of Christmas morning.'

'Any thoughts on how it might have played out?'

'Well, the fact that Mr Bateman is still clinging to the shotgun would seem to suggest that he used it to kill himself. But in scenes like this that I've attended in the past the shotgun was always found on the floor or ground next to the body. However, it could be that Mr Bateman's thumb got caught in the trigger guard when he went down. So, I'm afraid it's going to be for you to work out if this is a set-up or not.'

James felt his chest expand as he let out a breath and turned to look again at the corpses.

At least now they could focus on a more specific timeline. On Christmas Eve Robert Bateman visited a pub in the village, and it was highly likely that he came straight home from there with the drinks he'd bought.

So, what happened at that point? Did the family get into a fierce argument that ended in their deaths? Or did an entirely different scenario unfold, one that involved someone who fled the scene after taking steps to confuse the police?

James thanked Dr Flint and decided to go and stage another impromptu briefing with his team. But as he stepped outside, he saw DC Abbott hurrying towards him.

'They've found something in the cellar that you need to come and see, guv,' she said when she reached him. 'And if you were thinking that this case is already pretty weird ... well, it just got a whole lot weirder.'

CHAPTER NINE

There was an exterior entrance to the cellar on one side of the house where a short flight of concrete steps led down to an oak door that stood open.

The cellar itself was large and soulless, with a low ceiling from which hung a single uncovered light bulb.

It cast a soft glow that revealed heavy duty metal shelving units crammed with storage boxes, plastic jerry cans, empty bottles and bags of vegetables.

A long metal workbench stood against one wall and on top of it were various tools, several sacks of topsoil and a few tins of paint.

Exposed beams criss-crossed the ceiling and the timber floor had fallen victim to dry rot in places.

James noticed that a SOCO was taking photographs of something in one corner and as he followed DC Abbott further inside, he saw that it was a grey marble memorial stone of the kind usually found only in cemeteries. It was about the size of a football and rested on a small, squat display unit. James stopped for a closer look and saw an inscription on the stone which read:

You will never be forgotten.

He assumed it had been placed here by the Batemans in memory of the couple who were found dead in the cellar twenty-four years ago. He also assumed that it was what Abbott was so keen for him to see. But he was wrong.

'You have to go up the stairs, guv,' she said, pointing ahead of her to a wooden staircase that climbed up through the ceiling.

'Well, that's not something I expected to find down here,' he said. 'I'm sure there's no door to the cellar inside the house. Or, if there is, I didn't spot it.'

'There isn't,' Abbott said. 'It was replaced.'

She stepped to one side at the bottom of the stairs and waved him on.

'A forensic officer is up there to show you what's been found, guv. There's no room for me as well so I'll wait down here.'

James's curiosity was aroused as he mounted the stairs. Halfway up he stepped over an evidence marker that had been placed next to a dark stain on a step, and he made a mental note to find out what it was.

There was another open door at the top of the stairs, and beyond it a small enclosed space where a SOCO stood holding a torch.

'Welcome to my cosy cubbyhole,' the officer said from behind his mask.

James felt the hairs on his neck stir as he stared inside. It was about five feet from the door at the top of the stairs to a plasterboard wall opposite, and ten feet from left to right, but the ceiling sloped dramatically and filled much of the space. The only object that James could see was a plastic step stool tucked up against the wall.

'Is this some kind of cupboard or storeroom?' he asked as the officer waved his torch around to illuminate the room.

'It could be used as such, and probably has been in the past,' the officer said. 'But as you can see it's empty now, except for the stool.'

'So, what have you found that's got my detective so excited?'

The officer placed a hand on the plasterboard wall.

'This is not part of the original structure,' he explained. 'It was put here to replace a door that used to allow access to the cellar from the living area. It's not uncommon for home owners to block off cellar doors like this, especially those that are located beneath interior staircases.'

James realised then why the ceiling was at such a steep angle – they were standing beneath the stairs that were located in the living room.

'So, what's so unusual about this?' he asked.

The officer pointed to a spot on the wall and shone the torch at it. James saw a small, dark circle about an inch in diameter.

'This, Inspector, is a hidden peephole. It's made of brass and is similar to those used in front doors. And by looking through it you can see what's going on in both the living room and kitchen. You just have to stand on this stool.'

He invited James to step forward and check it out. James stepped on the stool and put his eye up against the device to peer through it. What he saw surprised him.

The peephole gave an elevated wide-angle view that was slightly magnified. He could see Dr Flint and the SOCOs working away, unaware that he was looking down on them. But not only that. He could also hear them clearly as well.

'Believe it or not it's almost impossible to spot it from the inside,' the officer said. 'I checked, and even though I knew what I was looking for, it took me a while to locate it.'

'And why is that?' James asked.

'The wallpaper under the stairs has a garish raindrop design. The peephole has been carefully placed in one of the drops.'

'Bloody hell.'

'Now step back down, Inspector, but be careful where you place your shoes.'

When James had done as he was asked, the officer shone the torch beam at the floor.

'I also spotted these,' he said. 'They're breadcrumbs, and they're just days old at the most. Which tells me that someone has been in here recently to spy on the family.'

James felt his spine stiffen. 'This is crazy. And there was me thinking that this case couldn't possibly throw up any more surprises.'

'Well actually, there's more,' the officer said. 'Come and see.'

James followed him out of the cubbyhole and the officer shone his torch at the stain on the stairs next to the evidence marker as they passed it.

'I'm pretty certain that's blood and it hasn't been there long. We'll scrape if off in the hope that we can extract some DNA. But at this moment there's no way of telling if it belonged to any of our three victims.'

By now James's mind was leaping all over the place and adrenaline was pumping through his veins.

'Keep up the good work, officer, and turn the cubbyhole and the cellar inside out. My gut is telling me that piecing this all together isn't going to be easy,' he said.

DC Abbott was waiting for him at the bottom of the cellar steps.

'So, what do you make of it, guv?' she said.

James shook his head. 'It's yet another intriguing development that's going to make our job even more difficult. I've never known a case like it.'

'Me neither. Shall I tell the rest of the team what we've found?'

'Get them together again while I pop back inside the house. I want to have a look at the wall under the stairs.'

Less than a minute later he was staring up at the raindrop wallpaper and looking for the peephole. The SOCO was right, he realised. It wasn't easy to locate.

Eventually he saw it though, framed by one of the large raindrops about fifteen inches down from the ceiling.

Who had put it there, he wondered. And why? Did the Batemans ever know it was there? Could the ghostly sounds that Mary Bateman told people she heard coming from behind the walls have been made by the person who was watching them through the peephole?

CHAPTER TEN

James checked his watch and found it was one o'clock already. He didn't usually stay so long at a crime scene, but the time had positively flown by because Oaktree Farm was the strangest crime scene he had ever visited. Three dead bodies, shoeprints in blood, a sinister peephole in a wall, and the fact that something disturbingly similar had happened there decades earlier.

James touched on all these points and more with his team and they were as baffled by it all as he was.

'Okay, it's time we shifted the investigation away from the crime scene. We know that Robert Bateman was at The King's Head pub in the village on Christmas Eve,' he said. 'I intend to go there now. I know the couple who run it so hopefully they'll remember seeing him. I'd like you to go with me, DC Abbott. DS Stevens, you stay at the farm and oversee the forensic sweep. There's a lot to be done and we need answers quickly,' he said. 'I'll arrange for someone to relieve you later.'

The other two detectives were ordered to work with the uniformed officers and visit the properties closest to the farm to find out if anyone had any useful information to offer up.

'Then go into the village and ask around, but try not to say too much about what's happened,' he said. 'Mind you, by now I expect the media vultures will have got wind of it and it won't be long before it hits the airwaves.'

James got Stevens to give Abbott the keys to the pool car and then phoned headquarters with an update. He was just about ready to depart the scene when his phone rang. He saw it was Annie calling and feared that she had somehow learned about the killings.

'A news alert just came up on my phone,' she said. 'The BBC are reporting that the police in London are searching for Andrew Sullivan in connection with a murder. Did you know?'

'I heard when I got to the office this morning.'

'Then why didn't you tell me?' James thought she sounded more anxious than angry.

'I've been busy, Annie. I was going to mention it this evening. But you really shouldn't worry. I don't reckon it will be long before he surfaces and the Met pulls him in.'

'But if he's on the run he could be anywhere. Even here in Cumbria.'

'No way, Annie. I know how these things work. Sullivan will be desperate to stay one step ahead of the law. The last thing on his mind will be getting even with me. And that's assuming he still intends to.'

His wife drew a breath, and after a long pause, said, 'Okay, I'll try not to let it get to me, but whenever I hear the bastard's name mentioned it freaks me out.'

'I know, and you shouldn't allow it to.'

'That's easier said than done. But fair enough. I'll force myself not to think about him. Meanwhile, should I expect you home at a reasonable time? I can make us a nice dinner.'

He hesitated before answering. 'Actually, I'll probably be late. We're working on a big case.'

'Really? What's happened?'

He didn't want to tell her but he knew she'd find out soon enough.

'I can't say too much, Annie,' he said. 'But brace yourself for some bad news. It turns out that this Christmas was not without another bout of bloodshed after all.'

James knew it was against protocol to share information about a case with his spouse but he took the view that it didn't make sense never to talk about his job with the person closest to him. There were boundaries, of course, and what he did share with Annie was never anything that could be considered highly confidential.

On this occasion, he told her that three people had been found dead in suspicious circumstances on a farm near Kirkby Abbey, but left out the gory details.

He did reveal their identities, however, just in case she'd known them and could provide useful insight, and because his team were already on their way to speak to other villagers anyway.

'I'm sure my parents knew them,' she said. 'Their names sound familiar and I probably did come across them. But what a dreadful thing to have happened. I feel sick to my stomach.'

'Try not to let this worry you either,' James said before they said goodbye.

As James drove away from Oaktree Farm with DC Abbott, that short and difficult conversation with his wife played on his mind. He knew that what he'd told her had come as an unwelcome shock and he feared she wouldn't be able to stop thinking about it.

Annie was a worrier at the best of times, and pregnancy had heightened her emotional responses to just about everything, but James had to accept that there was nothing he could do about it for now. He pushed it from his thoughts and focused on the job at hand.

Of the two pubs in Kirkby Abbey, The King's Head was James's favourite. He liked the rustic charm and the way the landlord and landlady made customers feel so welcome.

When he and Abbott got there, Luke Grooms and his wife Martha, along with a couple of staff members, were busy serving the lunchtime rush. Everyone seemed to be relaxed and enjoying themselves, and the place still buzzed with festive spirit.

James wasn't looking forward to being the bearer of bad news again. He knew that as word spread, the village would be consumed by a deep, dark cloud. But what had happened at Oaktree Farm wasn't something they could keep a lid on.

Luke was chatting to a group at one of the tables and Martha was standing behind the bar. When she spotted James, she smiled and waved him over.

'Hello there, James,' she said. 'Didn't you tell me when I last saw you that you were going back to work today?'

'I am at work, Martha,' he replied. 'This is my colleague, Detective Constable Abbott, and we'd like to have a word with you, if we may.'

A frown puckered Martha's brow. 'That sounds ominous. What's it about?'

'First, I need to know if you and Luke were here between about six and seven on Christmas Eve.'

'Well I was, but my husband was visiting his mother in Sedbergh. Why do you want to know?'

'Can we go and talk somewhere more private, Martha?' James asked. 'And I think it would be a good idea if Luke joined us.'

The couple told their two staff members to cover the bar and tables and then retreated to a back office with James and DC Abbott. When Luke and Martha were seated, James said, 'Now what I'm about to say will come as a shock. As of this moment it isn't public knowledge but it soon will be, and until it is, I'll ask you to please keep it to yourselves.'

'You're scaring us, James,' Luke said, his eyes anxious. 'Can you please get to the point?'

'All three members of the Bateman family have been killed in an extreme act of violence at Oaktree Farm,' James said carefully.

Martha's hand flew to her mouth and her face creased as shock spread across her features. Luke put an arm around her and mumbled something incomprehensible.

'The reason that we've come to see you is that we know Robert Bateman was here on Christmas Eve,' James said. 'We found a receipt at the farm for drinks he bought shortly before seven o'clock.'

Tears welled up in Martha's eyes and she wiped them with her sleeve.

'I was the one who served him,' she said. 'He bought two bottles of wine and a bottle of sherry to take out.'

'Was he here with anyone?'

She shook her head. 'He was by himself, which wasn't particularly unusual. He said he'd been to see his bank manager in Kendal and popped in for a quick pint. He spent quite a while in the bar nursing his drink before he decided to leave. It was busy here that evening so I didn't get the chance to have a chat with him.'

'Did anyone else?'

'I don't think so. I did ask him if we would see him and Mary over Christmas and he said he wasn't sure.'

'Do you know for certain if he was going straight home from here?' DC Abbott asked.

Martha had to cough to clear her throat, and it was some moments before she recovered her composure enough to continue.

'Th-that's what he told me,' she stammered. 'He said he only popped in for a swift one and had to get home to Mary.'

'And have you any idea how they were planning to spend Christmas?' James pressed.

'Well, I don't think they were intending to go anywhere. He said Mary had got a load of food in and they had Charlotte and her boyfriend Neil staying with them.'

The mention of Neil's name prompted Luke to lean forward, eyes almost bulging out of their sockets.

'Neil, did you say? Neil Savage?' He then turned to James and added, 'Was he there? Is he dead too?'

'Not as far as we know, Mr Grooms,' James replied. 'His

body isn't at the farm, and until now we didn't even know for certain that he was spending Christmas there.'

'Then you need to find him,' Luke said. 'The guy's a nasty bastard, and I've always thought it was only a matter of time before he did something really bad.'

CHAPTER ELEVEN

As James came away from The King's Head a glimmer of hope blossomed in his chest.

At least they now had a prime suspect: Neil Savage.

'I'm surprised that we've never heard of the guy,' DC Abbott said as she drove them towards Kendal. 'From what Mr Grooms said about him being a thug and small-time drug dealer it sounds like he should have come to our attention long before now.'

'I've had two encounters with him,' he'd told the detectives. 'The first was when he was here in the pub with a couple of his mates about eight months ago. I saw him hand some pills to a young lad who lives in the village so I confronted him and told him to leave. He threw his glass on the floor and threatened to beat the shit out of me. His friends pulled him away and took him outside, but not before he spat at me. I could tell he was either pissed or drugged up.

'I came across him again about two months later when he was with Charlotte. I was driving through the village and the pair of them stepped off the kerb in front of me. I had to brake hard to avoid hitting them. Instead of thanking me, the guy gave me a load of verbal abuse and banged his fist against my side window. But what really got me was that Charlotte, who I've known since she was a little girl, thought it was funny.'

'Did Charlotte's parents know what Savage was like?' James had asked Grooms.

Luke had nodded. 'Of course. Robert told me once that he couldn't stand the guy and had tried to persuade his daughter to break up with him. That was when she left the farm and moved into his flat in Kendal. There was an upside to that though – since then he's rarely appeared in the village.'

As Abbott drove James called the office to learn the name had already been run through the criminal records database.

Neil Miles Savage, aged twenty-five, had form for possession of drugs, assault and theft. He'd been punished with fines and community service orders. Further checks had established that he was unemployed and lived in a flat in the centre of Kendal. A warrant to search the flat had been requested.

Savage's mother also lived in the town but his father was one year into a five-year prison sentence for a string of burglaries.

'Sounds like Savage junior decided to follow in his father's footsteps,' James said.

Abbott nodded and replied without taking her eyes off the road. 'I hope that he's at home when we get there, guv.'

'You and me both,' James said.

As they ploughed on towards Kendal, James noticed that the clouds had reclaimed the sky, blotting out the sun and turning the day grey and oppressive.

The market town of Kendal was known mainly as a centre for tourism and boasted two castles, two museums and a multitude of pubs and restaurants.

James had grown to really like the town since he'd started working there, even though – or maybe especially because – it was a world away from what he'd been used to in London. The air was cleaner, the streets safer and the din of traffic nowhere near as loud and annoying.

Savage's flat was in a small, unimpressive block close to the River Kent, which passed through the town. There was a patrol car parked outside when they got there and two officers in high-visibility vests were waiting on the pavement, having been told that detectives were on their way.

The flat was on the second floor and they got no response when they rang the bell so James took the decision to force their way in, instructing one of the officers to get a battering ram from the car. It took just one blow to force the door open.

The interior was small and unkempt, littered with empty crisp packets, beer bottles and overflowing ashtrays. Within seconds they established that the place was empty. There was just one bedroom, a lounge, a separate kitchen and a bathroom.

The bed was unmade and there was unwashed cutlery in the sink. James got the clear impression that the flat hadn't been occupied for several days and that Savage had left in a hurry.

He noted that Charlotte's clothes took up most of the space in the wardrobe and drawers, but there were no photos of her or Savage anywhere and not a single Christmas decoration.

They found several pairs of men's shoes – all a size ten – but none of them showed any obvious signs of blood on the soles, or had a pattern to match the shoeprints left at the farm.

'It could be he's still wearing them,' Abbott suggested.

James agreed and told her to call control and arrange for a forensic team to come to the flat.

As they waited he conducted a quick search, finding a bag full of cannabis capsules and some other pills that looked to be drugs of some kind. But he didn't come across anything that could be linked directly to the killings at Oaktree Farm. Or anything that told them where Savage was.

There were two other flats on the same floor and by now the police presence had attracted the interest of the occupants. A middle-aged man and a young woman had been asking the uniforms in the hallway what was going on. The man, who said his name was Tom Leyton, lived next door to Savage and one of the officers asked him to tell James what he'd told him.

'I haven't seen Neil since Christmas Day,' Mr Leyton said. 'I was downstairs when he drove into the car park about lunchtime, and I saw that his car was damaged. I asked him about it and he said he'd been involved in a collision but he wasn't hurt.'

'So where did he go then?' James asked.

'He came up here to his flat. But he didn't stay long. I know because an hour or so later I happened to be looking out of my window when I saw him walking off down the street. He had his rucksack on his back so I assumed he was going back to Charlotte's parents' farm. That's where he'd told me they were spending Christmas.'

'And Charlotte definitely wasn't with him on Christmas Day?' James said.

Mr Leyton shook his head. 'No, she wasn't. I haven't seen her around since early on Christmas Eve. So, what's going on? Is the lad in trouble again?'

'I'm not at liberty to say at this time, Mr Leyton. I can only share that we need to talk to him in connection with an incident. In the meantime, I'd appreciate it if you could come downstairs and show us which is his car.'

The car was a relatively old Peugeot 307 and there was extensive damage to the offside wing. It was badly dented and scratched, and the headlight was broken.

James noted the registration and called it in. He told control that he wanted to know if there were any reports of the car being involved in an accident on Christmas Eve or Christmas Day anywhere in this part of Cumbria.

He didn't have to wait long to hear back. A woman had called police around 7.20 p.m. on Christmas Eve to say that a vehicle rammed into the back of her car when it was over-taking, forcing her off the road and into a dry-stone wall. The driver of the other vehicle failed to stop and drove off at speed.

The woman was badly shaken but not hurt, and the officers who responded arranged for her car to be towed away and then gave her a lift home.

She didn't get the number or make of the offending vehicle but James believed there was a strong possibility that the other driver was Neil Savage. Not least because of where the incident took place – about two hundred yards from the entrance to Oaktree Farm.

CHAPTER TWELVE

It was three o'clock already so as James and DC Abbott waited at Savage's flat for the forensic team to arrive they took the opportunity to have a late lunch in the form of takeaway coffees and sandwiches from a small café across the road.

When they appeared, James briefed the SOCOs on the situation and got them to open Savage's car so that he could check the interior before it got transported to the labs. He didn't spot any signs of blood, but told the SOCOs to pay particular attention to the footwell and pedals.

'If it was Savage who left his bloody shoeprints at the farm then there might be traces,' he said. 'That's assuming that his shoes weren't wiped completely clean when he walked across the snow from the house to his car.'

More uniforms turned up to monitor the movement of people going in and out of the building, and to be there should Savage return. With James happy that everything was covered, he and Abbott set out for Savage's mother's house on the northern edge of the town. It took the detectives just over ten minutes to get there and on the way James received a text from the office with more background information.

Neil's mother and father had divorced three years ago and she'd reverted to her maiden name of Weldon. Neil was her only child and she was a partner in a firm of local accountants.

Her home was a modest terraced house with limestone walls and a tiny front garden, and alarm registered on her face when she opened the door and saw the warrant card in James's hand.

'Are you Miss Gillian Weldon?' he asked.

'Yes.'

'I'm Detective Inspector Walker and this is Detective Constable Abbott. We're here in the hope that you can help us locate your son, Neil, Miss Weldon. We've just been to his flat and he's not there. We need to speak with him as a matter of urgency in relation to an ongoing investigation.'

She was a diminutive woman with sallow skin and curly red hair. And when she spoke, her voice was high-pitched.

'Well I can assure you that he isn't here,' she replied. 'In fact, I'd like to know where he is myself. I was expecting to see him yesterday but he didn't come over and didn't bother to call me. I've tried ringing him but his phone is off. And so is his girlfriend's.'

'We would still like to ask you some questions so may we come in?' James said.

She managed a nervous smile. 'I suppose so. But I'm really not sure I can be of help.'

They followed her into a small, neat living room and she

invited them to sit on the sofa while she lowered herself onto the armchair facing them.

'You're lucky to catch me in,' she said. 'The office is closed for the rest of the week so I'm not working. That's why I was hoping to see Neil on Boxing Day. I know he spent Christmas Eve and Christmas Day at Charlotte's parents' farm. But yesterday we were meant to exchange gifts.'

'Is your son in the habit of making himself scarce?' James asked her.

She nodded. 'The fact is I don't see much of him these days. I suppose we have what you would describe as a strained relationship. He's too much like his father – bone idle and irresponsible. And he resents it when I try to discourage his bad behaviour. We don't always see eye to eye.'

'I can tell you that he's not with his girlfriend at the moment and he's not at home. So, where do you think he might be?'

'I have no idea. He has a habit of disappearing for days at a time. He could be anywhere.'

'We're aware that he has a criminal record, Miss Weldon,' James said. 'But would you say he's a violent person?'

'He can be when he's had too much to drink or is off his head on pills. He gets it all from his lowlife father who you probably know is in jail. I just don't want Neil to wind up there too, and I fear he will if he doesn't sort himself out.'

'Has he mellowed at all since he started a relationship with Charlotte?'

She shook her head and her eyes glistened with repressed anger.

'That's half the problem. She's as bad as he is. A right

stroppy mare at times. They wind each other up so much I'm surprised they've stayed together this long. If you want to know where Neil is you should ask her.'

James and Abbott exchanged a look and Miss Weldon picked up on the unspoken message that passed between them.

'You might as well tell me what sort of trouble he's in,' she said. 'Is it dealing drugs, stealing things or has he hit someone again? You're not the first police officers to have come here asking about him. I'm quite used to it by now.'

The blood quickly retreated from the woman's face as James told her what they had found at Oaktree Farm.

'We know from speaking to one of his neighbours that Neil returned to his flat on Christmas Day,' he said. 'We also know that he'd had a minor collision in his car, which is still parked over there. There's damage to the front offside wing and light, but the neighbour said he didn't appear injured himself. The same neighbour saw him walk away from the block about an hour after he arrived – he was carrying a rucksack – and it doesn't appear that he's been back there since.'

There was a faraway look in the woman's eyes now, as though she was unable to comprehend what she had just heard.

'I need to be clear with you that at this stage what happened at the farm remains a mystery,' James continued. 'But your son's disappearance inevitably implies guilt, and we need to find out if he was involved in any way.'

Miss Weldon shook her head slowly and a deep furrow entrenched itself in her brow.

'Neil would never kill anyone,' she said. 'He does stupid

things that get him into trouble. But he's most definitely not a murderer.'

'Then why do you think he's dropped out of sight?' James asked.

'I don't know. Perhaps he's scared and in a panic. Or perhaps something bad has happened to him as well.'

Tears filled her eyes then and she started to blink rapidly.

DC Abbott, who had been taking notes, leaned forward, elbows on knees, and said, 'We have to know if you've been totally honest with us, Miss Weldon. Has Neil been in contact with you?'

'No, he hasn't,' she replied, her voice hostile. 'If you don't believe me you can check my phone and search the house. I don't care. All I care about now is finding my son and hearing him tell me that he had nothing to do with those killings.'

She broke down then in a paroxysm of tears. Abbott got up and offered her a tissue, then crouched beside the woman and tried to console her.

They stayed with her for another forty-five minutes, during which time she let James look around the house. There was no sign of her son, but there were several framed photos of him, though none of them with Charlotte. He was tall and sinewy, with a narrow face and hair that was dark and spiky.

Miss Weldon allowed them to take one of the pictures away with them after James explained that they would need it if and when they launched an appeal for information on his whereabouts.

She also gave them Neil's mobile number and told them that Charlotte worked in a charity shop in the town centre.

'Do you know if that's how Neil and Charlotte managed

to pay for the flat? We understand he's currently unemployed,' James said.

'No, I top up his benefits with a monthly allowance,' she said. 'He refuses to stay here and I can't bear the thought of him sleeping rough on the streets. But I'm not stupid. I know he uses some of the money to buy drugs.'

CHAPTER THIRTEEN

When they left Gillian Weldon's house the sky was rushing towards darkness and it was much colder but at least it wasn't snowing.

First stop was the charity shop where Miss Weldon had said Charlotte Bateman worked. But it was closed, as were most of the other retail outlets in the town.

As the two detectives headed for police headquarters, James asked Abbott what she thought of Neil Savage's mother.

'I'm sure she told us the truth, if that's what you mean, guv,' she said. 'But I'm not convinced that she believes her son is incapable of killing someone. I reckon she's just hoping and praying that he is.'

James nodded. 'I'd agree with you. And she did lend weight to what Luke Grooms said about the guy. He's prone to violence, especially when dosed up with drink and drugs. And there was plenty of both found at the farm.'

James did not intend to stay long at the office but he wanted to get across what had been happening and ensure that the officers who'd be working through the night would have enough to keep them busy. However, he was in for an unpleasant surprise even before he entered the building.

There waiting for him when he climbed out of the car was a man he'd been hoping wouldn't appear until at least tomorrow.

'Hi there, Inspector. I thought I might bump into you if I waited around here long enough.'

Gordon Carver was a reporter with the *Cumbria Gazette* and James encountered him more often than he did any other hack because he happened to live in Kirkby Abbey. He was sharp-featured and in his late twenties, with close-cropped reddish hair and a forceful manner.

James saw no point in fobbing him off given that he might need his help during the course of the investigation.

'I can guess why you're here, Gordon,' he said.

'Before you refer me to the press office, you should know that I've already spoken to them,' Carver said. 'But what they've told me wouldn't fill half a page in my notebook.'

'And you're hoping that I'll give you an off-the-record briefing.'

Carver shrugged. 'You know by now that you can trust me, Inspector. I thought we had a quid pro quo arrangement.'

James told Abbott to go on ahead of him, then turned back to the reporter. 'So the story's out there, is it?'

'It hit the wires a couple of hours ago, but the official line is lacking so much detail that it's got our imaginations running rampant.'

'What do you know exactly?' James asked.

'Well, the statement that's been issued says that three members of the same family have been found dead at a farm in Cumbria. The location is given as close to Kirkby Abbey. Their identities have not been disclosed, but the statement makes clear that they died in violent circumstances and two of the victims suffered fatal gunshot wounds.'

'Then surely that's enough to be getting on with,' James said.

Carver grinned. 'Come off it, Inspector. You won't be surprised to learn that my phone hasn't stopped ringing. This is Cumbria, not London. I already know that it happened at Oaktree Farm, the home of Robert and Mary Bateman, so I'm assuming they're the victims along with their daughter, Charlotte.'

James blew out a breath. He should have known that it'd be impossible to manage the release of information.

'I also have a personal interest in this story,' Carver added.

James raised an eyebrow. 'Oh?'

'I've met Robert Bateman a few times and I even went to the farm once to interview him for a feature about the problems facing farmers in the county,' Carver said. 'I therefore find it strange, as well as quite unsettling, that such a thing has happened, and I'm desperate to know more.'

James mulled this over for a few moments before confirming that the bodies were indeed those of Robert and Mary Bateman and their daughter.

'I'll speak to the press office about releasing the names,' he said. 'There's no reason to hold them back now, and I won't object to you having a head start.'

'So, who was shot?' Carver asked.

'The parents.'

'And Charlotte? How did she die?'

'I can't release those details at this time.'

'So, what the fuck went on there?'

'We're still trying to work that out.'

'Do you think it was purely a family affair, or was someone else involved?'

This was where James had to tread carefully. He wanted to pick and choose what information was fed to the media at this early stage in the investigation. But he knew that once the floodgates were open it was always hard to control things.

He decided to throw caution to the wind and get Carver on his side. The reporter lived locally and had his ear to the ground. James was pretty sure he would be a useful source on information in the days ahead.

'Have you heard of a guy named Neil Savage?'

Carver rolled out his bottom lip as he thought about it.

'No, I don't think I have. Is he a suspect?'

'He's Charlotte's boyfriend. They lived together and we believe he was at the farm for Christmas, but he seems to have disappeared.'

'I'll sift through our files to see if he's there,' Carver said. 'Can I go with this and also offer it to the nationals?'

James nodded. 'I'll square it with the press office when I go inside. The sooner his name is out there the better as far as I'm concerned. We need to know where he is and I'm sure there's someone out there who can tell us.'

'What line should I take?'

'The usual. The police are anxious to speak to the guy because they believe he was at the farm at some point during the weekend, and they're hoping he might be able to help them with their enquiries. But don't quote me directly,' James said.

'When exactly did it happen?'

81

'That's yet to be confirmed, but we believe it was late on Christmas Eve.'

James waited for Carver to scribble it all in his notebook, then said, 'In return for this heads-up I'll expect you to let me know what you unearth in the coming days, Gordon. I'm sure that with your knowledge of the village and the people in it you'll find some things out before we do.'

'That goes without saying, Inspector. Now, as a matter of interest, are you aware of the history of Oaktree Farm?'

'I take it you mean the killings that took place there in 1997.'

'That's right.'

'Yes, I know about that, although I didn't before today.'

'I suppose it would be stretching it to think that there might be a connection, apart from the fact that Robert Bateman worked on the farm back then.'

'It seems unlikely on the face of it,' James said. 'But there are striking similarities between what happened then and what's happened now. Two married couples killed at the same remote location. In each case the husband died from a shotgun wound. Plus, one daughter disappeared and the other appears to have been murdered. So nothing can be ruled out. How well did you know Robert Bateman?'

'We were on first name terms, but to be honest our paths rarely crossed,' Carver said. 'He was an unassuming bloke and whenever I saw him with his wife, they seemed pretty happy together.'

'Can you think of anyone in the village who didn't get on with him or bore a grudge for whatever reason?'

The reporter chewed on his bottom lip while he gave it some thought. After about thirty seconds, he tilted his head to one side and said, 'Actually someone does spring to mind. Someone who fell out big time with Robert. In fact, I was in The King's Head one evening when the pair almost came to blows. I remember how the other guy flew at Robert when he walked into the pub. He yelled at him, claiming that he'd ruined his life and that he would make him pay. Some of the other customers had to get between them and calm things down.'

'Who is this other guy?'

'His name is Kenneth O'Connor. He was a farmhand at Oaktree but was sacked earlier this year and took it badly. You might even know him since he lives a few streets away from you in Kirkby Abbey.'

CHAPTER FOURTEEN

The office was teeming with detectives and civilian staff when James walked in. A bunch of them had been drafted in from other stations to lend support to the investigation.

It was half past four and the Christmas calm had been well and truly shattered. James hadn't seen the team so anxious and determined since they were hunting down the serial killer in Kirkby Abbey a year ago.

He clapped his hands to get everyone's attention and told them he would hold a briefing in ten minutes.

First, he wanted to make a couple of calls. He began with DS Stevens who was still overseeing things at Oaktree Farm. He told him that Neil Savage was now their prime suspect.

'No one seems to know where he is,' James said. 'And from the sound of it he's a right bad one.'

James ran through the interviews that he and DC Abbott had conducted with Luke and Martha Grooms, and Savage's mother.

'I was also cornered a few minutes ago by Gordon Carver, the reporter with the *Cumbria Gazette*,' James said.

'The press has been quick to latch onto this one, guv,' Stevens responded. 'A photographer and a television camera crew turned up here about an hour ago. We blocked the lane but they've been filming and taking pictures from the road.'

'That'll only get worse, but to be fair we need to work with the media on this one. Carver has already tipped me off about someone who also has to be a person of interest to us. And that's why I'm ringing you now rather than later. The guy in question lives in Kirkby Abbey, and I want you to go and see him right away. His name is Kenneth O'Connor and he worked as a farmhand for the Batemans but was fired earlier this year.'

James relayed the conversation he'd had with the reporter and passed on O'Connor's address.

'Take a couple of uniforms with you,' he went on. 'We need to establish what his movements have been since Christmas Eve. And if whatever he says doesn't sound right then bring him in for formal questioning. How are things going at the scene now?'

'Nothing new has been uncovered and much of the farm still hasn't been processed,' Stevens replied. 'There are fewer forensic officers here now, but they'll be back in force in the morning. Meanwhile, the bodies have been taken away and Dr Flint said she'll crack on with the post-mortems as soon as she can tomorrow.'

James ended the call by saying he would send someone to take over at the farm through the night.

His second call was to DCI Tanner, who was still travelling back from Scotland. After being updated, Tanner said he would talk to the press office about issuing a more detailed statement, and he'd tell them to be ready to release the photo of Neil Savage.

'I agree with you that it makes no sense to hold stuff back,' Tanner said. 'We need a quick resolution to this case for all our sakes. A media firestorm is building and if it drags on for any length of time the powers-that-be will pile on the pressure.'

James covered much of the same ground during the team meeting, explaining why Neil Savage was in the frame, but stressing that they did not know for sure if the bloody shoe-prints belonged to him.

'What appears to be in no doubt is that he went to Oaktree Farm with Charlotte on Christmas Eve,' James said. 'But we believe he drove away from there later in the evening and that just a couple of hundred yards from the farm his car collided with another vehicle, which was shunted off the road. He drove on without stopping but we have no idea where he went. What we do know is that on Christmas Day he returned to his flat here in Kendal around lunchtime, but only stayed for a short time before he was off again on foot and carrying a rucksack. We need to trawl CCTV cameras to see if we can find out where he went. His mother has given us his mobile number but attempts to ring it tell us it's switched off. We need to alert the techies so they can track it if it starts trans-mitting again.

'In the meantime, Savage's car, and the vehicle whose owner reported the accident, are being examined by forensics, and we do have another potential suspect,' James continued. 'Kenneth O'Connor used to work for the Batemans at Oaktree Farm but was sacked six months ago. He apparently took it hard. According to Gordon Carver, O'Connor blamed Robert Bateman for sending his life into a downward spiral. The journalist actually saw O'Connor threaten Bateman one evening in a village pub. DS Stevens is currently on his way to O'Connor's address to question him and find out if he had an alibi for Christmas Eve and Christmas Day. Does anyone else have any developments to add? Have the next of kin been traced and informed?'

'We've managed to reach Robert's brother in Ireland,' someone said. 'But so far we haven't been able to contact Mary's sister in France. We've asked the French police to assist.'

The latest news from forensics was that the two mobile phones found at the farm had been delivered to the lab along with various blood samples, including the one found on the stairs in the cellar.

There followed a brief question and answer session before James dished out assignments for the following day and decided who would work through the night.

'We'll kick off tomorrow with a briefing at eight,' he said. 'By then we'll have all the crime scene photos and forensic reports.'

He was about to leave the office when his mobile rang. It was Stevens calling to tell him that he'd visited Kenneth O'Connor's house, but there was no one there.

'I spoke to his neighbours but they haven't seen him for a couple of days and don't know where he is,' Stevens said. 'And none of them has his mobile number.'

'We'll go back tomorrow,' James said. 'You might as well call it a day. We have a briefing scheduled at eight in the morning.'

James hung up and sent a text to Annie telling her that he would soon be on his way home. Just as he finished, his phone rang again. This time it was one of the officers working with the SOCOs at Neil Savage's flat.

'I thought you should know that they've found something interesting, sir,' she said. 'It had been dumped in Savage's bin.'

'What is it?'

'A plastic bag, sir. Inside were several photographs of Charlotte Bateman that had been ripped up. In one she's standing between her parents. In another she's sitting on Savage's lap and kissing his cheek. There was also a Christmas card from her to him that has been torn to shreds. Forensics is going to try to put them all back together.'

James felt his pulse escalate. 'It suggests to me that he'd fallen out with her.'

'That's the obvious conclusion to draw, sir,' the officer said. 'But it's not the sort of thing one does after a minor tiff. He must have been mightily pissed off with her for some reason. Maybe she'd cheated on him. Or perhaps she'd told him that their relationship was over.'

'Well, I know one thing for sure,' James said. 'The evidence against the guy is stacking up.'

CHAPTER FIFTEEN

James could feel the tiredness creeping up on him as he finally left the office. At the same time, pressure was forming behind his eyes and he hoped it wasn't the onset of one of his tension headaches. He'd been having them for years, and sometimes they were so severe that it felt like a spike was being hammered into his skull.

There was a lot to think about during the drive home, and as soon as he hit the road, he started mentally adding things to his to-do list.

The last instruction he gave to the team was to pull out all the stops in an effort to find Neil Savage. The guy's photo had been circulated to every force in the country and attempts were being made to trace all those who knew him.

As usual, James felt a frisson of guilt for going home at the end of day one of an investigation. But he'd learned a long time ago that tired coppers make mistakes. During his time in the Met, he'd come across dozens of detectives who were reluctant to delegate. They'd ignore their body clocks and work until they dropped. Invariably this caused tempers to flare, arguments to break out and vital clues to be missed.

As senior investigating officer, James couldn't allow his mind to get fogged up by sheer exhaustion. He owed it to everyone to make sure that his batteries were fully charged at all times.

It wasn't as though it hadn't been a long, gruelling day. It was 8 p.m. when he got home and by then his eyes felt dry and heavy, and the pounding in his head filled his ears.

Annie was waiting for him in the hallway as he stepped through the front door. There was a smile on her face, but he could tell from her eyes that it was pasted on for his benefit.

'There's a large whisky waiting for you in the kitchen,' she said. 'And I've put a ready meal in the microwave. You can get stuck in while you tell me about your day, which I guess has been pretty horrendous.'

'You've guessed right, my love,' he said as he removed his coat and shoes and walked up to her.

He snaked an arm around her waist and pulled her to him. She was wearing his favourite perfume, the one with a heady fragrance of jasmine.

'I'm sorry I couldn't get home any sooner,' he said. 'Are you okay?'

'Of course. And there's no need for you to apologise.'

She lifted her head so that he could kiss her on the lips and afterwards she took his hand and led him into the kitchen.

'I've got a splitting headache,' he said. 'I'll need to take a couple of painkillers with the whisky.'

'Make yourself comfortable and I'll heat up your dinner,' Annie said.

He got a packet of paracetamol from the cupboard and

popped two tablets into his mouth, washing them down with the whisky as he sat at the table.

He wasn't really hungry – he would have been quite happy to have had just a couple more stiff drinks before sloping off to bed – but he knew that Annie was desperate to know how the investigation was going and whether the people of Kirkby Abbey had another killer in their midst.

She started the ball rolling after dishing up his meal and pouring herself a soft drink.

'It's been on the news,' she said. 'And I've already had two of my colleagues ring me. It's shaken everyone to the core and they can't believe it's happened.'

James picked at his food as he spoke, and he tried to ignore the dull, deeply embedded ache behind his eyes.

When they lived in London Annie never took that much interest in the cases he worked on. Most of the crimes were committed in places she wasn't familiar with, and there was nothing linking her to the victims. But here in this close-knit community it was different. Extreme acts of violence were rare and their impact was felt by everyone.

Annie listened in silence, her teeth tugging at her bottom lip, her features creased with emotion. She already knew much of what he told her, having monitored the news throughout the afternoon.

He ran the names Neil Savage, Gillian Weldon, and Kenneth O'Connor by her but the only one she recognised was O'Connor.

'I've never spoken to him, but I know he lives around the corner from here and according to gossip his partner walked out on him not long ago. Do you think he had something to do with what happened?'

James shrugged. 'We don't know. But we do know he had a falling out with Robert Bateman because he lost his job at the farm. He wasn't at home when we called round today but we'll try again tomorrow.'

James was going to mention the first bloodbath that took place at Oaktree Farm twenty-four years ago, but Annie beat him to it.

'The news feeds are making a big thing of it,' she said. 'They've dug up some old photos of the Roth couple. And the strange thing is I can actually remember how it freaked me out at the time. You see, my parents were friends with the Roths, and I even held their baby, the one who went missing.'

The revelation came as a bolt from the blue. As he listened to Annie, the photos he'd seen online of baby Megan and her parents flashed through his mind.

'I was twelve or thirteen at the time,' Annie told him. 'Mum and I were coming back from the store when we saw Amanda Roth pushing her pram. It was only a couple of weeks after she'd given birth and Mum invited her back for a cup of tea. While she was here, she had to feed the baby and afterwards she asked me if I wanted to hold her. I remember how small she was and how cute. But they didn't stay for long and we never saw either of them again.'

Annie's bottom lip quivered as she spoke and her eyes glistened with sadness.

'The news about the killings broke about a week later,' she went on. 'I remember how upset Mum was and how my dad joined in the search for Megan around Oaktree Farm. For a while it was the only thing people talked about. Then came the funerals at the church and I insisted on going along. But the turn-out was poor because by then the suspicion that Simon Roth had killed his wife before killing himself had taken root. And the conclusion the police came to was that one or both of them probably killed their baby and her body was hidden somewhere.'

'So, the Roths are buried in the village churchyard,' James said.

Annie nodded. 'That's right. Their graves share the same headstone. I recall attending a memorial service there to mark the first anniversary of the killings. Then, years later, my own parents were buried close by.'

James told her about the memorial stone in the cellar at Oaktree Farm.

'Well, that was where the bodies were found,' Annie said as she drew a tremulous breath. 'All credit to the Batemans for marking the spot.'

Annie lowered her eyes then and lapsed into sullen silence.

James pushed his plate to one side and reached across the table to take her hand.

'What I don't understand, Annie, is why you've never told me about this before now. It was obviously an event that made a big impression on you.'

She looked up and as she did so her eyes seemed to go out of focus.

'I suppose because it was a memory that I chose to bury,' she replied. 'A lot was going on in my life back then and people eventually stopped talking about it. Over time it became one of those things that I pushed to the back of my mind. And it would still be there if the Batemans hadn't been killed.'

CHAPTER SIXTEEN

Thursday December 28th

Somehow, despite being taunted by images from the crime scene and the story that Annie had told him the previous evening, James managed to get six hours sleep.

He came awake at 6 a.m. to find that he was alone in the bed, but there were sounds of movement coming from the bathroom.

He switched on the bedside lamp but stayed where he was for a few minutes, thinking about the day ahead and wondering if there had been any significant developments overnight.

Then the bathroom door opened and Annie appeared.

'I didn't realise you were awake,' she said. 'I tried to be quiet.'

'It wasn't you,' he told her. 'I've got a lot on my mind. Why are you up so early?'

She pulled a face. 'A bout of morning sickness. I just managed to reach the loo before throwing up.'

She was wearing her dressing gown, and as she stepped

towards the bed, he saw that her skin was flushed from the heat of the shower.

'Did you have a bad night?' he asked her.

She nodded. 'I couldn't stop thinking about what's happened to the Bateman family. It's like the grisly sequel to a horror movie that was set in the same location.'

It was a fair analogy, James thought as he hauled himself out of bed. He gave Annie a hug and told her that she smelled really nice. But he couldn't say the same about how she looked and that concerned him. Her face was lined with emotion and fatigue, and red veins laced the whites of her eyes.

This was just what she didn't need during the early stages of her pregnancy. It was bad enough having to deal with all the mental and physical issues that having a baby brought up.

'I'll go and make some coffee,' she said. 'Have you got time for breakfast before you go?'

'Maybe just some toast,' he said. 'I've called a meeting for eight but I need to sort stuff out before it starts and catch up with where we are.'

'Then you go and have a shower and the coffee and toast will be ready when you come down.'

Even after his shower, James could still feel the tension in his limbs. But at least he had managed to sleep off his headache and was raring to crack on with the investigation.

Before heading downstairs, he put in a quick call to the office and discovered that not much had happened during the night. Neil Savage still hadn't turned up, but his name and photo had been released to the media. In addition, photos of the crime scene had been delivered to the office and would be pinned to the evidence board in advance of the morning briefing.

James found that his breakfast was already on the table when he walked into the kitchen.

'How's the headache?' Annie asked him.

'It's gone, thankfully,' he said, as he sat. 'What about you? Do you still feel sick?'

'A little, but it'll pass.'

Before sitting down opposite him she switched on the TV and used the remote to turn to the BBC News Channel. The presenter was in the middle of an interview with a prominent politician; something about the latest economic forecast for the UK.

'So, what does your gut tell you about what happened at Oaktree Farm?' Annie asked. 'You didn't really say what you thought last night.'

James blew steam off his coffee and said, 'That it's not as straightforward as I would like it to be. I can't even be sure that Robert Bateman took his own life, even though that's how it initially looked. We need to speak to Neil Savage. I think he's the only person who can shed light on it for us.'

They were both suddenly distracted by the mention of Cumbria on the TV. Sure enough, the presenter was now speaking as aerial footage played of Oaktree Farm which looked like a tiny stain against the snowy white landscape surrounding it.

'*Police have now confirmed that three members of the same family were found dead at the farm yesterday morning,*' the presenter was saying. '*Robert and Mary Bateman, along with their daughter Charlotte, who was in her twenties, are believed to have been there since Christmas Eve. It's understood that*

Mr and Mrs Bateman were shot and that Charlotte suffered a fatal knife wound.

'Detectives leading the investigation are anxious to speak to a man named Neil Savage – Charlotte Bateman's boyfriend – who lives in Kendal and was due to spend Christmas at the farm with the family.'

The aerial shot was replaced by the photo of Savage that his mother had given the police, which was then replaced by an old newspaper cutting that included a picture of Simon and Amanda Roth.

'People living in the area have been quick to point out that Oaktree Farm was the scene of a similar tragedy in 1997 when the bodies of the previous owners were found in the cellar. The investigation at the time concluded that Mr Roth had shot himself after killing his wife. The Roths' daughter – three-week-old Megan Roth – disappeared on the same day. Police have long believed that she was sadly killed. We hope to bring you more on this story later today.'

Annie picked up the remote and muted the TV. She snapped her head towards James and a flash of panic passed over her face.

'I think I'm going to be sick again,' she said, clapping a hand over her mouth as she jumped to her feet and rushed out of the room.

James got up and put the coffee mug and plate in the dishwasher. He was about to go and see if Annie was all right when he heard the doorbell ring. It struck him as odd because they rarely had callers at this time of the morning.

Annie was in the downstairs toilet so he called out to let her know that he would answer the door. When he did, he was greeted by a squat, bullish man of about forty who was

97

bundled into a heavy grey overcoat. He had a blunt, square face and hardly any hair, and although James didn't know him, he was sure he'd seen him around the village.

'Hi there,' James said with a smile. 'Can I help you?'

'I'm here to help you, Detective Walker,' the man said. 'I live just a couple of hundred yards from here and when I got home late last night my neighbour told me I'd had a visit from the police who wanted to talk to me. And he said he suspected it was in connection with the killings at Oaktree Farm. So, I thought I'd save you the trouble of dropping in on me again later. The name's O'Connor. Kenneth O'Connor.'

James was totally thrown and it made him slow to react.

This was the first time a suspect had ever turned up at his home, either here or in London.

It felt like a huge and uncomfortable invasion of his privacy, as well as a dangerous precedent.

'You should have called the station in Kendal,' James said. 'Arrangements would have been made to interview you either there or at your home.'

O'Connor's expression showed irritation.

'But we're virtually neighbours, and when I heard that you were in charge of the case, I decided to do you a favour and pop round. Is that a problem?'

'Well it's unconventional, Mr O'Connor,' James said. 'I prefer to conduct interviews at the station and when I have a colleague with me, as per protocol.'

O'Connor shrugged. 'Then I'll take that to mean that you're not in a hurry to ask me any questions. But just so you know, I'm off to Carlisle today and won't be back until tonight.'

As he started to turn away, James said, 'Hold on a sec, Mr

O'Connor. I do need to talk to you about your relationship with Mr Bateman and it is urgent.'

'Okay, then. Do you want to do it here?'

'No. I was about to leave for the office. Would it be possible for you to return home and I'll follow you there? I have the address.'

O'Connor gave another shrug. 'I'm off in half an hour myself so if you can make it quick, I'd appreciate it.'

O'Connor walked off and James closed the door. When he turned, Annie was standing in the hallway looking anxious.

'That was a bit weird,' she said. 'I'm glad I wasn't here by myself. I wouldn't have known what to tell him.'

'I don't suppose he thought anything of it,' James said. 'And it might be something that we should expect to happen whenever a crime is committed on our doorstep and I'm put in charge. After all, this isn't London. Here every victim, witness and suspect will know where I live.'

CHAPTER SEVENTEEN

James called the office and pushed the morning briefing back to nine o'clock. Then he phoned DCI Tanner to tell him that he was going to talk to Kenneth O'Connor before setting off for Kendal.

'Is there any evidence to indicate that the guy was involved in what happened?' Tanner asked.

'Not so far, guv. All we know is that he had it in for Robert Bateman. I'll find out if he has an alibi and we'll take it from there.'

Before leaving the house, James asked Annie what she had planned for the day.

'I've got a pile of school work to get through before the new term starts,' she said. 'And I'm still trying to decide what to put in the baby's room.'

'That's great,' James said. 'Just avoid thinking about all the other stuff.'

Annie forced a smile. 'And by other stuff I take it you mean the fact that another killer could be living in the village, that our old friend Andrew Sullivan has disappeared and that my head is filled with painful memories that have just been unlocked?'

James didn't know what to say so he just smiled back.

'Come and kiss me goodbye, Detective Walker,' Annie said, holding out her arms. 'And then go and solve another bloody crime so that we can all feel safer.'

James's drive to O'Connor's house took him all of two minutes. On the way a light snow started to fall, filling the air with what looked like thousands of winged insects.

It was a dark day, the colours muted and pale, but the forecasters were expecting it to brighten up later.

There was a For Sale sign outside O'Connor's small semi-detached home, and the first question James asked him when he opened the door was whether he was moving away from Kirkby Abbey.

'As soon as I can find somewhere else to live,' he said. 'That's why I'm going to Carlisle today. There are some properties I want to check out and I've got some job interviews lined up there. I rent this place but the owner wants to sell it and since my partner moved out, I've been struggling to get by.'

Inside, it was cramped and in need of a facelift. The acrid smell of tobacco lingered in the air, and James got the impression that O'Connor did not spend much time or money looking after things.

James turned down the offer of a hot drink before O'Connor took him into the living room.

Now that the guy had removed his coat James could see that he had a pronounced beer gut and an indistinct tattoo on his right forearm.

When they were sitting down, O'Connor said, 'I'm assuming my name has come up because I used to work at Oaktree Farm and had a couple of run-ins with Robert after he fired me.'

James nodded. 'That's correct, Mr O'Connor.'

'In that case, let me begin by saying that although I came to dislike the guy, I swear I did not kill him or his family. Whoever did it must be a fucking psycho.'

'We believe it happened on Christmas Eve,' James said. 'So, can you tell me where you were on that day and where you've been since?'

'I was here by myself most of Christmas Eve,' he replied. 'At about eight I drove to Windermere to spend Christmas with my brother who lives there.'

'And what time did you arrive there?'

'Just before nine. I'll give you his number and you can ask him.'

'And did you go out before you left for your brother's house on Christmas Eve?'

He shook his head. 'I wasn't in the mood so I stayed in.'

'Why didn't you go to your brother's much earlier then?'

'Because he was working and didn't get home until half eight or so.'

'And there was nobody here with you?'

'That's correct. But I didn't go to Oaktree Farm. I haven't been there in months.'

O'Connor's eyes were intent under dark eyebrows and his voice was strong and steady. He held James's gaze the whole time and did not come across as nervous or unsure of himself.

'When was the last time you saw Mr Bateman?' James asked.

O'Connor didn't have to think about it. 'That would have been a couple of weeks ago at the Saturday market. He was there with his wife and we bumped into each other. By then I'd realised that it was a waste of time getting into arguments with him, so all we did was acknowledge each other.'

'Can you explain to me why you harboured such a grudge against him? Presumably he had no choice but to make you redundant given the state of his finances.'

He drew a breath and held it for a while before speaking.

'But that's the thing. He didn't get rid of me because he couldn't afford to keep me on. He was paying me a pittance anyway. The real reason was that he thought I was stealing from the house.'

'And were you?'

'No way. I told him so but he wouldn't believe me.'

'So what prompted him to make the allegation?'

He shrugged. 'Some things went missing over a period of time. A bottle of whisky. A CD. A watch. Mary was convinced it was a ghost because she claimed objects were being moved around as well. But Robert just assumed it was me. When he confronted me, I told him that his daughter was probably the culprit because she needed cash to buy drugs. And that made him really mad. A few days later he gave me my marching orders.'

'That must have made you very angry,' James said.

'It did my head in and I got myself into a right state. I took it out on my girlfriend and she eventually had enough and broke off with me. I suppose I blamed Robert for that too, but not enough to go over there and slaughter the entire family.'

James was thinking fast, mental gears whirring. He didn't know the man well enough to tell if he was lying. Instinct told him that he wasn't, but that was hardly enough to give him the all clear.

By his own admission he had no one to support his story about not going out on Christmas Eve until late. And on the way to his brother's place he might well have stopped at Oaktree Farm to pay the Batemans a visit.

Further enquiries would have to be carried out, but right now James wanted to extract as much information as he could about the family and the farm.

'Do you know anything about the cellar at the farmhouse? We found a concealed internal door leading from the cellar into the house – any chance you know when it was blocked off?' James asked.

O'Connor shrugged. 'That was long before my time, but Robert did tell me once why they had it done. It was for two reasons apparently. The first was because Mary was uncomfortable knowing that the previous owners died down there. Robert kept promising to replace the door with a wall but he didn't get around to it until some years after they moved in. The second reason was that both the outside and inside doors to the cellar were left open one day and a fox wandered in and gave them all a fright.'

'And are you aware that there's a small enclosed space behind the wall that was installed below the stairs?'

'That's news to me,' O'Connor said. 'I know there's a door at the top of the cellar steps but it was always locked. I assumed there was nothing beyond it but the wall.'

'Then you know nothing about a peephole in that wall? We believe it was used to spy on the family.'

He seemed genuinely shocked. 'Why the fuck would anyone do that?'

'That's what we'd like to know.'

'Well it wasn't me and I can't begin to imagine who it would be.'

'Did many people have access to the cellar?' James asked.

'Only the family. It was kept locked most of the time and I rarely went in there, which suited me because I found it a bit creepy.'

'Would I be able to take a look at your shoes, Mr O'Connor?' James asked suddenly.

O'Connor cocked his head on one side and frowned. 'What's that got to do with anything?'

James explained that shoeprints were found at the scene of the crime.

'We're going to be examining the shoes of everyone we talk to,' James said. 'By taking pictures of the soles we can help eliminate the owners from our enquiries.'

O'Connor pointed to the shoes he was wearing. 'All I've got are these, plus a smarter pair out in the hallway cupboard and some wellies. You're welcome to take photos, and if you suspect I might be hiding some then feel free to look around.'

James took him up on both offers. He photographed the soles of the shoes O'Connor had on as well as those in the hallway, and noted they were all size tens. Then he went from room to room until he was satisfied that there weren't any more hidden away.

Finally, he asked O'Connor if he would mind providing a DNA sample, which he had no problem with.

'Thanks for being so helpful, Mr O'Connor,' he said after he took down the man's mobile number. 'I really appreciate it.'

As James stepped outside, he pointed to an ageing Vauxhall Corsa that was parked at the kerb in front of the house.

'Is that your car?' he asked.

O'Connor said it was and James made a note of the number. As he walked back to his own car, he checked to see if there was any damage to the front of the vehicle. There wasn't.

CHAPTER EIGHTEEN

James made it to Kendal by eight forty-five. He'd already phoned ahead with Kenneth O'Connor's details so background checks could be carried out and someone could contact his brother in Windermere to check his alibi.

A warrant to search his home would also be secured so it'd be ready and waiting if they needed to execute it.

A shirt-sleeved DCI Tanner had been overseeing things and James almost didn't recognise him at first because he had shaved off his goatee beard.

'It was a Christmas present to my wife,' Tanner said. 'She never liked it and it finally got to the point where I realised that it didn't suit me.'

Tanner was a thick-set middle-aged man and James had a good working relationship with him, partly because the DCI preferred paperwork to legwork. More often than not he was happy to take a back seat while those detectives who reported to him got on with the grind of an investigation.

'I've brought myself up to scratch with the case,' Tanner

said. 'It makes sense for you to continue leading it since you live out that way and know more about the community than the rest of us.'

It had been the same with the serial killer investigation a year ago, when James was appointed SOI because the murders were taking place in Kirkby Abbey.

At nine sharp the team was assembled in the open plan office, armed with notepads and coffees. The room was packed and the atmosphere charged.

They were still waiting for the full forensic report from the scene and there had been a delay in unblocking the two mobile phones found at the farm but Tanner had been told they would be delivered within the hour.

They did have all the photographic evidence, though, and DS Stevens and DC Abbott had taken on the task of collating and then displaying it across two large whiteboards that had been set up.

On one were the photos of the crime scene. They showed the three bodies in situ, the bloody shoeprints and the layout of the room from various angles. There were also several external shots of the farm which looked as though it had been smothered in cotton wool with all the snow.

On the other whiteboard were photos of Robert, Mary and Charlotte Bateman, a photo of Neil Savage, and various images from the cellar, including the cubbyhole behind the wall and the memorial stone with the inscription: *You will never be forgotten.*

There were also the photos and the Christmas card taken from the rubbish bin in Savage's flat. Forensic technicians had done a good job of putting the bits back together.

A hush descended on the room as James took the team

through each photo, using a ruler to point at them. He was aware that about half of those present weren't at the briefing the previous evening so he'd be repeating much of what was said then.

'The initial thinking was that this was a murder-suicide,' he told them. 'As you can see in the photo Robert Bateman is still holding the shotgun, making it appear that he had shot his wife and then himself. But the bloody shoeprints cast doubt on that scenario. Someone walked out of the house after the killings, which could mean the scene was staged to make it look like a murder-suicide. And there's also the question of who stabbed Charlotte. Was it one of the parents or the person who fled the scene?

'We know that Robert Bateman was alive just before 7 p.m. on Christmas Eve because he visited The King's Head pub, meaning the killings took place some time after that.'

James then tapped the photo of Neil Savage with the ruler.

'This man, Neil Savage, was Charlotte's boyfriend and we've been told by two people that he was spending Christmas at the farm. However, there's compelling evidence to suggest that he drove away from there on Christmas Eve and was in such a hurry that his car collided with another vehicle. Given the evidence – which is currently being examined by forensics – we'll assume for now that Savage did flee the farm in a panic,' James continued. 'But we don't know where he spent that night. We do know that he turned up back at his flat here in town on Christmas Day and that's when a neighbour noticed the damage to his car. He only stayed a short while, though, and was then seen walking off with a rucksack on his back. Have we had any luck finding Savage on CCTV footage? Do we know where he walked to or if he was picked up by someone in a car?'

'Not so far, guv,' someone responded.

'Well, keep on it and let me know as soon as we find anything.'

James drew everyone's attention back to the photos and Christmas card found in Savage's flat.

'The card was from Charlotte to Savage and inside she wished him a merry Christmas and told him she loved him. And she sprinkled it with kisses. The photos are mostly of her and there's one of her with her parents. It's pretty clear that these were ripped up and thrown away by a very angry young man,' he said. 'We need to know what caused that anger.'

James then passed things over to DC Abbott so that she could share the notes she'd taken during the interview with Savage's mother.

When she was finished, James gave the team the headlines from his conversation with Kenneth O'Connor and asked who had been instructed to carry out the follow-up enquiries.

DC Colin Patterson raised his hand and said he had already phoned O'Connor's brother and he'd confirmed that he spent Christmas with him and arrived late on Christmas Eve.

'I've put in a request for a warrant to search O'Connor's home,' Patterson said. 'I've also sent the photographs you took of his shoes to forensics.'

James nodded his thanks and swiftly moved on to the aspect of the case that made it so intriguing – namely the potential link to the killings that took place at Oaktree Farm twenty-four years ago.

None of the officers in the room had been with the Cumbria

Constabulary when the bodies of Simon and Amanda Roth were found, but he reminded them that their former colleague, Giles Keegan, had been in charge of the case.

'The conclusion he drew was that it was a murder-suicide,' he said. 'Simon Roth hit his wife with a hammer and then killed himself with a shotgun blast to the head. Giles also strongly suspected that this took place after the death of their baby whose body has remained undiscovered. But he was never a hundred per cent certain that that is what happened. How could he be? Of course, we don't know yet if that case is relevant to our own investigation but the similarities can't simply be ignored. Who knows? Maybe this is the work of a copycat killer. Or perhaps Robert Bateman was so desperate about his precarious financial situation that he decided to do what his former boss did all those years ago.'

James pointed to the picture of the memorial stone in the cellar and read out the inscription.

'It's perhaps not surprising that the Batemans felt obliged to pay tribute to the Roths by placing this in the cellar. After all, Robert worked on the farm at the time and he took it upon himself to buy the place and keep the business going. But this whole thing gets even stranger when you take into account the wall that was installed to replace the interior cellar door. It created this small inner space that's reached via the cellar steps. At some point in time a tiny peephole was inserted into the wall. It's almost impossible to see it from inside the house, but it gives a view of the living room and kitchen. So, we need to find out who was spying on them and why. And whoever it was may well have been doing it this past week because fresh breadcrumbs were found on the floor there.'

He was about to throw the session open to questions when the office door was pushed open and Tony Coppell, the chief forensic officer who had attended the crime scene at Oaktree Farm, entered the room.

When he realised that all heads had turned towards him, he held up a file he was holding and said, 'I'm sorry for the delay, Detective Walker, but I've now got a summary of the forensic report. And you'll be particularly interested in what we found on the two mobile phones that were taken from the house.'

CHAPTER NINETEEN

Coppell walked to the front of the room and stood next to James. It wasn't often he made an appearance without being covered from head to toe in crime scene attire, and this morning he was looking trim in a tapered blue suit and a white shirt that was open at the neck.

He took some documents from his file and said, 'We're about to circulate this lot by email and create a series of slides, but I thought it best to brief you on the contents straight away.'

He began with the bloodstain that was found on the stairs in the cellar.

'It was fresh blood, only a couple of days old, and tests have shown that it's not a match for any of our victims.'

That drew an immediate response from DC Abbott, who said, 'So that's another mystery lobbed into the mix. As if there weren't enough already.'

Coppell nodded. 'We're running the DNA through the system now to see if we get a result. Meanwhile, the other thing to note is that the breadcrumbs found in the space at the top of the cellar are only about three or four days old. My guess is they fell to the floor while someone was eating a sandwich in there.'

The significance of this wasn't lost on James or anyone else. It pointed to someone spending a prolonged amount of time in the wall space spying on the family through the peephole.

'It could be that whoever it was decided at some point to go into the house and wreak havoc.' This from DCI Tanner who was on his feet and having a close look at the photos of the cellar on the whiteboard.

'That is a distinct possibility,' Coppell replied.

He then held up another document labelled 'Fingerprint Analysis'.

'We found quite a few prints on the shotgun,' he said. 'Most are Robert Bateman's, but a couple belong to his daughter. It means that at some point she held the weapon, but it might well have been long before Christmas Eve.'

'What about the knife used to kill Charlotte?' James said.

Coppell shook his head. 'Again, we only found a couple of her own prints and the handle was badly smeared with blood where she probably held onto it as she struggled to remove it. That doesn't mean she stabbed herself, of course. And it could be that someone else's prints got smudged. We also found Charlotte's prints on some of the fragments of glass that were scattered across the floor around the bodies. As you may already know, they were from a broken wine bottle. But there were other prints on the glass as well and these belong to her boyfriend, Neil Savage. He's been arrested a number of times and his prints are in the system so we were able to match them quite quickly.'

'So that's further confirmation that he was there,' James said. 'Are you sure his prints weren't also on the weapons?'

'I'm sure,' Coppell said. 'But he could have wiped them off, of course.'

He answered a few more questions from the other detectives and then moved on to the bloody shoeprints, sharing that his team had managed to identify the type of shoe that left them.

He moved nearer to the whiteboard and put a finger on one of the photos showing the impressions.

'These are most definitely a size ten, which as you might know is the average size for males in the UK,' he said. 'They're known as Commando style shoes or boots and they're perfect for hiking and climbing. They're thick and waterproof, and this particular design is called Vibram Roccia. It's very common in this part of the country because of its rugged, outdoorsy profile.'

James was disappointed to realise it wasn't going to be easy to trace the wearer through local retailers or the manufacturer.

'But I've got more positive news from the mobile phones,' Coppell went on. 'We only found two phones in the house and they belonged to Mr Bateman and his daughter. I'll start with Charlotte's.' He looked down at another document. 'She received a call at five minutes past seven on Christmas Eve from someone named Heather Redgrave who appears in her contacts list. The call lasted for four minutes. Charlotte then called her back fifteen minutes later and that call lasted five minutes.

'Now just after that second call ended Charlotte sent a message to Neil Savage saying: *How could you do this to me?*

I should have known not to trust you. I'll come get my things after Christmas. You're dead to me.'

'We need to speak to this Heather Redgrave,' James said. 'I want to know what prompted Charlotte to send that message to her boyfriend. Remind me when that accident that Savage may have been involved in was reported?' James said.

'Just after twenty past seven on Christmas Eve,' Stevens answered. 'I read it in the notes a little while ago.'

'So, Charlotte is on the phone with Heather for four minutes starting at five past seven. Fifteen minutes later, at 07.24 p.m., she calls Heather back and they speak until 07.29, at which point she messages Neil, confirming he is not with her at that time,' James said. 'I suppose it's possible he went straight back there after he received the message and that's when things went bad.'

'But he would have had to drive past the car he'd shunted off the road and it doesn't seem likely to me that he would have done that,' Stevens said.

James turned back to Coppell. 'Have we ascertained the exact time the killings took place?'

Coppell shook his head. 'But it would almost certainly have been between seven-thirty and midnight.'

'We'll have to work with that then. Meanwhile can you come back to us as quickly as possible with the results of the forensic examination being carried out on Savage's car and the other vehicle?'

'I'll make it a priority,' Coppell said. 'There was another text message I think will be of interest, this one on Robert Bateman's phone. Mr Bateman received it at 04.30 p.m. on Christmas Eve and he didn't reply to it. It was sent by a man named Dean Foreman – who is listed among his contacts – and it said: *I've had enough now and I'm not going to take any more of your shit. You're about to discover that I don't make empty threats, Bateman.'*

CHAPTER TWENTY

The progress with the forensic evidence had upped the pace of the investigation. Suddenly there was another suspect as well as new questions about how events might have unfolded at Oaktree Farm on Christmas Eve.

James adjourned the briefing so that things could be set in motion without delay, letting everyone know they would reconvene in half an hour. In the meantime, he wanted to know who Dean Foreman was and why he had sent a threatening text to Robert Bateman.

He also wanted to know what relationship Heather Redgrave had with Charlotte and what had been said during their phone conversations to provoke Charlotte into sending the text message to Savage. Did it have something to do with the reason he tore up her photos in his flat?

There was a sudden burst of frenetic activity in the room. Those who didn't go straight to their phones or computers started chatting animatedly amongst themselves.

'This case gets more interesting by the hour,' DCI Tanner

said as he sidled up to James. 'Right now I'm mightily confused.'

'Join the club,' James said. 'Just when we think we might be getting somewhere we're sent racing off in another direction.'

Tanner nodded. 'But one thing is becoming clear. Robert Bateman wasn't universally popular among those who knew him. We know that Kenneth O'Connor had a serious grudge against him. And now there's this Dean Foreman, whoever he is.'

'It's easy to make enemies when you're in a financial shithole,' James said. 'Maybe that text he received from Foreman relates to some money issue between the two men.'

'That's quite possible, but you have to wonder how many other people there are who Bateman got on the wrong side of. From what I've learned about the state of his finances there could be quite a few.'

'I'll get someone to try and pull together a list of those he owes money to – we should have access to his bank accounts by now. His bank manager has confirmed he had a meeting with Bateman here in Kendal on Christmas Eve, at which he spelled out the dire state of the man's finances, including a large overdraft. He said Bateman was down in the dumps when he left to go home.'

Tanner nodded then retreated to his office and James took a few moments to pull his thoughts together.

He turned instinctively to the whiteboards, and his eyes were drawn to the photos of the victims. They sparked a wave of heat that rose up his neck. Suddenly he was back at Oaktree Farm with all the blood and the cloying aroma of death.

It was obvious to him now that the crime scene was holding back more than it was offering up. The farmhouse itself was an enigma, and he couldn't help wondering if echoes of the past had somehow had a bearing on the Christmas Eve carnage. The previous owners were killed and their daughter vanished, and then twenty-four years later the current owners were slain and their daughter died with them. Was it just a creepy coincidence, or was it something more?

He switched his gaze from the photos of the bodies to those of the cellar. The small concealed space, the peephole in the wall, the breadcrumbs on the floor, the bloodstain on the step. What the hell did it all mean? And was it connected to the killings?

He had never worked on a case that involved a perpetrator hiding inside the walls of a house, but he was aware that it had happened before.

One notorious case came to mind because it had featured in numerous true crime documentaries, podcasts and magazine features over the years.

James dredged from his memory the name of the man involved – Daniel LaPlante – so he went to his computer and typed it into Google. There was an abundance of information and he focused on part of an article that appeared several years ago in the online edition of an American newspaper.

Daniel LaPlante was sixteen in 1986 when he became obsessed with two teenage girls in his home town of Townsend, Massachusetts in the US. Their mother had recently died of cancer and they were living with their father.

LaPlante went on a date with one of the girls but it didn't work out and she dumped him. He then began stalking her and one day managed to sneak into her home when it was empty. The story goes that while searching through a built-in wardrobe below the stairs he discovered a hidden gap that gave access to an empty space between the walls. He decided to hide and spy on the girls.

It was widely reported that he inserted several peepholes in the walls and lived in the space for about two months without the family knowing. However, during that time he saw an opportunity to torment the girl who had rejected him and spent weeks creepily tapping on the walls, causing the girl and her younger sister to think that the ghost of their dead mother was haunting the house. LaPlante eventually got caught by police after a confrontation with the girls' father.

He was arrested and spent time in a juvenile detention centre.

James couldn't be sure how much of the story was true and how much was urban legend. But it was impossible to ignore the fact that the elements that made it so spine-chilling were replicated at Oaktree Farm – the hidden wall space, the peephole, the fact that Mary Bateman claimed she heard noises coming from behind the walls, which led her to believe that the farmhouse was haunted.

James went on to read what LaPlante did after he was released from the juvenile detention centre, and it sent a cold rush of blood through his veins.

The bastard went on to rape and murder a mother before

drowning her two young children in the bath. And for that he was still in prison serving multiple life sentences.

When James was ready to continue the briefing, he pushed the ghoulish story of Daniel LaPlante to the back of his mind. But he had an idea it would resurface again in the days ahead.

The team had managed to achieve quite a lot in half an hour and the first to provide an update was DS Stevens, who had followed up on the text message sent by Dean Foreman to Robert Bateman.

'Foreman lives in Penrith where he runs a food wholesale company,' Stevens said. 'He's not visible on social media, but his company does have a website that includes a photo of him, and he looks to be in his late forties or early fifties.'

'Liaise with the team in Penrith and get them to bring him down here for questioning,' James said. 'Or better still, go there yourself. It'll only take half an hour. Don't forget to check his shoes. And make sure you have backup. We've no idea what to expect from the guy.'

Next up was DC Abbott. She had obtained an address for Heather Redgrave.

'She lives here in town,' Abbott said. 'I rang her number but her mother answered and said Heather had left her phone behind while she went out for a run. She's expecting her back in about twenty minutes and I told her we'd be sending someone around to talk to her about Charlotte. The woman confirmed that Heather and Charlotte were friends.'

'And had Heather heard the news?' James asked.

'Apparently so, which is why she didn't go to work today. She's very upset and went for a run to clear her head.'

'Well, fingers crossed she can tell us stuff about Charlotte that we don't already know,' James said. 'You and I will pay her a visit this morning. And we'll also drop in on the shop where Charlotte worked. Hopefully it will be open today.

'Do we have an update on Neil Savage?' James asked.

'His phone still isn't transmitting a signal and though we've traced a number of his friends they all claim not to know where he is,' DC Wendy Mitchell said. 'The forensic sweep of his flat is complete though and there's an unmarked pool car outside the block keeping an eye out for him.'

'The Constabulary has agreed to stage a press conference at eleven. I'll front it so that you can crack on,' DCI Tanner said to James. 'We can agree on what should and shouldn't be said before you go out.'

Tony Coppell shared the very latest from forensics.

'My team at the farm is back to full strength and they're now working their way through the barn and outbuildings as well as the house. I can also confirm that it was indeed Neil Savage's Peugeot that was involved in the collision close to Oaktree Farm on Christmas Eve,' he said. 'We matched paint from the Peugeot to paint found on the rear bodywork of the other car.'

'Well that's good to know,' James said. 'But now we need to find out what happened following the shunt and whether Savage drove back to the farm after receiving the angry text message from Charlotte.'

'I can't help you with that,' Coppell said. 'But what I can tell you is that no blood was found in the footwell of Savage's car or on the pedals. That could either mean he wasn't the one who walked through the blood or the soles of his shoes were wiped clean by the snow.'

CHAPTER TWENTY-ONE

James had just climbed into the pool car with DC Abbott when he had a call from Gillian Weldon.

'You told me you'd let me know what was going on,' she said, her voice cracking with emotion. 'But I haven't heard from you, and I still don't know what's happened to my boy.'

'I was going to call you later today, Miss Weldon,' James said. 'Unfortunately, we still haven't been able to trace Neil.'

'And that's why I'm so angry as well as worried,' she fumed. 'I keep seeing his picture on the television and people are ringing me up asking me if he killed that family. It's just not fair. He's being labelled a murderer and he might be lying dead somewhere himself.'

'We had no choice but to issue an appeal for him and release the photograph you gave us,' James said. 'He might be the only person who can tell us what happened at Oaktree Farm. We know he was there on Christmas Eve and that he left in a hurry.'

'That doesn't mean he killed them.'

'I'm aware of that, Miss Weldon. And that accusation has not been levelled against him. Nonetheless, he is a suspect and we can't rule him out until we're able to speak to him.'

She started to respond but her words turned into a sob.

'We really are doing everything we can to find your son,' James said. 'But nobody we've spoken to so far knows where he is, or if they do, they're not telling us.'

Miss Weldon cleared her throat and said, 'What about the reprobates he usually hangs around with? The layabouts who get him to go along to their drink and drugs benders? They're the ones you need to talk to.'

'Do you have any names?'

'Of course not. He would never share that information with me. But I'm sure they all have police records, so it shouldn't be hard for you to find out who they are.'

'I assure you we're working on it,' James said. He paused to let her respond, and when she didn't, he continued. 'There is something we know now that we weren't aware of when we spoke to you yesterday. On Christmas Eve Charlotte sent an angry text message to your son telling him that she intended to end their relationship and move out of the flat. The message was short and sharp and though your son didn't respond we have evidence to suggest that he wasn't happy about it.'

'What kind of evidence?'

James told her about the ripped-up photos and Christmas card found in the bin at Savage's flat.

'Have you any idea why Charlotte decided to end it with Neil?' he asked.

'All I know is that they were always falling out, Inspector.

I told you yesterday how they used to wind each other up. And I know they've called it a day on their relationship at least twice before, only to get back together soon after.'

James assured her again that he and his colleagues were working flat out to find her son.

'In the meantime, try not to think the worst,' he said. 'In all probability he's somewhere safe and might even be unaware of what has happened.'

He then gestured for Abbott to start the car and told Miss Weldon that he had to go.

'But I promise to let you know as soon as I hear anything,' he added. 'And if your son does contact you then for everyone's sake please don't keep it to yourself.'

Heather Redgrave lived in a small development of terraced houses close to Kendal College.

The woman who answered the door had clearly been expecting the police to call and introduced herself as Heather's mother, Judith Redgrave. She was about fifty and of medium height, with short brown hair.

She invited James and Abbott in after telling them that her daughter was in the shower.

'She was sweating when she got back from her run,' the woman said. 'She won't be long, though. You can wait in the lounge. Would you like something to drink?'

They both shook their heads, and James said, 'That's very kind of you but we both got well caffeinated before we left the office.'

There were two small sofas in the lounge and when they were seated facing each other, James asked if anyone else lived in the house with her and her daughter.

'Only my husband,' she replied. 'He's on a post-Christmas visit to his parents in Wigan. He'll be back tomorrow.'

'You mentioned to me on the phone that Heather has taken the day off,' Abbott said. 'As a matter of interest where does she work?'

'In a small boutique hotel not far from here,' Mrs Redgrave said. 'Usually on reception or in the back office. But she really wasn't up to it today.'

'And how long had she and Charlotte Bateman been friends?'

'Oh, since they were at school together. You see, we used to live in Kirkby Abbey before we moved here five years ago. They stayed in touch and they've seen more of each other since Charlotte moved in with her boyfriend.'

'Do you know him – Neil Savage?' Abbott asked.

She shook her head. 'And from what I've heard about him I don't think I ever want to. By all accounts he's a nasty piece of work.'

Abbott was about to ask another question when the door opened and a young woman wearing jeans and a T-shirt walked in.

'This is my daughter, Heather,' Mrs Redgrave said. 'Heather, these are detectives Abbott and Walker.'

Heather was about five foot six with a model's figure and dark, unruly wet hair. She had a thin, angular face and eyes that were heavy and red, presumably from where she'd been crying.

She sat next to her mother and fixed James with a nervous stare.

'Is everything they've said on the news true?' she said. 'Was Charlotte stabbed?'

James gave a slow nod. 'Sadly, she was, Miss Redgrave, but

I can't really say anything beyond that. The reason we're here is that we know you had two telephone conversations with your friend shortly before she was killed on Christmas Eve. We'd like to know what they were about.'

She took a deep breath and pushed her fingers through her hair.

'I want you to know that I was going to call the police when I heard that you were looking for Neil, but I was too scared,' she said.

'And why was that?' James asked.

She looked at her mother, who wore a puzzled expression, and then turned back to James.

'Because I didn't want to be blamed for what happened there,' she said. Tears suddenly broke free from her eyes and she buried her head against her mother's shoulder.

'What on earth are you talking about?' her mother said, clearly shocked. 'What haven't you told me?'

Heather sobbed for almost a minute while her mother stroked her hair and the two detectives waited patiently for her to stop. When eventually she did, she sat up straight and wiped her eyes with the back of her hand.

'I'm sorry but I can't stop thinking that I shouldn't have phoned Charlotte when I did,' she said. 'If I hadn't told her what Neil did … she might still be here.'

James exchanged a look with Abbott and then leaned forward, noting the pain on Heather's face.

'You need to understand, Miss Redgrave, that we don't know who killed the Batemans,' he said. 'Neil Savage is one of several people we're hoping to question.'

'When I saw his picture on the news, I thought he must have done it and that's the reason he's run away.'

James shook his head. 'It's not as simple as that. So please don't blame yourself for anything. But you do need to talk us through what you said to Charlotte.'

Her mother put an arm around her shoulders. 'It's important that you tell the police everything, darling,' she said. 'And there's no need to be scared.'

It was another thirty seconds before the words tumbled out of Heather's mouth.

'Charlotte was working in the charity shop on Christmas Eve,' she said. 'She phoned me from there in the morning to wish me a merry Christmas. I was still here because I wasn't working that day. But a couple of hours later I was walking into town to meet a friend for lunch and I saw Neil. He was coming out of a pub and he wasn't alone. He was with his ex – a girl named Amy Bell. They walked off together and I had an idea where they were going, so I followed them.'

'And where did they go?' James asked.

'To Amy's flat, which is just a few streets away from the pub. It's on the ground floor and I know she lives there by herself. Anyway, I watched them go in together, and before they did, he pulled her to him and kissed her. And when she opened her front door, he grabbed her arse and pushed her inside. They were both laughing.'

'Did you hang around?' Abbott asked her.

Heather shook her head. 'I couldn't. I had to meet my friend across town. But I stewed on it all afternoon. I hated the thought that the fucker was cheating on my friend even though I'd long suspected that he did. But at the same time, I didn't want to ruin her Christmas by telling her.'

'So, what did you do?' Abbott prodded her.

'Well I decided I would wait until after Christmas before

breaking it to her, but then I went to a party that evening and I got a bit drunk. And that was when I changed my mind and phoned her.'

'And what was her reaction?'

'She was gutted and also furious. She told me she was going to end it with him because it wasn't the first time that he'd done it.'

'Was he with her at the time at Oaktree Farm when you called?' James said.

'Yes, he was. And about twenty minutes later she called me back to tell me that she'd confronted him. He didn't deny it and so she told him to go, which he did.'

'And was that the last you heard from her?' James asked.

She nodded. 'I tried calling her on Christmas Day and Boxing Day, but she didn't pick up and now I know why. And after I heard that Charlotte and her parents were found dead, I thought that he must have gone back to the farm after she sent him packing and then took it out on all the family.'

She lost it then and buried her face in her hands. This time she cried for much longer.

CHAPTER TWENTY-TWO

When James and Abbott left Heather and her mother, they were armed with Amy Bell's address. James found it hard to suppress his excitement as they headed towards the flat of Neil Savage's former girlfriend.

The investigation had taken a significant step forward and they had a better idea now of some of what had happened at Oaktree Farm on Christmas Eve.

Heather's call had obviously come as a bitter blow to Charlotte and she had reacted by insisting that Savage leave the house. After he'd done so she sent him a message, making it clear what she thought of him.

But what happened after that? Did Savage return to the farm following the collision he was involved in? Or did someone else appear on the scene and slaughter the family?

'At least we're making progress, guv,' Abbott said, as she steered the pool car through the town's busy streets. 'We know now why Savage might have blown a fuse that night. And hopefully his ex-girlfriend will know where he is. I suppose he could even be staying with her.'

As luck would have it they arrived at Amy Bell's flat just as she was stepping out of the front door. She was wearing a smart knee-length black overcoat and woollen hat, and was taken aback when they approached her.

'Am I right in assuming that you are Miss Amy Bell?' James asked her.

'Yes, I am,' she replied, her face fisting into a frown.

They both took out their warrant cards and showed them to her.

'We're police officers, Miss Bell. I'm Detective Inspector Walker and my colleague here is Detective Constable Abbott. We'd like to have a word with you about Neil Savage, whom I believe used to be your boyfriend.'

'Well if you're going to ask me where he is, I honestly don't know. We're not together anymore.'

'You may not be together but you're still seeing him, aren't you?' James said. 'In fact, he was here with you on Christmas Eve, wasn't he?'

'How do you know that?' she snapped at him.

'You were seen leaving a local pub together,' James said. 'And naturally it's made us wonder if you know where we can find him. I take it you're aware that he's gone missing?'

'Yes, I've seen the news. But I swear I haven't seen him since Christmas Eve.'

'Nevertheless, we'd like to ask you some questions. So, may we come in? It's rather cold out here.'

She swallowed hard and blew out a breath.

'Can't it wait? I've got an appointment at the opticians in twenty minutes.'

James forced a smile. 'I'm sure they won't mind if you're a little late or even if you cancel. We'd like to satisfy ourselves that you're telling us the truth about your contact with your ex. For all we know he could be hiding in this very flat.'

'He's not here,' she said, with a note of panic in her voice. 'Come in and see for yourselves. I promise I'm telling the truth.'

Once inside, she took off her coat and hat and said she was happy for Abbott to look around the flat while James went with her into the kitchen to start asking questions.

She stood with her back to the sink and invited him to sit at the small table that was sandwiched between a large fridge-freezer and a cupboard.

She was wearing a brown jumper, black trousers, and a large leather belt that accentuated her narrow waist.

'Do you live here alone, Miss Bell?' James asked her.

'I have since Neil moved out,' she replied. 'That was about eighteen months ago.'

'How long were you together?'

'Just over a year. And before you ask, I was the one who ended it.'

'And why was that?'

'Well he just wasn't committed enough to the relationship, and I felt that I was being used. He kept promising to get a job but never did, and all he was ever interested in were drink, drugs and sex.'

'So why are you still seeing him and how long has it been going on?'

She shrugged. 'It's not serious. We've got together about half a dozen times since he started seeing Charlotte. And it was only ever for a couple of hours. We had sex and a laugh and it suited me because I've been by myself since the break up and I get bored and lonely at times. I don't feel proud of myself, but then I don't feel guilty either. He was the one who was cheating on his partner. Not me.'

'So why did you meet up with him on Christmas Eve?'

'Oh, it wasn't pre-planned. I work as a cleaner and I did an early shift that day. I popped into a supermarket on the way home and we came face to face in the booze aisle. He suggested we went for a drink since it was Christmas and one thing led to another. He said Charlotte was working and that he'd be spending Christmas with her mum and dad at the farm.'

At that moment Abbott entered the room.

'There's no one else here, guv,' she said.

'That's what I told you,' Amy was quick to point out. 'And believe me if he is the one who did that to Charlotte and her parents then I don't want him anywhere near me.'

'Do you think he's capable of doing something like this?' James asked. 'We've been told he can be violent at times, especially when he's drunk or high.'

'I've never thought he's as bad as people make out,' she said. 'He would shout and swear but I'm glad to say he was never violent towards me. I wouldn't have stood for it.'

Abbott stepped further into the room and stood next to Amy.

'Where do you think he might be now, Miss Bell?' she asked. 'He was last seen on Christmas Day at his flat. His mother hasn't heard from him and his phone seems to be switched off.'

'Well if he's hiding from you guys, he could be anywhere

in the country. But if not then he might well be on one of his benders, or parties or whatever you want to call them.'

'His mother mentioned to us that he has a habit of disappearing for days at a time,' James said.

Amy nodded. 'He does, but he's not the only one. It's become a big thing around here during the past couple of years. Small groups get together and chill out, usually during holidays or over long weekends. I went with Neil once but I hated it.'

She lifted her head suddenly and squeezed her features as though a thought had occurred to her.

'I've just remembered something,' she said. 'When he was here on Christmas Eve he mentioned that a few of his mates had something planned that was starting on Christmas Day, but he couldn't go because he was going to be with Charlotte at the farm. And he sounded disappointed.'

'Do you know where it was and who was going?'

'I don't know who was going, but he said it was the same place he took me to.'

James felt his body tense. 'And where was that?'

She shrugged again. 'I haven't a clue. I was just a passenger in the car when he drove me there and I didn't pay much attention. It's an old house in the middle of nowhere. It must have been a farm at one time because there's a barn next to it that's been converted into living accommodation. I'm sure it was north of here and it took us about fifteen minutes to get there.'

'Is there anything else you can tell us about it?'

She pulled her lips tight and squinted in concentration.

After a few beats, she said, 'All I remember is that some old guy lives there. He's like a recluse, and he lets people like

Neil stage parties in the barn which has some bedrooms and an open plan living area. They give him a few quid and basically take over the place. It suits them because there's no phone signal there and nobody around for miles to complain about the noise. As I recall the barn's kitted out with a bar, a music system and a widescreen TV. And they can do pretty much whatever they want. The old guy just leaves them to it.'

'Do you think it's possible that Neil decided to go there on Christmas Day?' he asked.

'I suppose so,' Amy said. 'And if he did then that might be why you can't find him. Once those parties are in full swing it's all about getting drunk and stoned. You sleep it off and when you wake up it starts all over again.'

CHAPTER TWENTY-THREE

James and Abbott came away from Amy Bell's flat with plenty to think about. The possibility that their prime suspect may well have gone on some drink and drugs bender needed to be explored further.

If he had then was it in a desperate bid to escape reality? Did he regard it as a final hurrah before facing up to what he'd done? Or was he not planning on coming back from it, instead intent on filling his body with lethal amounts of mind-blowing substances?

'As soon as we're back at base we'll get the team onto it,' James said. 'There can't be many places around here like the one Amy described. And there's every chance we've had call outs there before.'

'It doesn't ring any bells with me, guv,' Abbott said. 'But I do know that those types of blowout benders have become quite popular with young folk. It's partly because unemployment is so high and drugs have never been so cheap. I remember reading about one that lasted eight days. Some kid held it in his house when his parents were away on holiday. The house was completely trashed and it ended badly when two of his mates died from dodgy ecstasy tablets.'

'It's a scary thought that the recluse who Amy mentioned is probably just one of many who are cashing in on the craze,' James said. 'Letting out properties to groups who want to get wasted is an easy way to make money. But I suppose it's not that different to the illegal raves that take place on private land. That's been big business for ages now.'

They talked through what else Amy had told them as they drove across town to the charity shop where Charlotte Bateman had worked.

The streets were busier now and James guessed it was partly because the day had brightened up. Locals and visitors were out in force, reminding him that Kendal was a vibrant commercial hub, with high street brands thriving alongside a collection of independent shops and dining options.

Between scattered clouds the sky was a flawless blue, but the sun wasn't anywhere near strong enough to melt the snow that lay across the rooftops and open spaces. James expected that to be a feature of the landscape well into next week. He just hoped that it didn't turn really bad like it had last Christmas and New Year when Cumbria was hit by brutal blizzards that brought the county to a virtual standstill.

James was pleased to see that the charity shop was open. They parked the car around the corner and walked back to the small shop, which sold everything from used books to second-hand clothes. There were no customers when they entered, but a grey-haired woman who was probably in her sixties was stacking shelves.

James went straight up to her and introduced himself.

'Is this about poor Charlotte?' she asked, her voice laced with despair.

'It is,' he said.

She hesitated a weighty second before she found her voice again.

'I've been wondering if the police would drop by,' she said. 'It's all so upsetting. I cried when I heard the news. She was due back in today and I can't believe I won't see her again.'

Her face was drawn and pale and there were dark circles under her eyes.

She gave her name as Fiona McCarthy and told them that she last saw Charlotte on Christmas Eve.

'She was fine when she left here and told me she was going to spend Christmas with her parents and boyfriend.'

'And how long had she worked here?' Abbott asked her.

'Just over two and a half months,' Fiona said. 'She used to work at a local factory but lost her job when they made cutbacks. We had a vacancy for a paid member of staff and she applied for it and was taken on.'

'We're trying to find out as much as we can about the Bateman family, so what can you tell us about Charlotte?' James said.

Fiona pursed her lips. 'Well, she was a good worker, but at the same time she was clearly a troubled individual.'

'What makes you say that?'

'Her moods were so unpredictable. One day she would be bright and cheerful and the next she'd be morose and would hardly speak to me. Take a few weeks ago, for example. I came back from lunch and caught her sobbing in the office out back. She was holding an envelope and when I asked her why she was so upset she said it was because she'd received some bad news to do with her family. I asked her what it was but she didn't want to tell me and I didn't push it.'

'That's certainly something we'll try to find out more about,' James said. 'Is there anything else you can tell us about her?'

'Only that she did seem to have problems in her private life, but again she wouldn't open up about it.'

James pressed her. 'Can you be more specific?'

'Well, her boyfriend, the one you're looking for, was unemployed and still is as far as I know. He came here several times trying to get Charlotte to give him things for free. She always refused, but once he looked like he was drunk and swore at her in front of me before storming off. And then another time a bloke she used to go out with popped in to wish her well in her new job. He seemed nice enough, but when he was gone Charlotte told me that he gave her the creeps. She said he had never fully accepted that their relationship was over, and turned up wherever she went.'

James felt his adrenaline spike. 'Do you know the name of this former boyfriend?'

'I'm sure she said it was William. That's right. William Nash. I made a mental note to remember it in case I saw him lurking around outside the shop.'

'And do you know if he lives here in Kendal?'

'I know for sure that he doesn't,' she replied. 'I distinctly recall Charlotte telling me that he lives in Kirkby Abbey and that they used to go to school together.'

CHAPTER TWENTY-FOUR

James was feeling cautiously optimistic as they arrived back at the station.

They now had a couple of new leads to follow up as well as some more useful information on Charlotte. But he had to remind himself that she was only one of the victims of the Oaktree Farm killings. They still needed to find out more about her parents, especially her father, as he'd recently become the target of some animosity.

The first question he asked when the team was back together was where they were with Kenneth O'Connor and Dean Foreman.

'We now have a warrant to search O'Connor's home and car,' DC Patterson said. 'As soon as you give the go-ahead, guv, we can exercise it.'

James didn't hesitate. 'I think we should. Contact him by phone and tell him what's happening so he can come back from his property search in Carlisle. And I want the house subjected to a full forensic sweep. Despite what he told me he has to be a serious contender for three reasons: he lives in Kirkby Abbey so he's pretty close to Oaktree Farm, he recently fell out with Robert Bateman and he doesn't have anyone to confirm his claims he was at home for most of Christmas Eve before driving over to Windermere to visit his brother about the time the killings might have taken place. If he's lied about anything then there might well be something in the house that gives him away.'

'On that note, forensics have come back to say that the photos you took of his shoe soles have been compared with the impressions found at the house and they're not a match, although they are the same size,' Patterson said.

'That doesn't surprise me,' James said. 'We have to accept that whoever did walk through the blood probably realised their mistake and got rid of the shoes afterwards. But it's worth checking the inside of his car for traces.'

'Definitely. In regards to Dean Foreman, DS Stevens just phoned to say that the guy's agreed to come in to be interviewed,' he said. 'Apparently he refused to answer any of the questions that were put to him by DS Stevens and said he'll only do so when his lawyer is present. He's arranged for the brief to meet him here and Stevens is bringing him back now.'

'Do we know if he has form?' James asked.

'He doesn't, but he did appear on our radar about a year ago when we received a call from his wife who accused him of hitting her. She had a cut lip so we hauled him in and were in the process of pursuing a domestic abuse inquiry when she suddenly withdrew the accusation and told us she'd over-reacted and that it was an accident. So, he walked.'

'Do we know his shoe size?'

'We do. A ten. Same as the bloody shoeprints.'

'Give me a sheet with the details on so I've got them when I talk to him,' James said.

He was then told that DCI Tanner had gone to Penrith to front the press conference that was due to start in half an hour. Also, Dr Flint had sent through preliminary results from the post-mortems. There were no surprises, though. Mr and Mrs Bateman had died from shotgun wounds and their daughter from severe internal injuries and loss of blood caused by the knife wound. There were no defensive wounds on any of the bodies and toxicology showed that they had all consumed varying amounts of alcohol and, in Charlotte's case, a significant amount of weed.

It was then James's turn to tell them about his and Abbott's conversations with Heather Redgrave, Amy Bell and Fiona McCarthy. He referred to his notes throughout and said he would write them up and circulate them.

'So, I want you to open up three new lines of inquiry,' he said. 'Track down the recluse who rents out his barn to bunches of drunks and druggies. See if you can find out why Charlotte was so upset a couple of weeks ago. Was it possible that the bad news she received had something to do with the killings? And finally, dig up whatever you can on this William Nash, the ex-boyfriend. He lives in Kirkby Abbey apparently. And he strikes me as someone we should talk to.'

As the team set to work, James went to his desk and called Tanner. After he had given him an update, the DCI said, 'So it doesn't change the line I'm taking, which is the appeal for information on the whereabouts of Neil Savage.'

'That's correct, sir. And as agreed, we make no mention of the bloody shoeprints or the hidden space above the cellar.'

'No problem. Let me know if anything else comes in while I'm here. I've got a meeting this afternoon with the Chief Constable.'

After hanging up, James phoned Annie. He wanted her to know about the press conference so that she could tune in to it. But he also had a question for her.

'Have you heard of a bloke named William Nash? I've been told he lives in Kirkby Abbey.'

'He does,' she said. 'I gather he's the village handyman. He's done a few jobs at the school this past year and the staff call him Mr Fixit.'

'Can you describe him?'

'Well he's tall, in his twenties, and a bit nerdy. Why do you want to know?'

'He used to go out with Charlotte Bateman but she told someone that he'd been stalking her recently.'

'I wouldn't know about that, but are you saying that makes him a suspect?'

'At this stage he's just someone we need to talk to. Do you know where we can find him?'

'I think he's got a small yard over near the petrol station so his contact details must be online or in the phone book.'

'Thanks, I'll check. And please don't repeat what I've said to anyone.'

Annie clucked her tongue. 'You really don't have to say that, James. You know I never have and I never would.'

James spent the next half an hour typing up his notes from the various interviews. Once he'd shared them via a group email, he watched a feed of the press conference with the rest of the team.

It was being held at police headquarters in Penrith and was going out live on the BBC News Channel.

Tanner sat behind a table next to one of the press officers and as usual he looked supremely confident. Unlike James, Tanner revelled in the attention, always happy to put himself in the spotlight.

He began by reading out a pre-prepared statement for the hacks in which he stressed that the police still weren't sure exactly what had happened at Oaktree Farm.

'But we are certain that Neil Savage, Charlotte Bateman's boyfriend, was spending Christmas there with her family. He hasn't been seen since and so naturally we're anxious to speak to him. Anyone who has information as to his whereabouts should contact us without delay.'

When he opened it up for questions, they came thick and fast. The first few focused on Savage and the Bateman family. It was Gordon Carver of the *Cumbria Gazette* who brought up that other dark day in the history of Oaktree Farm.

'Can you please confirm, Detective Chief Inspector, that you're investigating possible links between these killings and those of the previous owners of the farm who were found dead there twenty-four years ago?' he said.

Tanner nodded. 'Of course, it's something we're looking at because, as you know, there are some striking similarities. But it does seem highly unlikely that there's a connection.'

But that was never going to be enough to deter the media from making the most of the fact that a total of at least five people had now died in violent and mysterious circumstances at the farm. It was an angle that was guaranteed to draw in more readers, viewers and listeners.

As the questions continued, James realised that there was

still a lot that he himself didn't know about those first killings. He hadn't yet had time to go and see Giles Keegan who knew more about them than anyone else. So he decided to go online and print off some material while the press conference rumbled on.

A few taps on the keyboard took him to a plethora of newspaper stories and photographs. There was even one picture of a young Keegan speaking to reporters in a field with Oaktree Farm in the background.

As he continued to trawl through the reports that had been archived by various news outlets, he stumbled on a photo that came as quite a shock.

It showed a large group of people standing outside St John's Church in Kirkby Abbey at a memorial to mark the first anniversary of the deaths of Simon and Amanda Roth. He remembered Annie telling him that she'd attended that memorial service and he stared at the picture for perhaps a full minute before he realised that he could see her standing there between her mum and dad.

CHAPTER TWENTY-FIVE

TWENTY-THREE YEARS AGO

It's a crisp autumn day in Kirkby Abbey, just like it was a year ago when they came here for the funerals.

Now they're here again to mark the first anniversary of the deaths of Simon and Amanda Roth.

The memorial service has just finished inside the church and the forty or so villagers who attended are gathered around the headstone above the graves.

Father Silver, the priest of St John's, is saying a final prayer for the couple, and for their daughter, Megan, who is still missing and presumed by many to be dead.

Robert and Mary Bateman are among those with their heads bowed as they listen to the priest's words. Charlotte is between them in her pushchair, totally oblivious to what is going on.

It's proving a tough day for everyone as the memories of what happened at Oaktree Farm come flooding back. But Robert and Mary feel it more keenly than the others because they now live there and it's never been far from their minds.

Robert still doesn't regret buying the place from Simon's

brother, even though Mary wanted to move elsewhere. He believes it was the right thing to do and he's hopeful that his wife will eventually come around to accepting that.

He's just glad that they've been able to keep the business going to save the animals, and at the same time secure a better future for themselves. It would have been much easier to have walked away, and he's sure that most people in their position would have. But Robert has always prided himself on never taking the easy route. To him it was a challenge as well as a way to keep the Roths' legacy alive.

Robert becomes aware that his wife is quietly sobbing again so he reaches for her hand and gives it a gentle squeeze.

He knew she would find today hard going. Even before they left the house she was in tears after they reminisced about the last time their two families were all together. It was such a delight to see the two babies lying side by side on the sofa and to talk about how they would grow up together.

But that was before tragedy struck and everything changed.

Robert feels the tears press against his own eyes and a familiar ache fill his chest.

He needs a distraction so he lifts his head and looks at the people around him.

Simon's brother Mark is standing behind the headstone with his wife. They've come all the way from Sevenoaks in Kent to be here.

To their left stand Grace and Richard Kellerman and their teenage daughter Annie. He hasn't seen them since the funerals and he remembers Grace telling him something he didn't know – that Amanda took Megan to their house in the village not long before she and her husband were killed.

Behind them Robert can see Giles Keegan, the detective who

was in charge of the investigation into the deaths. He was the one who phoned to tell the Batemans what had happened at Oaktree Farm. And to his credit, he had worked tirelessly in pursuit of the truth about the killings and Megan's disappearance.

Robert recognises most of the other people in the churchyard, but some he doesn't, including a photographer from the Cumbria Gazette who has been snapping away throughout.

The story no longer features in the national press or on the TV news, but every now and then the local rags return to it and the headlines usually go something like 'SO WHERE IS MEGAN?' and 'IS MISSING MEGAN DEAD OR ALIVE?'

Father Silver finishes his prayer and makes the sign of the cross on his chest. Then he thanks everyone for coming and tells them to keep a place in their hearts for the Roth family.

As they all begin to disperse, Robert hands Mary a handkerchief from his pocket so that she can dry her eyes.

'Some people are going to The White Hart for a drink,' he says. 'I think we should join them. Charlotte will be awake by then and she'll enjoy it.'

'I'm not sure I'm up to it,' Mary replies. 'I'd rather go back to the farm.'

Robert leans into her and kisses her cheek.

'You'll be fine once we're there, sweetheart. It'll do us both good and we don't have to stay long.'

Mary blows out a breath and nods. 'Very well.'

They head for the gate with Robert steering the pushchair. As they step out onto the pavement, Detective Keegan is waiting to speak to them.

'I just want to ask how things are going at the farm,' he says to Robert. 'It's been a long time since I last spoke to you.'

'Well, it's not easy but we're making a go of it,' Robert tells him. 'I like to think that Simon and Amanda would be pleased with what we're doing.'

'I'm sure they would be,' Keegan says. 'From what I've heard you're doing them proud.'

'And what about you, Inspector? Are you still investigating the deaths?'

Keegan shakes his head. 'That part of the case is concluded. All the evidence suggests that Simon killed his wife and then committed suicide. But the search for their daughter continues. We'll never stop looking for her. And hopefully one day we'll find her and solve the mystery of her disappearance.'

CHAPTER TWENTY-SIX

When the press conference ended James went back to his desk and reflected on the fact that his wife's parents had known the two couples who had died at Oaktree Farm. It was a curious thing and it made the case all the more disturbing.

In London he had always managed to keep a distance between his own family and the cases he worked on. The only exception was the Andrew Sullivan investigation because the bastard made threats that had to be taken seriously. So seriously that he and Annie felt that it was no longer safe to live in the capital.

This was different, of course, but nevertheless it was beginning to unsettle him. And it must have shown on his face because DC Abbott asked him if he was all right.

He hadn't noticed that she was standing in front of his desk, her face pinched with concern.

'Of course I am,' he said. 'Why do you ask?'

'Because I've been trying to get your attention and it's like you're in a trance.'

'I'm sorry, Jessica. I was thinking about the Roth killings and their missing baby. It's such a tragic story.'

'I know it is, guv. I've been reading about it too.'

'Anyway, you now have my full attention. What is it you want?'

'I came to tell you that Dean Foreman has arrived and so has his lawyer. DS Stevens is sorting out the interview room.'

'I'll go along then. While I'm there can you liaise with Penrith on what response there's been to the press conference? I'm hoping it'll generate more than a few calls.'

'I'm on it, guv.'

'Thanks. Oh, and I've got some info on William Nash. According to my wife he works as a handyman in Kirkby Abbey, doing all kinds of odd jobs. Pass it on to whoever is checking him out. We need an address, and you and I will go and see him later this afternoon.'

DS Stevens was waiting outside the interview room when James got there.

'Dean Foreman and his lawyer are inside,' he said. 'The brief's name is Peter Haig and I haven't come across him before.'

'Anything else I should know?' James asked.

'Foreman was at home with his wife and not at his wholesale food warehouse. As soon as I told him I wanted to talk about the text he sent to Robert Bateman he clammed up and wouldn't say anything without a lawyer.'

'What do you make of the guy?'

'He's big and arrogant, and when I asked him if he'd heard about what had happened at Oaktree Farm, all he did was nod. It was as though he didn't think it was a big deal.'

'Sounds like a right charmer,' James said.

The two men were sitting next to each other when James entered the cramped and windowless interview room and he could tell straight away who was who.

The lawyer was a smart gent wearing a sober grey suit and an earnest expression. He had neat, short hair that was parted with surgical precision.

His client couldn't have been more different. Dean Foreman was a burly guy with a broken nose that pressed up against the rest of his face.

James introduced himself as he and Stevens sat opposite them across the table. He opened a folder and extracted several documents from it.

'I'd like to start by thanking you for coming in today,' he said. 'I know it's very short notice and I appreciate your cooperation.'

'Do us a favour and dispense with the bullshit, Detective,' Foreman replied, his voice clipped. 'Just get the hell on with it.'

Foreman then bared his teeth in what passed for a smile, and crossed his arms.

James took an instant dislike to the man. His demeanour reeked of malevolence and he came across as a nasty piece of work.

James knew from the note he'd been given that Foreman was forty-seven and married. He had rust-coloured hair that was receding at the front and long at the back, and his jawline was rough with stubble.

He'd made no effort with his appearance, and the shabby leather jacket and baggy jumper he had on made him look like someone who'd spent the day begging on the streets.

James felt a flare of anger, but pushed it down and pressed on with the pre-interview formalities, which included explaining why they were there for the benefit of the tape.

'My first question to you is this, Mr Foreman,' James said. 'Do you know why you're here?' Foreman grinned again and this time it produced deep creases around his eyes.

'Well, you seem to have got it into your heads that I had something to do with the killings at Oaktree Farm,' he said.

'And did you?'

'Of course I bloody well didn't.'

'But you did make a serious threat against Mr Bateman on Christmas Eve, which is when we believe the killings took place.'

James picked up one of the documents from the folder. 'The message was sent at half past four and this is what you wrote, Mr Foreman: "*I've had enough now and I'm not going to take any more of your shit. You're about to discover that I don't make empty threats, Bateman*".'

James sat back and waited for a reaction. Haig started to speak first, but Foreman raised a hand to stop him.

'There's a simple explanation for that,' he said. 'Bateman owed me money. Five thousand quid to be exact. I loaned it to him over a year ago because he begged me to help him out until his business picked up. We were good mates then so like a fool I gave it to him after he promised to pay me back within months. But then he announced he had cash flow problems because the farm was no longer making money. That was when I discovered that the main reason he was in debt was because he'd acquired a gambling habit.

It really pissed me off. I told him to pay me back in instalments, but he kept making excuses as to why he couldn't. Then, on Christmas Eve morning, he finally admitted he would never be able to pay me back. I was furious and told him I wouldn't let him get away with it and that I'd be coming to the farm to take away whatever I could in lieu of the money. He told me to fuck off and put the phone down on me. And that was why I sent the message. I had every intention of doing what I said I'd do, but not until after Christmas. Now the bastard won't have to pay off any of his debts.'

'So how do we know that you didn't threaten to hurt him, or kill him even? And that you didn't go to the farm at the earliest opportunity to carry out the threat?'

Foreman aimed unblinking eyes at James and shook his head.

'I had a legitimate reason to be angry with him, Detective. He took me for an idiot even though we were mates. It's probably obvious to you now that I have a short fuse and I'm full of bluster. But I'm not a fucking murderer. I did not go to the farm on Christmas Eve or any other day. I haven't been there in months.'

'So where were you on Christmas Eve?' This from Stevens.

'I was at home all day with my wife. I closed the warehouse the day before and we're not due to open again until tomorrow. I was also at home on Christmas Day.'

'And can anyone else apart from your wife verify that?'

For the first time he hesitated before responding, and James got the impression that he suddenly wasn't so cocky and confident.

'We spent Christmas by ourselves,' he said. 'The only time I left the house was on Boxing Day to go into town to pick up some groceries. You can ask my wife.'

'Is this the same wife who accused you of hitting her a year ago, Mr Foreman?' James asked.

He wasn't surprised when the lawyer slammed his hand down on the table in protest.

'That accusation was withdrawn, as you well know, Inspector,' he said. 'To bring it up now is completely out of order. It's irrelevant in respect of the matter at hand.'

'I don't agree, Mr Haig,' James said. 'I've been involved in numerous cases where a wife was forced to provide her husband with a false alibi.'

'Well I can assure you that's not true in this case. And your aggressive line of questioning makes it clear why Mr Foreman was absolutely right to refuse to speak to you without legal representation.'

'They're out to stitch me up,' Foreman broke in. 'It's as clear as day.'

'That's nonsense, Mr Foreman,' James said. 'I'm merely drawing attention to the fact that your explanation is not as convincing as you seem to think it is. And for that reason, we will need to speak to your wife and carry out a search of your home and car.'

Foreman's jaw tightened and bulged. 'You've got to be joking. I had nothing to do with what happened to that family. And my wife doesn't live in fear of me or do things just because I tell her to.'

'Even so, you threatened Mr Bateman in writing only hours before he and his family were killed. We can't simply take your word for it that your only intention was to seize some of his belongings as payment for an outstanding debt. It warrants further investigation.'

'So, what do you intend to do now?' the lawyer asked.

'Your client will remain here in custody until checks have been carried out,' James made clear. 'We'll be interviewing his wife and obtaining a warrant to search his home. I believe that to be a reasonable step to take in the circumstances.'

'Well, I don't,' Foreman interjected. 'It's fucking outrageous. I've told you the truth.'

'Then you shouldn't have a problem with us talking to Mrs Foreman and confirming your account of things.'

'But I do have a problem with it.'

'That's just too bad, Mr Foreman. We're investigating the deaths of an entire family, and contrary to what you believe, we have not determined exactly what happened at Oaktree Farm and are therefore pursuing all possibilities.'

'So, how long will my client be expected to remain here?' Haig asked.

'As long as it takes us to do what has to be done,' James said. 'You know how it works, Mr Haig, and you know that we can hold a suspect for a significant period before we have to charge or release them. Your client made an overt threat against Mr Bateman shortly before he and his family were killed. That's reason enough to arrest him on suspicion of an offence.'

The lawyer then insisted on having a private chat with his client so James paused the recording and he and Stevens left the interview room for about five minutes. When they returned, Foreman's face looked as though the blood had been sucked out of it. The arrogance was gone and his eyes were dull with shock.

'My client accepts that he needs to remain here for the time being, given the circumstances,' Haig said. 'But he wants me to be present when you interview his wife. And he would like you to do it in their home so that she doesn't have to be brought here.'

'That won't be a problem,' James said. 'And I hope he appreciates that we can't allow him to contact his wife beforehand.'

The lawyer nodded. 'He does.'

'Good. But before we get things moving there are just a couple more questions I'd like to ask.' James referred to his notes before continuing. 'Can you tell me how long you've known Robert Bateman, Mr Foreman?'

Foreman sat up straight and pushed his shoulders back.

'We met twelve years ago when we both joined the same pheasant shooting club,' he said. 'I lived here in Kendal back then and the pair of us got on well and we socialised quite a bit. We also went on a lot of shoots together.'

'And how well did you get to know his wife and daughter?'

'Not at all well. I only met them a few times.'

'What about Neil Savage, his daughter's boyfriend?'

'You mean the bloke you're looking for?'

'That's right.'

'I'd never heard of him until his picture came up on the telly.'

'And were you acquainted with Simon and Amanda Roth, the couple who lived on Oaktree Farm before the Batemans? Did you have any business with them?'

'No. The first I heard of them was when their names were all over the papers back when they died.'

'And finally, do you know anyone else Robert Bateman owed money to?'

Foreman shook his head. 'I'm sure there must be others, though. I can't believe I was the only fool to succumb to his sob story and lend him money that he no doubt squandered on online gaming sites.'

CHAPTER TWENTY-SEVEN

As James left the interview room, his thoughts were gnashing in his head.

He wasn't sure what to make of Dean Foreman, or whether to believe what he'd said. The guy was clearly an arrogant prick, and James was willing to bet that he was also mentally and physically abusive to his wife.

But would she cover for him if she suspected he had committed murder? James knew it was possible given the sheer number of women he'd seen in court who had done exactly that.

'D'you want me to go and see the wife, guv?' Stevens asked. 'I've already met her because she opened the door when I arrived at their house.'

'And how did she strike you?'

'The nervous type. Polite and timid, and quietly spoken. If she's hiding something, I don't think it will take much to get her to crack.'

'Then go for it,' James said. 'And see how quickly you can

get a forensic team there. But before you go, get Foreman's DNA and prints, and an impression of the soles of the shoes he's wearing.'

'And where are you off to, guv?'

'Kirkby Abbey. We're ready to see if Kenneth O'Connor's house will throw up anything interesting. And hopefully we can drop in on Charlotte Bateman's ex-boyfriend, William Nash.'

Back in the office, DC Abbott had some news for James.

'Three things, guv,' she said. 'First, I've spoken to Penrith and they're still receiving calls in response to the press conference. So far none stand out or offer a credible clue as to Neil Savage's whereabouts.'

'Well I'm sure the appeal will be repeated during the rest of the day and into the evening, so there's still a chance we'll strike lucky. What are the other things?'

'I've now got William Nash's address so we're ready to roll. And I can confirm that he doesn't have a criminal record. But, of course, that doesn't mean he's clean.'

Before they set off for Kirkby Abbey, James called the team together to tell them about the interview with Dean Foreman.

'DS Stevens will go to Penrith to talk to Foreman's wife and oversee a search of their house,' he said. 'DC Abbott and I will go to Kirkby Abbey to talk to Charlotte's ex-boyfriend, William Nash, and see where we are with Kenneth O'Connor.'

Several other members of the team gave updates saying they now had access to Robert Bateman's bank accounts and these were being examined, but no progress had been made in the search for Neil Savage, or the isolated house where he attended drink and drugs benders. And nothing new had turned up during the forensic sweep of Oaktree Farm.

So, it seemed they were making some progress on various fronts, but not enough to convince James that they were close to finding out why and how the Bateman family had met such violent deaths.

James and Abbott grabbed a late lunch snack from the vending machine before heading out to Kirkby Abbey. James drove his own car because he didn't plan on returning to Kendal this evening, so DC Abbott followed him in a pool car.

Heavy clouds were building and the sun had all but disappeared. The brightness had been short-lived and Cumbria was bracing itself for some heavy overnight snow showers.

The forecasters were expecting the Lake District to be hit the hardest, but they were predicting that some areas might escape the worst of the weather altogether.

William Nash lived on a plot of land behind Kirkby Abbey's only petrol station. It was set back from the road, which was why James had never noticed it before.

Inside a low perimeter fence was a small detached cottage, a garage that had been converted into a workshop and a semi-circular yard paved in asphalt, which was large enough for several vehicles.

When James arrived just before 3 p.m. there was a motor scooter and a small transit van parked on the asphalt. On the side of the van were the words: *WILL NASH (MR FIXIT) Handyman Services.*

James parked on the road and waited for Abbott to pull up behind him. Then they both walked through the yard to the front door of the cottage. There was no bell so James used the heavy metal knocker to get the attention of whoever was inside.

The man who answered was wearing tight, drainpipe jeans and a soiled blue T-shirt, and he fit the description that Annie had given James – tall, in his twenties and a bit nerdy.

'Are you Mr William Nash?' James asked.

He ran his tongue over thin lips and nodded. 'Yes, that's me.'

Both detectives flashed their warrant cards and James explained who they were.

'We've come to ask you some questions about your former girlfriend, Charlotte Bateman. I take it you're aware of what's happened to her and her parents.'

A shadow crossed his face and James noticed that his eyes were red and inflamed.

'Of course I have,' he said, his voice gravel-edged. 'It's been on the news and it's all anyone in the village is talking about. I keep telling myself that it can't be true. I don't want it to be true.'

'Well I'm afraid it is true, Mr Nash, and as part of the investigation into what happened we need to know as much as we can about each member of the family. And we're hoping that you can help us in respect of Charlotte. So, may we come in?'

He stood aside and waved them through to a small, low-ceilinged living room, which should have been cosy but wasn't. There was no sofa, just two armchairs, an old TV, an open fireplace and a sideboard. The floor was cluttered with cardboard boxes and carrier bags.

'Excuse the mess,' Nash said. 'I made an effort this year and put up some decorations because I thought my parents were coming for Christmas. But they pulled out at the last minute.'

'So, you live here alone?'

He nodded. 'Mum and Dad moved to Spain two and a half years ago. I didn't want to go so they left me the cottage and the business. I'm mortgage free and make enough money to keep me going. I can't complain.'

He invited them to sit on the armchairs while he stood with his back to the fire which was smouldering away.

Without being prompted, he said, 'It might sound odd to you, but I haven't been able to function properly since the news broke. I've had to cancel two jobs, and I can't stop thinking about Charlotte. She didn't deserve for this to happen to her.'

His eyes filled with tears but he blinked them away and did his best to remain composed.

'It seems to me as though you still had strong feelings for her,' James said.

Nash swallowed. 'I did. That girl meant the world to me and I never wanted our relationship to end.'

'So how long had you known each other?'

'Just under ten years. We met at school, but we didn't start going out until three years ago. At first it was great, but she gradually drifted away from me, mainly because she started mixing with people who she should have stayed clear of, people who were into drugs and that. At the same time, she was having problems at home, especially with her mother. There were lots of arguments and she kept threatening to move away from Kirkby Abbey.'

'What did they argue about?' Abbott asked.

'Anything and everything,' Nash replied. 'They just didn't get on. Charlotte had a better relationship with her father. He was like a calming influence on her. Once she even said to me that she would have preferred it if it was just the two of them.'

'So, when did you and Charlotte break up?' James said.

'That would have been just over a year ago.'

'And when was the last time you saw her?'

'About six weeks ago. I'd heard that she'd got a new job at a charity shop in Kendal. I was in town so I dropped by to wish her well.'

'We actually heard about that, Mr Nash,' James said. 'Apparently Charlotte told her colleague that she thought you were stalking her because you couldn't accept that your relationship with her was over.'

He shook his head. 'That was what Savage tried to make her believe. He started telling it to people before Charlotte moved in with him and was still living here in the village. He didn't like the fact that I tried a couple of times to persuade her to leave him. I knew he wasn't good for her. And it turns out I was right.'

'What do you mean?'

'Well he got her into drugs and God only knows what else. And now we're being led to believe that he killed her and her family.'

'We don't know that for certain, Mr Nash.'

'Then why wasn't his body also found at the farm? The police have made it clear that he was with the family on Christmas Eve.'

'That's a good question and one that we can't answer as yet,' James said. 'Would you have any idea where he might be?'

'None at all. If I did, I'd tell you, but I only know him by reputation. I'm glad to say I never met him.' Emotion suddenly overwhelmed him and the tears came out in huge, racking sobs. He pulled a rag from his pocket and pressed it against his eyes.

'I keep trying to hold it in, but I can't,' he sobbed. 'It's really got to me. I just don't understand it.'

He was visibly shaking now and started to cough.

DC Abbott shot to her feet and offered to get him some water. He mumbled a thank you and pointed to the door that led to the kitchen.

James stayed where he was and tried to determine whether the man's grief was genuine. It certainly seemed to be. But then people often became consummate actors when they were desperate to hide something.

Abbott came back with a glass of water that she handed to Nash. He thanked her and started drinking.

'Do you need more time or can I start asking you a few more questions?' James said.

Nash swallowed a mouthful of water and asked James what else he wanted to know.

'I'd like you to tell me how well you knew Charlotte's parents. Did you spend much time at Oaktree Farm when you were together?'

'Not really,' he replied. 'Charlotte preferred to come here, and at the time she was working at a factory in town so it was more convenient for both of us.'

'So, did she live here with you?'

'We didn't get that far. She stayed over quite often and I tried to persuade her to move in but she wouldn't.'

'Were you aware that her father was having financial problems with the farm?'

'It's been an open secret in the village for a while, but when I was with Charlotte it never came up.'

166

'And what about the relationship between Charlotte's parents? Was it a healthy one?'

'Most of the time, I think it was. Charlotte didn't talk about it much except when she moaned that her mum was nagging her.'

'And would you know if Mr and Mrs Bateman had any enemies?'

'I wouldn't. Like I told you, I didn't see much of them.'

'Okay. Now, did you ever have reason to go into the cellar when you were at the farm?'

Nash wrinkled his brow. 'No. Charlotte told me it was out of bounds to most people.'

'Is that because the previous owners were found dead down there?'

He nodded. 'Charlotte wasn't made aware of that until she was in her teens and it creeped her out. She said her parents even put up some kind of memorial in there.'

'And did you know that there was an internal door that led from the cellar into the house? And that it was blocked with a wall?'

'I did, but only because Charlotte told me. The wall was installed when she was a toddler.'

'And do you happen to know who carried out the work?'

'I've no idea.'

'Mr Nash, would you mind providing us with fingerprints and DNA samples?' James's question provoked an immediate and strong reaction.

'Why do you want those?' he demanded. 'Does it mean I'm a suspect? You said you wanted me to tell you about Charlotte. Not that you think I might have killed her.'

'The intention is to eliminate you from our enquiries, Mr Nash,' James said.

167

'So, you're not arresting me?'

'No, we're not.'

'Well I know that if you don't have any grounds to arrest me you can't force me to give you fingerprints and DNA samples. I've never been in trouble so I don't want them on your files, and I resent the fact that you think I would have murdered the woman I loved.'

'Look, there's no need for this hostility, Mr Nash,' James said, but the man was already striding across the room to the door. He grabbed the handle and pulled it open.

'I want you to go now please,' he said, his voice thick with emotion. 'I've answered your questions and now I want to be alone.'

The detectives stood and James took out one of his cards and placed it on the sideboard.

'It would help if you cooperated with us willingly, Mr Nash, rather than us having to force you to. We'll be in touch again tomorrow and by then I hope you'll have calmed and will realise that making things difficult for us is not in your best interest.'

Nash said nothing as they walked past him and out the door, which he slammed shut behind them.

When they reached the road, James said, 'We'll give him the benefit of the doubt for now, and assume that it all just got a bit too much for him. But he stays in the frame because I've got the feeling that he's not being entirely honest with us. If he doesn't come through tomorrow, we'll either arrest him on suspicion or get a court order to force him to cooperate. We need his prints as soon as possible in order to compare them with those found at the farm.'

Abbott's face slid into a half smile as she reached into her coat pocket and pulled out a clear evidence bag. Inside it was a small glass.

'It was on the kitchen side when I went to get the water so I helped myself to it,' she said. 'His prints are all over it.'

James arched his brow as he took the bag from her and peered at the glass.

'I know it's technically theft, guv, but I could tell he was in a state and thought he might not be willing or even able to cooperate.'

James grinned. 'Well, that's certainly an impressive display of initiative, Detective. I'm therefore willing to turn a blind eye in this instance.'

'Thanks, guv. I'll be back on my best behaviour tomorrow.'

'But bear in mind that this just gives us a head start. We'll still need to take his prints through the formal process.'

He gave her back the bag and looked at his watch. Almost four o'clock.

'You might as well knock off,' he said. 'Drop that at the office for the forensics team on the way home.'

'And where are you going?'

'To check on what's happening at Kenneth O'Connor's house. I'll see you in the morning.'

CHAPTER TWENTY-EIGHT

Kenneth O'Connor's place was on the other side of the village, but James didn't go straight there.

Curiosity compelled him to stop on the way at St John's Church in order to see for himself the headstone marking the graves of Simon and Amanda Roth.

It would soon be dark so he reckoned that now was as good a time as any, and at least it would be another box ticked.

He couldn't shake the thought that there was something he wasn't seeing. Something that connected the two crimes other than the fact that they both took place at Oaktree Farm and involved the families who lived there. Was there more to it than mere coincidence? That was the million-dollar question and he couldn't yet answer it.

He parked in front of the church and climbed out of the car. The air felt raw and a noisy wind was dancing through the streets of the village.

As he walked through the gate into the churchyard, an

empty ache touched the pit of his stomach as it always did when he came here. That was partly because two of the people murdered by the Kirkby Abbey serial killer a year ago were buried here. And their deaths continued to press heavily on his conscience because he hadn't been able to save them.

Their graves were at the back of the church and he wouldn't be paying them a visit this evening. Instead, he squeezed the memory of what happened to them to one side and went looking for the headstone he had come to see. He knew from the photo he'd downloaded of the anniversary service that it was at the front of the church and to the right of the path, pretty close to the graves of Annie's parents.

He found it easily enough, but because of the fading light he had to use the torch on his phone to read the epitaph.

In loving memory of Simon and Amanda Roth – together in life and death. Their daughter Megan will always be in their hearts.

James read it through twice and the words evoked a strong emotional response inside him. There was a deep sense of sadness, as well as an element of frustration because their deaths, and what happened to their daughter, were still mysteries after all this time.

He wondered what secrets Simon and Amanda took to their graves. Did they know before they died what had happened to Megan? Was she the reason their lives came to such an abrupt and brutal end?

It felt to James as though he was investigating two crimes that were committed twenty-four years apart.

The deaths of Robert, Mary and Charlotte Bateman were

just as mysterious as those of Simon and Amanda Roth. And James feared that if he didn't solve this latest crime it would be history repeating itself, with people still asking two decades from now what had happened at Oaktree Farm on that fateful Christmas Eve.

It seemed incongruous to James that as the evening closed in a wide range of Christmas lights started coming on throughout Kirkby Abbey. Windows sparkled, elves and reindeer figurines flashed on and off in front gardens, and the huge multi-coloured tree lit up the market square.

It was a grim reminder that before the bodies were discovered at Oaktree Farm, the villagers had been determined to make the most of the festive period. Last year it was ruined by the string of murders, and this year they had hoped, and expected, things to be different.

He couldn't imagine that anyone would be in the mood to celebrate the New Year that was just four days away. He and Annie had nothing planned, but it was just as well as there was a good chance he would still be bogged down with the investigation by then.

When he drew close to Kenneth O'Connor's home the street outside was awash with high-visibility vests. As a result, O'Connor's neighbours had come out of their homes to see what was going on, and several small groups were gathered on the pavements. He was surprised because he'd expected the team to take a low-key approach.

James found a place to park and walked up to the house. He got another surprise when he saw two uniformed officers dragging Kenneth O'Connor out through his front door. He was yelling at them to let him go, but they ignored him and marched him over to a waiting patrol car. He was bundled into the back seat while still remonstrating with them.

James noticed that he was cuffed and so had presumably been arrested. He experienced a surge of adrenaline and wondered if this was a breakthrough of some kind.

He spotted DC Patterson standing next to the patrol car and hurried straight over to him.

'What have I missed?' James said. 'Has O'Connor been arrested?'

As Patterson turned, James saw that blood was dripping from his nose.

'Jesus, Colin,' he blurted. 'What the hell happened to you?'

Patterson dabbed at the blood with a tissue he'd been holding.

'The fucker punched me,' he said. 'He arrived back from his visit to Carlisle just as we got here. When I told him that we had a warrant to search the house he started to kick up a fuss and told me we had no right to. Then he stood in front of the door and refused to move. I grabbed his arm and he hit me and then rushed inside and locked the door. The guys had to break in and pull him out.'

'You need to get that nose checked,' James said. 'It might be broken.'

Patterson shook his head. 'I'm sure it isn't. But it hurts.'

'Either way, we'll charge him with assaulting a police officer.'

'And with resisting arrest. But what I'm keen to know is why he felt so strongly about not letting us in. It suggests to me that he has something to hide.'

James decided to have a word with O'Connor before they hauled him off to Kendal.

He stepped up to the patrol car, pulled open the back door and stared down at him.

'Care to explain why you don't want this search to take place?' he said. 'What is it you don't want us to find?'

O'Connor's face was flushed with anger and blood vessels bulged at his temples.

'I'm not hiding anything and I've already let you look around,' he responded. 'I thought that would be it. But then I suddenly got a call to tell me you're sending the fucking troops in. I've done nothing wrong so I don't see why I should let you tear my place apart.'

'That explanation is just not convincing,' James said. 'You're clearly worried that my officers will turn up something that will either embarrass or incriminate you. So, what is it?'

'You've got it wrong. Honestly. I just panicked and hit out.'

James shrugged. 'Suit yourself, Mr O'Connor. You're going to be formally charged with assaulting a police officer and tomorrow morning I'll be talking to you at the station – and confronting you with whatever we find here.'

James shut the door and signalled for the officers to take him to Kendal.

He then instructed the SOCOs, who had been waiting in the forensic van, to go into the house.

DC Patterson was one of two detectives who had come from the office. The other was DC Dawn Isaac. James told her to take charge and ordered Patterson to go and get his nose seen to.

Then to Isaac, he said, 'I live just around the corner from here so if you need me don't hesitate to call.'

Before calling time on the working day, James phoned

Tanner to update him on the interview with William Nash and the situation with O'Connor.

The boss had just arrived back in the office from Penrith and said he would make a point of talking to O'Connor when he was brought in.

'I'd keep a close eye on him, sir,' James said. 'He used to work on Oaktree Farm. Robert Bateman sacked him for allegedly stealing from them. O'Connor was furious and they fell out. It almost came to blows between them at least once, and there's something just not sitting right about it all.'

'Thanks, James. I'll get someone to dig out whatever else we have on the guy and will let you know if anything comes of it.'

James made one more call before going home, this time to DS Stevens, who told him that the search of Dean Foreman's house in Penrith was still under way.

'I've spoken to his wife and she's very upset,' he said. 'But she insisted that she's not covering for him. She claims he did not leave the house on Christmas Eve or on Christmas Day. It's impossible to tell if she's lying. She also reckons she's not a victim of domestic abuse and that she was wrong to have accused her husband of hitting her a year ago. She said it was all a misunderstanding, whatever that means.'

'Okay, well, give me a full briefing in the morning unless you find something significant in the house.'

James ended the call and pocketed his phone. Then he returned to his car and drove home.

CHAPTER TWENTY-NINE

Annie was waiting for him in the kitchen. She offered him a warm smile and a glass of freshly poured white wine.

'I was at the window and saw you pull up,' she said. 'How come you're so early? I didn't expect you until much later.'

'I came back to the village to interview William Nash, and to check on the team searching Kenneth O'Connor's house,' he said, taking the wine. 'There was no point driving back to the office.'

They kissed and he asked her how her day had gone.

'I've got most of the school work done and I went for a long walk,' she said. 'But I felt exhausted afterwards and had a nap on the sofa.'

'Did you watch the press conference?'

'Of course. Have you managed to find Neil Savage?'

'Not yet, but we're gradually making progress on that front.'

He sat at the kitchen table and loosened his tie. It was good to be home but it would take a while for his mind to settle, and he needed some quiet time to rein in his scattered thoughts.

'I was going to raid the freezer for dinner,' Annie said. 'Is there anything you fancy?'

'I wouldn't mind having you on a plate,' he joked.

She gave her head a slow shake. 'Well, I'm most certainly not on the menu tonight, honeybun. I'm too knackered. But I can dish up a nice lasagne. It won't be as tasty but I'm sure you'll enjoy it.'

So, lasagne it was and they ate it at the table after James had changed into some casual clothes.

They both made an effort to steer the conversation away from the Oaktree Farm killings, but it proved impossible.

Annie said several people stopped her to ask about it on her walk through the village earlier.

'They all assume that you tell me everything,' she said. 'And I can't convince them that you don't, probably because it's not true.'

'What is the mood like out there?' James asked.

She shrugged. 'Everyone is shocked and bewildered. And I was told that quite a few people are afraid to leave their homes. It's just like it was last Christmas when the murders were taking place. No one knows if there will be more killings this year.'

'I don't think we're dealing with a serial killer this time,' James said.

'But that's the problem isn't it? You don't really know what you're dealing with. Uncle Bill called today. He'd heard about the Batemans on the news,' Annie said. Her uncle Bill lived alone in Penrith and had dementia. They had learned of his condition a year ago and since then it had gradually worsened, although he still managed to cope without a carer or having to go into a home.

'He was apparently a friend of Robert Bateman's, but he also knew Simon and Amanda Roth quite well. He said they were a lovely couple and he never did believe what everyone said about Simon killing his wife. He's always been convinced that there was more to it than that.'

'I don't think he's the only one,' James said. 'But the problem for the investigators at the time was the lack of witnesses. Plus, there was no obvious motive and no potential suspects.'

James was about to tell Annie that he had visited the churchyard to see the Roths' headstone but as he started to speak his phone rang.

His heart shunted up a gear when he saw that the caller was Leo Freeman, his former colleague in the Met.

'I'd better take this in the other room,' he said, rising quickly to his feet.

Annie's eyes narrowed inquisitively as he rushed out of the kitchen clutching his phone.

He didn't press the answer button until he was in the hallway, and before Leo spoke, he said, 'I assume you've got an update for me on our friend?'

'That I have, James, and I'm afraid you're not going to like it.'

James experienced a blast of anxiety, and suddenly his throat was too tight to speak.

'We still don't know where he is,' Leo carried on. 'But we just came across a couple of burner phones that were hidden in his home. On one of them were some photographs of you and your wife and your house in Cumbria. It looks like they were taken about two months ago by whoever sent them to Sullivan. I'm about to send them to you.'

James squeezed his eyes shut and pinched the bridge of his nose between forefinger and thumb. This was just what he didn't need right now – a raising of the threat level from the villain who effectively drove he and Annie out of London with his terrorisation.

'Do you know who took the photos?' he asked.

'We do. His name is Stuart Ross and we're about to pull him in. He's one of Sullivan's foot soldiers based here in London. The note that accompanied the photos makes it clear that Sullivan sent him north to Kirkby Abbey to snap the pair of you along with your house.'

'That can mean only one thing, Leo,' James said. 'Sullivan got wind of where we are and has decided it's time to settle the score.'

CHAPTER THIRTY

James didn't want to tell Annie about the photos on Sullivan's phone, but she had a right to know.

He had mistakenly believed that the threat they'd faced from Sullivan had receded over the past year. But clearly it hadn't. And now he had to decide how seriously to take this latest development and what, if anything, to do about it.

Before facing Annie, he slipped into the downstairs loo and opened up the photos that Leo had sent him.

The first was an exterior shot of their house. The second showed he and Annie coming out of the front door. The third was of the pair of them walking arm in arm through the village.

For a few minutes he was lost in silent thought as a knot of dread formed in his stomach. When he walked back into the kitchen, his heart was pounding in his chest.

Annie hadn't moved from the table and the look she gave him told him that she knew that something was up.

'That was Leo Freeman in London,' he said, deciding that

there was no point beating about the bush. 'He had some news about Andrew Sullivan.'

'Please tell me they've collared him,' she said.

He shook his head. 'They're still looking, but they found something when they searched his house.'

Alarm shivered behind Annie's eyes as she stared at him, slack-jawed.

'Well don't keep me in suspense,' she said. 'What did they find?'

When he told her, and showed her the photos, she sucked in a breath and her eyes grew to the size of saucers.

'I knew the bastard wouldn't leave us alone,' she said, her voice trembling. 'But I can't believe he sent someone to take pictures of us. Why would he do that?'

'It could be he was planning to send them to me in order to scare us,' James replied.

Annie jammed her tongue to the side of her mouth and thought about it.

'I think it more likely that he was checking out the lie of the land before making his move,' she said. 'If he's decided to come here, he'll want to know what to expect.'

James swallowed, trying to moisten his throat.

'What we shouldn't do is panic,' he said. 'Sullivan is wanted in connection with a murder and he's on the run. Like I said to you before, he's got enough on his plate to keep him busy. I really don't think he'll bother to show his face here.'

'But that might not stop him from sending someone else to do his dirty work for him.'

James knew that she was right and that it was going to be necessary to take some precautions.

'Look, I'll talk to Tanner and arrange for a unit to be stationed outside the house until we have a better idea of what we're dealing with. And just to be on the safe side, you should probably avoid going out for a couple of days.'

Annie's face suddenly took on a fiery intensity and her hands clenched into fists on the table.

'This is totally ridiculous, James. That man is the reason we moved here, and even now, more than a year on, he still poses a threat. We can't go on like this.'

'I know that Annie, but at least we now know what he's been up to so that when he's eventually caught, he can be confronted with it and we'll have him. Meanwhile, we just have to be careful. And short of moving again there's not much else we can do.'

James was suddenly glad that he'd had a state-of-the-art burglar alarm fitted in the house with security cameras at the front and back that were linked to their mobile phones. It gave him a modicum of comfort.

He got up and walked around the table to his wife. She looked up at him, her eyes moist. He felt his heart swell as he cupped her face in his hands.

'I won't let him or anyone else harm you, Annie,' he said. 'I promise. But you have to do your best to remain calm and strong for both our sakes and for the baby's.'

As Annie began to cry, he eased her to her feet and held her in his arms. She was still sobbing as he led her into the living room and planted her on the sofa.

'Try to relax while I go and call my boss,' he said. 'I'll make you a tea whilst I'm at it.'

Back in the kitchen he called Tanner and put him in the picture.

'I'll arrange for a car to come straight there and stay all night, James,' he said. 'That won't be a problem, and we can talk tomorrow about what we do longer term. But I need to know if this will hinder your ability to continue with the Oaktree Farm investigation. If so, I can take over as SOI.'

'You don't have to worry about that, sir, I'll be fine. I'm not as worried as my wife and I need something to keep my mind occupied.'

'Okay, but keep me posted if anything changes. I had a word with Kenneth O'Connor when he arrived at Kendal, by the way. He answered no comment to every question I put to him,' Tanner said. 'We can have another go at him in the morning.'

James put the kettle on and while he waited for it to boil, he used his phone to bring up the latest news stories on Andrew Sullivan. There were plenty of them and they all focused on the fact that he was wanted by the police.

It was in connection with the murder of a man named Kyle Ramsay, who used to be one of Sullivan's inner-circle henchmen. The guy had been shot dead outside a South London pub and witnesses saw a man matching Sullivan's description fleeing the scene. Sullivan made himself scarce shortly after.

As James made Annie's tea, his mind raced and his heart beat rapidly. He hoped he wouldn't regret assuring Tanner that this wouldn't hinder his ability to cope with the current investigation.

The truth was he didn't know for sure how much of a distraction it would prove to be going forward. He guessed it would depend on how many more bombshells landed on him.

Later that evening a blizzard hit Kirkby Abbey with a vengeance and James and Annie lay in bed listening to the howling wind and the snow lashing their bedroom window.

But it wasn't the only thing that kept them awake. Andrew Sullivan was still foremost on their minds and the arrival of the patrol car now parked across the road provided little comfort.

It was after midnight before Annie finally dropped off, but for James sleep proved more elusive. His overactive brain refused to rest and Sullivan's face was just one of a number that demanded his attention. The others belonged to the individuals who figured in the Oaktree Farm investigation – everyone from the three victims to the characters who were emerging as credible suspects.

The case was proving to be a real challenge and to solve it he needed to be fully focused. But he wasn't convinced that was going to be possible now that he had to put more effort into making sure that Annie was safe. It was an added burden and one he could have done without.

It was just after three in the morning when he finally dropped off to sleep and barely an hour later the ringing of his phone jolted him awake again.

It was DC Dawn Isaac on the line and she sounded excited.

'I know I've probably woken you up, sir, and I'm really sorry,' she said. 'But you told me to call if we came up with anything inside Kenneth O'Connor's house that might link him to the farm killings. Well, we have, and I thought you'd want me to tell you about it straight away.'

CHAPTER THIRTY-ONE

Friday December 29th

The call from DC Isaac also woke Annie, and James told her to stay in bed as he got up and pulled on some clothes.

'I won't be long,' he said. 'I've got to pop around to Kenneth O'Connor's place. I'll come back before I go to the office and if you're still awake I'll make you some breakfast.'

He didn't bother to wash or shower, but he did prepare himself for the harsh weather outside by putting on his thermal-lined parka and his hiking boots.

About four inches of snow had come down overnight, but thankfully it had stopped falling. A biting wind continued to whip through the village, though, and this made it feel colder than it was.

Before heading to O'Connor's house, James crossed the road to tell the two officers in the unmarked pool car where he was going. He was glad to see that they were both awake and seemed fully alert.

As he then set off on the short walk, he wondered if this was going to be the breakthrough he'd been waiting for. DC

to tell him about the development with the jewellery box. The DCI was already up and getting ready to head for the station himself.

'This sounds like a game changer,' he said. 'If we're going to formally interview him this morning, I'll get onto it and make sure there's a duty solicitor around.'

A fizz of excitement was running through James when he arrived at the station. Some team members were already in and so he was able to get things moving straight away.

The custody sergeant was told to prepare Kenneth O'Connor for the formal interview and James asked officers to dig up more information on the man. He wanted someone to talk to his former girlfriend and run a check on his bank and social media accounts.

By 7.30 a.m. most of the team were in and James brought them up to date. The discovery of Mary Bateman's jewellery box was the only lead that showed any promise as they hadn't got any further in the hunt for Neil Savage and the search of Dean Foreman's house had proved fruitless.

James gave the go-ahead for Foreman to be released from custody but instructed two detectives to stay on his case.

'The threatening text message he sent to Robert Bateman on Christmas Eve still troubles me,' he said. 'And we only have his wife's word for it that he stayed with her at home the whole time. So, we need to keep up the pressure. Let's talk to his friends and colleagues, and also members of the shooting club that he and Bateman belonged to.'

After the briefing, and before the interview with O'Connor, DCI Tanner asked him what the latest situation was with Andrew Sullivan.

'He's still on the run as far as I know, sir,' James answered.

'I'll be informed as soon as there's a development. Meanwhile, thanks for arranging for the car to come over.'

'I've made provision for a crew to be outside your house for the rest of the week. And they'll be armed. We'll review it then or before if anything changes.'

'That's great, sir. But to be honest I really don't think Sullivan would be stupid enough to come here. He'll be too busy trying to stay out of sight.'

'I agree with you there, James,' Tanner said. 'But it's better to be safe than sorry, especially in view of what happened to Jack Hannah.'

It was a good point, James thought. Detective Inspector Hannah had led an investigation into a large drugs ring in Liverpool at the start of the year. When one of the ringleaders was convicted by a court and sent down for a long stretch Hannah received an anonymous call threatening revenge. Sadly, he didn't take it seriously and neither did his superiors. Three weeks later he was enjoying an evening at home with his wife when someone rang the doorbell. Hannah answered it and was shot dead by a man who ran off and was never found.

His death ensured that all threats against police officers were now being taken a lot more seriously.

CHAPTER THIRTY-TWO

It was just after eight when James and DC Abbott entered the interview room.

Kenneth O'Connor had already been introduced to the duty solicitor, Christian Lee, a regular at the station, and the pair were seated at the table.

James got a shock when he saw O'Connor. The guy looked like death warmed up. His face was gaunt and colourless, the eyes dark rimmed and bloodshot.

James turned on the recorder and went through the motions of saying who was present in the room. After that it was the lawyer who spoke first.

Christian Lee was an old hand at this. He'd been a brief for years and had a commanding presence. He was somewhere in his late forties with prominent cheekbones and bushy hair peppered with grey.

'I'd like to make clear at the outset that Mr O'Connor bitterly regrets striking that detective last evening,' Lee said. 'If the matter proceeds to court he will argue that he was under extreme duress at the time and hit out in a panic when he felt threatened.'

James turned straight to O'Connor, and said, 'Why did you feel threatened, Mr O'Connor? You'd already told me that you had nothing to do with what happened at Oaktree Farm. So, was it because there was something in your house that you didn't want my officers to find?'

O'Connor didn't respond for several seconds, his eyes fixed on his hands, which were joined together on the table.

It was clear to James that he wasn't sure what to say because he didn't know if the search team had found anything in his house.

When eventually he looked up and spoke, his voice was dry and hoarse.

'I've got nothing to hide, Inspector. I made that clear to you last night. I didn't see why I should just let the police invade my privacy. That detective was aggressive, and he grabbed me first. I reacted instinctively. But for what it's worth you can tell him that I'm sorry.'

James gestured for DC Abbott to open the folder she'd brought in with her. She did so and took out a photograph of Mary Bateman's jewellery box, which she placed face up on the table.

'For the benefit of the tape Mr O'Connor is being shown a photograph marked exhibit number two,' she said.

James waited a second before saying, 'Do you recognise that, Mr O'Connor? Or are you going to pretend that you've never seen it before?'

O'Connor clamped his top lip between his teeth as he looked down at the photo. When he saw what it was, he closed his eyes and dragged in a long breath.

The solicitor picked it up and said, 'So, what's the relevance of this?'

James shrugged. 'Well since your client seems to have lost his voice, I'll tell you. That jewellery box and its contents belonged to Mrs Mary Bateman, who as you know was killed on Christmas Eve along with her husband and daughter. Her name is embossed on the box and inscribed on a piece of the jewellery. The question is, what was it doing in your client's bedroom drawer?'

O'Connor's eyes sprang open and he started blinking rapidly while shaking his head.

'It's not what you think,' he said. 'I did take it from the house but it wasn't on Christmas Eve. It was weeks ago.'

'Are you telling us that you stole it?'

'I still have a key to the farmhouse. I've been desperately short of money since I was sacked so I decided to go back there and take a few things. I felt they owed me.'

'I take it this wasn't the first time you stole from them?' James said. 'When Robert Bateman accused you of pilfering before he was right, wasn't he?'

O'Connor pulled a slightly pained expression and nodded. 'I did it because they were paying me shit wages and I knew the business was gradually going under. So, when I saw things lying around that I thought I might be able to sell I helped myself to them.'

'And how many times have you burgled the house since you were sacked?'

'Just the once. I waited until I knew they were both out. I didn't go looking for the box but I found it when I started going through their stuff. It was the only thing that looked as though it might be worth something.'

'So why should we believe you, Mr O'Connor?' DC Abbott asked him. 'After all, you lied to us when you insisted you had nothing to hide.'

'Well, I knew you would jump to the wrong conclusion, and it turns out that I was right,' he said. 'But I'm not lying to you now. It's true I stole the jewellery and that was stupid of me. But I did not kill anyone. You have to believe that.'

'I'm not sure what to believe right now,' James said. 'Just look at it from our point of view. You used to work at Oaktree Farm so you knew the family well. Then you had a major falling out with Robert Bateman because he accused you, rightly, as it turns out, of stealing from him. And as a result, you harboured a serious grudge. You then broke into the farmhouse after he'd sacked you and stole his wife's jewellery. And to top it all there's no one to corroborate your movements on Christmas Eve before you arrived at your brother's house.'

'That's circumstantial evidence at best,' the solicitor said. 'You haven't produced anything that directly links Mr O'Connor to the killings. I understand that none of my client's footwear matches the bloody shoeprints you found at the farm and I'm sure that if you had any incriminating DNA or fingerprints you would have told us by now.'

'Not all the evidence from the crime scene has been processed yet,' James said. 'For instance, the cellar is still being examined, along with the hidden space at the top of the cellar stairs.'

Lee raised a hand. 'Permit me to stop you there, Inspector. This is the first I've heard about the cellar and any hidden space.'

James apologised and told him about the wall with the peephole.

'Breadcrumbs only several days old were found on the floor on the cellar side of the wall,' he said. 'It makes us believe that someone was in there spying on them in the run-up to Christmas. And we have to consider the distinct possibility that it's been going on for weeks, months or even years.'

James turned to O'Connor. 'You told me when we first spoke that you didn't know about the hidden space or the peephole. But if that was a lie, we'll soon know it when we have the results of the fingerprint search. So, now's your chance to come clean. Were you spying on the family and is that how you knew the house was empty before you burgled it?'

O'Connor sucked air between his teeth and shook his head again.

'You won't find my prints in that place because I've never been inside it,' he said. 'And I'll repeat what I said before – I had no idea it was there.'

James was about to ask a follow-up question when the door to the interview room was pushed open and DS Stevens stepped in.

'We need you both outside,' he said, looking from James to Abbott. 'Something important has come up.'

James turned off the tape and offered his apologies to O'Connor and his solicitor.

When they were outside in the corridor, Stevens said, 'We think we know where Neil Savage is. A young man who knows him responded to the televised appeal. He said he was invited to a drink and drugs binge party on Christmas Day at a place called Bash Barn, north-east of Kendal. He couldn't go himself but he's pretty sure that Savage was also invited.'

James punched the air with his fist. 'At last. Did he tell us how to find the place?'

'He did better than that. He told us the home owner is a bloke named Damien Porter and he lives in a house next to the barn. It took us minutes to track down the address. I've already put a rapid response team on standby.'

James felt his heart lurch in his chest. He quickly stepped back into the interview room and explained to Lee and his client that the interview was being suspended until later in the day.

Lee started to object but James ignored him and stepped back out. He signalled to the uniformed officer standing in the corridor to take O'Connor back to the custody suite. Then he turned to Stevens and said, 'How far away is this place?'

'About five miles, guv. It's just this side of Grayrigg.'

'Then let's get going.'

CHAPTER THIRTY-THREE

Two Ford Transit police vans, a patrol car and an armed response vehicle tore along the A685 towards the village of Grayrigg. James, Abbott and Stevens followed in a pool car.

The road ran through miles of undulating countryside with steep, rugged hills in the distance on both sides. There was plenty of snow, but not enough to slow them down.

'Let's just hope we're not wasting our time,' Abbott said from the back seat.

'I'm optimistic. The description the caller gave of the place was similar to the one you got from Amy Bell,' Stevens, who was driving, said. 'There's an old farmhouse, plus a converted barn which is let out to groups who want to hold parties and raves. That must be why the owner calls it Bash Barn.'

It sounded promising, and James was hoping to God that Neil Savage would be there. He was still their main suspect as the evidence against Dean Foreman and Kenneth O'Connor remained inconclusive. There certainly wasn't enough to persuade the Crown Prosecution Service to press ahead with a case against either of them.

Their destination wasn't hard to find. After coming off the A685 just before Grayrigg, they followed a narrow lane for about half a mile and there it was. The place was extremely remote and surrounded by a winter wonderland of fells and moors.

There was no gate, just an opening in the hedge that led to a spacious yard and a stone-built house with an attached garage. Off to the left about fifty yards away stood the two-storey converted barn, which was twice the size of the house. There were three cars parked outside it, plus a motorbike.

The police vehicles pulled up in front of the house. Within seconds the yard was packed with uniforms and a man wearing a startled expression could be seen staring out of one of the ground-floor windows of the house.

The same man then pulled the front door open just as James reached it. He was short and plump, and James guessed he was at least seventy.

'What the fuck is going on?' the man said.

'Are you Mr Damien Porter?' James asked, showing his ID.

'Yes I am. Why are you …'

James cut him off. 'I need to know if your barn is occupied at the moment.'

Porter's eyes darted between James and the armed officers who were fanning out across the yard.

'I don't get it,' he said. 'That lot haven't been any trouble. And there are no other houses for miles, so who the hell has complained?'

'We're not here because of a noise nuisance, Mr Porter. We're looking for a man named Neil Savage, who might well be dangerous. And we've reason to believe that he could be among the group who are here.'

'Well I wouldn't know that. I only get the name of whoever makes the booking and pays me. And I've only seen the rest of them from a distance.'

'So how many are there?'

'Seven. Four young men and three young women. They're due to leave today. As soon as they're gone, I'll go in and clean up the place.'

'And am I right in saying that you allow them to take drugs?'

He shrugged. 'I don't care what they do as long as they enjoy themselves and come back. I had the place converted so I could run it as a bed and breakfast, but I made no money because not enough people came to stay. But when I read about a bloke in the Lake District who lets young'uns use his barn for parties, I started doing the same, and it brings in a nice little income.'

'So, are all seven of them in the barn now?'

'They should be, but they're probably not awake yet. They're usually at it all night and then sleep for most of the day. I'll be turfing them out this afternoon.'

'Well we need to go in to see if our man is there,' James said.

'Do you have a warrant?'

'No, but if I was you, I'd think twice about making things difficult for us, Mr Porter. I'm sure that if we look into what you're doing with this place we'll find all manner of misdemeanours.'

The old man thought about it for all of five seconds and then puffed out his chest.

'Fine. I'll get the key.'

Minutes later they descended on the barn. The armed officers rushed in first and there was a lot of shouting followed by a couple of screams.

James and his colleagues entered when they were told that it was safe for them to do so. They couldn't be sure that any of the partygoers did not have a weapon and there was no point taking chances.

In any event there proved to be nothing to worry about. The seven youngsters posed no threat. They had all been asleep and had got a rude awakening.

One guy had been lying fully clothed on the sofa and next to him on the floor were two empty bottles of beer and an ashtray full of the remains of joints.

Another guy had been dead to the world on an armchair in just a T-shirt and pants when the officers stormed in. The air around him stank of cigarette smoke and something more potent.

The rest of the dopeheads were upstairs. A guy and a girl who looked to be in her teens had been sleeping together naked in one of the bedrooms, their clothes scattered about the floor along with used condoms and a colourful bong.

In another room the officers roused two girls who'd been sharing a bed with an array of sex toys. They looked to be barely out of their teens and one of them appeared to be covered in her own vomit.

The fourth guy was by himself in the third bedroom and when James entered a uniformed officer was talking to him.

He was sitting on the bed with his back resting against the headboard, his chest bare above his tracksuit bottoms and his face was expressionless, eyes blank and vacant. It looked as though he wasn't fully awake.

James's mind flashed on the photo they'd circulated of Neil Savage and he knew right away that this was their man.

'Hello, Mr Savage,' he said. 'I'm Detective Inspector Walker and I'm here because I need to ask you some questions, but before I do you should know that you do not have to say anything, but it may harm your defence if you do not mention when questioned something which you later rely on in court. Anything you do say may be given in evidence.'

Savage shook his head. 'I don't get it. What's this about?'

James cleared his throat. 'My questions relate to Charlotte Bateman and her parents.'

'What about them?' Savage replied groggily.

James stepped closer to the bed. 'I want to know if you killed them.'

Savage's mouth dropped open. 'Is this a joke? If it is, I'm not fucking laughing.'

'It's no joke, Mr Savage,' James said. 'And are you seriously telling me that you didn't know they were dead?'

'Why are you saying that? They aren't dead. How can they be? I was with them on Christmas Eve.'

'I know you were. And that's when they were killed. Charlotte was stabbed to death and her parents were both shot. But then you know that, don't you?'

Savage shook his head again. 'I don't know what you're talking about. You can't be serious.'

'Oh, but I am, Mr Savage. It's been all over the news so I don't understand why you're acting surprised.'

'I'm not acting. There's no phone signal here and the telly is never on. We cut ourselves off so that we can party and do other ...' His words dried up and a shocked expression froze on his face.

200

'You need to get dressed and come with us to the station,' James told him. 'You've got a lot of explaining to do.'

Savage's lips started to tremble and his nostrils flared.

'Oh my God it's true, isn't it?' he spluttered.

James nodded slowly, which prompted the young man to let out a strangled sob. A moment later his face crumbled and his body seemed to collapse in on itself.

CHAPTER THIRTY-FOUR

Neil Savage didn't cry for very long. He pulled himself together as soon as James told him he was going to be taken to Kendal to be formally questioned in connection with the killings at Oaktree Farm.

It made James wonder if his reaction to what he'd been told had been an act. Or perhaps it had been fuelled by the drugs in his system.

His rucksack and clothes contained nothing that linked him to the killings and a quick check of the shoes he was wearing showed that the soles were entirely different to the bloody shoeprints found at the crime scene, though they were a size ten.

He kept insisting that he hadn't known that Charlotte and her parents were dead. But James said nothing further, waiting until they were back at the station to grill him properly. There was too much commotion going on around them and it was a huge distraction.

Savage's pals were all making a noise and protesting about

having their sleep disturbed. It didn't seem to bother them that they were facing charges for possessing drugs. A quick search of the barn revealed a variety of substances and pills including weed, ketamine, cocaine and ecstasy.

James arranged for Savage to be transported back to Kendal in a patrol car and got DS Stevens to go with him. Once there he'd be checked over by a doctor and his prints would be taken along with a DNA swab.

He and DC Abbott then set about talking to each of the others before decisions were taken on what to do with them.

They all claimed that they were above the age of consent and had come to Bash Barn simply to have a blowout Christmas party. And it wasn't the first time for any of them.

They all reiterated what Savage had said about not watching the television or being able to use their phones. They insisted they hadn't heard about the farm killings or about anything else that had gone on in the world since Christmas Day.

One of the girls was Kerry Duncan, a petite nineteen-year-old blonde, and she echoed what the others said about Savage.

'We didn't expect him to come along because we'd been told that he was spending Christmas with Charlotte's parents,' she said. 'But he'd had a row with her and they'd split up. That was all the excuse he needed to come and have a blast with us.'

'And did he seem upset about the break up?' James asked her.

'Not at all. He was really up for enjoying himself. That's what coming here is all about. Letting our hair down and getting wasted. Life is shit for most of us so why shouldn't we?'

James was suddenly beset by a stream of conflicting emotions. The girl's words made him feel sad, angry and frustrated. He wanted to shake some sense into her but it wasn't his place to. He just hoped that she and her mates would eventually find a way off the path to self-destruction.

He took down the names and addresses of all six of them and left them in the hands of the uniforms. He and Abbott then headed back to the pool car. On the way he put in a call to Gillian Weldon, Savage's mother.

Her voice was filled with dread when she answered, evidently fearing that James was going to impart bad news.

'We found your son and he's fine,' he said quickly and he heard her gasp into the phone. 'He was with some pals on a bender, just as you suspected. He's now on his way to the station in Kendal where he'll be formally questioned.'

'Thank you for letting me know,' she said. 'I'll arrange for a lawyer to go there. Will I be able to see him?'

'Not straight away, I'm afraid. But once we've talked to him, I'll see what can be sorted.'

During the return trip to Kendal, James asked Abbott what she made of Neil Savage.

'Well I think he put on a good show for us, guv,' she said. 'But he failed to convince me that he didn't know anything at all about the killings. He's clearly a shady character and I have no doubt he's perfected the art of lying.'

James grinned. 'I actually don't disagree with any of that. I've seen what drugs can do to people when they suddenly have to deal with stressful events such as the end of a relationship. When I was in London, I was involved in at least four investigations where doped-up guys brutally attacked their partners after they were given the elbow. Two of those partners were murdered. One was stabbed and the other beaten to death.'

'There was plenty of weed found at the farm,' Abbott said. 'And we know from the tox report that Charlotte had a fair amount in her system at the time of her death. No doubt Savage did too.'

'Drugs and booze are a heady mix,' James said. 'That's probably why Savage was involved in a collision as soon as he left the farm. He was in no fit state to drive.'

'I'm looking forward to hearing what he's got to say for himself, guv. And I hope he'll shed some light on those mysteries that are doing my head in.'

'I take it you mean the bloody shoeprints and the peephole in the wall.'

'Exactly.'

James nodded. 'I'd also like to find out if he can tell us anything about Kenneth O'Connor and Dean Foreman. And I'm curious to know if he's aware that William Nash was still pining for Charlotte. We need more clarity right now. We've got four suspects but not nearly enough concrete evidence.'

CHAPTER THIRTY-FIVE

There was a real buzz at the station when they arrived.

Finding Neil Savage had boosted morale and encouraged the team to believe that the investigation was gaining momentum.

Reporters had already begun calling the press office to find out if the story of Savage's discovery was true.

'This will relieve the pressure on us from upstairs,' DCI Tanner said. 'I'll come and do the interview with you. Together we can hopefully get a confession out of the bastard so we can close the case.'

'I'm not sure it's going to be as simple as that, sir,' James replied.

Tanner sat back in his office chair and removed his reading glasses. 'Well let's just look at what we've got. The lad was there at the farm on Christmas Eve. He's confirmed that himself. We know that Charlotte confronted him about cheating on her after she received a phone call from her friend. She threw him out and he drove off. He was then in a collision with another vehicle near the farm. But we can't be sure that he didn't go back to the farm after Charlotte sent him the message telling him their relationship was over.'

'That's about the size of it,' James said. 'It's quite possible that he did go back, given that he'd been drinking and probably taking drugs as well so was likely feeling quite emotional and reckless. And let's not forget that he has form for assault and possession.'

'And we still don't know where he stayed that night.'

'I haven't asked him that yet. But we know that he didn't turn up at his flat until Christmas Day. And that's when he ripped up the photos of Charlotte along with the card that she'd given him.'

James then gave Tanner a detailed account of what they'd found at Bash Barn and what Savage's pals had said about him.

After that he checked with DS Stevens to see if Savage had been processed.

'He's in a holding cell, guv,' Stevens said. 'We've got his prints and taken a DNA swab. We've also heard from a firm of solicitors who've been retained by his mother. They're sending someone over now.'

While waiting to crack on with the interview, James updated the team and issued some new instructions.

He also asked DC Abbott to continue questioning Kenneth O'Connor, who was still being held.

'Check with forensics first to see if they've found his prints in the hidden space above the cellar,' he said. 'And let's also find out where his former partner is, the one who dumped him. She might have something useful to tell us.'

James was then given the news that Mary Bateman's sister

had finally been contacted in France and would be coming to the UK as soon as she could. She said she hadn't spoken to or heard from Mary for about six months.

James asked DC Patterson, who was sporting a red, puffy nose, to liaise with the sister and Robert Bateman's brother.

It was 3 p.m. when they were told that Savage's lawyer had arrived. At the same time James's phone rang with a call from Gordon Carver, the journalist at the *Cumbria Gazette*. He chose not to answer it and turned his mobile to silent mode as they headed for the interview room.

CHAPTER THIRTY-SIX

Savage's lawyer was a woman James had encountered before named Harriet Mason. A formidable brief, her age was difficult to peg, but she had short fair hair, sharp facial features and a deep voice.

They put her in the picture before they gathered in the interview room with her client, so she was well aware why Savage had been hauled in. She briefly talked it through with him and told him that his flat had been searched and his car taken away because the police knew it had been involved in an accident.

James and Tanner had furnished her with information that had not been made public, including details about the crime scene and the concealed space at the top of the cellar stairs.

Once they were seated at the table and the recorder was on, James began by asking Savage to confirm that he clearly understood what was going on.

The man looked dreadful. His face was slack and listless, the eyes pouchy and raw.

'I'm here because you suspect me of killing three people,' he said, his voice barely above a whisper. 'But I didn't. I've already told you that.'

Tanner had decided that James should take the lead so he flipped open his notebook to the list of questions he'd jotted down.

'Just for the record I'd like to start by having you tell us how long you and Charlotte were an item,' he said.

Savage shifted nervously on his chair and stroked the stubble on his chin.

'We started going out just under a year ago,' he said. 'Then six months ago she moved in with me.'

'And did you love her?'

'In my own way, I suppose. We weren't about to get married anytime soon, if that's what you mean.'

'But she loved you.'

'She said she did, but I'll never know now if she really meant it.'

'How did you get on with her parents?'

'I didn't have a lot to do with them because they didn't like me much. Charlotte told me that they thought I wasn't good enough for her. That I was a bad influence.'

'Did you ever fall out with them?'

He shook his head. 'It never came to that. Besides, I tried to avoid going to the farm. I didn't like it there and neither did Charlotte. She said it was creepy and her mum reckoned it was haunted. And there was always a bad atmosphere, mainly because Charlotte and her mum didn't get on. Mary was always telling her what a disappointment she was, partly because she chose not to go to uni and because she didn't want to follow in Mary's footsteps and become a nurse.'

'We've been told that Charlotte was a bit of a handful,' James said. 'And that she made life difficult for both her parents. Does that ring true to you?'

'They were too strict with her. They tried to tell her who she should and shouldn't spend time with and she didn't like it.'

James paused for a beat to glance at his notes, then said, 'I'd like to come back to the family dynamics later, but for now, can you tell me why you went to Oaktree Farm on Christmas Eve if you didn't like being there?'

'Charlotte banged on about it for weeks because the place was being sold and it was going to be the family's last Christmas there,' Savage said. 'They were all making a big deal out of it so I agreed to go even though I didn't fancy it.'

'And what time did you arrive?'

'About five. Charlotte finished work at the charity shop and she came back to the flat. We set off soon after.'

'And what happened when you got there?'

He shrugged. 'Nothing much. Mary was by herself because Robert was in Kendal seeing his bank manager. She opened the wine and told us to relax. The plan was to eat when he got home. But that's not how it worked out.'

He was breathing more heavily now and beads of sweat were popping up all over his forehead.

'We'd been there for a couple of hours when one of Charlotte's friends phoned her,' he went on. 'Heather, she's called. She told Charlotte that I'd been shagging someone else.'

'And was it true?' James asked, to see if Savage would lie to him.

He didn't; just pushed out a sigh and nodded. 'It was an

211

ex of mine. Her name's Amy. We met by chance earlier on Christmas Eve when I was in town and ended up back at her flat. Heather happened to see us together and then thought it would be a good idea to grass me up.'

'And how did Charlotte react?' James asked.

'She went fucking crazy. It didn't help that she was fucked. She screamed at me and called me all kinds of names. I tried to tell her it wasn't true, but she picked up an empty wine bottle and threw it at me. I jumped out of the way and it smashed against the breakfast bar.'

His voice was trembling now as he struggled to speak and breathe at the same time.

'And then her dad suddenly arrived back from Kendal,' he continued. 'He came storming into the house wondering what the hell was going on. Charlotte told him I'd cheated on her. Then her mum made things worse by telling him that Charlotte was bladdered. Charlotte screamed at her and called her a bitch. At this point Robert grabbed her arm and pushed her towards the stairs. He told her to go to her room and calm down.'

'And did she?'

'Well she went upstairs, but she didn't calm down.'

'And is that when you left?'

'Not right then, no. I hoped I wouldn't have to because I'd had a lot to drink and, like Charlotte, I'd popped some pills.'

'So, what did you do?'

'I just stood there waiting for Mary and Robert to lay into me. I think Mary was about to, but Robert interrupted her and asked us both if there was anyone in the cellar. It was a strange thing to say and Mary looked at him as though he was mad.'

'Did he explain what he meant by that?' James asked.

'He said that before he came into the house, he saw shoe-prints in the snow leading from the lane to the outside door to the cellar. But there were none coming the other way and the door was closed. He assumed it was because someone was in there but just as he was about to go and check he heard Charlotte scream and rushed indoors.'

James and Tanner shared a look. This was an unexpected revelation and James felt his heart bounce in his chest.

'And were you aware of anyone being in the cellar?' he asked.

Another shake of the head. 'I wasn't and neither was Mary.'

'So, you didn't notice any shoeprints in the snow when you arrived two hours earlier?'

'No, but that was probably because we parked further away from the cellar door.'

'What happened then? Did Robert go and investigate?'

'He was going to, but Charlotte came flying down the stairs again. She was holding her dad's shotgun, which I know he kept on top of the wardrobe in his bedroom. When she got to the bottom, she aimed it at me and told me to fuck off out of the house. She said that if I didn't, she would blow my brains out. Her dad went ballistic and rushed towards her, but she pointed the gun at him and it stopped him dead in his tracks.'

He paused there and pressed the heels of his hands against his eyes.

'What happened next?' James said.

Savage cleared his throat before responding.

'We all pleaded with her to put the gun down but she wouldn't. It was a crazy situation and I was afraid she was fucked enough to pull the trigger, so I decided to leave. My overnight bag was still in the car so all I had to do was get my coat and walk out. And that's what I did.'

'And can you clarify something for me?' James said. 'When you walked out, were they all standing between the kitchen and the lounge area?'

'They were, yes.'

Savage leaned forward across the table and wiped a palm across his sweaty forehead. His lawyer poured him a glass of water from the jug on the table and told him to drink it.

James and Tanner watched him as they digested the information about the shotgun. Assuming he was telling the truth, it was a real turn up for the books. It hadn't occurred to either of them that it was Charlotte who had introduced the weapon. But it did explain why her prints were on the gun along with her father's.

Savage gulped down the whole glass of water and then assured his lawyer that he was okay to continue.

'We need to be clear about what happened after you left the house,' James said.

'I drove away from the farm but my head was spinning and I couldn't focus properly,' he replied. 'It hit me all at once – the shock, the drink, the pills. I gather you know that I ran into the back of another car, but it was nothing serious so I didn't stop because I didn't want to be done for driving whilst drunk.'

'Where did you go?'

'I knew it'd be too risky to drive all the way to Kendal so I went straight to a mate's house in Kirkby Abbey. He lives with his parents but he'd told me they were away for Christmas.'

'We need his name and address,' James said.

'His name is Craig Lawrence and he lives on Tindell Street. Number five.'

'And what happened when you got there?'

'I told him I'd been kicked out by Charlotte and that I didn't want to risk driving home because I'd already been involved in a shunt. He said I could stay. That was when I saw the text message from Charlotte telling me that it was all over between us. I showed it to Craig and he just said that I was better off without her.'

'And you didn't return to the farm that evening?'

'No, I didn't. Not the next morning either. And you can check that with Craig. We both got sloshed and fell asleep in the living room. But not before he told me he was going to Bash Barn on Christmas Day. I'd forgotten it was happening so I said I might as well join them. He called Floyd Tasker who was organising it and that was that.'

'Then Craig Lawrence is one of the guys you were with this morning?'

'Yeah. He's the one with the bald head and tattoo on his face.'

James suddenly remembered talking to the guy in the barn.

'And on Christmas Day you returned to your flat around lunchtime, didn't you?' he said.

'That's right. I needed to get the car home so I left before Craig. After I'd packed a bag, I walked up to the end of the street and he picked me up there.'

So, that was why he hadn't turned up on any CCTV cameras, James thought.

'We found photos of Charlotte in the bin at your flat,' James said. 'They'd been torn up. Was that you?'

'Yeah. I was really pissed with her and if she'd been there,

I would probably have slapped her.' His eyes suddenly filled with a cold fury and he banged his fist down on the table.

'She'd still be alive if she hadn't threatened to shoot me,' he said. 'I would have got her to see sense. It's her own fucking fault that she's dead.'

His lawyer put a hand on his arm to stop him from continuing and he started to sob.

'I think my client needs to have a break,' she said. 'And perhaps a hot drink would be a good idea.'

James turned off the recorder and told her they would come back in fifteen minutes.

CHAPTER THIRTY-SEVEN

James left the interview room and arranged for some coffee and biscuits to be sent in. He then asked about Craig Lawrence and was told that he'd been brought to the station and was waiting to be processed.

'Why don't I go and talk to him while you finish up with Savage?' Tanner said.

James nodded. 'That makes sense, sir. If he corroborates Savage's alibi, we'll have to decide whether we believe him. If we do then it means Savage is in the clear and the killings must have taken place shortly after he left the farm as the broken glass from the bottle was still on the floor and the bodies were positioned roughly where he said the three of them had been standing when he left.'

'And this is where we have to wonder about the shoeprints in the snow that Robert Bateman claimed he saw,' Tanner said. 'Does it mean there was someone in the cellar the whole time? Hiding out in the space behind the wall?'

'Once Savage had walked out, he could have decided for

whatever reason to go into the house and cause carnage,' James said. 'And then left another bunch of bloody shoeprints in his wake, this time in the blood of his victims.'

'Let's pick this up after I've spoken to Craig Lawrence,' Tanner said. 'We can't yet rule out the possibility that the guy is prepared to cover for his mate or even that they went back to the farm together while off their heads on drugs. And we'll need to search Lawrence's house.'

James got DS Stevens to go back into the interview room with him after fifteen minutes.

Savage had calmed by then and was hunched over a mug that was half filled with coffee.

James introduced Stevens and explained that DCI Tanner was interviewing Lawrence.

'I now intend to ask some more questions about the Bateman family,' he said. 'And I'll start with Charlotte. Was what she did on Christmas Eve out of character?'

'She did have a problem controlling her temper but it was over the top, even for her,' Savage said. 'She hit me over the head once with a frying pan during an argument and I needed a couple of stitches. Another time she punched a girl in the face at a party because she saw her flirting with me.'

'Sounds like she had anger management issues,' James said.

Savage nodded. 'That's what her mum used to say to her. Most of the time she was okay, though.'

'This problem she had with her mum. Did it go back years?'

'I think so. She never had a good word to say about her. But then something happened recently that made things even worse.'

'What was it?'

'She told me she'd found out that Mary had been unfaithful to Robert. She wouldn't tell me how she knew and she wouldn't say when it was or who it was with. And she made me promise not to tell anyone. But it really upset her.'

'Did she confront her mum about it?'

'She decided not to for Robert's sake. She didn't want to give him something else to worry about on top of his money problems.'

For James it was another nugget of information to add to the intrigue surrounding the case. Mary Bateman had been having an affair behind her husband's back? And if so, could it have had something to do with what happened on Christmas Eve?

'We know that the farm was running at a loss and they were being forced to sell it,' James said. 'What impact was it having on the family?'

He heaved his shoulders. 'Charlotte told me it was causing a lot of tension between Robert and Mary. She picked up on it whenever she went back there. Just weeks ago, they had a big row because Mary accused him of selling off her jewellery to bring in some money. It was in a box that went missing and included bracelets and necklaces that belonged to her mother and grandmother.'

'And what did Robert say?'

'He denied it, but Charlotte suspected he was lying because he was desperate to raise some cash.'

James chose not to disclose that Robert actually hadn't lied and that it was Kenneth O'Connor who took the box.

'Did you ever meet the man who worked as a farmhand at Oaktree, Kenneth O'Connor?'

'A couple of times. I didn't like him. Charlotte said he was always ogling her when she lived there and it made her uncomfortable.'

'Were her parents aware of that?'

'She told them but they said she'd imagined it.'

James made a note of that.

'Do you know of anyone who might have wanted to hurt any member of the family?' he asked.

'Well O'Connor, for sure,' Savage said. 'You should find out what he was up to on Christmas Eve. But other than him I can't think of anyone else.'

'Can you tell me how much you know about William Nash, who was Charlotte's boyfriend before you?'

'He's a weirdo for one thing and Charlotte did well to get shot of him,' Savage said. 'He was obsessed with her and tried to break us up by telling her I was no good for her. I wanted to go and punch his lights out but she wouldn't let me.'

'Do you think it's possible that he might have had anything to do with the killings?'

This made Savage smile. 'The guy's a pathetic prick. He wouldn't have the guts to do something like that. Even when he was with Charlotte, she treated him like shit. She told me he was like a pet and she only stayed with him until someone better came along. Guess that someone was me.' He smirked.

James found it interesting to note how Savage's demeanour had changed quite dramatically. He was sitting up straight now and had stopped trying to avoid making eye contact. Clearly the shock had worn off and he was back in control of his emotions.

'Finally, I'd like to know if you ever went into the cellar below the house,' James said.

Savage shook his head. 'I never had cause to. But I do

know the previous owners died down there and Charlotte told me that her parents had some kind of memorial installed.'

'And were you aware that there used to be an internal door that led down to it from inside the house, but it was replaced by a plasterboard wall a number of years ago?'

'No, I wasn't. Charlotte never mentioned it.'

James continued to press him on the subject of the cellar but he carried on denying that he had ever ventured down there.

When James called a halt to the interview, he told Savage that he would be held in custody while further enquiries were made and he was warned that he might face drugs charges. Neither he nor his lawyer raised any objections.

When he left the interview room, James thought about what he'd been told. The answers Savage had given seemed convincing enough. But he had his doubts about the claim that he had never been inside the cellar and was not aware that the internal door had been blocked off.

Somehow it just didn't ring true.

CHAPTER THIRTY-EIGHT

TWELVE YEARS AGO

The call from the school comes two days before Charlotte's twelfth birthday.

Mary answers the phone and the head teacher tells her that her daughter is upset and needs to be picked up and taken home.

'I regret to inform you that a fellow pupil has told her what happened to the previous owners of Oaktree Farm,' Mrs Wilkinson says. 'I know it's something you've deliberately tried to keep from her and with good reason. But Charlotte is pretty shocked and she's being teased over it. It's Friday so I'm hoping that it won't be such a hot topic by Monday.'

Mary and Robert had known that Charlotte would find out about the Roths eventually. They've managed to keep it from her for twelve years, but she's now at an age when it's far more difficult to shield her from the ugly realities of life.

It had helped that people living in and around Kirkby Abbey had long ago stopped talking about it. They no longer mark

222

the anniversaries of Simon and Amanda's deaths, and have given up all hope that Megan will ever be found alive.

Mary drives to the school alone because Robert is busy shearing sheep. It's one of the many jobs that makes life on Oaktree Farm so tough and time consuming.

She's used it by now, but still regrets allowing her husband to talk her into taking it over. And it was never just because of what happened to the Roths, as everyone assumed. She's always felt that they should have moved away from the area and started a new, simpler life elsewhere.

But Robert had always wanted to run his own farm and so he seized the opportunity when it was presented to him.

And when it comes to decisions, he's usually the one who makes them.

Charlotte is sitting on a chair in Mrs Wilkinson's office when Mary gets to the school. A ball of sadness explodes in her chest when she sees how troubled her daughter looks.

Her eyes are red and slightly swollen, and she's clutching a moist tissue on her lap.

'Come here, angel,' Mary says and holds her arms open. 'I'm going to take you home.'

Charlotte gets up and rushes into her mother's embrace.

Mrs Wilkinson comes out from behind her desk and says, 'Thank you for coming so quickly, Mrs Bateman. I didn't want you to panic, but the poor girl is quite shaken. I thought it best she didn't return to the classroom.'

Mary feels an uncomfortable tightness in her chest as she steps back and looks down at Charlotte. There are tears in the girl's eyes and her breath is unsteady.

'Is it true, Mum?' she says.

'Is what true, angel?'

'That two people were killed in our house and their baby went missing. Andrea said her dad told her about it and showed her pictures on the Internet. And Lucy said that their ghosts must live in our house because people always haunt the places where they die.'

For a moment Mary doesn't know how to respond. Her mouth goes dry and a deadbolt twists in her stomach.

She and Robert had often talked about this moment, when Charlotte would ask about her home's dark past. But they had never got around to deciding how best to approach it.

'It is true that the couple who used to live at Oaktree Farm died there,' she said carefully. 'But there are no such things as ghosts so you shouldn't listen to what Lucy says. She's just trying to scare you.'

'Then why don't you like me to go into the cellar, Mum? Andrea said that's where the bodies were found.'

'We've told you about the cellar before. It's not safe because of all of your father's tools and chemicals. Plus, there are rats down there.'

Mary is anxious to get away so she turns to Mrs Wilkinson and thanks her for being so considerate.

'My husband and I will have a long talk with Charlotte over the weekend,' she says. 'We'll put her young mind to rest and I'm sure she'll be ready to return to school on Monday.'

'I do hope so,' Mrs Wilkinson says. She then turns to Charlotte and adds, 'Don't forget what I told you, Charlotte. You should never let things that happened in the past bother you now.'

On the drive home Charlotte asks lots of questions and Mary does her best to answer them. But she continues to lie *about Oaktree Farm not being haunted even though she firmly believes that it is.*

Robert has told her time and again that it's all in her imagination and he doesn't take her seriously when she says she can feel a hostile presence. She's had the same response over the years from her doctor. But Mary is convinced that they're both wrong, and that Simon and Amanda have decided to hang around.

Perhaps it's their way of getting revenge for the terrible things that were done to them.

CHAPTER THIRTY-NINE

What Neil Savage told them had thrown the case wide open. James said as much to the team when they got together after DCI Tanner had finished questioning Craig Lawrence, who had confirmed Savage's Christmas Eve alibi.

'Lawrence insists that Savage went to his house in Kirkby Abbey after he left the farm and then stayed there all night,' James said. 'If true it means that he wasn't at Oaktree Farm when the killings took place. We won't just take Lawrence's word for it, of course. We'll search his house, run a background check and speak to neighbours. But it seems likely that we've lost our prime suspect.'

He then ran through all the points raised during the interview, starting with Savage's description of Charlotte's reaction after Heather Redgrave called to tell her that her boyfriend had cheated on her. James then referred to the shoeprints in the snow that Bateman apparently claimed he saw just before entering the house.

'He told Savage and Mary that they led from the lane to

the exterior entrance to the cellar, but there were none coming the other way. It made him believe that someone was down there. But before he had time to investigate, he heard Charlotte scream inside the house, which sent him rushing in. Now what we don't know is whether he went to check the cellar after Savage had left. If he didn't then perhaps whoever was down there came into the house and killed them all.'

At this point DC Abbott mentioned that forensics had found a number of fingerprints in the cellar and the concealed space at the top of the stairs.

'Most belong to Robert Bateman,' she said. 'None so far belong to Neil Savage, Dean Foreman or Kenneth O'Connor. But there are several other prints that haven't yet been processed.'

'What about the bloodstain on the stairs?' James asked.

'That's still being analysed, guv.'

'Then it remains a bloody mystery – excuse the pun. Whose blood is it and how did it get there?'

'We'll keep working on it for now. In the meantime, I managed to track down and speak to O'Connor's ex-partner. She told me that he became impossible to live with after losing his job at the farm,' she said. 'He couldn't find other work and he was angry most of the time. She knows he lied to the Batemans about not stealing their personal belongings because she found a watch in his pocket that didn't belong to him. However, he denied it when she confronted him and then things between them went from bad to worse. A few weeks later she decided she'd had enough and walked out. She now lives in Lancaster and hasn't heard from him in months.'

'I don't want to give up on O'Connor just yet. Let's hold off for now on charging him with assaulting a police officer,' James said. 'I'd rather keep him here than have him appear in court and be shunted off to prison on remand. At least we'll have easy access to him while we carry out further enquiries.'

James then moved on to what Savage had said about the friction between Charlotte and her mother, and the revelation that Mary may have been unfaithful to Robert.

DC Patterson interjected to share that he'd been speaking to the family's GP, Dr Kevin Prior.

'The most interesting thing he had to say was about Mary Bateman, who he described as socially awkward and troubled,' Patterson said. 'She'd been a regular visitor to his surgery for years as she suffered frequent bouts of depression and periods of psychosis during which she had hallucinations, including hearing voices. He reckons she lived in a state of anxiety most of the time but refused to see a psychiatrist, although she was on anti-depressants. And she had regular panic attacks. The doctor says her problems began soon after she and her husband took over the farm following the deaths of the Roths. She convinced herself that their ghosts were haunting the farm.'

The more James learned about the family the more dysfunctional they appeared to have been. The father had a gambling addiction, the daughter was dangerously unruly, and the mother was beset by psychological disorders. How much of it, he wondered, had played a part in their deaths?

Before ending the briefing, James decided that it was only fair to explain to the team why two officers in plain clothes were watching his house from a patrol car parked outside. He was sure that the word had already spread but no one had yet approached him about it.

He kept it brief and told them of the long-running threat posed by London crime boss Andrew Sullivan, but stopped short of saying that he was the reason James and Annie had moved out of the capital.

'He's an old adversary who is currently wanted in connection with a gangland murder,' James said. 'My former colleagues in the Met discovered that he got someone to come to Cumbria to take photographs of my wife and I. We don't know why but we have to assume they weren't to put in an album. My house is therefore under surveillance as a safety measure. But I'm determined not to let it distract me or any of you from our investigation.'

He answered a few questions and addressed a couple of concerns then ended the briefing and went and got himself a coffee. While he drank it, he called Annie to make sure that she was all right. She assured him that she was and asked him if he'd heard any more about Sullivan.

'No, I haven't, but I'm expecting to hear back from Leo soon and when I do, I'll let you know,' he said.

'When will you be home?'

'A couple more hours.'

'I'm just planning on having a sandwich for dinner. What about you? Shall I cook you something?'

'No, love. A sandwich will be fine.'

James spent the next hour typing up his notes and reading through the statements that had been taken. He also phoned Savage's mother to update her and tell her that she wouldn't be able to see her son today. He informed her that Neil was being charged with possessing drugs, but she already knew that because she'd talked to the lawyer.

The longer that James sat at his desk, the less positive he felt about the investigation. Suspects were falling by the wayside while at the same time questions were piling up.

How much of what Neil Savage had told them was the truth? Was someone spying on the family through the peephole in the wall when it all kicked off? Was that someone Kenneth O'Connor, the man who used to work at the farm and made a habit of stealing things?

James hadn't entirely ruled out the murder-suicide theory. But it was challenged by one significant factor – the bloody shoeprints.

There was also the fact that Charlotte was stabbed to death. It seemed inconceivable that either of her parents would have done it, so did she do it to herself or was someone else responsible?

There were so many ways in which the scene might have been played out. But no single scenario was glaringly obvious based on the evidence they had to work with.

James got up from his chair and walked over to the whiteboards, hoping that something he'd missed until now might jump out at him.

He ran his eyes over the photographs of the crime scene. The bodies, the blood, the shotgun, the shoeprints. Then the faces of the initial suspects – Neil Savage, Dean Foreman, Kenneth O'Connor. There was as yet no photo of William Nash, Charlotte's ex-boyfriend, who had been desperate to get back with her. His name was on the board though, along with a note saying that he'd refused to provide fingerprints and a DNA sample. No mention of the fact that DC Abbott had swiped a glass with his prints on from his kitchen, which James knew was now with forensics. He was on the list to be interviewed again tomorrow and would be forced to cooperate if necessary.

Someone had added photos of the Roth family to the collection – Simon, Amanda and baby Megan – and yet again James couldn't help but wonder how weird it was that such brutal killings should have taken place in the same farmhouse twenty-four years apart. It was almost surreal.

Two married couples who knew each other.

One husband who was employed by the other.

Both men appeared to have committed suicide by blasting themselves with shotguns.

Two daughters, one killed and one missing.

James was still mulling all this over when his phone rang. By a strange coincidence the caller was Giles Keegan.

'Hello, Giles,' he said. 'I know I told you I'd pop over for a chat at some point but I just haven't had the time.'

'No problem, my friend,' Keegan said. 'It's just that I've remembered something that I thought you might find interesting. It doesn't relate directly to the current investigation, and for all I know you might already be aware of it. But if not, I think you ought to be.'

'Well, you've got my attention, mate. What is it?'

'Do you remember when we last spoke, I mentioned all the talk about Oaktree Farm being haunted?'

'Of course. You said that Mary Bateman was convinced of it.'

'That's right. But I forgot to tell you that she called in a psychic medium on a couple of occasions to hold séances there. Her name is Lisa Doyle and it's possible she might be able to tell you things you don't know about the family and about Mary's state of mind.'

'That's actually not a bad shout, Giles. How do you know the woman?'

'Well, she's a bit of a celebrity in these parts. I've seen her at various events over the years and then I got in contact with her after my own wife died. I was confused back then and I found it comforting to talk to her even though I'd never believed in all that stuff. We've stayed in touch ever since.'

'And did she help you?'

'In a way she did. And before you ask it wasn't about calling up my wife's spirit. Lisa seemed to really understand what I was going through and that made things easier for me.'

'Interesting. So, is she based in Kirkby Abbey?'

'No. She's over in Ravenstonedale. She's a widow and lives by herself.'

'Then why don't I drop by your place on my way home and you can tell me more about her.'

'Great. And you can update me on the case.'

'I'll see you in about an hour then,' James said.

CHAPTER FORTY

James made the team aware of what Giles Keegan had told him and asked if any of them had heard of the psychic Lisa Doyle. No one had.

'I might pop over to Ravenstonedale tomorrow to find out what she can tell us about the Batemans,' he said.

'Does this mean we're buying into the idea that there's a supernatural aspect to the case?' Abbott asked with a smile.

James rolled his eyes. 'Absolutely not and the last thing we want is for the press to think we are. So, I want you all to keep your lips buttoned on this one.'

He ended the meeting with a quick catch-up on all the other leads they were following.

'Let's hope we can make better progress tomorrow,' he said, as he grabbed his coat and headed for the door.

On the way to Kirkby Abbey, James phoned Leo Freeman at Scotland Yard to find out if they'd managed to collar Stuart

Ross. Freeman didn't answer, but he did ring back five minutes later.

'I'm sorry I missed your call,' he said. 'I was in a team meeting.'

'I'm just wondering what's happened with Stuart Ross,' James said.

'That's what we were discussing. The guy was brought in a few hours ago and we've just finished interviewing him.'

'And what did he have to say for himself?'

'Well, when we raided his flat, we found a revolver and a quantity of Class A drugs. So, we already had him by the balls before we showed him Andrew Sullivan's phone and the photos of you and your wife. He coughed up straight away after we told him that it would play well with the judge if he cooperated.'

'Did he confirm that he took them?'

'He had no choice. They were still on his own phone. He reckoned that Sullivan had decided that it was time to settle some old scores. While in prison he drew up a list of people he wanted to get his own back on. The guy he shot last week was on it along with several other blokes who disappeared over the last couple of months. You're the final name on the list. You're lucky in a way, because he fucked up with the guy before you and he's now on the run.'

'Does Ross know where he is?'

'He says he doesn't, but he probably has an idea. There is some good news, though. We now have CCTV footage of Sullivan close to the scene of the shooting shortly after it happened. It means we've got a solid case against him so once he surfaces, he'll be going back inside for sure, and this time he won't be coming out again.'

* * *

James made it to Giles Keegan's detached house just after six. Bright exterior lights shone down on the snow-covered forecourt and the ageing Mini Cooper that he was often seen driving around the village in.

Keegan had spent his entire career with the Cumbria Constabulary and had worked his way up to detective chief inspector before retiring. He'd lived alone since his wife succumbed to cancer six years ago.

He greeted James with a pat on the back and waved him through to the living room which was warmed by the heat from a large open fire.

He pointed to a bottle of whisky on the sideboard and asked James if he would like a glass.

'I've love one, Giles,' he said. 'It's been a tough day and I've been up since four.'

'Are you heading home after this?'

James nodded. 'Annie's preparing dinner so I can't stay for long. But I'm keen to know more about your psychic friend, Lisa Doyle.'

James sat on the sofa and Keegan started telling him about her as he poured two neat whiskies.

'First I should point out that it's my understanding that Lisa went to the farm on two separate occasions,' he said. 'They were both a number of years ago, and Robert made no secret of it. It came up in a conversation I once had with him and Lisa also mentioned it to me.'

'Do you know what actually happened?'

Keegan shrugged. 'Only that Lisa was asked to contact the spirits that Mary believed were haunting the house.'

'And did she manage to?'

'I don't know. At the time she regarded that kind of

information as confidential. But I can tell you that Robert described it as total nonsense. He only went along with it because Mary kept on.'

'And did Lisa pass on any interesting or disturbing facts about the family?' James asked.

'Not that I recall, but I didn't pick her brain about it because at the time I wasn't particularly interested.'

James thought about it as he took a mouthful of whisky, which burned a track down the back of his throat.

'Do you think it'd be worth me having a word with her?' he said.

Keegan shrugged. 'That depends on what you hope she can tell you.'

'I'm not sure really, but given the awful things that have happened at Oaktree Farm I feel I need to find out as much as I can about the place and the family.'

'Well she's a nice lady and I'm sure she's following the latest story with interest. I can give you her contact details and if you like I can ring her to see if she's up for talking to you.'

'I'd appreciate that, Giles. I could pop along to Ravenstonedale in the morning before going to the office if that's convenient for her.'

'I'll find out and call or text you,' Keegan said. 'Now, I realise you're in a hurry to get going but before you do, I'm desperate to know how things are progressing with the case.'

James grinned. 'You also know that I'm not supposed to tell you.'

'But I'm sure you will if I top up your drink.'

CHAPTER FORTY-ONE

When he got home, James made a point of engaging with the two officers who'd been sent to keep an eye on the house. Their unmarked car was parked in front of a gated entrance to the field across the road.

He was relieved to be told that they hadn't spotted anyone acting suspiciously or matching Andrew Sullivan's description. They also let him know they'd spoken to two of the neighbours who had expressed concern about their presence, telling them that they were there so they could be at DI Walker's beck and call 24/7.

'Can you pass on our thanks to your lovely wife, sir?' one of them said. 'She's made sure we've been comfortable by plying us with coffees and cakes.'

James said he would and went into the house happy to know there would be dessert waiting for him. Baking was one of the things that Annie had been doing to keep herself busy. The result tonight was a plate full of James's favourite Eccles cakes and Chelsea buns. He tucked in after devouring the two cheese and pickle sandwiches she'd prepared for him.

Annie barely touched her food though, saying she had filled herself up by picking at the baked goods throughout the day. But James suspected the truth was that she'd suddenly lost her appetite after he told her that he was on the list of people Andrew Sullivan wanted to settle scores with, and that was why he'd got one of his henchmen to come to Cumbria to take the photos. He hadn't planned on breaking the news until later but she'd insisted on an update.

'That man really is a monster,' she said. 'I just hope that he's banged up or buried long before our baby is born.'

As she spoke, she placed a hand over her stomach and gave it a gentle rub.

Inevitably the conversation moved from Sullivan to the Oaktree Farm investigation. Annie had been watching the news again so she knew that Neil Savage had turned up.

'He insists that he didn't know that we were looking for him or that the Batemans had been killed,' he said. 'He claims they were alive after he left the farm following a row with Charlotte.'

'And do you think he's telling the truth?'

'I fear he might be, and that presents a problem because it means we're rapidly running out of suspects.'

The rest of the evening passed fairly quickly. After dinner they retired to the living room and watched television for an hour or so but as there was nothing on that either of them was interested in they both ended up paying more attention to their mobile phones.

James received a text from Giles Keegan saying that he had

talked to Lisa Doyle and she said she was happy to talk to him tomorrow morning at nine. James then sent a message to DCI Tanner and the team telling them that the early briefing would be at ten. He didn't expect to be with Ms Doyle for long and it would only take him about half an hour to get to Kendal from Ravenstonedale.

Annie went to bed before James did. Although he was limp with fatigue, he wanted some time alone to think about where they were with the case and how to move forward with it.

The first thing he did was to check if Lisa Doyle had an online presence. It surprised him to discover that she had her own website. There was a photo of a woman who looked to be in her forties or fifties, with a round face and dark, wavy hair that kissed her shoulders.

She described herself as a psychic medium and clairvoyant based in Cumbria, adding: *I act as a conduit to help people hear from their loved ones who have parted this world.* Further down the page she went on: *Services include online chats, same day psychic readings, home visits, energy healing and séances.*

James had never believed in such things and he certainly didn't think that there was anything supernatural about the deaths of the Bateman family. But one of the many weird aspects of the case was that Mary Bateman was convinced that Oaktree Farm was haunted, and she'd told people that she heard noises coming from behind the walls.

It was therefore possible, James reasoned, that this in some way had a bearing on what had happened on Christmas Eve. And if so, then it was a line of inquiry that could not be ignored.

CHAPTER FORTY-TWO

Saturday December 30th

The new day was draped in billowy white clouds as James drove north to Ravenstonedale. More snow was in the forecast but it wasn't expected until late afternoon.

As always, the rugged beauty of the landscape lifted his spirits. It never ceased to amaze him how spectacular it all was. The frosted hills and chilled lakes, the windswept fell tops and distinctive stone walls. It was no surprise to James that the stunning scenery had served as inspiration for so many poets and artists.

The unspoilt picturesque village was situated on the watershed between the River Lune and the River Eden and Lisa Doyle lived in one of the many scattered dwellings on the periphery. James was there just before nine o'clock and she was waiting for him.

After James introduced himself, she said, 'It's nice to meet you, Inspector. I hope you had a pleasant journey here.'

She looked much older than she did in the website photo which had probably been taken years ago. He reckoned she was in her late sixties. She had an open, welcoming face and eyes that were sharp despite the shadows beneath them.

James politely declined her offer of a hot drink, and when they were seated at the table in the dining room, she said, 'Giles explained why you wanted to meet me. I just hope I can be of help.'

'And that's why I'm so glad you've allowed me to come and talk to you, Ms Doyle,' James said. 'We're struggling to understand what led to the killings at Oaktree Farm on Christmas Eve.'

She shook her head. 'I still can't believe what's happened. It's totally shocking, especially following on from the terrible events that took place in the village this time last year.'

'Indeed, it is,' James said. 'I'm hoping that the more we learn about the family the closer we'll get to solving it.'

'Well, I know that Giles made you aware of my visits to the farm. The first was actually nine years ago and the second was just four years ago.'

'And it was Mary Bateman who contacted you. Is that right?'

'That's correct. She first approached me when I held one of my psychic evenings at the village hall in Kirkby Abbey.'

'And what did she say?'

'She was of the firm belief that Oaktree Farm was haunted and she wanted me to confirm it and, if possible, to contact the spirits.'

'And that led to the first visit?'

She nodded, and then grinned. 'I feel compelled to ask if you're a sceptic when it comes to the supernatural, Inspector.'

He smiled back. 'I'm afraid I am, but I fully appreciate that a great many people believe in such things and find comfort in that.'

She nodded again. 'And Mary Bateman was one of them. She truly believed that she was sharing her home with the couple who died there over twenty years ago.'

'As a matter of interest, did you yourself know Simon and Amanda Roth?'

'No, I didn't. But I knew *of* them, of course.'

'Okay, so what happened when you went to the farm that first time?'

'I was asked to hold a séance and both Mr and Mrs Bateman joined me at the table. But Mr Bateman was very anxious and made it clear to me that he was only there to keep his wife happy.'

'What impression did you have of the couple?'

'Well, there was obviously a degree of friction between them over the issue. Mr Bateman insisted that the house was not haunted and he hadn't heard any strange noises. But Mary was convinced the spirits were those of Simon and Amanda Roth.'

'Did the séance settle the matter?' James asked.

'Unfortunately, no. Although I sensed a strong spiritual presence, I wasn't able to make contact for some reason. Mary was bitterly disappointed and got very upset, and Robert described the whole thing as a waste of time and money and stormed out of the room.'

'How would you describe Mrs Bateman's state of mind?'

'It was clear to me that she was struggling with life at the time. And I also got the impression there were things she wanted to tell me but couldn't.'

'Did you stay in touch after that?'

'No. As I said, it was another four years before she approached me again and asked me to come back to the farm,'

Ms Doyle said. 'She told me that she was hearing more strange noises and these were coming from the cellar as well as from behind the walls. To be honest, her behaviour made me think that she might be on the verge of a mental breakdown. She said her life was a mess and she was having to keep secrets that were tearing her apart. She even revealed to me that she'd considered committing suicide.'

'So why did she want you to return?'

'She wanted me to try again to make contact with whatever spirits were in the house. But this time it was just the two of us. Robert was away and so was their daughter.'

'And how did that go?'

'It was strange and quite upsetting,' Ms Doyle said. 'You see, I did manage to make contact, but not with Simon and Amanda Roth.'

'Who then?'

'That's the thing. My head filled with the sound of a baby crying. And when I closed my eyes, I saw a tiny, indistinct figure wrapped in a blanket floating in the air in front of me. I know you'll find that hard to believe, but it's true. I've managed to reach a great many spirits since I realised I had the gift but this was by far the most upsetting encounter I've ever had. I was quite shaken by it.'

James felt his stomach roll.

'How did Mary react?' he asked.

'She broke down. I tried to console her, but I couldn't. She lost it completely and asked me to go. And that, Inspector, was the last time I saw her.'

When James left Ms Doyle's house, he told himself that the visit hadn't been a complete waste of time.

He'd learned that Mary Bateman's state of mind had been such that she had even contemplated suicide. And she had also admitted that she was having to keep secrets that were tearing her apart.

Could any of that have been a factor in what led to the Christmas Eve killings? James wondered.

Just as intriguing was Mary's apparent reaction to what the psychic told her about seeing and hearing a crying baby.

Was it just shock that brought on a flood of tears or did it trigger an unpleasant memory?

Ms Doyle insisted that she hadn't made it up and that she truly believed she had made contact with the spirit of an unidentified child.

It left James wondering whether Mary Bateman had jumped to the conclusion that the baby was Megan Roth. If so, then did it mean she knew or believed that Megan had also died in the house twenty-four years ago, along with her parents?

Maybe that was one of the secrets she was keeping.

Before James drove away from Ravenstonedale, he called Tanner to tell him he was on his way to the office, but he didn't get a chance to tell him what he had learned.

'Your timing is perfect, James,' the DCI said. 'I was just about to phone you.'

'Has something come up?'

'You bet it has. We've found out that Dean Foreman lied to us when he said he didn't leave his house on Christmas Eve.'

'Did someone spot him?'

'It's better than that. We've got traffic camera footage that shows him driving south along the M6 from Penrith at just after nine that evening. He then turned off onto the A684 slip road that would have taken him through Sedbergh to Kirkby Abbey and after that Oaktree Farm.'

CHAPTER FORTY-THREE

It was another dramatic development in a case that had more twists and turns than a big dipper and the discovery of the traffic camera footage triggered a swift response. Officers from police headquarters in Penrith were dispatched to pick up Dean Foreman and his wife and take them to Kendal for questioning. They were instructed to tell them that new evidence had come to light in the Bateman case, but not to specify what it was.

James took it upon himself to call Foreman's lawyer, Peter Haig, to let him know what was going on. The sooner he got to the station to represent his clients, the sooner they could get started.

While they waited for Foreman and his wife to arrive at the station, there was time for James and the rest of the team to view the traffic cam footage.

The images were clear and showed his car on the M6 and A684 late on Christmas Eve. What's more, in a magnified freeze frame the man himself could be clearly identified behind the wheel.

'That's much better than we could have hoped for,' Tanner said.

James briefed the team on what would happen next. He and DC Abbott would question Foreman and DS Stevens and DC Patterson would interview the wife.

'After we're done, we'll meet up to consider the state of play,' James said. 'But let's not build our hopes up too much. We thought we had it in the bag with Neil Savage and Kenneth O'Connor. Dean Foreman might still be able to prove that he did not go to Oaktree Farm on Christmas Eve. If so, we'll be right back to square one.'

James was back in the interview room just after midday and it struck him that Dean Foreman did not look so sure of himself this time around. His face was as grey as a headstone and there was a glint of sweat on his brow.

As soon as James switched on the recorder, Foreman's lawyer demanded to know why his client had been hauled in for further questioning so soon after being released from custody.

'You're about to find that out, Mr Haig,' James said. 'I'm going to—'

'And what about my wife?' Foreman cut in. 'Why has she been brought here? She's being treated like a common criminal and it's not right.'

'We have reason to believe that she wasn't altogether truthful with my colleague when he spoke to her on Thursday,' James said.

'Then she needs to have a lawyer with her. I don't want you lot putting words into her mouth.'

'Your wife is being represented by the duty solicitor, Mr

247

Foreman. And Mr Haig here has raised no objection to that. So, can we now carry on?'

Foreman twisted his mouth, searching for words, but Haig touched his arm and cautioned him against saying any more.

James had placed a folder on the table and now he opened it and pulled out several sheets of paper.

'As you're aware the last time you were here in this room, the interview we conducted with you was recorded,' he said. 'This is the transcript and it shows that you stated clearly that you and your wife did not leave your home in Penrith on Christmas Eve and Christmas Day. Do you recall saying that, Mr Foreman?'

He shot his lawyer a look before fixing James with a cold, implacable stare.

'I remember saying it because that's what happened,' he said, his voice glacial. 'And whoever is telling you otherwise is a bloody liar.'

'So, you did not go for a drive in your car on Christmas Eve.'

James spotted it immediately. The flicker of hesitation in his eyes. The swallowing of a lump that appeared to be the size of a golf ball.

'I told you that I didn't,' he said. 'So why are you asking me again?'

James took two photographs from the folder. They were stills from the traffic camera footage. He dropped them on the table between Foreman and his lawyer.

'I asked you again because I thought you might see sense and tell us the truth,' he said. 'Those pictures are proof that you lied to us before and you're lying to us again. These images are from traffic cameras and they show that you drove your car south along the M6 on Christmas Eve around 9 p.m. You took the slip road onto the A684, then headed east towards Oaktree Farm. As far as we know the family were still alive at that time.'

The shock was evident on both their faces. Haig leaned forward for a closer look at the photos while Foreman let out a ragged breath and shook his head.

James then plucked a third photo from the folder and placed it on top of the others.

'And before you tell us that you weren't behind the wheel, this is a close up of the vehicle and either that's you driving it or you have a double.'

Foreman reacted by screwing his eyes shut and squeezing his lips together. His lawyer sat back and heaved a loud sigh.

'We're showing these same photographs to your wife, Mr Foreman,' James said. 'And I'm looking forward to hearing what she has to say about that night and what you did.'

Foreman opened his eyes then and from his expression it looked as though a huge weight had been lifted from his shoulders.

'Look, it's all my fault, Inspector,' he said. 'I talked my wife into lying for me so she really isn't to blame.'

'What have you concealed from us, Mr Foreman?' James asked.

A deep intake of breath. Then Foreman swallowed another lump before the words fell from his mouth.

'It's true that I did go to Oaktree Farm,' he said. 'But I promise you I did not kill anyone.'

CHAPTER FORTY-FOUR

The interview was paused briefly so that Haig could have a private conversation with his client. Foreman's admission had clearly come as a shock to the lawyer.

When they got going again, he said, 'For the record, I've advised my client to request a longer break so that I can consult him further, but he insists we continue so that he can get things off his chest.'

'I'm glad to hear it,' James said. 'Now let's start with why Mr Foreman decided to go to Oaktree Farm on Christmas Eve.'

Foreman scrunched up his face as though in pain and several seconds passed before he began to speak.

'I worked myself up into a fury that day,' he said. 'After I sent the text message to Robert, I realised that he probably wouldn't take it seriously. I imagined him laughing at me while he celebrated with his family. It got to the point where I wanted to make sure that he didn't enjoy Christmas, so I told my wife I was going to the farm to teach him a lesson.

I wanted him to know that I wasn't going to let him get away with not paying back what he owed me. Linda tried to stop me but I ignored her and set off.'

'You must have arrived at Oaktree Farm shortly after nine then,' James said.

Foreman nodded. 'I think so. I didn't pay much attention to the time.'

'What happened when you got there?'

'I pulled up in front of the farmhouse. The lights were on inside and the only other vehicle there was Robert's Land Rover. I went up to the door and rang the bell. No one answered so I banged on it a few times and shouted out that I wouldn't leave until I'd spoken to Robert. When there was still no answer, I tested the door to check if it was locked and found that it wasn't. I pushed it open and walked straight in. And that was when I saw the bodies on the floor and all the blood.'

'Then you're telling us that the Batemans were already dead when you got there,' James said.

'Exactly. It was shocking. I just froze on the spot and stared at the mess.'

'How far did you venture into the room?'

'I didn't. I could see from where I stood just inside the door that they were all dead. There was so much blood and Robert no longer had a face.'

'Then you didn't walk across the room and out of the back door, leaving your bloody shoeprints?'

'No, I did not. What with the threats I'd made, I knew it would look bad once the police started to investigate. But I also knew it would look much worse if you found out I'd been there.'

'Then what did you do?'

'I just walked straight back out of the house and closed the door behind me. I made sure to wipe my prints from the handle before going to my car and driving back to Penrith. I was in such a state that it didn't occur to me that my car would show up on any traffic cameras until much later. And although I deleted the text I sent to Robert from my own phone, I realised that you'd find it on his.'

'Did you tell your wife what you found at the farm?'

'Yes, and she pleaded with me to go to the police, but I told her that if I did, there was a good chance I'd get the blame. I did keep thinking about it over Christmas Day and Boxing Day, but I convinced myself I was doing the right thing. And then when the news broke, I knew I'd left it too late to change my mind anyway and would have to keep schtum.'

'Did you ever go down into the cellar when you were at the farm?' Abbott asked.

He shook his head. 'I told you what happened. After I saw the bodies I turned around and left. I couldn't get away from there quick enough.'

'And does that mean you didn't see anyone else at or near the farm?' she pressed him.

'It was otherwise deserted as far as I could tell,' he answered.

James got Foreman to repeat what he'd said and they pumped him with more questions. He stuck to the same answers, but the longer it went on the more emotional he became.

At one point a giant sob escaped him and he said over and over that he was sorry.

'I know I made a huge fucking mistake by not calling you

as soon as I entered the house,' he said, his voice close to hysterical. 'But I panicked and the longer I left it the more guilty I knew I'd look. Please believe me when I say I didn't kill that family. I don't have it in me to do something like that.'

CHAPTER FORTY-FIVE

The interview with Dean Foreman concluded at 1 p.m. and he was taken to a cell to be held in custody.

Detectives Stevens and Patterson had already finished questioning his wife by then and she was also in a holding cell.

'She got really upset after we showed her the traffic camera photographs,' Stevens told James. 'But she eventually calmed and admitted that she'd lied for her husband. She insists he said that the Batemans were dead when he got to the farm and she believed him. And still does.'

'We'll let them both stew for a while and then have another crack either later today or tomorrow morning,' James said. 'In the meantime, send a team back to the house to make sure we didn't miss anything the first time around. And we should also visit Foreman's warehouse. We might find something there.'

Before briefing the troops, James had a one-to-one with DCI Tanner in his office. He filled him in on the interview with Foreman and told him what the wife had said.

'Sounds to me like we've got him bang to rights,' Tanner responded. 'He had motive for wanting to hurt Robert Bateman, we know he went to the farm around the time of the killings to reinforce the threat he'd already made, and then he went on to lie to us. He's also had plenty of time to cover his tracks by cleaning his car and dumping the shoes he was wearing. We can go ahead and charge him with murder, then wear him down until he fesses up to the rest of it.'

'My advice is to hold fire on any charges, sir,' James said. 'There's still too much we don't know and that worries me.'

Tanner's brow knitted. 'Give me some examples.'

James shrugged. 'The crime scene, for one thing. It might have been staged to make it look as though Robert killed himself after shooting his wife, but that doesn't explain why their daughter was stabbed to death. It's also hard to believe that Dean Foreman arrived at the house, did all that damage, and then left no trace of himself behind. And if he got there around nine and the Batemans were still alive when he arrived then surely the broken glass from the bottle Charlotte threw at Savage earlier would have been cleared up by then. But it wasn't. And then there's the cellar with the bloodstain on the stairs and the peephole in the wall. Plus, the shoeprints in the snow that Robert saw leading to the outside cellar door. It makes me think that there was someone else at the farm on Christmas Eve. Someone other than the Batemans and Neil Savage.'

'Okay, I understand. So, tell me, who else is still in the frame?'

'I haven't entirely ruled out Savage,' James said. 'If he returned to the farm with his pal and they were high on drugs there's a chance they let rip. And Kenneth O'Connor has got no one to verify his movements before he arrived at his brother's place in Windermere around nine. And even then, we can't be sure that his brother isn't covering for him. Finally, there's Charlotte's ex-boyfriend, William Nash. She claimed he was stalking her and we're in the process of getting a warrant to search his home in Kirkby Abbey. Any one of them might have played a part in what happened.'

Tanner shot his cuff and checked the time on his watch. 'I've got a conference call with the Chief Constable in half an hour. I was hoping to tell her that we've solved the case. Instead, I'll just say we've arrested three people and we're in the process of questioning them.'

James then told Tanner about his meeting with Lisa Doyle in Ravenstonedale and how she went to Oaktree Farm twice to stage séances at Mary Bateman's request.

'It was useful in that I learned a couple of things about Mary,' he said. 'She told the psychic that her life was a mess. She also said she was having to keep secrets that were tearing her apart and it could be that one of those secrets relates to the missing baby, Megan Roth.'

James went on to describe what Ms Doyle had said about seeing and hearing a crying baby and how Mary had reacted.

'It could just be that she didn't get over what happened all those years ago and had always believed that Megan was still alive. Maybe what the psychic told her finally convinced her that she was dead and it hit her hard.'

While Tanner prepared for his conference call with the Chief Constable, James gathered the team to bring them up to speed.

He covered the same ground as he had with Tanner and

kept it short. Afterwards he went and got a sandwich from the canteen and took it back to his desk. He was just about to bite into it when his phone rang. It was Gordon Carver, from the *Cumbria Gazette*. This time James decided to take the call.

'Good afternoon, Inspector,' Carver said. 'I've been trying to reach you since yesterday.'

'I know and I'm sorry I wasn't able to respond. It's been manic.'

'I bet it has. It's just that I wanted you to know that your press office is being less than helpful. For instance, I have it on good authority that you've arrested a businessman and his wife in connection with the Bateman killings. But I can't get it confirmed. I'm hoping that since we have an arrangement, you'll tell me if it's true.'

James was happy to confirm it since that snippet of information would be released soon anyway. But he wouldn't be drawn on the details.

'I appreciate it, Inspector. Now what about Neil Savage, the most wanted man in the country until yesterday when you tracked him down to that isolated party destination? According to one of my contacts he's presented you with an alibi which presumably means he's no longer a suspect.'

'I'm afraid your contact is jumping the gun,' James said. 'Mr Savage remains in custody and will face further questions.'

There was a time when James used to get worked up over police officers leaking information to the media but he'd come to accept that there was nothing anyone could do to stop it. And, of course, he himself had slowly become more than happy to provide reporters like Gordon Carver with off-the-record briefings when it suited him.

He told Carver that he'd be the first to know if there were any major developments and then ended the call.

James ate his sandwich while sifting through his emails and the various reports that had landed on his desk. He then started making lists of all the jobs that needed doing and all the questions that needed to be answered. But he didn't get far before he was interrupted by DCI Tanner who came rushing out of his office with an excited look on his face.

'I've just taken a call from the chief forensic officer,' he said. 'You need to get out to Oaktree Farm right away, James. The team over there has found something.'

James felt his heart jump. 'Did he say what it is?'

Tanner nodded. 'The skeletal remains of a baby. Buried beneath the cellar.'

CHAPTER FORTY-SIX

James headed straight out to Oaktree Farm with DC Abbott in tow. He left it to Tanner to arrange for a forensic anthropologist to meet them there.

He or she would have to analyse the remains and try to determine how long they'd been there and if the skeleton was that of a male or female.

James was already convinced that it would turn out to be a girl. And that the mystery of where Megan Roth had been for the past twenty-four years had been solved.

It seemed as though she had died before her parents and had been concealed under the floorboards in the cellar. But the grim discovery threw up a fresh bunch of questions.

How did she die?

Did one of her parents kill her?

Why wasn't her body found when police and forensic officers searched the farm at the time?

James felt a flare of unease when he thought back to what Lisa Doyle had said about the crying baby that she 'contacted' during the second séance at the farm. Did it mean that in future he should be less sceptical about all things paranormal?

'Ever since I heard about the Roth case, I've suspected that their baby was dead,' Abbott said. 'But I didn't expect this. It's so sad and horrible to think that the little mite has been there under the farmhouse all this time. And Robert and Mary Bateman obviously had no idea.'

'Perhaps they did,' James said.

Abbott turned to look at him. 'Are you serious, guv? Surely if that had been the case, they would have made it known.'

James shook his head. 'It's time we stopped making assumptions about this case. It's throwing up too many surprises. And the more we learn about the farm itself the more inclined I am to believe that it was never just a cosy little nook in the middle of the dales.'

'You're not the only one to draw that conclusion, guv. DS Stevens reckons that if someone decided to write a book about the creepiest places in Cumbria Oaktree Farm would have to be included.'

James nodded. 'Well think about it. Just over two decades ago the couple who ran it were found dead in the cellar and their three-week-old baby went missing. Then Mary Bateman started telling people it was haunted and they covered the cellar door with a wall to stop spirits from coming up into the house. Later someone inserted a peephole in that same wall to spy on the family. Then came the killings on Christmas Eve, again in mysterious circumstances. And as if all that wasn't enough to chill the blood, we've now discovered the skeletal remains of the missing baby in the cellar.'

'When you lump it all together like that, I don't feel I'm far wrong in believing that the place is cursed,' Abbott said.

James raised a faint smile. 'I've always scoffed at such beliefs. But now I see how they can take hold when a single property is the location for so many appalling events that can't be fully explained.'

Dark clouds were gathering on the edges of the grey sky as they approached Oaktree Farm.

James hadn't been back since his initial visit but SOCOs had continued to beaver away, carrying out forensic sweeps of the house, the barn, the outbuildings and, of course, the cellar.

The moment the farm came into view those ghastly images from the crime scene pushed their way into his mind once again, causing a knot to tighten in his throat.

It was among the worst he had attended in all of his years on the force. An entire family slaughtered. So much blood and gore. A true Christmas nightmare.

As they drew up in front of the farmhouse, a cold, crawling sensation ran down his spine, and as James climbed out of the car the bitter air shuddered in his throat when he took a breath.

The pair headed straight for the entrance to the cellar where a constable in a high-viz jacket was standing guard.

'The chief forensic officer is waiting in there for you, sir,' he said to James.

They both walked down the short flight of steps to the open door of the cellar and James felt a creeping dread as they stepped inside.

He noticed immediately that it was much less cluttered

than it had been when he was last here. The storage boxes and bags of rotting vegetables had been removed from the metal shelving units along with the stuff that had been piled up on the workbench.

Tony Coppell was deep in discussion with one of his team when he saw James and Abbott.

'It's over here,' he said, pointing at the floor. 'We found it by chance when we moved the display unit. The boards beneath it had been cut at some point in time and slipped back into place without being screwed down. I assumed something could be hidden down there and I was right.'

James felt the blood stiffen in his veins as he stepped forward. He saw that two short sections of floorboards had been removed and a small galvanised steel box had been taken out. It sat a few feet away with the lid open. Inside was the skeleton of a tiny baby. The skull and bones rested on a dark blanket and the sight of them caused a ball of sadness to expand in James's chest.

Abbott shook her head ruefully and said, 'This is another sight that will be with me for the rest of my life.'

She turned away then and gnawed at her lower lip.

'How long would you say this has been here?' James asked.

'The forensic anthropologist will be here soon and he'll be able to give you an accurate assessment, but my guess is at least a couple of decades,' Coppell replied. 'It fits the timeline of when Megan Roth went missing.'

'But can you be sure that we're looking at a female?' James said.

Coppell shook his head. 'This child lived for only a few weeks and sexual dimorphism is slight in pre-adolescent children as the bones are not sufficiently developed for gender differences to emerge. So, determining the sex will be difficult in this case, although we'll probably get something from a DNA extraction.'

'But I think it's fairly safe to assume that this was baby Megan,' James said. 'Are there any indications as to how she might have died?'

'There's nothing obvious from what I can see. The skull's intact and none of the bones are broken.'

'And was the skeleton wrapped in the blanket?'

Coppell nodded. 'I think she was laid to rest with great care and that again would suggest that it was her parents who put her here.'

While they'd been speaking Abbott had moved across the cellar to where the squat display unit was now positioned. The memorial stone with the inscription *You will never be forgotten* was still resting on top of it.

'It raises the question as to whether the Batemans knew that the baby was buried under the floorboards when they placed the unit and the memorial stone on top of it.'

'But I don't see how they could have,' James said. 'They weren't here when Mary's parents were killed. According to Giles Keegan they were at Robert's mother's house in Sunderland. It was Giles who broke the news to them by phone.'

'There's another issue that needs to be considered,' Coppell said. 'The bodies of Simon and Amanda Roth were found here in the cellar. Therefore, the forensic team would have searched it thoroughly, and I'm sure they would have noticed that two of the floorboards had been tampered with and could be lifted out. They would have done what we did, which was to check to see what was underneath.'

'Then what does that tell you, Tony?' James asked.

'That's a no-brainer, Inspector. It means you have to consider the possibility that the baby's body was placed here after the farm had been searched and the investigation had been wound down.'

CHAPTER FORTY-SEVEN

THREE YEARS AGO

Charlotte has been looking forward to today. For the first time in ages her parents have left her alone in charge of the farm.

It's only for the afternoon and all the chores have been carried out so there's nothing for her to do – except spend some quality time with her new boyfriend William.

He's due to arrive any minute now that her parents have set off for Penrith. They're attending the funeral of someone her mum used to work with during her time as a nurse.

It means Charlotte can chill out for a bit after another rough week. She's between jobs so they've kept her busy on the farm and it's not something she enjoys.

In fact, she hates working outside in the cold with all the mud and the bucket loads of shit from the cows and sheep. It's all so disgusting and smelly. She was never cut out to be a farmer.

She knows that her parents are disappointed in her, especially her mum. That's why there are so many arguments. They reckon she's lazy, ungrateful and disrespectful. But the truth is she feels trapped in a life that makes her miserable.

Now that she's no longer a teenager she finds it easier to stand up for herself. She doesn't take as much crap as she used to and she's more careful when it comes to staying out of trouble.

It's been two years since she was given a police caution for stealing four packs of cigarettes from a store in Kendal. And a year since her dad found the joints in her bedroom and went apeshit.

She can't help that she has a rebellious streak and finds living in the wilds of Cumbria so fucking boring. She's determined to move away as soon as she can afford to. Manchester or London. Somewhere she can be herself.

Far too often she's consumed by a tidal wave of self-pity. It's why she got into drugs and drinks more than is probably good for her.

And why she's forever in the doghouse and being told she doesn't act her age.

It doesn't help that she has always felt uncomfortable in the only home she's ever known. Oaktree Farm is such a cold and creepy place. Even before she was told about the bodies in the cellar, she felt that there was something not right about it.

She doesn't blame her mad mother for believing it to be haunted. She's heard plenty of strange noises herself, especially at night. Her dad insists that it's to be expected in an old farm building that is constantly being battered by the elements. And she knows he's right. But that doesn't stop her imagination from running riot at times.

She still can't forget the nightmare she had after she read

about Simon and Amanda Roth and what happened to them and their baby nearly twenty years ago.

It began with her walking into the cellar to fetch a tin of paint for her father. But then she heard a baby crying. It was coming from beyond the door at the top of the steps that leads to nowhere.

She went and pulled the door open and there was tiny Megan, lying on the floor, naked and covered in blood. And she was still crying even though it was clear that she was already dead.

That was the first and only time that Charlotte has ever woken up screaming in the middle of the night.

And she hopes it will never happen again.

She's only ever told one person about the baby nightmare, and that's William Nash, or Mr Fixit as she likes to call him. They weren't an item then, but they were friends and tended to confide in each other.

It was inevitable that he would eventually summon up the courage to ask her out. For years he had made it obvious that he was besotted with her. But he was always too shy and scared that she'd turn him down.

However, a month ago he invited her to lunch in one of the pubs in Kirkby Abbey, and while there he'd made it known how he felt. She suddenly saw him in a new light. He'd matured and came across as a lot less geeky. So, when he went to kiss her afterwards, she let him.

They'd had sex four times since then. Twice at his house when his parents were away. Once in his van. And once in a field. Today will be his first visit to Oaktree Farm, even though their families have known each other for some time.

Charlotte has always been reluctant to entertain her friends here, partly because her mum invariably goes out of her way to make them feel unwelcome. She doesn't like visitors even though she won't admit it. It's as if she's ashamed of the place and doesn't want others to know how eerie and unpleasant it is.

William rolls up in his van at just after one o'clock. He's taken over the Mr Fixit business from his father who has recently retired and plans to move to Spain soon with his wife. It means William's now his own boss and can skive off whenever he wants to.

Charlotte is very fond of William, but she can't imagine spending the rest of her life with him. He's not a very exciting or interesting person, and he's a bit straightlaced. He's already urging her to give up the drugs and stay off the drink. But he'll do for the time being. At least he makes her laugh and doesn't give her too much grief. Plus, she's already finding it pretty easy to control him.

She's been feeling horny all morning so she insists that they have sex before she gives him a grand tour of the farm. She's also worried that her parents might find a reason to return earlier than expected and catch them at it.

They do it on her bed and after they're dressed, she shows him around the house and makes a point of referring to the wall beneath the stairs. She explains that it replaced the door to the cellar and tells him why it was installed.

'My mum is a barmy old cow. She's worried that ghosts will come up into the house. And it's never occurred to her that if ghosts actually exist, they're bound to be able to pass through walls.'

'Actually, I'm sure it was my dad who installed the wall,'

William says. 'I've seen the receipt for the work in the files and I seem to remember he mentioned it to me once.'

'Well, what do you know?' Charlotte replies, surprised. 'Come on, let me show you what it's like down there.'

As soon as they step into the cellar, she can see that he's slightly in awe of it even though it's grim and untidy.

'This is where the couple were killed then,' he says, his eyes stretching.

Charlotte points to the memorial stone on the small display unit.

'That ugly thing is a shrine to them,' she says. 'It makes my stomach turn every time I see it, which is why I don't often come down here. I've told Mum and Dad that we should get rid of it because it feels like we're living above a cemetery, but they won't listen.'

'It is a bit strange and creepy,' William says.

Charlotte pulls a face. 'It's just one of the strange things about this farm. Would you believe I caught my mum down here talking to herself the other day? Proper weird, because she hates the place more than I do. And Dad only stores things that he rarely uses.'

William moves closer to the memorial stone and reads the inscription.

'I wonder what really happened to the Roths and their baby,' he says. 'My dad has always said that he never believed the husband killed the wife and then himself.'

Charlotte has long thought that her own parents know more about what happened back then than they've ever let on. She's convinced it's one of the many secrets they keep from her.

She often hears them whispering when they don't think she

can hear them. A few times she heard the names Simon and Amanda mentioned, along with Megan.

As always, she regrets coming down here and can't get out quick enough.

'Let's go back upstairs,' she says. 'I think we've got time for another session before my parents get back.'

CHAPTER FORTY-EIGHT

James could not take his eyes off the skeletal remains in the steel box.

He was confident that DNA analysis would soon identify them as belonging to three-week-old Megan Roth. But he was not at all sure how or when her body had been buried beneath the floorboards.

The fact that it hadn't been discovered during a search by police twenty-four years ago had led the chief forensic officer to suggest that it might have been placed there afterwards. But it was always possible that the forensic team hadn't done a thorough job back then. Perhaps it wasn't obvious that the floorboards had been tampered with or the spot was covered by a piece of heavy furniture that didn't get moved.

It raised a whole series of new questions that hummed like high-voltage electricity through James's head.

'I have to keep reminding myself that we're trying to find

out what happened here on Christmas Eve,' he said to Abbott. 'Not what took place here over twenty years ago.'

'But it does support the theory that they might somehow be connected,' she responded.

James nodded. 'And that's one of the aspects of this case that makes it so challenging. I won't be at all surprised if another credible suspect suddenly turns up out of the blue.'

They were still discussing it when Dominic Martin, the forensic anthropologist, arrived. He was a bulky man with a fleshy, nondescript face and a nasal edge to his voice.

After a brief look at the bones in the steel box, he said, 'I agree with Tony that they belonged to a very small baby and have been here for twenty years or more. The remains are well preserved but I very much doubt that I'll be able to determine the sex from them. However, we should be able to extract some DNA samples. These can then be compared with the profiles we have on the database of the couple you suspect were her parents.'

James used his phone to take a couple of photos of the skeleton, then asked Coppell if his team had found much else during their search of the farm.

'Nothing that you'll find particularly useful,' he replied. 'The bloodstain on the stairs over there still hasn't led us anywhere, and the prints found in the cubbyhole at the top don't match any on the system, or those of Kenneth O'Connor, Neil Savage or Dean Foreman.'

James asked Coppell and Martin to fast-track the DNA tests and he and Abbott then went back outside.

'There's no point us hanging around here,' he said. 'Let's get back to the station and pull our thoughts together. I'll put in a call to Giles Keegan on the way and tell him what we've found.'

The former detective was shocked to hear what had been unearthed in the cellar at Oaktree Farm.

'That's really upsetting,' he said. 'I've always clung onto the faint hope that she didn't die and has been living a full life somewhere, oblivious to what happened to her parents.'

'This is probably a stupid question, Giles, but was a full forensic search of the cellar carried out at the time?' James asked.

'I'm sure it must have been. I wasn't there while the sweep took place, but I'm convinced that if it had looked as though the floorboards had been moved, they would have been taken up.'

'Then it's another mystery,' James said.

CHAPTER FORTY-NINE

They arrived back in Kendal just as it began to snow. James could feel his pulse beating high up in his throat as he walked into the office, and at the same time dark thoughts were swimming through his head.

The case was beginning to grind him down, especially the way it kept hurling him back through the years. It was making him believe that the answers to some of the outstanding questions lay in the past. But if he was wrong, he ran the risk of wasting valuable time by searching for them.

He gave Annie a quick call before deciding what needed to be done, and told her he wouldn't be home until much later.

'Janet has popped over to see me,' she said. 'We're having an afternoon tea together and she's helping me decide what we should have in the baby's room.'

Janet Dyer was Annie's closest friend in the village. She was a single mum to twin boys and worked as a carer.

'I made a casserole earlier,' Annie went on. 'All you have to do is heat it up when you get in.'

'Are the officers still outside keeping an eye on the place?' he asked.

'Yes, they are. I forgot to tell them that Janet was visiting and one of them gave her quite a scare when he approached her on the doorstep.'

'Andrew Sullivan won't be an issue soon and they'll be pulled off.'

'I do hope so,' Annie said. 'I really don't like living like this.'

After disconnecting the call, James went to Tanner's office and showed him the photos he'd taken on his phone of the baby's skeletal remains.

'Giles Keegan believes the cellar was subjected to a rigorous forensic sweep after the bodies of Mr and Mrs Roth were found,' he said. 'But we can't be certain that it was thorough enough and so have to entertain the possibility that they simply failed to find the baby's body beneath the floorboards.'

Tanner gave a thoughtful nod. 'On the other hand, it's also possible the baby was killed at a later date and then hidden there.'

James shrugged. 'That's what Tony thinks, but then where would she have been when her parents died and why the hell didn't her killer bury her in a place where she'd be unlikely ever to be found?'

The office was packed to the rafters with detectives and support staff for the end-of-day debrief.

There was a lot to get through and James kicked off with the latest shocking discovery at Oaktree Farm.

No one quite knew what to make of it, or how it impacted on the case they were working on, but it fed into the general disquiet that was growing within the team. Like last year's serial killer case, disbelief and confusion added to the pressure on everyone.

James summed up where they were with the investigation and outlined a plan of action for the following day.

'We have four suspects in custody,' he said. 'Dean and Linda Foreman, Neil Savage and Kenneth O'Connor. The Foremans will be held overnight and I intend to interview them again tomorrow. We therefore need to make them aware of that along with their lawyer. Now what's the situation with the other two?'

'Neil Savage hasn't yet been charged with any drug offences because there was some confusion over exactly what he had in his possession when he was collared at Bash Barn with his mates. There was so much lying around that uniform still haven't worked out who owns what,' DS Stevens said. 'We're leaving them to sort it out while we hold onto him.'

'And where are we with the alibi his pal Craig Lawrence gave him?'

'They're both sticking to it. We've searched Lawrence's house and found nothing, and I spoke to his father an hour ago. He and his wife are on a Christmas break in Jersey. They knew nothing about the bender at the barn but did know that their son was into drugs. They say he's never been in trouble with the police before and I can confirm he's not on the database. They're returning home to Kirkby Abbey tomorrow.'

'And what about Kenneth O'Connor?'

'No change there, guv,' Stevens said. 'We're holding onto him and he's got the assault charge hanging over his head.'

'DC Patterson, where are we at with the next of kin?' James asked.

'Robert Bateman's brother is travelling over from Ireland tomorrow. I've arranged for him to come here first thing so that we can talk to him about his brother and explain what's going on with the investigation,' Patterson said.

'I'd like to be in on that conversation so let me know when he arrives,' James told him.

'Any update on Charlotte's former boyfriend, William Nash?' he asked the room at large.

'We're still waiting to be granted a warrant to search his home in Kirkby Abbey,' one of the team supplied. 'Intel and background checks on the man have failed to come up with anything that suggests he's anything other than an upstanding local businessman and member of the community though.'

'Thanks. Did you want to add anything, sir?'

'Yes, another press conference had been scheduled for tomorrow at eleven. You don't need me to tell you that the level of interest in this story continues to rise,' DCI Tanner said. 'And as per usual it's proving difficult to manage the release of information. I've just heard that the press has already been tipped off about the discovery of the skeleton and I'm having to pull together a statement. I don't know if any member of this team put it out there but I want to remind everyone that only myself and DI Walker are authorised to decide what does and doesn't get released.'

As soon as James wound up the meeting, he received a call on his phone from Gordon Carver at the *Cumbria Gazette*.

'Word is you've found the remains of the Roth baby, Inspector,' Carver said. 'Is it true?'

'We've found a small skeleton, but we can't be sure it

belonged to Megan. Forensic tests will need to be carried out in the lab.'

'But I understand the discovery was made in the cellar at Oaktree Farm, right where her parents were found dead. So surely it must be her.'

'You'll be told more at the press conference tomorrow,' James said.

'Can I quote you?'

'I don't see why not.'

Before leaving the office James wrote up his report. He always made a point of keeping on top of the paperwork because he didn't like it to build up. Once it was complete, he emailed it to the rest of the team, CC-ing DCI Tanner.

On the way home he reflected on another day that had been full of surprises and he wondered what tomorrow would bring.

Janet Dyer had gone by the time he reached home and he found Annie watching television. He poured himself a glass of wine while she heated up some of the casserole she'd made.

Earlier she'd spotted a newsflash on her phone about the skeleton in the cellar and naturally had questions about it, but it didn't dominate the conversation during the rest of the evening, and James got the impression that she wanted to lighten the mood.

She was clearly finding the whole thing very upsetting, and that was on top of learning that Andrew Sullivan had been stalking them.

So much for the quiet life in Cumbria, he thought as he tucked into the casserole and listened to his wife talk about what she wanted to do with their baby's room.

He couldn't help wondering if deep down she regretted leaving London. After all, they'd been happy there before Sullivan was released from prison and made threats against them.

They had moved north in order to secure a safer and better life, in a place where crimes were few and far between and where they expected all of their neighbours to be honest and friendly.

But so far Kirkby Abbey had failed to live up to their expectations, and living here was proving to be more stressful than it had ever been in the big, bad city.

CHAPTER FIFTY

Sunday December 31st

For James it was another night blighted by dreams and troubled thoughts.

At one point a noise woke him and he got it into his head that Andrew Sullivan had broken into the house. He even climbed out of bed and went downstairs to investigate.

Needless to say, his nemesis hadn't made an appearance and the noise was caused by the wind crashing against the back door. It was blowing a gale outside and at least a couple of inches of snow had fallen, settling on the lawn like a thick grey carpet.

He checked out the front too and was relieved to see that the surveillance team hadn't deserted their post. But his relief was tempered by the fact that he knew that Tanner couldn't post them there indefinitely. And even though they were armed, they really didn't offer that much protection. A ruthless villain like Sullivan could surprise them by wrenching open a door and incapacitating both officers with a stun gun or taser. He had always been one of the most violent and devious of

London's crime bosses, and it was rumoured that he had killed more than a dozen people and ordered hits on many more.

It wasn't helpful having him as a distraction at this time, but it was impossible for James to banish him from his thoughts. The threat he posed was real. It was especially disturbing to think that he had sent someone to Cumbria to take photographs of them.

The first thing James did when he got up at five was to text Leo Freeman, asking if the Met had made progress in the hunt for Sullivan.

Leo replied an hour later, just as James was about to leave the house.

Nothing to report, mate. We're following up a couple of leads and several unverified sightings. I'll let you know as soon as there's news.

Annie stayed in bed while James showered and dressed, but she was awake so he made her a cup of tea.

'Happy New Year's Eve, my love,' he said. 'I'm sorry I had to disturb you, but I need to go in early.'

She smiled up at him. 'Not a problem. Hopefully I'll go back to sleep. I feel really tired.'

He gave her a kiss and said he'd call her later.

Before leaving, he made up a flask of coffee and took it across the road to the two officers who were watching the house. They both looked tired and stressed out and told him they were due to be relieved in about an hour.

The drive to Kendal wasn't as bad as James had feared it would be. It had stopped snowing and the gritters had already been out clearing some of the roads.

As he drove, he listened to the local news on the radio and it came as no surprise that the lead story was the discovery of the baby's skeleton.

… Police believe it to be that of three-week-old Megan Roth, who disappeared when her parents were found dead at Oaktree Farm in 1997. The remains were discovered by officers investigating the Christmas Eve killings of Robert and Mary Bateman and their daughter Charlotte. Police still don't know if anyone outside the family was involved, however, a number of people have been questioned and we understand that four individuals are currently being held in police custody.

James was sure the report would encourage most listeners to believe that the police were close to solving the crime. But he knew that not to be the case as they didn't yet have enough evidence to charge any of the suspects. And they still didn't know exactly what had occurred on Christmas Eve at Oaktree Farm.

Or why an entire family was wiped out.

James just hoped that today he and his colleagues would hit upon the breakthrough that they so desperately needed.

CHAPTER FIFTY-ONE

James had been at the station for three hours and still there was no breakthrough.

He'd held a team briefing and re-interviewed the four suspects who had been in custody overnight. He went in hard in the hope that he could trip them up or get them to change their stories. But his approach had proven unsuccessful.

Dean Foreman continued to insist that when he arrived at the farm on Christmas Eve the Batemans were already dead. And his wife repeated exactly what she'd said during the last interview.

Their home had been searched again and the staff at Foreman's warehouse had been spoken to, but nothing new or incriminating had surfaced.

The same went for Kenneth O'Connor. They'd thought they had him with the discovery of Mary Bateman's jewellery box in his home but according to Neil Savage it had been stolen from the farmhouse weeks ago. And his were not the prints found in the space behind the wall in the cellar.

As for Savage, it was unlikely they would get the CPS to press charges as Craig Lawrence had provided him with an alibi.

It didn't help that all three male suspects had the same shoe size.

Decisions would now have to be taken on what to do with them. Was it worth charging Savage with drug offences? Now that whatever pills or substances he'd taken over several days had finally been flushed through his system, he seemed genuinely grief-stricken over what had happened to his girlfriend. A court would have to take his previous convictions into account and he'd almost certainly receive a custodial sentence but James wasn't convinced the guy deserved it at this point in time, despite the fact that he clearly wasn't a very nice person.

There was also a decision to be made over whether to drop the assault charge against Kenneth O'Connor. Even his victim, DC Patterson, was saying he wasn't bothered either way. And James was only too aware that O'Connor's lawyer would argue strongly that the attack wasn't premeditated and that his client had acted instinctively when in a state of panic.

These were all sensitive issues that James decided to give more thought to later. Right now his mind was on the press conference that was about to start.

He watched it on the live feed from Penrith with the rest of the team and was glad that he hadn't been asked to front it.

DCI Tanner began by giving an overview of the investigation, confirming that Neil Savage was among the four suspects in custody and that he was arrested following the appeal for information on his whereabouts.

'I don't intend to disclose the identities of the other individuals at this stage,' he said.

He then touched on the subject of the skeletal remains found in the cellar at the farm.

'We strongly believe it to be the skeleton of Megan Roth whose parents died there in 1997. As you're all aware she was only three weeks old at the time and has been missing ever since. However, we won't know for sure if it is her until a thorough forensic examination has been carried out.'

After Tanner's summary came the questions, and the first was from Gordon Carver of the *Cumbria Gazette*.

'Have you managed to establish how the baby died?' he asked. 'Is there evidence to suggest that she was murdered?'

'It's too early to say at this time,' Tanner replied. 'And it's possible, of course, that we will never know, given how long ago it happened.'

The questions that followed veered between the past and the present.

'How likely is it that Robert Bateman shot himself after killing his wife and daughter?'

'Do you believe that baby Megan was murdered by her parents?'

'You made it known that Neil Savage was with the family on Christmas Eve. So, has he told you what happened?'

'Why has it taken so many years for the baby's remains to be found?'

'Is it true that the Batemans were having severe financial problems, which is why the farm was up for sale?'

'A rumour is now circulating that Mary Bateman was having an affair. Is that true?'

The presser lasted for fifty minutes and James felt that

Tanner gave a solid performance but it was clear that the journos had been hoping to hear that much more progress had been made with the investigation.

James knew it would heap further pressure on the team and no doubt the Chief Constable would be wanting to know why none of those arrested had so far been charged.

He spent the next half an hour in one of the soft interview suites with DC Patterson and Robert Bateman's brother Todd who had flown in from Ireland.

The man had a long face and deep-set eyes, and it looked as though he hadn't slept in days. He was four years older than Robert and had moved to Dublin seven years ago after marrying a woman he met on a business trip there.

'Farming was never for me,' he told them. 'I much prefer living and working in the city. But Robert loved it and when he first took over Oaktree Farm, he made a real go of it. It became a struggle in recent years though, same as it did for a lot of farmers in this part of the world.'

'Did you see much of him?' James asked.

Todd shook his head. 'We last got together about nine months ago when I came for a visit. He told me then that he was finding it really hard to make ends meet. I was the one who urged him to sell up because I could see it was taking a toll on the family. Mary was stressed to bits and Charlotte was going off the rails. But I don't believe for a second that it got so bad that my brother decided to kill his wife and daughter and then himself. Robert loved them and when I spoke to him by phone a few weeks ago he was relieved that he and Mary were about to embark on a new life. He'd finally accepted that the farm was being sold and they were looking forward to settling down some-where else.'

'We've been told by Neil Savage that Charlotte claimed she'd found out that her mother had been unfaithful to her dad,' James said. 'Do you know if there's any truth in that?'

'I really don't, but I would have thought it was extremely unlikely. She hardly ever left the farm and when she did it was usually with Robert.'

Todd said he had spoken to Mary's sister and neither of them expected to gain financially from the sale of the farm as they were both aware that Robert had accumulated substan-tial debts.

'I didn't know about the gambling, though,' Todd said. 'My brother kept that to himself. And I have no idea if he had any enemies. The suspects you've mentioned are just names to me and I never met Simon and Amanda Roth. Before I moved to Ireland I was based in Leeds and so we led separate lives.'

James ended the informal interview by asking Todd what he thought could have led to what happened on Christmas Eve.

The man's eyes flared with emotion. 'There can only be one explanation. Someone went into the house and killed them. It was not a murder-suicide, as some people are suggesting. Of that I'm certain.'

James headed back to the office feeling disappointed. Todd Bateman had merely confirmed much of what they already knew about his brother. He hadn't provided any information that would move the investigation forward.

When James reached his desk, he started making a list of the decisions that needed to be made as soon as possible. But after a minute or so DC Abbott rushed up to him.

'I think we might have got that breakthrough we've been waiting for, guv,' she said. 'The lab just called to say they've identified the fingerprints found in the concealed space above the cellar. The ones that didn't belong to Robert Bateman.'

'Are they a match for any of our suspects?' James asked her.

She nodded excitedly. 'They match those on the glass I swiped from William Nash's kitchen.'

James jumped to his feet. 'The ex-boyfriend! The guy Charlotte thought was stalking her.'

'The very same, guv. And by sheer coincidence the warrant giving the go-ahead to search his house has just been signed off.'

CHAPTER FIFTY-TWO

DC Abbott was back in the driving seat when they set out for Kirkby Abbey in the pool car.

James sat next to her with his mobile phone clamped to his ear as he updated DCI Tanner on the latest development.

'We're on our way to William Nash's house now,' he said. 'A patrol car is also heading there.'

'So, his prints have been found in the hidden space above the cellar,' Tanner said.

'That's right. But he told us he'd never set foot inside it, which means he lied. It's a sure bet he was the one spying on the family through the peephole. Or rather, he was keeping an eye on his ex-girlfriend.'

'It sounds promising, James. I'll soon be on my way back to Kendal so keep me in the loop.'

James cast his mind back to the chat they'd had with Nash. He'd said that Charlotte's death had broken his heart because he'd never wanted their relationship to end. He'd also denied stalking her, but admitted that he still had strong feelings for her.

James also recalled how Neil Savage had described Nash as a 'pathetic prick' and a 'weirdo', and that he'd claimed that Charlotte treated Nash like a pet when they were together.

'I wonder how much time he spent behind that wall,' Abbott said. 'And whether there was ever anyone with him.'

'I don't think it's a group thing,' James said, and then went on to tell her about the case of Daniel LaPlante.

'I'm sure I read about that,' she said.

'The perv was living inside the walls of that house for months while spying on the girl he fancied and her sister. Perhaps Nash got the idea from him.'

'What are you thinking, guv, that Nash was in the cellar space and suddenly decided to go into the house and carry out the killings after Neil Savage left?'

'That's one possible scenario. Another is that he was hiding there and witnessed what happened through the peephole.'

'But wouldn't he have called us?'

'Not necessarily. By raising the alarm, he'd have put himself in the frame, and he wouldn't have wanted that.'

'Which is what Dean Foreman claims prevented him from calling the police.'

'Another possible scenario is that Foreman is lying and did go into the house where he got into a fierce argument with Robert Bateman. It then turned nasty and he went berserk and stabbed Charlotte and shot her parents. If Nash witnessed everything, he could have been too shocked and scared to do anything about it, and as he likely had no idea who Foreman was he decided to go home and keep quiet in the hope that he wouldn't be drawn into it.'

Abbott let her breath escape in a slow whistle. 'Whatever the truth, guv, I'm pretty sure that people will be talking about this case in years to come. And eventually someone might even turn it into a book.'

They arrived at Nash's place at the same time as the patrol car, and followed it down the short driveway into the yard.

'His van isn't here,' Abbott observed. 'Probably means he's out.'

'That won't stop us going in now that we've got a warrant,' James said.

The two cars came to a stop in front of Nash's cottage. There was no sign of the man and no response when James knocked on the door.

'We need to get forensics here,' he said.

'Should we call Nash?' Abbott replied. 'I've got his number.'

James was about to respond when the sound of an engine seized his attention.

He spun round and saw that a vehicle had pulled off the road and had come to an abrupt halt halfway along the driveway.

'That's his van,' Abbott blurted, and they could both see the familiar figure of William Nash beyond the windscreen.

The van suddenly went into reverse, backing out onto the road with a loud screech of tyres.

'He's doing a runner,' James yelled. 'We need to get after him.'

As they rushed towards the pool car, James asked for the keys and Abbott grabbed them from her pocket and handed them over. Before he got behind the wheel, James shouted to the patrol officers to follow them.

Seconds later he stamped on the pool car's accelerator pedal and spun the wheel so they were heading back across the yard towards the driveway.

Nash had taken a right turn and was now driving away from the village. James followed, his pulse galloping in his head as he switched on the siren and instructed Abbott to get on the radio and alert control to what was happening.

Nash was well ahead of them, but it was a narrow, twisting road and the conditions were treacherous.

The guy was obviously desperate to avoid being questioned again so God only knew how fast he would go and how many risks he was prepared to take.

James couldn't remember the last time he'd been in hot pursuit of another vehicle and his heart felt as though it was trying to punch its way out of his chest.

The patrol car stayed with them, blue light flashing as they raced along the slippery road.

Fortunately, traffic was light and the few cars they came across pulled over to let them pass.

They spotted Nash's van after about two miles and that was only because a bunch of sheep being herded across the road slowed him down. He was honking the horn and recklessly forcing his way through them as James closed the gap.

An irate farmer was gesticulating wildly and at least one of his sheep nearly got flattened beneath the van's tyres. Thankfully the rest of the herd quickly scurried onto the narrow verges either side of the road, allowing James to steer a path between them.

As soon as the sheep were behind them, James stamped on the accelerator again and the car lurched forward.

'There's a T-junction up ahead,' James told Abbott. 'Let's

hope he turns right. It'll take him further away from the village and along another few miles of straight road with no homes.'

Abbott placed both her hands against the dashboard, as though bracing herself for the moment the pool car came to a sudden stop.

'This is sod's law, guv,' she said. 'If we had arrived just sixty seconds later, we'd have cornered him in the yard.'

'But what he's doing is pointless as well as dangerous,' James said. 'He must know he can't outrun us in the bloody wilds of Cumbria. The roads are few and far between and there aren't many built-up areas. In a city he'd be able to nip round any number of side streets, park up and hurry away on foot. But here his options are limited and he's probably wondering now what the hell he's going to do.'

The van's brake lights came on and James immediately saw why. A road sign indicated the junction up ahead. James knew that Nash would have to slow down significantly as he approached it so when the van's brake lights went off again, he felt a stab of panic.

'The idiot is going even faster now,' he shouted. 'He'll never make the turn at that speed.'

'Oh God, I don't think he's going to try,' Abbott shrieked.

It happened in the blink of an eye, but to the two detectives it seemed like it was in slow motion.

The van must have been racing at sixty miles an hour as it entered the junction.

It tore across the empty road, mounted the verge, and slammed into a dry-stone wall on the other side.

The crash sounded like an explosion and drowned out the screech of the pool car's tyres as James slammed on the brakes.

CHAPTER FIFTY-THREE

James stared through the windscreen in disbelief. The van they'd been chasing was a total wreck and the sight of it robbed him of air.

He'd brought the pool car to a juddering stop in the middle of the road and as he leapt out the smell of burning fuel and rubber caused his nostrils to flare.

'We have to get to him,' he cried, fearing the van would burst into flames at any second.

As he approached it, the extent of the damage shocked him. The front end was crushed up against the wall, and several large stones had tumbled onto what was left of the bonnet.

The windscreen was shattered, and James could see that William Nash was pinned between the back of his seat and the buckled steering wheel, which had been pushed up against his body. The airbag had been deployed but it hadn't saved him from being injured. His eyes were closed and blood was pouring from several wounds to his face and head.

Smoke rose from the chaos of broken parts that were covered in oil and petrol.

James turned and yelled for the officers who were climbing out of the patrol car to bring over an extinguisher and summon the fire brigade and an ambulance.

Then he set about trying to extract Nash from the van. But the door was buckled and wouldn't open. He yanked at the handle, swearing under his breath as he did so.

'Try the other side,' he yelled to Abbott, but she was already on her way there.

'This is stuck too,' she called out after she failed to open it.

By now one of the patrol officers was at the back of the van and pulling open the rear doors. Luckily there was no divider panel between the storage section and the front seats, which meant he was able to scramble on board and get to Nash.

James jumped in with him while the other officer smothered the smoking engine with foam and stopped the whole thing going up in flames.

'He's alive,' James announced after leaning close to Nash and hearing him breathe. 'But it won't be easy to get him out of here.'

They started by pulling back the seats, but they only went so far and Nash's legs remained trapped under the dashboard.

'If we're not careful we'll do more harm than good,' James said. 'Find out how quickly the firefighters can get here and warn them they'll need to perform an extrication.'

While they waited James climbed into the passenger seat next to Nash and used a first aid kit provided by Abbott to tend to his facial injuries.

He wiped away the blood and kept assuring Nash that the rescue services were about to arrive.

At one point the man's eyes flickered open briefly and he let out a groan, but he did not regain full consciousness.

The ambulance arrived first and one of the paramedics took over. James got out of the van and stood with Abbott, who had been on her radio keeping the team updated.

'I don't think there's any doubt that he tried to kill himself,' James said to her.

She nodded. 'So, he chose to die rather than face being questioned by us again.'

'That's how it looks,' James said. 'It probably means he won't make it easy for us to save his life.'

When the firefighters arrived, they got straight to work on the van. It took them fifteen minutes to remove the driver's side door and adjust the seat so that Nash could be released. As he was being placed on the stretcher James asked one of the paramedics if he was likely to live.

'That all depends on how quickly we can get him to hospital and the trauma team can set to work,' the paramedic replied. 'It looks like he suffered a severe blow to the head when he hit the windscreen. We won't know if there are any internal injuries until he's been X-rayed. But I can tell you his right leg is broken and at least a couple of ribs are too.'

'So where are you taking him?'

'The Royal Lancaster Infirmary. It's got the nearest accident and emergency department.'

James turned to Abbott and told her to go with them in the ambulance.

'Keep me informed of his condition,' he said.

'And what about you, guv?'

'I intend to go and check his house. Maybe there's something there he didn't want us to find.'

Before heading off, James removed Nash's key from the van's ignition. There were four other keys on the fob and one of them looked like it would open his front door.

James also took Nash's mobile phone and wallet from his jacket pocket and placed them into evidence bags, which he took with him.

CHAPTER FIFTY-FOUR

On the way back to William Nash's house James arranged for DS Stevens and a forensic team to meet him there.

He had no idea what he expected to find, but he was sure it would be something that linked Kirkby Abbey's Mr Fixit to the Christmas Eve killings.

Why else would the man have sped away when he saw the patrol car? And what else could have encouraged him to try to kill himself by driving into the wall?

If he doesn't die then we might well get to find out the answers, James thought. But if he does die then his secrets will never come out.

They already knew he'd lied about never going into the hidden space behind the wall. And it was a safe bet that he was the one who'd been spying on the family through the peephole. But that did not necessarily mean that he was there on Christmas Eve. Or that they were his shoeprints in the snow that Robert Bateman spotted going towards the exterior cellar door.

Nash's actions had propelled him to the top of the list of suspects. And it was time they found out much more about the man.

James's heart was still in a sprint as he drove. Watching Nash plough into the dry-stone wall had shaken him up more than he cared to acknowledge. The sight of the damaged van and the man's blood-covered face kept pushing itself into his thoughts. Bearing witness to something so traumatic was bound to have an impact. What he needed was a hot drink to calm his nerves, or perhaps something stronger.

But there was no time for that right now. It would have to wait until they'd found out if there were vital clues waiting to be discovered inside William Nash's home.

James got there before anyone else but didn't venture inside until DS Stevens and the forensic team arrived. They were accompanied by two patrol cars, each containing two officers.

James briefed them all in the yard as a sharp easterly wind whipped up the snow around their legs.

He told them about the crash and about Nash's prints being discovered in the space above the cellar at Oaktree Farm.

'The guy panicked when he saw us here and I'm hoping the answer to why he did it is here in his cottage or workshop,' he said. 'So, let's get suited up and try to find it.'

Stevens and three SOCOs followed him in while the other three SOCOs and two of the patrol officers went to search Nash's workshop.

The cottage interior looked the same as it did when James was here before, except that the cardboard boxes and carrier bags stuffed with Christmas decorations had been removed from the living room. Despite that, the house still appeared cluttered and untidy. But given that Nash lived here by himself that came as no surprise to James.

There was little in the way of comfort items, unwashed crockery filled the sink and fast-food packets were piled high in the fridge.

But nothing struck James as out of the ordinary until he went upstairs and walked into Nash's bedroom.

It was like a shrine to Charlotte Bateman.

Photographs of her virtually covered the wall behind the double bed and it looked to James as though many had been taken without her knowledge.

In one she was walking through the village in a summer dress and in another she was standing outside a pub in Kendal with her friend Heather Redgrave.

A dozen more photos were in frames and these were displayed on the tops of the bedside tables, the chest of drawers and a shelf above the radiator.

'This is ruddy creepy,' Stevens said when he entered the room. 'The bloke obviously has an unhealthy obsession with his ex.'

'We'd already been told that,' James said. 'And when I spoke to him, I got the clear impression that he'd loved her dearly and was grief-stricken by her death.'

'But that doesn't mean he didn't decide to kill her, along with her parents, as punishment for her leaving him.'

James nodded. 'You're right, but if that is the case then we need more evidence. These photos and the prints in the cubby-hole are not going to be enough to get a conviction.'

The search continued and the detectives learned quite a bit more about William Nash. It seemed he was a history buff and had dozens of books on everything from the Roman Empire to the American Civil War. He was also something of an artist, and a spare room was filled with drawings and watercolours of the Cumbrian fells and familiar landmarks in Kirkby Abbey.

Nash had used another room as an office and paperwork relating to his handyman business was filed away in a steel cabinet. On his desk was a framed photo of him and Charlotte together. He had his arm around her shoulders and they were both smiling at the camera.

In the desk drawer James found an address book that included contact details for his customers and acquaintances. James was poring through it when Stevens suddenly drew his attention to a sheet of paper that he'd plucked from the waste-basket next to the desk.

'Holy fuck, guv,' the DS said. 'You need to read this. It looks like Nash started to write a suicide note to his parents but decided not to finish it.'

James took the crinkled note in his gloved hand and his stomach knotted with tension as he read the neat handwriting.

Mum and Dad,

Please forgive me for taking the coward's way out. It's just got too much. The police have been to see me and I'm sure it's only a matter of time before they find out that I lied to them.

My life is no longer worth living and I can't risk going to prison. But first I want you and the world to know how and why my beloved Charlotte was killed. I swear it wasn't me who did it, but unless I'm dead I fear I won't be believed. It's such a horrible story and it starts with what really happened at Oaktree Farm twenty-four years ago.

I can't ...

James finished reading the page and instinctively looked at the wastebasket, which was now empty.

'It was the only thing in there,' Stevens told him. 'And it was screwed into a ball.'

'So, he either changed his mind or this was the first attempt at a note and he finished it on another sheet of paper.'

'It's a real eye-opener, guv,' Stevens said. 'We really need to know what else he was going to say.'

James nodded. 'Too bloody right we do. It sounds like William Nash can help us solve not only this crime but also potentially the one that took place at Oaktree Farm over two decades ago.'

CHAPTER FIFTY-FIVE

SIX MONTHS AGO

Charlotte Bateman can't believe that this day has finally arrived. There have been times over the past few years when she'd convinced herself that it never would.

As she zips up the last of her bags, she feels an overwhelming sense of freedom. At last, at the age of twenty-three, she's moving away from Oaktree Farm in order to embark on a new and more fulfilling life.

She doesn't know if her relationship with Neil Savage will stand the test of time and in truth she doesn't really care. She's just grateful that he's invited her to move into his flat in Kendal. It'll give her a chance to assert her independence and learn how to survive beyond the shadow cast by her parents.

She knows they don't approve of Neil because they've told her more times than she cares to remember. But in her eyes that makes him all the more appealing.

She also knows that they'll both be glad to see the back of her. And not only because her behaviour infuriates them and causes so much tension. With her gone they won't have to take her into consideration when it comes to selling the farm. It'll make it easier for them to decide where to move to. And she's in no doubt that once they shed the burden of their troublesome daughter their own relationship will improve.

Charlotte lifts her bag and looks around her bedroom, knowing she's not going to miss it. She's stayed for this long because deep down she feared she could never hack it by herself. But not anymore. Now she's ready to face the big bad world. She'll be back, of course, but only for the occasional overnight stay before the farm is sold.

According to her dad, that will probably happen before the end of the year. He can't afford to keep it going much longer and that's partly his own bloody fault because of the gambling.

Her mum will be pleased, though. She's never liked living here alongside the ghosts the silly woman believes haunt the place.

Charlotte shakes her head and smiles to herself as she heads for the door. Her parents are waiting for her downstairs and she's hoping they won't make a big deal of her departure.

If they're expecting her to shed a tear, they're going to be sorely disappointed.

For Robert Bateman it's the end of one of the worst weeks of his life. As he waits for Charlotte to come down the stairs, he swallows another shot of whisky.

He's sitting on the sofa feeling flat, unsettled, disconnected. And once Charlotte has left, he intends to drink himself into a stupor. At least then he'll be able to stop dwelling on how miserable he is.

Things have been bad for a long time now, but the events of this week have pushed his anxiety to a new level.

First, he was forced to sack that scumbag Kenneth O'Connor for stealing from them for who knows how long.

And then the true scale of his financial problems was laid bare by their financial adviser who made it clear that the farm would have to go.

Now there's Charlotte's departure, which fills him with dread. He can't bear to think what will become of her when she's shacked up with that drug-addled delinquent, Neil Savage.

They've tried to talk her out of moving in with him but without success. It's a bad move on her part, but there's nothing they can do to stop it happening.

He pushes down the sadness that is threatening to overwhelm him and gulps back some more of his drink.

At the same time, he studies his wife over the rim of the glass as she waits for Charlotte to come down.

She's standing with her back to the breakfast bar, arms folded across her ample chest, and her body stiffens when Charlotte appears on the upstairs landing.

Robert knows that this is just as difficult for Mary despite the fact that she and Charlotte have had such a fractious relationship for so many years. And he's glad that today at least they're both on their best behaviour.

He smiles when Charlotte reaches the bottom of the stairs and she and Mary step into each other's arms. It's a touching moment and one that Robert intends to share with them. He drains his glass and gets to his feet so that he can join the embrace.

'Your mother and I will miss you, Charlotte,' he says. 'And we will always be there for you.'

'I know, Dad,' Charlotte replies, stepping back from them. 'But I'll be fine. It's not as if I'm moving far away. You really *don't have to worry. Most of the girls I know who are my age flew the nest years ago.'*

Minutes later they say their goodbyes and wave to Charlotte as she drives out of the yard and away from the farm.

'Well, at least there's one good thing about her moving out,' Mary says, turning to Robert. 'There'll be less chance of her ever finding out the secret we've been keeping for all these years.'

CHAPTER FIFTY-SIX

William Nash's unfinished suicide note was yet another baffling development. After placing it in an evidence bag James sent a photograph of it to DCI Tanner and the rest of the team.

He also emailed over contact details for Nash's parents in Spain, which they found in his address book. Someone would have to inform them that their son had been rushed to hospital and that he was a suspect in a murder investigation. They'd be advised to travel to the UK as quickly as possible.

'His parents are in for quite a shock,' Stevens said. 'Let's hope he survives, if only for their sakes. I'm sure they'll have as many questions for him as we do.'

'You're not wrong there,' James replied. 'In the note he tells them that he didn't kill Charlotte. But he says he knows how and why she died. Could that really be true? And what does he mean when he claims that it all starts with what happened at Oaktree Farm twenty-four years ago? What the hell can he possibly know about the deaths of Simon and Amanda Roth, and the disappearance of their baby?'

'And if he really didn't kill Charlotte, then who did?' Stevens said.

James shook his head and blew out a breath. The question was still playing on his mind fifteen minutes later when he left Nash's house. Stevens stayed behind with the SOCOs to see what else they could find.

The City of Lancaster was twenty odd miles south of Kirkby Abbey, but it was a straight run along the M6 motorway. James was there in less than half an hour and DC Abbott was waiting for him in the A&E department of The Royal Lancaster Infirmary.

'Nash is still unconscious but they're describing his condition as stable rather than critical,' she told him. 'He's got severe concussion, two broken ribs and a broken left leg, plus a bunch of cuts and bruises. But it seems that no damage was done to any internal organs.'

'Are they expecting him to wake up soon?'

'When I last spoke to the doctor about forty-five minutes ago, she said it was too early to tell. But we should get an update soon.'

While they waited, they got themselves a coffee each and discussed Nash's note. And they were still discussing it when a Dr Amara Khan came to talk to them.

'I'm pleased to inform you that Mr Nash has regained consciousness and we're confident he hasn't suffered any brain damage,' she told them. 'However, he's had to be sedated because of his various injuries, including whiplash and broken bones. He's in extreme pain and not yet able to communicate coherently.'

'So, when do you think we'll be able to talk to him?' James asked.

'Not until tomorrow at the earliest,' the doctor replied. 'He's in no fit state to respond to questions at this stage.'

James nodded. 'You need to know that your patient is a suspect in a murder investigation and he deliberately drove into a wall to avoid being questioned. It means I'll have to arrange for an officer to stay close to him overnight.'

'That won't be a problem, Inspector. Can I leave it to you to inform his next of kin?'

James nodded. 'It's in hand. His parents live in Spain so I don't know how long it will take them to get here.'

'We'll be ready for them.'

'And what about his clothes and shoes? Presumably they've been removed.'

'Of course.'

'Then we need to take them with us so that they can be checked over in the lab.'

The afternoon was giving way to evening as James and Abbott headed back to Kendal. Abbott drove while her boss made various phone calls. He spoke to DS Stevens who was still working with the forensics team at Nash's house.

'There's nothing else so far,' Stevens said. 'I'm still sifting through his paperwork, but I've checked his shoes and none of the soles match the bloody prints at the crime scene.'

'We've got the pair he was wearing today so they can be handed over to forensics when we're back.'

He told Stevens to hang on there for the time being and then arranged for a uniformed officer to be sent to the hospital to keep them posted on any changes to Nash's condition overnight.

After coming off the phone, he said to Abbott, ' What do you think the chances are we can wrap this case up before the start of the new year?'

Abbott raised her brow. 'Well, I reckon the odds have shortened in the past couple of hours, guv. But it really depends what our new prime suspect tells us when we eventually get to talk to him.'

CHAPTER FIFTY-SEVEN

The news about William Nash's unfinished suicide note had generated a high level of excitement among the team. They hung onto James's every word as he described the car chase and its dramatic end.

'I'm hoping we'll be able to talk to him tomorrow,' he said, before going on to list the man's injuries.

'Sounds to me like he's lucky to be alive,' DCI Tanner said. 'Although I don't suppose he'll see it that way when he comes around.'

James then told them about the photos of Charlotte on Nash's bedroom wall.

'Some of them were taken from a distance and clearly without her knowledge since they broke up over a year ago,' he said. 'We can assume he's been stalking her and spying through the wall that was installed between the farm's living area and the cellar. His fingerprints testify to that. But we can't assume his obsession with Charlotte became a motive for murder. And if we're to believe what he wrote in the note then he didn't kill her.'

'So, we can't rule out any of the other suspects just yet,' Tanner said.

James shook his head. 'We need to keep hold of them for now. If necessary, we'll apply for custodial extensions.'

'That shouldn't be a problem,' Tanner said. 'Leave it with me.'

'Guv, the police in Spain have contacted Nash's parents at their home on the Costa Blanca. They're making arrangements to fly to the UK as soon as possible and they've been given a number to ring at the hospital,' DC Patterson said. 'They've been told that their son was involved in a car accident, but not that he tried to kill himself. And the father confirmed that they hadn't seen William since July and had been planning to come here for Christmas but were forced to change their plans.'

'Great. Let's try to keep a tight lid on this latest development,' James said. 'I know there'll be lots of pressure because the discovery of the baby's remains has put the story right back at the top of the news agenda, but if they get a sniff of this then things will get out of control again and we don't need it.'

There was nothing new to report on the other suspects since none of them had changed their stories and no evidence had come to light to suggest any of them had lied.

Just before James called time on the briefing DS Stevens – joining the meeting via speakerphone – offered a final update.

'I've found something interesting in Nash's office filing cabinet,' he said. 'There are about thirty folders with the names of people and companies his firm has done work for. One is marked Oaktree Farm.'

'How far back do they go?' James asked.

'Quite a few years before Nash took over the business from his father. And here's the thing. It turns out it was Nash's father who replaced the interior door to the cellar with the plasterboard wall. The work was actually carried out sixteen years ago.'

'Then Nash lied to us.'

'He did, but there's more. There's also a receipt for work done eighteen months ago. Nash was called out to put up shelving units in the cellar and to repair the cellar's external door. Then weeks later Robert Bateman got him to paper the internal wall below the stairs. And get this – Nash was the one who supplied the raindrop paper that makes it hard to spot the peephole from the inside.'

'This would appear to be another mystery solved,' James said. 'It seems obvious to me that he used the opportunity to insert the peephole in the wall. He would have made sure to position it so that it couldn't easily be seen by the family. At the time he was dating Charlotte so it was a way of keeping an eye on her when she wasn't with him. He must have had his own keys cut so that he could access the cellar and the space behind the wall whenever he felt the need.'

'But surely it can't have been that easy,' someone said. 'Wouldn't the family have known when he turned up at the farm?'

James shook his head. 'He could easily have reached the exterior door undetected. He owns a motor scooter and he could have left it in a nearby field and then approached the house on foot. Once inside the cellar he could have stayed for hours without being detected. It's likely he did make some sounds and these might have helped convince Mary Bateman that the farm was haunted.'

James then brought up the subject of Daniel LaPlante and told the team how the man spent months hiding behind a wall and nobody knew he was there. Some of them had heard the story and others like it. One support staff member mentioned the case of a small hotel owner in London who put up a partition wall in a large bedroom and then installed a small hole through which he spied on and filmed female guests. He got away with it for several years and it only came to light after he suffered a fatal heart attack while watching a couple having sex.

Before James ended the meeting, he brought the discussion back to Nash's unfinished suicide note.

'It raises two important questions,' he said. 'Was he a witness to what happened at the farm on Christmas Eve? And was he aware that baby Megan was buried beneath the cellar?'

James spent the next hour typing up notes and finding out as much as he could about William Nash. He spoke again to DS Stevens who said the SOCOs would soon be wrapping up for the day but were planning to return at six in the morning. He told Stevens to head for home when the SOCOs left.

When James left the office he was feeling physically and emotionally exhausted. He promised himself a relaxing evening and an early night because he was sure that tomorrow was going to be another long and challenging day.

But as soon as he climbed into his car, he received a call from Leo Freeman in London. And even before his former colleague spoke, James knew his stress levels were about to rise.

CHAPTER FIFTY-EIGHT

'I've got an update for you on Andrew Sullivan,' Leo said.

James groaned. 'From the sound of your voice I'm guessing you're not going to tell me that you've collared him.'

'I'm sad to say we haven't, James. But I think the net could be closing in on him. You see, we've discovered that seven months ago he took out a three-year lease on a house in Scotland. It's a remote property a few miles south of Dumfries.'

'How did you find that out? Did his lawyer finally decide to distance himself from him?'

'It wasn't arranged through his brief. Sullivan kept it away from his legal team and his minions.'

'So, he intended it to be his secret bolthole for when he needed somewhere to hide out?'

'That's what we believe. And you'll know yourself that it's something most of the organised crime lords have been doing for years.'

'Then how did you get wind of it?'

'Quite by chance. We found out that he's been using two

post office boxes that were registered under an alias. We obtained a warrant to open them and in one there was a letter from a property management company in Dumfries informing him that the monthly check on the house had been carried out and everything was in order.'

'So, you don't even know if he's been there,' James said.

'Oh, he has, but only the once and that was back in June. He signed the lease that day after viewing the property. He paid for the full three years in advance with a single bank transfer from an offshore account we didn't know he had.'

'And presumably he showed them fake documents.'

'Indeed, he did. Passport, utility bills for a phony address and a false driving licence. Everything he would have had on tap.'

'Have you been there yet?'

'We have, but he's not there. That doesn't mean he won't soon turn up, though. Those who know him believe he'll flee abroad as soon as he can, but we're convinced he's still in the UK. That's why we placed the house under surveillance. And it's why I thought you needed to know as you might want to take extra precautions.'

'I don't understand,' James said, before the penny dropped.

'Think about it,' Leo told him. 'To get to that part of Scotland he'll almost certainly drive through Cumbria. And he might not be able to resist a short detour to Kirkby Abbey.'

On the way home James's thoughts were spinning in all directions. The threat posed by Andrew Sullivan had reared its ugly head again and he wasn't sure how to respond to it.

There was no way of knowing if the guy would head for the house he was leasing near Dumfries, which was only eighty miles away from Kirkby Abbey. And even if he did then surely the odds were against him making a pit stop in Cumbria – unless he was determined to exact his revenge before it was too late for him to do so. It was a grim possibility that could not be ignored.

The only way for James and Annie to be completely safe would be for them to move away for a while. But that wasn't really an option at the present time. So, they would just have to carry on being vigilant, at least until the Bateman case was solved. He could then seriously consider more drastic action such as taking Annie on an extended holiday in the hope that the Met would either find Sullivan or be able to confirm that he'd left the country.

James exhaled long and hard, trying to release the knot of tension inside him. But it wasn't easy with so much going on.

Before he got home, he came to the decision not to pass on to Annie what Leo had told him. It would serve no purpose other than to make her far more anxious.

But he did make a point of having a word with the surveillance team outside their house. He explained the situation and asked them to be even more on their guard.

'It's still extremely unlikely that Sullivan will turn up here,' he said to them. 'But the man's a psycho, so you can never be sure what he'll do, even if it's something the rest of us would consider totally stupid and reckless.'

As soon as James walked into the kitchen and saw Annie standing there, he could tell she'd had a bad day. Her face was pale against her dark hair and the muscles around her eyes were tight.

'Is everything okay?' he asked her.

'Not really,' she replied, her voice flat. 'I have chronic indigestion and painful constipation, and I've been sick no less than three times this afternoon.'

'Should I take you to the hospital?'

She forced out a smile and shook her head. 'No, it's all part of the pregnancy process. I've spent hours reading up on it again. Some women suffer much more than others and it appears that I'm one of the unlucky ones.'

'You poor thing,' James said as he took her in his arms. 'Why don't you go and relax in a hot bath? I'm sure it will make you feel better.'

'I doubt that. What I need is a good night's sleep.'

'Then go to bed now.'

'It's too early, and besides I want to hear what you've been up to today. I've heard from two people who said that something happened in the village and one of them saw you in a car with the siren blaring. There's a cottage pie in the oven. You can tell me all about it while you get stuck in.'

At least what he had to tell her took her mind off her own problems for a while. But alarm flashed across her face as he described how they pursued William Nash before he drove his van into the dry-stone wall.

'My God, that's awful,' she said, her hand over her mouth. 'Did he survive?'

James nodded. 'He's in hospital, battered and bruised but alive. I'm hoping to be able to question him tomorrow.'

'I feel guilty now for being so pathetic,' she reacted. 'You've had a much worse day than I have.'

'Don't be daft. I'd rather have the adrenaline rush of a car chase than suffer the discomfort and indignity of not being able to poo.'

She laughed out loud and stretched across the table to tap the back of his hand.

'You really do have a knack for saying the right thing at the right time,' she said.

'Well at least it's put a smile on your face. Now is there anything else I can say or do to cheer you up?'

She thought about it for a moment and said, 'You can try to switch off work mode and then after you've eaten you can come into the living room and listen to what I've decided to do with the baby's room. How does that sound?'

He grinned. 'It sounds like the perfect way to spend an evening.'

She tapped his hand again. 'That's exactly what I hoped you would say.'

James felt he did a good job of feigning interest in what Annie showed him. It wasn't that he didn't care about the colours and the furniture that would bring their baby's bedroom to life, it was simply that his thoughts were so scattered he found it hard to concentrate. But at least it helped get rid of the lead weight in his chest.

Annie was pleased that he agreed with all of her choices and he didn't balk when she told him how much it was going to cost.

'Our baby will be worth it,' he said, and then gave her a long, lingering kiss.

It made him realise yet again just how big an impact the job had on his private life. It was never easy to wind down and free himself from the distraction of an ongoing case.

Thankfully, despite everything that had happened, including

the threats from Andrew Sullivan, their relationship remained strong. He just hoped that would never change.

They went to bed early after deciding not to see the New Year in at midnight. They were both too tired and so were anxious to get as much sleep as possible. But before going upstairs, James called The Royal Lancaster Infirmary again to check on William Nash's condition. He was glad to hear that he was continuing to improve. The news did not make it any easier for him to sleep, though, and he had another rough night.

A riot of images filled his mind as he tried to fall asleep and made him sweat. There was Nash crashing his van into the wall. The baby's skeletal remains in the steel box. The bodies of the Bateman family on the floor at Oaktree Farm. The bloody shoeprints. The peephole in the wall. And the unfinished suicide note that raised more questions than it answered.

In sleep there was no peace either. He had a graphic nightmare in which Andrew Sullivan found his way into their home armed with a revolver which he pointed at Annie.

She screamed for him not to pull the trigger, but he did anyway and there was a loud bang, which was when James woke up.

CHAPTER FIFTY-NINE

Monday January 1st

The first day of the new year brought with it a cloudless blue sky. No fresh snow had fallen overnight and the forecast was for a dry, bright day.

James woke up at six and showered downstairs so as not to wake Annie. Before taking her up a cup of tea he called The Royal Lancaster Infirmary and was told that William Nash's condition remained unchanged. However, he was being weaned off sedation and his doctor was confident he'd be fit enough to be interviewed by mid-morning.

Annie appeared in the kitchen just as James came off the phone. She was wearing her dressing gown and fluffy indoor slippers and looked shattered.

'I was about to bring you up some tea,' James said. 'How are you feeling?'

'Well, I've been to the loo and I haven't been sick yet,' she replied. 'So, I'm happy about that.'

'Then why not stay in bed?'

She shook her head. 'I'm awake now and I don't think I'll

be able to get back to sleep. I might as well make the tea while you go and get dressed.'

James gave her a kiss and they wished each other a happy new year. He then hurried upstairs to get ready. When he came back down the tea was poured and she'd made him some toast.

'I'm guessing it's going to be another long day for you,' she said.

He nodded. 'I've spoken to the hospital and they reckon we'll be able to talk to Nash later this morning.'

'And what do you think he'll tell you?'

'I wish I knew. I just hope it will help us bring the case to a close.'

For a moment James was tempted to tell her that Andrew Sullivan had taken out a lease on a house just across the border in Scotland. But he chose not to. Annie hadn't mentioned the man last night and he didn't want her to spend today worrying about him.

He left home at seven and decided to stop by Nash's cottage before making his way to Kendal. The forensics team had been due to resume the search around six and he wanted to see if they'd come up with anything new, but he got a surprise when he saw that the *Cumbria Gazette* reporter Gordon Carver had beaten him to it. Carver's car was parked by the roadside and he was standing at the top of Nash's driveway talking to a PC in a high-viz vest.

James cursed under his breath as the constable waved him through. He brought the car to a stop in the yard behind the forensic van and the officer approached him as he got out.

Flicking his head towards Carver, he said, 'The guy's a

reporter and reckons you know him, sir. He just turned up and started asking questions.'

'No problem,' James said. 'I'll go and have a word with him. Has anyone else turned up apart from the SOCOs?'

'No, sir. It's been really quiet.'

James walked up the driveway towards the reporter, who was making notes.

'Good morning, Inspector,' Carver said as James approached him. 'I was actually planning to give you a call in a little while.'

'Well now you won't have to bother,' James said. 'What are you doing here?'

'I'm trying to find out exactly what happened yesterday. It's all over the village that William Nash was involved in an accident while being pursued by police. But no one seems to know for sure why he was fleeing. The assumption is that you wanted to question him about the Oaktree Farm killings. Is that so?'

James sighed. He should have known that with Carver being a resident of Kirkby Abbey it'd be impossible to keep a lid on what had happened.

'Shouldn't your first question have been how badly hurt is he?'

Carver grinned. 'I already know that, Inspector. I've got a couple of contacts at the Royal Lancaster and they told me he's got a bunch of broken bones and a head injury, but that his condition isn't critical.'

'And have you got the jump on everyone else with this story?'

'I think so. I checked the wires before I came out and there's no mention of it anywhere. But it's a hot topic among the villagers so it won't be long before the word spreads.'

'Have you called the press office?'

'I did late last night, but they only confirmed that there'd been an accident. They didn't release the driver's name.'

'Try again in a couple of hours then. They'll have more to tell you by then.'

'I'll do that, but in the meantime, I intend to run the story with what I know.'

'And what do you know?'

Carver consulted his notebook. 'That handyman William Nash was badly hurt when his van crashed into a wall while he was being chased by you guys. That he's the former boyfriend of Charlotte Bateman, who was killed along with her parents on Christmas Eve. And that you suspect he might have carried out the killings, which is why a forensic team is at his home today.'

James mulled this over and said, 'Well, as a favour to you, Gordon, I won't contradict anything you've told me.'

'So, does that mean I can file the story in the knowledge that it's entirely accurate?'

James stifled a grin. 'You can. But don't quote me. And I hope you get credit for coming up with yet another scoop.'

'Oh, that's a given, Inspector. I'll be in touch. And thanks.'

With that, he turned and walked to his car.

James knew it would have been a waste of time asking him to hold fire on the story. The guy had got lucky because he happened to live in the village. But at least he didn't know that Nash had tried to kill himself or about the unfinished suicide note. That was a relief and James took it to mean that the information had not been leaked by a member of his team.

James couldn't be bothered to get suited up in a forensic gown so he didn't go inside the cottage. He could see from the doorway that the SOCOs were still hard at it. Transparent plastic stepping plates were dotted about the floor and finger-print dust hung in the air.

He was briefed by the team leader who said they hadn't come across any trace evidence linking Nash to the farm killings.

'A lot of his stuff has been sent to Kendal,' he said. 'As well as his laptop and paperwork, there are three bags full of his clothes.'

James thanked him and checked his watch. Seven forty-five. He called the office and told them to prepare for a team meeting at nine.

He was on the road when his phone rang and he was surprised when Dominic Martin, the forensic anthropologist, asked him if he was free to talk.

'I'm driving, but you're on speaker,' James said. 'What have you got for me?'

'Something I did not expect to find,' Martin said. 'My team has been working around the clock and the final results have just come through on the DNA from the baby's skeleton.'

'And do they confirm that it's Megan Roth?'

'No, they don't. They show that the baby buried in the cellar was not Megan because the DNA from the bones does not match the profiles we have on file for Simon and Amanda Roth.'

Martin's words sucked the air out of James's lungs and every muscle in his body grew tense.

'But that doesn't make sense,' he said. 'Megan disappeared at the same time they were killed.'

'I know that,' Martin responded. 'And it's why I decided to cross check the DNA with those of Robert and Mary Bateman.'

'And?'

'And they're a match. The baby who was placed in the steel box and buried under the floorboards belonged to the Batemans.'

'You're kidding me.'

'No, Inspector. It's true. As you know they had a child, a little girl, just a few weeks before Amanda Roth gave birth to Megan.'

'Then it means that the girl who grew up on Oaktree Farm and died on Christmas Eve was not the real Charlotte Bateman,' James said. 'She was Megan Roth, who went missing twenty-four years ago when she was just three weeks old.'

CHAPTER SIXTY

There was a murmur of disbelief when James broke the news to the team. Shock was etched on the faces of everyone in the room as they tried to process what he was saying.

'This is yet another unexpected development,' he said. 'Robert and Mary Bateman must have known that the baby they brought up was not their own. It begs the question as to what the hell happened back in 1997. We know that Charlotte and Megan were born several weeks apart and that the families spent a bit of time together socially. But when Simon and Amanda Roth were killed, and their baby was reported missing, the Batemans were staying with Robert's mother in Sunderland, and by all accounts their own child was with them.

'So, we need to know when and how the real Charlotte died. When she was buried in the cellar. And why the Batemans pretended to the world that baby Megan was their own child.'

'Do you think that Charlotte knew that Robert and Mary weren't her real parents?' DC Abbott asked.

James shook his head. 'I very much doubt that they told her. It would have been far too risky.'

'We've heard that the girl had a difficult relationship with her mother. Perhaps that was the reason.' This from DCI Tanner.

'It's possible,' James said. 'Another mystery to me is how they managed to pull it off back then. Surely the two babies would have looked different. At the time Charlotte was six weeks old and Megan was three weeks old.'

'Because babies grow and change appearance so quickly all they had to do was keep Megan away from people for a while,' Tanner said. 'It wouldn't have been that difficult, especially as their home was fairly remote.'

'Well, I'm hoping we'll get some of the answers from William Nash when we speak to him,' James said. 'He wrote in his note that he wanted the world to know what really happened back then. We can only assume that he somehow found out. And maybe that led to what happened to the Batemans on Christmas Eve.'

Among the things they went on to discuss was the memorial stone that had been placed over the cellar floorboards above the skeleton.

'It makes sense now why the names of Amanda and Simon Roth are not on it,' DS Stevens said. 'The Batemans must have put it there as a tribute to their real daughter. But I can't help wondering how and why she died, and whether they might have killed her.'

Someone else pointed out that the body of baby Megan, or rather Charlotte, was probably placed in the cellar when the Batemans bought the farm and moved in, which was why it wasn't discovered during the forensic search. Before then it must have been hidden elsewhere, perhaps in the couple's original home or somewhere close to it.

The longer they talked about it the more bizarre it sounded. Tanner told them that he would ask the Chief Constable whether it should be made public.

'I suspect the answer will be yes,' he said. 'The media vultures are aware that the skeletal remains are being subjected to DNA analysis and the pressure will be on us to announce the findings.'

'Then if it's all right with you, sir, I'll put in a call to Giles Keegan before I leave for the hospital,' James said. 'The guy deserves to know before it's out there. The fact that he and his team never found the missing baby still bothers him.'

The ex-copper could barely contain himself when James told him.

'I can't believe it,' he said. 'Are you absolutely sure?'

'The lab techs are convinced based on DNA analysis of the bones,' James replied. 'Megan Roth never actually went missing. Her name was unofficially changed to Charlotte Bateman and the baby she replaced was put into a box and buried in the cellar.'

'That was never something we considered at the time,' Keegan said. 'It's fucking extraordinary. And sick.'

'Did you ever see the Batemans with their baby?' James asked him.

'Several times, but only from a distance, and she was either in her cot or wrapped in a blanket in Mary's arms.'

'And what about their house? Was it searched?'

'Of course, along with the homes of a number of other people. As soon as they returned from Sunderland we went in and they didn't have a problem with it. But we found nothing. And the couple didn't do anything to arouse my suspicion. They were upset and confused over what had happened to Simon and Amanda Roth and I didn't get the impression it was an act.'

James then took him into his confidence in respect of William Nash. Keegan had heard about the crash and had jumped to the obvious conclusion that the handyman was in the frame for the Oaktree Farm killings.

'There's more to it than that, Giles,' James said. 'The guy drove into the wall deliberately.'

'Jesus.'

James then told him about the unfinished suicide note. He felt that Keegan deserved to know since he'd been so helpful during the investigation.

'This gets more surreal by the day,' Keegan said. 'Could it possibly be true that he really does know what happened all those years ago?'

'I'm hoping he does,' James said. 'And I'm also hoping he can tell us what led to the Christmas Eve carnage and who was responsible.'

'Be sure to let me know then, James. And I do appreciate you keeping me informed. It almost makes me feel like I'm part of the team again.'

CHAPTER SIXTY-ONE

James took DS Abbott with him in a pool car to The Royal Lancaster Infirmary. They arrived at eleven-thirty and it came as a relief when they were told that William Nash was in a fit state to be interviewed.

'We're very pleased with the progress he's making,' Dr Amara Khan said. 'He had a good night and is now fully awake and able to communicate. However, he still needs painkillers and is clearly mentally traumatised.'

'Has he spoken to you about what happened to him?'

'Not yet. I tried to get him to open up this morning but he wouldn't and I didn't push it.'

'Does he know we want to talk to him?'

'I told him myself and he seems resigned to it. Also, just in case you haven't heard, his father rang the hospital late last night and he and his wife aren't able to get here until tomorrow morning at the earliest.'

Dr Khan took them to Nash's room, which he had to himself. A uniformed police officer was standing outside and he recognised them so there was no need to show their IDs.

James was surprised to see Nash sitting up in bed. His left leg was in plaster and raised on a pillow, and dressings covered wounds to his forehead and left cheek.

His skin was white, almost translucent, and his eyes were sunken and shadowed. They darted nervously between the two detectives.

'These are police officers and they would like to talk to you, Mr Nash,' Dr Khan said to him. 'Do you feel up to it?'

He gave a slow shake of the head which appeared to require some effort. 'Not really, but I might as well get it over with,' he replied, his voice low and raspy.

The doctor then left the room, saying she would be along the corridor if she was needed.

'Hello there, Mr Nash,' James said as he approached the bed. 'Do you remember us?'

He nodded. 'I don't recall your names, though.'

'I'm Detective Inspector Walker and this is Detective Constable Abbott.'

'Were you the ones who chased me?'

'We were. And you gave us quite a scare when you drove into that wall. You're very lucky to have survived.'

'I wouldn't consider myself lucky,' he said. 'It must have been obvious to you that I did it on purpose.'

'Would you care to tell us why you did it?' James said.

He answered without hesitation. 'Because my life has been shit for a long time and Charlotte dying made me realise that I don't want to carry on. It was the thought that we might eventually get back together that kept me going.'

'Why did you flee when you arrived home and saw us in the yard?' James asked.

'I don't really know. I just panicked.'

James frowned. 'That's not entirely true, is it, Mr Nash? You see, we found your suicide note. The one you didn't finish. In it you wrote that you feared it was only a matter of time before we found out that you had lied to us and that you couldn't risk going to prison.'

Nash stared at James, his eyes wide, the breath wheezing out of him. He started to speak but the words seemed to get stuck in his throat.

'It's time you came clean,' James said. 'We know you lied when you told us that you had never been inside the cellar at Oaktree Farm. It was your own father who replaced the inner door with the wall. Plus, we found a receipt for work you carried out to the doors and shelves. And your finger-prints are in the concealed space behind the wall from where you've been spying on the family, or I should say, spying on Charlotte.'

Nash wet his lips with his tongue and said, 'Are you arresting me?'

'Not unless you give us a reason to. This is an informal interview. You're not being accused of any offence. We just want to establish some facts. In the unfinished note to your parents, you swore that you did not murder Charlotte, but you wanted them to know that you knew how and why she was killed. That must mean you were behind the wall on Christmas Eve and bore witness to what happened. You also wrote, and I quote, "it's such a horrible story and it starts with what really happened at Oaktree Farm twenty-four years ago". Now, when your parents arrive later, we'll be showing them the note, and they'll likely be just as curious as we are to know what else you were going to tell them.'

'Did you finish the note on another sheet of paper?' Abbott asked him.

Nash shook his head again. 'I stopped writing because I suddenly wasn't sure I could go through with it. So, I binned the note and went for a drive to clear my head. When I came back you were there and I knew that you wouldn't believe anything I told you. When I arrived at that T-junction and saw the wall, I suddenly found the guts to do what had to be done. Only I fucked up.'

'And we're glad you did, Mr Nash,' James said. 'We've got lots of questions relating to the violent deaths of the Bateman family. And we won't stop asking them until you've provided the answers.'

Nash shifted his gaze towards the ceiling and was lost in silent thought for about half a minute. Then he turned back to James and said, 'I did not kill anyone, Inspector. But yes, I was there that evening and I do know what happened.'

CHAPTER SIXTY-TWO

James and Abbott looked at each other across the bed. Abbott then took out her mobile phone and switched on the recorder. In response, Nash clenched his jaw

'That's for your benefit as well as ours,' James explained to him. 'And if at any point you feel you can't continue then just say the word and we'll stop.'

Nash grimaced as though in pain and took a long, deep breath.

'Where shall I start?' he asked, a crack in his voice.

'First I'd like to know if it was you who installed the peep-hole in the wall,' James said. 'And tell us how you managed to do it.'

Nash twisted his mouth as he searched for words and when he spoke his voice was thick with emotion.

'It goes back to when I did the work for Robert in the cellar,' he said. 'It was the first time I'd been down there without Charlotte. I knew that the door at the top of the steps led nowhere, but I was curious to see what was beyond it. I'd been given a set of keys and one of them unlocked it. That's when I saw the concealed space between the door and the wall. As soon as I stepped inside, I heard Mary and Charlotte talking to each other in the living room. Their voices were as clear as day and I realised it was a way for me to find out what Charlotte really thought about me.'

He paused to gulp in some air before continuing.

'The space wasn't being used for anything and so I decided to make the most of it. I got my own key cut for the external door and stole the key to the internal door. Then for weeks afterwards I went there, usually late in the evening, and listened to their conversations. But it got to the stage where it wasn't enough and I wanted to see them too. So, I bought a peephole online. I knew that the paper they had on the inside of the wall had been there for years and so I went looking for something that I thought would camouflage the hole. I came up with the raindrop design. I offered it to Robert for free. He liked it and he paid me to put it up. At the same time, I inserted the peephole.'

'And how often did you go there to spy on them?' James asked.

'A couple of times a week. I wouldn't have had to if Charlotte had moved in with me. But she wasn't prepared to and so I was paranoid and insecure.'

'And did you stay in there for hours at a time?'

'I had nothing better to do and it always cheered me up when she said nice things about me to her parents.'

'But how did you get away with it for so long?' Abbott asked him.

A shrug. 'It was easy. I left my scooter behind a hedge on the road and approached the house from the rear. It was always in the evening so they were inside and I was able to slip into the cellar without anyone knowing.'

'And is that what happened on Christmas Eve?' James said.

Nash nodded. 'After Charlotte moved out, I didn't go there very often. But I always made a point of going when I found out she was visiting. And I'd heard she'd be there on Christmas Eve.'

'What time did you arrive?'

'About four. Mary was alone then and Charlotte and Savage didn't get there until much later. And Robert turned up after them at about seven.'

'We've been told that Robert saw shoeprints in the snow leading to the cellar. Did they belong to you?'

'They did. It was a stupid mistake on my part to have left them there.'

'Am I right in saying that while you watched everyone arrive you passed the time by eating a sandwich?'

He looked surprised. 'How did you know that?'

'There were crumbs on the floor.'

Nash rolled his eyes. 'Another stupid mistake.'

James felt his pulse quicken as he asked Nash to describe what led to the killings.

Nash began with the same account as the one Neil Savage had given them. Charlotte received a call from her friend Heather Redgrave who told her that Savage had been unfaithful. Charlotte then confronted Savage and threw a wine bottle at him. Her father came rushing into the house and made Charlotte go upstairs. That was when Robert mentioned the footprints in the snow.

'I thought he was going to come to the cellar, but then

337

Charlotte came tearing down the stairs holding his shotgun,' Nash said. 'She threatened to shoot Savage who had no choice but to flee the house.'

So far so good, James thought. Nash's description of what happened tallied with the one from Savage. Now they would hopefully get to find out what had followed Savage's departure.

'When we first spoke to you, Mr Nash, you came close to accusing Neil Savage of carrying out the killings. But now you're telling us he left the house.'

'I wanted him to be blamed because if he hadn't cheated on Charlotte, they would all still be alive. But I have to assume now that you know he didn't do it. I'm not proud of myself, Inspector. And it's another reason I wish I was dead.'

James mentally crossed Savage off their list of suspects and said, 'So now tell us what occurred in the house after Savage had driven off.'

Nash pressed his head back against the pillow and stared at the ceiling, his eyes squinting.

'As soon as he was out of the door Robert grabbed the shotgun from Charlotte and placed it on the breakfast bar,' he said. 'She burst into tears and ran upstairs again. Mary started crying too and Robert tried to console her. Nothing else happened for about twenty minutes. Then Charlotte came back down holding her phone. Her parents then had a go at her and it all kicked off again. I'd never seen Charlotte get so worked up and I suspected she'd been popping pills and putting away too much booze.'

'So, what happened then?' James prodded.

Nash blinked repeatedly as he struggled to get the words out.

'Charlotte learned the truth about who she was,' he said. 'And what followed will haunt me for the rest of my life.'

James leaned closer. 'Take your time, Mr Nash. Tell us exactly what you saw.'

CHAPTER SIXTY-THREE

CHRISTMAS EVE

Robert and Mary are sitting side by side on the sofa, still reeling from the shock of what happened twenty or so minutes ago.

When they hear Charlotte coming back down the stairs, they're expecting her to show some contrition. A grovelling apology would suffice.

But she doesn't. Instead, she ignores them both and goes straight to the fridge where she takes out a new bottle of wine.

Robert can feel the anger building inside him. She clearly doesn't give a toss that she's ruined their last Christmas here.

Mary is watching her with a contemptuous look on her face and Robert fears she'll explode at any moment. Instinct tells him it's going to get very ugly.

Mary's eyes follow Charlotte as she unscrews the cap on the wine bottle while making a point of not looking at them.

'You could at least clear up the broken glass on the floor before you have another drink,' Mary tells her.

Charlotte lifts her eyes and fixes Mary with a hard, unfriendly stare.

'I thought you would have done that by now,' she says. 'If you can't be bothered then I'll do it when I'm ready. Just avoid treading on it in the meantime. Wouldn't want you to hurt yourself.'

Mary shakes her head. 'Why do you always have to spoil things? Did you deliberately set out to cause trouble tonight?'

'That's typical of you,' Charlotte snarls through gritted teeth, her reaction clearly fuelled by alcohol. 'Blame me even though that shitty boyfriend of mine is the one in the wrong.'

Mary stands up and steps towards the kitchen.

'But what you did was completely over the top. It's time you learned to control that vile temper of yours. Do you realise what damage you could have done with that gun? You would have killed him if it had gone off.'

Charlotte's lips curl into a mirthless grin. 'It would have been no more than he deserves after what he did. I should never have brought him here. I shouldn't have come myself. It's not as if I ever feel welcome.'

'You're such an ungrateful girl,' Mary fumes. 'And if you move out of his flat don't think you can just move back here until we sell up because I won't let you.'

'Well, I have no intention of coming back,' Charlotte responds, slurring her words. 'Not now that I know what a lying cow you are and always have been.'

Now Robert jumps to his feet.

'That's enough young lady,' he yells at her. 'You apologise to your mother right now.'

Charlotte jabs a finger at him. 'You wouldn't say that if you knew what I know. Or maybe you do know and you don't care. If so then you're as bad as she is for keeping it from me.'

Robert has no idea what she's on about. He turns to Mary who looks just as confused as he is.

'What lies am I supposed to have told?' Mary asks. 'Or are you just spouting the first thing that comes into that drug-filled head of yours?'

There's a flash of hesitation on Charlotte's face as she looks from Mary to Robert. But it's quickly replaced by a dark, determined expression.

To Robert, she says, 'I wanted to surprise you with a special Christmas present this year. I remembered you once talked about paying for one of those ancestry tests. You said you thought it would be interesting to know about your distant relatives. But I know you never got around to it. So, I did it on your behalf and did one for myself at the same time. All I had to do was send in a used toothbrush with DNA on it. I swiped yours when I was last here.'

Robert remembers it going missing, but that's not important now. He feels his insides turn cold because he can see where she's going with this. He starts to speak but Charlotte raises a hand to stop him.

'A couple of weeks ago the results came back. I got a letter telling me that our DNA doesn't match. And I knew then that you are not my biological father.'

The shock slams into Robert like a steam train. He looks across at Mary who is standing there with her mouth open.

'I haven't talked to anyone about it, not even Neil, because I've struggled to accept it,' Charlotte continues. 'The reason I agreed to come here for Christmas was so that I could get some more DNA samples for more tests. But in my heart, I know it's true and the results will be the same.'

By now tears are pooling in Charlotte's eyes and her lips are

342

trembling. She turns to Mary. 'So, you might as well tell me now who my real dad is. Or was he just a one-night stand and you didn't even ask his name?'

The silence that descends is disturbingly palpable and it lasts a good ten seconds before Robert breaks it.

'They must have got it wrong, Charlotte. It's not true. You're my daughter and your mother has always been faithful to me.'

'You can't be sure of that,' Charlotte replies, her voice as rough as gravel. 'In those days she was a nurse and you were a farmworker. You couldn't possibly have known if she was shagging some doctor while she pretended to be on the night shift at the hospital.'

Her words ignite a fire inside Robert's stomach because it's clear that she's pushing Mary too far.

His wife puffs out her chest and for a few beats her face contorts with a fierce anger.

Then, in a slow voice dripping with venom, she says, 'How dare you? I give you a home, raise you like my own daughter, and you accuse me of this? You're right, you ungrateful cow. He's not your father, but I'm not your mother either. You aren't related to either of us, and thank God for that.'

Robert's heart drops. He can't believe that Mary has revealed their darkest secret, a secret they've kept for all these years. One they both agreed they would take to their graves.

'What are you talking about?' Charlotte asks, confused and suddenly wary.

Mary strides across the room towards her and Robert rushes forward to stand between them.

'Stop there, Mary,' he pleads. 'This has gone far enough. You should—'

But Mary pushes him out of the way with a violent shove.

343

'No, Robert. It's time she knew the truth, and I don't care about the consequences anymore. I'm just sick of all the shit she puts us through. These last few years she's made our lives a misery.'

Robert doesn't want her to say any more, but he knows she will. It'll be disastrous. But how can he stop her? It's obvious from her face and demeanour that she's consumed by an uncontrollable rage, the likes of which he hasn't seen before.

'Just give it a rest, Mary,' he shouts. 'You're talking nonsense.'

'No, she isn't,' Charlotte says. 'I want to hear what she has to say. And I want to know about my real parents and why I've been lied to all these years.'

'We didn't tell you because we didn't want you to know,' Mary says, her face red, features tight. 'You see, we had a daughter of our own and her name was Charlotte. She was perfect. But she died when she was just six weeks old. And that's why we adopted you. Or I should say, we abducted you.'

Robert realises there's nothing more he can say or do so he just stands there, completely paralysed as his wife proceeds to get twenty-four years of guilt off her chest. The floodgates are open and she seems determined to crush Charlotte and destroy all of their lives by taking them back to that fateful day.

CHAPTER SIXTY-FOUR

TWENTY-FOUR YEARS AGO

Mary doesn't want to get up, but she knows she has to. She needs to check on the baby and start thinking about what to cook Robert for dinner.

She's expecting him home about six, although there's a good chance he'll be late. He usually is on Fridays because Simon Roth, his boss at Oaktree Farm, likes to take him along on his weekly pheasant shoot. It's always just the two of them and Robert carries the birds and the lunch box, and acts as beater.

Mary rolls on her side and peers at the clock on the bedside table, which shows it's 1.10 p.m. It comes as a shock because it means she's slept for almost three hours.

She wishes someone had warned her how hard it would be to cope with a newborn. She loves Charlotte to bits but she's finding motherhood a real struggle. It doesn't help that she misses being a nurse and the opportunities it gave her to meet people and escape the isolation that is the downside of living in such a remote location. Their house is between Kirkby Abbey and Oaktree Farm and the nearest neighbour is over a mile away.

It wouldn't be so bad if Robert were more helpful, but he works a six-day week at the farm and is always knackered when he comes home.

She hauls herself up to a sitting position and looks across the room at the cot. Only then does it occur to her that Charlotte has missed a feed. She wonders if it's because her little darling is in a real deep sleep or because she's simply not hungry.

Mary can feel that her breasts are full and sees that milk has leaked onto her blouse.

'Damn it,' she says aloud as she swings her legs off the edge of the bed and stands up.

She pads barefoot across the room and leans over the cot. Charlotte is lying face down and looks to be warm and comfortable but when Mary reaches over and gently nudges her body in a bid to wake her, she suddenly realises that something is wrong.

Her baby is unresponsive, and as she turns her over, she sees that her face is blue and she doesn't appear to be breathing.

Panic seizes Mary's chest. She quickly lifts Charlotte out of the cot and immediately becomes aware of how cold she is.

'Oh, dear God, no,' she bellows when it suddenly becomes obvious to her what has happened.

She turns around and lays Charlotte on the bed. Her nurse training kicks in and she starts to administer CPR.

'Start breathing, sweetheart,' she pleads. 'Please wake up. Please.'

But she doesn't. And though Mary has spent enough time in hospital emergency rooms to know that she never will, for *ten minutes she carries on hysterically pumping Charlotte's chest and blowing air into her tiny mouth.*

When she finally accepts that her daughter is dead, she lets out a scream that it more animal than human and collapses onto the bed beside her.

The tears flow and she's swamped by a sense of loss that is so profound it feels like hot lead is flowing through her veins.

She knows that if she had found Charlotte sooner it might have been possible to save her. She could have kept her alive until the paramedics arrived, and once at the hospital the doctors could have worked their magic.

But she also knows that even then the odds would have been against Charlotte surviving, given that every year in the UK around two hundred babies die suddenly and unexpectedly.

It's clear to her now that Charlotte is a victim of sudden infant death syndrome, or cot death, as most people know it. Her body temperature and the colour of her skin suggest to Mary that she passed away at least a couple of hours ago ... while her mother was fast asleep only a few feet away.

The guilt she feels is overwhelming and it adds to the riot of emotions raging through her mind. She pulls her baby close and kisses her forehead.

'I'm so sorry I went to sleep,' she sobs. 'Please forgive me, my darling. I beg you.'

Even through the turmoil in her head she knows she's meant to call the police, but she doesn't want to. She doesn't want them to take Charlotte away. Not now. Not ever.

She will have to tell Robert that his daughter has died, though, and she can't bear the thought of it. The news will destroy him and in all likelihood their marriage as well.

He's bound to say it was her fault. That she should have been watching their baby.

It means she will have to lie and say it happened really quickly and there was nothing she could do. And she can't possibly admit to being asleep.

Suddenly she's overcome by a strange sensation, as though her mind has lost control of her body. It's happened to her several times in the past when she's been stressed out or suffered a shock.

Before she knows it, she's off the bed and heading for the door. She doesn't want to break the news to her husband over the phone. She needs to tell him to his face. She'll then know from his reaction if she's lost him forever as well.

Mary is on autopilot as she drives towards Oaktree Farm. She's numb with grief, shock and self-recrimination, and is only half-aware of the road in front of her.

But she's stopped crying and feels a peculiar need to act normal, to put on a brave face, as though nothing bad has happened.

Maybe it's all in her head anyway. A grim nightmare from which she will eventually emerge.

It's a thought that flashes through her mind but doesn't take root. How can it when she knows only too well that she's awake? The pain she feels is real and so is the sun that's shining down on the countryside around her.

She starts to hum a meaningless tune in an effort to drown out the shrieking noise in her ears. And she keeps it up until she reaches her destination.

Oaktree Farm.

Robert's car is parked in the front yard next to the barn,

and the sight of it brings on a violent urge to vomit. But somehow she manages to hold it in as she pulls her own ageing Vauxhall Corsa to a stop behind it.

The moment she kills the engine she hears a voice and turns to look through the side window.

Amanda Roth, Simon's wife, is standing at the top of the short flight of stairs that leads down to the cellar door. She's waving an arm and her voice carries through the glass.

'Hi there, Mary,' she calls out. 'I thought it was Simon and Robert returning from the shoot. I'm tidying up in the cellar. Come and join me.'

Amanda disappears back down the cellar steps and Mary struggles to decide what to do.

Robert isn't here so she's going to have to tell Amanda what has happened. But she doesn't want her friend to know. Or anyone else other than her husband.

She sits there without moving for perhaps a minute, her chest pumping, starved of oxygen. Eventually, as though in a trance, she pushes the door open and gets out. It feels almost as though her mind is detached from her body as she walks across the yard and down into the cellar. She's never been in there before and it's brighter than she imagined it would be thanks to the light on the ceiling.

Amanda is standing next to the long wooden workbench repotting house plants. She's wearing jeans, a jumper, and a pair of gardening gloves. Her dark hair is pulled back in a ponytail.

'This is a nice surprise, Mary,' she says. 'What brings you here today?'

Before the words can even register, Mary's attention is drawn to the carrycot on the floor behind Amanda. She can see baby

Megan inside lying on her back, eyes closed, mouth open. Not for the first time it occurs to Mary that she looks so much like Charlotte. They have the same fair hair and turned-up nose. The same chubby cheeks and full lips.

'Are you all right?' Amanda asks, concern in her voice. 'Is something the matter?'

That's when Mary snaps and her mind tells her that it's not Megan in the carrycot. It's Charlotte. And she now has another chance to save her daughter.

She rushes forward, barging Amanda out of the way. Her friend's body slams against the shelf and she falls to the floor after losing her balance.

Mary doesn't care, though. All she cares about now is keeping her daughter alive.

She drops to her knees next to the carrycot and reaches in to gently poke the baby.

'Wake up, Charlotte,' she yells. 'It's Mummy. Wake up. Please.'

The child doesn't stir, so she starts to poke a little harder.

'Wake up my darling. Don't die on me again. Please.'

When the baby's eyes flicker open, relief surges through Mary. But at the same time, she's suddenly wrenched backwards by her hair.

She screams with the pain as she's pulled across the floor by Amanda.

'Are you insane, woman?' Amanda screams. 'What the hell do you think you're doing? That's Megan. Not Charlotte.'

Mary's head drops to the floor as Amanda lets go of her hair.

Amanda then moves towards the cot, clearly intending to pick up the crying baby. But before she reaches it, Mary is on her feet and seizing her ponytail.

'How do you like it, you fucking bitch?' Mary yells as she pulls on it.

Amanda twists her body to face Mary, her eyes ablaze.

'Let me go, you mad woman.'

'I'm not mad,' Mary responds, her voice suddenly lower and more controlled. 'I know my own baby and I'll do anything to save her. And no way will I let you take her from me.'

Amanda reacts by reaching out and grabbing Mary by the throat. She forces her back against the bench and for several seconds the two women are locked in a violent struggle.

Mary just doesn't understand why this person she regarded as a friend would try to steal her baby. It's unbelievable. Monstrous.

The pressure on Mary's back forces her to release her grip on Amanda's ponytail so that she can reach behind her and support herself. As she does so her hand comes into contact with an object on the workshelf.

She knows straight away that it's a hammer and her fingers close around the grip.

By now she can barely breathe as Amanda's fingers dig into her throat. The woman is ranting about calling the police and Mary believes she therefore has no choice but to protect herself and her baby.

She manages to place her left hand on her attacker's chest and gives an almighty push.

As the gap opens up between them, Mary brings the hammer around from behind her back and lashes out with it.

One strike to the side of the head is all it takes to force Amanda to let go of her throat. As she stumbles backwards, Mary hits out again and this time the face of the hammer smashes into Amanda's forehead.

The woman collapses onto the floor where the blood starts to pool around her head. Her eyes stare at the ceiling and her features are frozen.

It takes a few moments for Mary to realise that Amanda is dead. And that she's the one who killed her. She feels dizzy and nauseous and her head is filled with the sound of a baby crying.

But at least that means her daughter is safe. And alive.

'Looks like your lovely wife is paying us a visit,' Simon observes as he and Robert arrive back from the shoot and see Mary's car in the yard.

'She probably stopped off on her way home from the village,' Robert replies.

'Well, it'll be nice to see her and Charlotte.'

When they step out of the Land Rover, Simon heads for the front door while Robert makes his way towards the cellar. He's carrying his boss's shotgun in one hand and two dead pheasants on a strap in the other. He'll hang the birds up and lock the gun away before going upstairs. All part of the Friday routine.

The cellar door is open, which makes him think that Amanda is down there. It's where she keeps her plants and vegetables and she likes to give them a daily dose of fresh air.

But the first person he sees isn't Amanda. It's Mary. She's crouched in a ball on the floor clutching a baby to her chest. Robert is about to ask her what's wrong when he catches sight of the body on the floor. It causes his breath to stall and his heart to trip.

But his brain is slow to respond and a couple of seconds pass before he takes in the blood and realises that he's looking at Amanda.

He drops the pheasants but not the shotgun.

'She's dead,' Mary tells him, her voice shockingly calm. 'I killed her but I had no choice.'

Robert snaps his stricken gaze towards his wife. 'My God, are you serious?'

She nods. 'She tried to take Charlotte from me but I wouldn't let her.'

'What did you do?'

'I hit her with the hammer over there. It was the only way I could get her to let go of my throat.'

Robert spots the hammer next to the body, the blood on the face of it, and he feels his jaw go tight, making it hard to speak.

'Please tell me it isn't true,' he manages to utter.

'It's not something I'd make up, Robert. It happened about twenty minutes ago and if I thought she could have been saved I would have called an ambulance. I did it in a moment of madness. I was trying to protect our baby.'

'What do you mean?' He steps closer to her. 'That's Megan you're holding. Not Charlotte.'

Something happens to Mary's face then. It's as though a sudden realisation has dawned on her and she isn't sure how to react to it.

'Oh my God,' she mumbles as she looks down at the baby in her arms. 'I made a mistake. I really thought … I thought she was Charlotte.'

Robert's heart is thudding out of control now and his throat is so tight he's struggling to get air into his lungs.

'What the hell is going on, Mary?' he manages. 'Where is Charlotte? Where is my daughter?'

Mary blinks back tears. 'Charlotte is dead, Robert. She passed away earlier and there was nothing I could do to save her.'

Disbelief shapes his features. 'No, that can't be right. You're lying. Please tell me you're lying.'

She shakes her head. 'It's true, my love. It was cot death. She died in her sleep. I came here to tell you and when I saw Megan, I thought she was Charlotte. As I went to pick her up Amanda attacked me.'

Robert's mind suddenly moves beyond the horrific scene before him and he realises the consequences of what has happened. Any second now Simon will come through the door to the cellar and find out that his wife has been murdered by her friend. The shock will be unbearable for him and Robert dreads to think how he'll react. He'll no doubt call the police and when they come Mary will be arrested and likely spend the rest of her life in prison. And that's not what Robert wants despite what his wife has done. He'll be left alone to grieve for his daughter. He'll lose everything and he's not sure he'll be able to cope by himself.

And the thing is, he knows that Mary is not a bad person. When she came here to the farm, she would have been a total mess after what had happened to Charlotte. Her head would have been all over the place, her emotions in turmoil. And despite what she's done, he can't help feeling a degree of sympathy for her.

He suddenly knows what he has to do. The survival instinct has kicked in.

He helps Mary to her feet, still holding the baby, and says, 'I want you to go out to the car and wait for me. Take Megan with you.'

'What about Simon?' his wife says.

'I'll deal with him. We can't let him live. He'll destroy our lives.'

354

Mary doesn't argue. As she rushes towards the door Robert tightens his grip on the shotgun and heads for the stairs.

But just then he hears Simon enter the cellar from inside the house.

'What's going on down here?' he calls out. 'Am I missing all the fun?'

Robert feels his mouth open but he says nothing. Instead, he steps to one side and waits for Simon to come to him.

CHAPTER SIXTY-FIVE

CHRISTMAS EVE

When Mary finally stops talking, Charlotte – Megan – is in a state of total shock.

She's listened to the horrific story without moving a muscle, as though her entire body has been filled with cement.

Robert is tempted to cross the room and take her in his arms, but he knows she won't welcome it. Not now that she's been told he murdered her real father.

A wave of impotent rage sweeps through him and at the same time a knife of guilt twists in his stomach.

His wife has completely lost the plot, just as she did twenty-four years ago. And once again she's caused untold damage.

The silence lasts for only a matter of seconds before she starts ranting again, and it's as though every word out of her mouth makes the burden she's carried for all these years that much lighter.

'You might imagine that we panicked, but we didn't,' she says, almost proudly. 'Instead, I went back into the cellar after I heard the shot and we stayed there for about an hour talking

through what we should do. The first decision we made was to stick together and the second was to take you with us and make everyone believe that you were Charlotte. Then we decided to leave the bodies there and go. First we made sure not to leave any trace of ourselves behind. We wiped our prints from the hammer and the shotgun and staged it to look like Simon killed Amanda and then himself. Then we took you home, packed up, and went to Sunderland where the police called us a couple of days later to tell us your parents had been killed and you were missing. Your nan was suffering early-stage dementia back then so it was easy to convince her we'd been there longer than we had. So, we didn't become suspects.'

A deep frown forms on Charlotte's face and tears glisten on her cheeks.

'I don't understand,' she says. 'If this all happened in the cellar why did you want to move here?'

'I didn't want to,' Mary replies, flicking her head towards Robert. 'He persuaded me to after your nan died and we came into some money. It was cheap and he liked the idea of being his own boss. But as you know, I've never liked living here. It creeps me out. That's why we eventually got the cellar door replaced with a wall. Plus, we couldn't risk you finding our real daughter.'

Charlotte's eyes widen with alarm. 'What do you mean?'

'We brought her here with us and buried her body beneath the floorboards,' Mary says. 'We wanted her close to us. The memorial stone down there is for her and not for your real parents. Nobody but us knows she's there.'

Mary falls silent again and she and Charlotte stare at each other. Charlotte is clearly devastated whereas Mary looks almost pleased with herself.

357

Robert switches his gaze between the two of them and it feels like his heart is being squeezed by an iron fist.

He knows there's no way back from this. Mary has seen to that. Her fragile state of mind, combined with her anger over Charlotte ruining Christmas, has pushed her over the edge and released a mass of inner demons. She probably feels that Charlotte has finally got what was coming to her. Payback for years of Mary having to tolerate her bad behaviour.

Suddenly Charlotte finds her voice. 'I hate you both so much. I've always suspected that I wasn't wanted and that you didn't love me. And now I know why.'

'What we did was wrong,' Robert tells her, his voice desperate. 'But you must believe that we've always loved you, always wanted you and we've tried our best to make you happy.'

'That's bollocks,' she shouts at him. 'You're both liars and murderers and you've destroyed my life.'

Robert takes a step forward and Charlotte responds by moving away from him.

'We have to talk this through,' he says to her. 'I'm sure we can make you understand that ...'

Charlotte bares her teeth and cuts him off. 'You're as fucking crazy as she is if you think I can ever forgive you.'

And then she does something that takes them both by surprise. She grabs a knife from the block on the worktop and threatens to cut her wrist with it.

'You told me not to shoot Neil, but I don't reckon you'll mind if I kill myself,' she screams at them. 'Because if I do, I won't be able to tell the police what you did. And you can then get on with your rotten lives.'

Robert is about to tell her to put the knife down when Mary

decides to take more decisive action. She hurls herself forward and tries to take the knife away from Charlotte.

But Charlotte resists and holds onto it. A fierce struggle ensues. The pair fall to the floor with Mary on top.

Before Robert can get to them Charlotte lets out a painful cry and her body goes limp.

It's not until Mary rolls off her that they see the knife buried deep in Charlotte's stomach and the blood spreading across her blouse.

Mary gasps. 'My God, I didn't mean for that to happen. Please believe me. It was an accident.'

CHAPTER SIXTY-SIX

It suddenly got too much for William Nash. After describing how Charlotte was stabbed, he broke down and tears pushed out of his eyes, accompanied by great racking sobs.

'I can appreciate how hard this is for you, Mr Nash,' James said. 'But I need to know what happened after that.'

James let out a slow breath. What Nash had told them had come as a huge shock, but he didn't doubt that it was all true. It was in line with all of the evidence from the two crimes.

Suddenly almost everything had fallen into place, and James now knew most of the answers to the questions that had been plaguing him.

It was no longer a mystery why Simon and Amanda Roth had died. Or why their daughter Megan had disappeared. Or why Charlotte suspected Mary had been unfaithful. The ancestry test result was obviously what had upset her that day in the charity shop when she received the envelope Fiona McCarthy mentioned.

But none of it filled James with any sense of satisfaction, even though he was in a position to bring one of his most challenging investigations to a successful conclusion.

It was another five minutes or so before Nash had pulled himself together enough to carry on with the interview. But it turned out that what he had to say was not what James was expecting to hear.

'I could see Charlotte lying on the kitchen floor with the knife in her stomach,' Nash said. 'I panicked because I wasn't convinced that Robert and Mary would take care of her. But when I pushed open the door from the room to the cellar, I was moving too fast and slipped on the top step. I went crashing to the bottom and smashed my head a couple of times.'

'So, it was your blood we found on the steps,' James said.

Nash nodded. 'I didn't realise how severe the blows were until I tried to get up off the floor and found I couldn't. I was dizzy and disoriented and when I touched the back of my head there was blood on my hands. I think I may actually have passed out for a few minutes. But while I was lying there, I heard two loud bangs and assumed they were shots being fired.'

'Are you telling us that you didn't actually see who fired them?' Abbott asked.

Nash shook his head. 'I'm afraid not. By the time I was able to stagger out of the cellar and around to the front of the house it was all over.'

'What did you do then?' James asked.

'The front door was unlocked, so I went in,' Nash replied. 'And I couldn't believe what I saw. It was like a slaughterhouse with blood everywhere. It seemed obvious to me that Robert had shot his wife and then himself.'

Nash paused to blow his nose and dab at the tears that were streaming down his cheeks.

'I went straight to Charlotte. She was lying on her back, her white blouse covered in blood from the knife wound,' he explained in a voice that cracked with emotion.

'Did you touch anything?' James asked.

'Only Charlotte's face,' Nash said. 'I prayed that she'd respond even though I could see she was dead.'

'So the bloody shoeprints belonged to you?'

'That's right. When I realised that I couldn't help anyone I just got out of there as fast as I could. I didn't think to check if I'd left any marks but I did throw my shoes away before I got home when I saw the blood on them.'

'Why didn't you come clean about all this before, Mr Nash?' James asked. 'You could have saved us all a lot of time and trouble.'

'I knew that if you lot found out I was there you'd assume I was responsible. And I'd have had to explain what I'd been doing behind the wall. Plus, I knew that if I went to prison it would be much harder for me to end my own life.'

James wrapped up the interview after explaining to Nash that he would remain under police guard – as well as suicide watch – while they considered whether he should be charged with any offence. Those being considered were withholding information from the police and perverting the course of justice.

'But you do believe me, don't you?' Nash said. 'I've told you exactly what happened and what I heard.'

James chose not to answer the question. He wanted to give

more thought to what they'd been told before coming to a decision.

DC Abbott played the recorded interview back on her phone as they drove to Kendal so James could use it to make notes and draw up a list of further questions he needed answers to.

William Nash's extraordinary revelations were making his heart beat at a rapid rate. What the man claimed to have seen and heard tied in with the evidence from both crime scenes and with what Neil Savage experienced before he was forced to leave Oaktree Farm on Christmas Eve.

The only thing missing was an eyewitness account of what had happened after Charlotte – Megan, he corrected himself – was actually stabbed.

It was a pity Nash had fallen down the cellar steps, James thought. But then if he had managed to get into the house minutes sooner than he did he might well have ended up dead himself.

'I'm still struggling to take it all in,' Abbott said once the recording had finished playing. 'That poor girl did not deserve what happened to her. And it beggars belief that the Batemans got away with what they did for so long.'

'That's what makes this so bloody shocking,' James said. 'It's hard to know how they lived with themselves. Between them they murdered two people and they replaced their own lost child with someone else's. It's fucking sick.'

'But it eventually came full circle, guv. The death of the child they abducted provoked Robert into killing his wife before turning the gun on himself.'

'I just wish we knew exactly how it played out at the end,'

James said. 'Did the pair exchange words while the girl was lying dead or dying on the floor? Or did Robert simply pick up the shotgun and kill his wife and then himself because he couldn't take any more and decided they'd be better off dead?'

'I'm guessing it's something we'll never know,' Abbott said.

CHAPTER SIXTY-SEVEN

James briefed the team as soon as he got to the office. There was a collective intake of breath as he relayed what William Nash had told them.

'So, in addition to solving the Bateman case we now know what happened to Simon and Amanda Roth and their baby, Megan,' DCI Tanner said.

'That's right, sir,' James replied. 'And it's all thanks to a bloke who was spying on his girlfriend through a wall.'

'And do you believe everything Nash said?'

James nodded. 'Most of it, yes. Evidence confirms he was there on Christmas Eve and witnessed what took place. And I don't believe he would have stabbed the girl – he loved her. In addition, he's connected a lot of the dots and we can now answer most of the questions that have troubled us. However, I intend to question him again tomorrow. There's one thing niggling me and that's what transpired after the girl was stabbed. He claims he heard the shots but didn't see what happened. I'm not convinced that's entirely true.'

'Any particular reason?' Tanner asked.

James shrugged. 'Just intuition. It's a bit too neat an ending. Have a listen for yourself.'

Abbott had transferred the interview file from her phone to her computer and played it through a speaker so the whole team could hear.

It generated a healthy discussion and raised lots of questions. The general consensus was that William Nash hadn't made it up, but that James was right to be suspicious about exactly how Mr and Mrs Bateman had died.

The team also agreed that Nash should be charged at the very least with obstruction of justice or withholding evidence. And a decision was taken to release the four suspects still being held in custody.

'I'll discuss with the Chief Constable how much information should be shared with the media, given that this story now goes way beyond the Christmas Eve killings,' Tanner said. 'It needs to be handled carefully and with some restraint on our part.'

James got Tanner's permission to break the news about the Roth killings to Giles Keegan. And he made a point of doing so straight after the briefing.

It came as yet another blow to the retired detective.

'It makes me sick to my stomach to know that I let them get away with it, James,' he said. 'I was really convinced back then that they had nothing to do with it.'

'No copper gets it right every time, Giles. You shouldn't let it get to you.'

'Oh, but it will,' Keegan said. 'And for the rest of my flipping life.'

*   *   *

James couldn't wait to get home. It was 7.30 p.m. when he left the station and he felt dog-tired.

At the same time a pulse hammered in his head as he tried to get to grips with the dramatic turn the investigation had taken.

A degree of luck as well as solid team work had got them to this point. If Nash had succeeded in killing himself when he crashed his van then they would still be flailing in the dark. And if he hadn't been eavesdropping on the Bateman family on Christmas Eve, he wouldn't have heard Mary spill her guts in what sounded like a fit of pique.

James ran through it all in his mind as he drove along the dark, deserted country road towards Kirkby Abbey.

He'd told Annie to expect him at about eight and he was looking forward to the stew she'd said she had prepared.

He was just over halfway there when another car drew up behind and started tailgating him. Its headlights were on full beam and James felt his hackles rise.

'Impatient prick,' he said out loud to himself as he lowered his side window, poked his arm out, and waved the other driver on.

The car was quick to overtake, but instead of surging ahead it braked sharply, forcing James to stamp on his own brake pedal.

It then stopped altogether at an angle across the road that made it impossible for James to get around.

He saw the driver jump out and rush towards him. It looked like a man but his head was lowered so his face wasn't visible.

James's first thought was that he must be a fellow officer who had a very good reason for forcing him to stop.

But as James pushed his own door open and stepped out, he got the shock of his life.

James did know him. But the guy standing before him wasn't a copper.

It was Andrew Sullivan.

And he was holding a revolver that was aimed at James's stomach.

CHAPTER SIXTY-EIGHT

James felt his insides freeze as he stared at his nemesis.

He'd recognised him instantly even though he looked very different to the last time he saw him in the flesh about three years ago.

He was wearing a baggy hoodie that covered his bald head and a thick beard coated his square chin. But the scar on his right cheek was still visible and so too were those deep, dark eyes that James had always found so unsettling.

He'd put on weight, but for a man who was approaching sixty he still looked fairly fit and threatening.

'Long time no see, Detective Inspector Walker,' he said with a crooked smile. 'Bet I'm the last person you expected to bump into.'

James felt his body grow rigid as he looked from Sullivan's face to the gun in his hand.

'Are you out of your fucking mind?' he said.

Sullivan shook his head. 'Surprised to see me? You probably thought I was no longer a threat to you, but I made it my mission to get even with you before I depart these shores.'

'Then you clearly are crazy,' James said, as he struggled to keep his panic in. 'Any sane person would have been long gone by now.'

'But I've never professed to be sane, Detective. In fact, as I recall it you described me in court as a "grade-A psychopath".'

'And now you want to kill me because you spent fourteen months inside?'

'You know very well that being banged up was only ever part of it. Because of you I lost my wife and kid. I have no fucking idea where in the world they are.'

'You've only got yourself to blame for that, Sullivan. You murdered someone and by putting you away I was only doing my job.'

'Well, that's not how I see it. I told you a year ago that we'd meet again at a time and place of my choosing. And this is it. I didn't want to have to rush it because you're the last on my list of scores to settle and I was looking forward to savouring it.'

'So, how did you know I'd be driving along this road tonight?'

'I followed you from the station in Kendal. It might surprise you to learn that I've been staying at a B&B in the town for a couple of nights. The intention was to sort you out before moving on to a little hideaway I have in Scotland. I know all about your new life in Kirkby Abbey and the plan was to drop in on you at home. But when I got there, I spotted the surveillance team outside and drove past. I clocked your car and the number plate, though, so I came up with another plan.'

'And what was that?' James asked, playing for time as he desperately tried to judge whether he could turn the tables.

'I went to the station this afternoon and saw your car out front,' Sullivan said. 'So. I parked nearby and waited. And the fact that you left so late this evening suited me perfectly because it's now dark and this road is bound to be empty for a while.'

'Then why haven't you pulled the trigger already?' James said.

'Because like I said, I want to savour this moment. It's been a long time coming, and it'll be my swansong. In a week or so I'll be on my way to Europe and then to South America. A new start. A new life. Fuck this shithole of a country.'

James saw the fire in his eyes now. He was excited, worked up. As he spoke spit flew off his lips.

'Before your lot get here I'll be swigging back whisky in my snug Scottish bolthole,' he said.

James saw an opportunity to dent his confidence and he went for it.

'Do you mean the house that you're leasing near Dumfries?' Sullivan's eyes narrowed. 'How the fuck ...'

It was James's turn to grin. 'They're waiting for you there, Sullivan. In fact, the Met warned me you might pay me a visit on your way up and it turns out they were right.'

His expression went from cocky and confident to confused. He pushed his shoulders back and was about to say something when he got distracted by the headlights of an approaching vehicle and then made the mistake of flicking his head towards it. The timing couldn't have been better for James. He saw it as the only opportunity he was going to get to avoid being shot and he went for it by lunging forward and swiping the gun with his right hand.

A shot rang out but the bullet went wide and momentum carried him forward into Sullivan, who dropped the gun and fell backwards onto the icy road.

James had the advantage and showed him no mercy. The first punch connected with Sullivan's nose and the second smashed into his mouth.

James managed to roll to one side and stand. Sullivan tried to grab his legs but James stepped back before he got a grip and then delivered a brutal kick to the forehead.

Sullivan wailed in pain and attempted to struggle to his feet. But by then James had picked up the gun and he brought it down hard on the back of Sullivan's head.

That was enough to leave the bastard writhing on the ground while James cuffed him.

As this was happening the unsuspecting driver who had saved James's life suddenly appeared on the scene.

'I'm a police officer,' James said. 'And this man is a dangerous criminal. Please go back to your car and wait until I've summoned backup.'

CHAPTER SIXTY-NINE

The first responders were on the scene within fifteen minutes. By then there were short queues of traffic in both directions.

James had used the time to lock Sullivan in his car after thoroughly searching both him and the vehicle. He left him lying on the back seat swearing and moaning about the throbbing pain in his head.

'Get used to it scumbag,' James told him. 'You've got years of suffering to look forward to when you're back behind bars.'

James put in calls to Leo Freeman and DCI Tanner to apprise them of the situation. He also rang Annie to let her know that he was running late, but he didn't tell her why. He knew that this was news that he needed to deliver in person.

It did not take long for the shock of what had happened to wear off but the adrenaline rush stayed with him. At last, his nemesis had been neutralised and it was down to the man's own stupidity. He'd been punching above his weight to think that he could easily pull off such a reckless stunt on a country road in the dark. All it had taken was a split second's loss of focus for him to come unstuck.

With patrols now on the scene both cars were quickly moved to allow traffic to flow and James handed Sullivan's gun, which he'd placed into an evidence bag, to a uniform.

Forty-five minutes after Sullivan launched his attack, he was in the back of a police van being taken to Kendal.

Unfortunately, that meant James had no choice but to return to the station so that he could make a statement and see that Sullivan was charged with the attempted murder of a police officer. He would spend the night in a cell and be formally interviewed in the morning, by which time a team from the Met would have arrived to question him about the murder he was believed to have committed in London.

When James finally got home just before midnight, he told the surveillance officers in the car across the road that they were no longer needed. They'd suspected as much, having heard what had happened on the road between Kendal and Kirkby Abbey.

'My thanks to you and the other crews for making us feel safer these past few days,' he told them.

Annie was waiting up for him, and the first thing he told her was that Andrew Sullivan had been arrested and would be going back to prison for many years.

Her response to this was to break down in tears of relief. But when he then told her how it had come about the shock hit her so hard that she had to rush to the sink and throw up.

'I can't believe he was going to shoot you,' she said afterwards. 'And right there in the middle of the bloody road.'

'I got lucky,' he said, and then told her that Sullivan's arrest wasn't the only reason to celebrate.

'We had a major breakthrough in the case today,' he said. 'Not only do we now know what happened to the Batemans. We also know what really happened at Oaktree Farm twenty-four years ago.'

CHAPTER SEVENTY

Tuesday January 2nd

James and Annie eventually went to bed at 2 a.m. but they continued to talk about Andrew Sullivan and William Nash for at least another hour.

Annie dropped off some time later, but James wasn't able to. His mind was far too active, with so many thoughts and questions demanding his attention.

Among them was whether William Nash had been completely honest with them. James didn't doubt that he had been up to the point where Charlotte – Megan – was stabbed during the struggle with Mary. But his account of what had happened after that was unfortunately less convincing.

The trouble was it was supported by the evidence. The shotgun was found in Robert's hand and the only prints on it belonged to him and Charlotte.

It was therefore only natural to conclude that it must have been a murder-suicide. But that was what Giles Keegan had done twenty-four years ago and he'd been wrong.

He was out of the door by six while Annie remained in

bed, and he promised her he would try to get home early so that they could spend the evening together to celebrate the new year and Andrew Sullivan's incarceration.

On the way to Kendal, he phoned DC Abbott and told her to meet him at the station as soon as possible.

'We're going to have another go at Nash,' he told her.

'I'll be there, guv,' she said. 'And I heard what happened last night. Are you okay?'

'I feel better than I have in a long time. Knowing that the threat from Sullivan has finally gone away is a huge weight off my shoulders.'

At the office he convened a short meeting of those who were in and various decisions were taken.

DCI Tanner and DS Stevens would formally interview Sullivan armed with James's statement and the evidence of the gun taken from him. They would also liaise with the team from the Met who were due to arrive at about ten.

Tanner had already talked to the Chief Constable and it had been agreed that a press release would go out in respect of Sullivan's arrest but they would hold back on the latest developments in the Bateman investigation until after James had questioned Nash for a second time.

Nash's doctor had been forewarned that they were coming but James had specifically asked her not to tell him.

He was awake when they entered his room and he looked as rough and pale as he had the day before.

He did not object when the doctor said the police wanted to talk to him again.

'We've come to ask you some more questions, Mr Nash,' he said, before proceeding to caution him. 'You do not have to say anything, but it may harm your defence if you do not mention when questioned something which you later rely on in court. Anything you do say may be given in evidence.'

Nash stiffened and his eyes came out on stalks. 'But I've already told you what happened.'

'We've given it a lot of thought,' James said. 'We do believe that you were spying on the family and heard what was said about events that took place in the past. But the story you told us about how Mr and Mrs Bateman died is less convincing, I'm afraid.'

'Why?'

'Well, for one thing, I'm sure they would have tried to save their daughter. After all, you said she was stabbed by accident while struggling with her mother.'

'But they didn't care about her,' Nash said.

'That's not strictly true though, is it, Mr Nash?' James said. 'Robert loved her as his own daughter, and I'm sure that Mary did too despite their difficult relationship. I can't believe they would have just let her bleed to death. And as you made it clear that even though you fell down the stairs and hit your head you still managed to get into the house within minutes, I struggle to believe that Robert decided to shoot his wife and then himself so soon after Charlotte was stabbed.'

'Well, that's what happened. I told you I heard the shots.'

Nash was becoming more agitated and his face wore a tortured expression. James could see he was on the defensive and so he kept up the pressure.

'It seems more likely to me that Charlotte was still alive when you rushed into the house,' he said. 'And I suspect they were desperately trying to save their daughter. Perhaps they were even about to phone for an ambulance. But for whatever reason you stopped them and that's why she died.'

'But that's ridiculous,' Nash responded indignantly. 'I loved her. She meant the world to me. But she was dead when I got there. That's why I want to kill myself. Without her there's no point carrying on.'

'Or it could be that the reason you want to commit suicide has more to do with guilt than grief. You blame yourself that Charlotte is gone.'

'No, no, no,' Nash cried, his face red, body shaking. 'They didn't even try to save her. She was dead, and they were arguing about what to—'

And that was it. The words were out of his mouth before he could stop them. As soon as Nash realised what he'd said he closed his eyes and pressed his lips together.

James looked at Abbott and winked. His ploy had worked and he'd managed to provoke an obviously unstable Nash into slipping up. He hadn't expected it to be so easy though.

'There's no going back now, Mr Nash,' he said. 'You've confirmed that Robert and Mary were both alive when you entered the house. Now tell us what they were arguing about.'

Nash opened his eyes and took a deep breath. 'If I'd succeeded in killing myself, I wouldn't have had to lie,' he said. 'I don't want to go to prison but I also don't want anyone to think that I did nothing to try and save Charlotte.'

'Then make us believe that, Mr Nash. Tell us what really happened.'

After a long pause, Nash said, 'The truth is that although I fell down the steps, I didn't lose consciousness. It took me less than a minute to get inside the house and when I did

379

Robert was screaming at Mary and telling her it was her fault that Charlotte was dead. And Mary was blaming Charlotte and saying to Robert that they would have to hide the body and cover up what had happened. They were thrown when I stormed in and both started yelling at me. I told them I'd heard everything that was said and that was when I saw Robert move towards the shotgun on the breakfast bar. But I beat him to it. Without thinking what I was doing I shoved the barrel up against his throat, told him what I thought of him, and pulled the trigger. Mary screamed, but didn't move, so I just turned the gun on her and shot her as well. They both deserved it. They had to pay for what they'd done. To Amanda and Simon. To their baby. And to Charlotte. *My* Charlotte. We were meant to grow old together. And they took that away from me.'

'And what happened next?' James asked quietly.

Nash cleared his throat and wiped the back of his hand across his forehead. 'I did to them what I heard them say they did to the Roths. I wiped my prints from the gun, and placed it in Robert's hand. Then I gave Charlotte one last kiss goodbye and got out of there as quickly as I could. Over the next couple of days, I started thinking about ending my own life, but for some reason I couldn't do it.'

Nash started to cry then and so James ended the interview and called the doctor. He told her that her patient might need some medication and that extra precautions would have to be taken because he was now even more of a suicide risk.

By coincidence, Nash's parents turned up just as they left the room and so it fell to James to explain to them that their son was going to be charged with two murders and that they wouldn't be able to speak to him just yet.

'William has confessed to what he did,' James said. 'So, I suggest you arrange for a lawyer to represent him.'

On the way back to the station James sent a group email to the team. It consisted of just two words.

Case solved.

EPILOGUE

EIGHT WEEKS LATER

It was a sombre afternoon in Kirkby Abbey, but at least the sun was shining.

James and Annie were among about fifty people who had gathered in the churchyard. Several reporters and a TV camera crew were also there to record the latest development in a story that the public couldn't seem to get enough of.

After William Nash's arrest came his appearance before a magistrate where he was charged with the murders of Robert and Mary Bateman. He was remanded in custody and was now awaiting a trial date.

What he'd revealed about the deaths of Simon and Amanda Roth hit the headlines a few days later and Cumbria Constabulary had already been approached by a BBC producer who wanted to make a documentary about the case.

Each of these events attracted more attention than the arrest of Andrew Sullivan, and James noted with a degree of pleasure that even his remand hearing, where he was charged with murder and the attempted murder of a police officer, failed to make it onto the mainstream news bulletins.

However, James knew that today's poignant service, during which Megan Roth had been laid to rest next to the graves of her real parents, would make the evening news.

Giles Keegan had volunteered to read the eulogy after Robert Bateman's brother said he couldn't handle it, and Keegan used the opportunity to also make a public apology on behalf of himself and the Cumbria police for not uncovering the truth twenty-four years ago. He told the assembled mourners that the skeletal remains of the real Charlotte Bateman were to be cremated along with the bodies of her parents in the coming weeks.

The ceremony lasted almost an hour and when it was over James and Annie headed for home, choosing not to go for a drink in one of the village pubs with their friends and neighbours.

Instead, they planned to start working on the baby's room in the hope that it would take their minds off what had been another dreadful day in Kirkby Abbey.

THE END

ACKNOWLEDGEMENTS

Once again, I would like to thank Molly Walker-Sharp, my editor at Avon/HarperCollins. She was my partner in crime on this book and her input was invaluable.

If you've enjoyed *The Killer in the Snow*, then why not head back to DI James Walker's first case?

A serial killer is on the loose in Kirkby Abbey. And as the snow falls, the body count climbs…

Read on for an exciting bonus chapter, exclusive to Asda...

BONUS CHAPTER

James was back behind his desk at Kendal HQ before sunrise the following morning.

He hadn't been able to stop thinking about Megan Roth's funeral. It had kept him awake for much of the night, unbeknownst to Annie who had slept like a log beside him.

He had a mound of paperwork to get through and he was hoping it would provide a much-needed distraction.

As expected, the funeral had featured on both the local and national TV news, and there was extensive coverage in most of the papers.

One paper contained an interview with Robert Bateman's brother, Todd, who said that a decision had yet to be made on the future of Oaktree Farm.

James was still finding it hard to come to terms with what had happened there. It was truly the stuff of nightmares and would be a dreadful blot on the beautiful Cumbrian landscape for many years to come.

'Morning, guv. You're in early.'

James looked up to see DC Abbott standing there smiling down at him.

'Couldn't sleep so I thought I might as well come and make a start on this lot,' he said, indicating the pile of papers on his desk.

'Great minds think alike,' she replied. 'I've got a lot of catching up to do as well. I can't believe it's still so dark outside. It's like the middle of the night.'

Abbott placed her bag on her chair and started removing her coat.

'At least we've only got to wait a couple of weeks before the clocks go forward,' she added. 'Coffee?'

He nodded, even though he'd only just finished one.

'Anything to eat, guv? I'm going to treat myself to a bacon butty.'

James shook his head. 'No thanks. I gorged on toast and marmalade before I left home.'

As Abbott set off for the canteen, James returned his attention to the document he'd been reading.

He was still ploughing through it when she came back a couple of minutes later – minus the coffees.

'I didn't make it to the canteen,' she said, her face taut and serious. 'We've just had an alert from control, and I think you're going to want to respond to it, guv.'

James felt his stomach tighten. 'Sounds pretty serious. What is it?'

'A report of a serious fire.'

'So why is that of interest to us?'

'It's the location, guv. According to the guy who called it in flames are tearing through Oaktree Farm as we speak.'

*   *   *

The pair of them headed for the farm in James's car with the siren blaring.

On the way, daylight began to penetrate the heavy cloud cover and a wind that had raged all night continued to gather strength.

'It has got to be arson,' James said, as he steered a course along the A684. 'The farm has been locked up and empty since the crime scene teams finished up there.'

'But it has attracted a lot of attention from curious folk, including tourists,' Abbott said. 'And the calls from the locals for it to be pulled down have been growing by the day.'

James nodded. 'I know. Just today there's an interview with Bateman's brother in one of the papers. He was asked what was going to happen to Oaktree Farm and he said no decision had yet been made.'

'Well, it could be that someone has decided for him.'

James recalled a conversation he overheard in The Kings Head pub about three weeks ago and it made his pulse jump.

'I was having a drink with my wife, so I didn't let myself get drawn into it,' he explained. 'A group of locals were discussing whether they should raise a petition demanding that the place be demolished. And someone, I can't remember who, actually suggested the quickest way to get rid of it would be to burn it down. At the time it didn't occur to me to take it seriously, partly because Annie thought it was a good idea. Like a lot of people around here, she believes the farm is cursed and if it remains intact it'll carry on attracting thousands of weirdos who get off on that kind of thing.'

'I can see her point,' Abbott said. 'It also serves as a constant reminder to those living around it of what happened there.'

'It's hard to disagree with that.'

'So, who was involved in this discussion?' Abbott asked.

James cast his mind back. 'Some very familiar faces actually. Kenneth O'Connor, along with Giles Keegan, and Luke Grooms, the pub landlord. Peter King, who runs the general store in the village, was also there.'

'Then if we're right and it is arson, I reckon they'll all be suspects.'

James nodded. 'I suppose so, along with thousands of other people in Cumbria.'

They were still a couple of miles from Oaktree Farm when they saw the smoke. It was being whipped into a frenzy by the wind as it curled up into the sky.

James hadn't been back there for at least a month and he cast his mind back to the layout: a stone-built house, a large wooden barn and two small outbuildings. As far as he knew the furniture had not been removed from the house and most of the Bateman family's belongings remained.

Its remote location several miles south of Kirkby Abbey made it an easy target for anyone intent on destroying it. There were no nearby neighbours, and it was set back a couple of hundred yards from the road.

According to control, a man driving past had spotted the fire at about five thirty, by which time it had already taken hold. He'd stopped his car and called the emergency services and was still at the scene waiting to provide police with a statement.

When they reached the farm, James parked in the field next to it that was reached through a gap in the dry-stone wall. A police patrol car was already there and one of the two uniformed officers told him they had arrived a few minutes ago at the same time as the fire crew who were just starting to get to work. It was already obvious that they would not be able to save the property.

Flames engulfed the house, rearing up through the thatched roof and out through the windows on both the ground and upper floors. The barn was also a raging inferno, along with the outbuildings, and the wind was showering the area with black ash and small bits of charred debris.

James was taken aback because he had never been this close to such a fierce fire. The fact that it wasn't confined to just one part of the farm appeared to confirm that it had been started deliberately.

'I've spoken to the man who phoned it in,' the uniformed officer said, pointing to a lone figure standing about twenty yards away from them. 'The guy says he saw a car pull out of the track and onto the road just after he spotted the flames and slowed down, but it headed in the opposite direction. At that point, he stopped his own car and called the three nines.'

'What can he tell us about the other car?' James asked.

'Only that it was small and white. He didn't register any other details.'

After alerting the chief fire officer to their presence, James and Abbott stood a safe distance away. As James stared at the burning buildings, he felt certain that after today Oaktree Farm would cease to exist, and that was going to please a lot of people – including Annie.

Five people had met violent deaths inside the house and a baby's body had been buried in the cellar. It seemed highly unlikely that another family would ever want to make it their home.

It took more than an hour for the fire fighters to dowse the flames and to start taking stock of the situation. The barn and outbuildings were reduced to piles of smoking wood and metal, and the thatched roof of the house was completely destroyed.

But despite that it didn't take long for the chief fire officer to confirm that the fire did not start by accident and that so far there was no indication that anyone had been inside any of the buildings.

'Petrol was used as an accelerant,' he told James. 'You can probably smell it yourself, and there are drops of it on the steps leading down to the cellar. The cellar door had been forced open and it seems our arsonist poured petrol around down there. It's my guess they also broke into the house through a window and started another fire inside, before starting on the barn and other buildings.'

But there were no obvious clues that might lead them to the person or persons responsible.

'We need to get forensics here as fast as we can,' James said. 'And we'd best start trying to trace a small white car that was almost certainly being driven by our arsonist.'

James started giving thought to how to take things forward. He decided that the obvious first step was to go straight to Kirkby Abbey and speak to the locals who had actually discussed the option of burning down the farm that evening in the pub.

He told Abbott to remain at the scene and call for back up.

'We need to be absolutely sure that there are no bodies inside,' he said. 'Once we know we'll decide how much time and effort to devote to the investigation.

First port of call for James was The King's Head. It was a hotel as well as a pub, so it was already open for business.

Luke Grooms was busy serving breakfast to the handful of guests in the small restaurant while his wife Martha was occupied in the kitchen.

'I need to have a chat with you, Luke,' James said. 'Can you spare me a minute?'

'Of course,' Luke responded, and then called on a young assistant to take over from him.

He led James to the small office behind the hotel reception desk.

'This is obviously not a social call,' Luke said. 'Is it about the fire at Oaktree Farm?'

James narrowed his eyes. 'You already know about it?'

Luke nodded. 'Everyone seems to. Three people have called me in the last hour and it's been on the local news. As far as I'm concerned it's a cause for celebration.'

James told him they were treating it as arson and then alluded to the conversation he overhead in the bar three weeks ago.

'I distinctly remember hearing one of you mention setting fire to the farm,' he said.

Luke's face registered shock. 'Are you seriously here to question me as a suspect?'

James shook his head. 'Not in any formal manner, but I can't pretend I didn't hear it and so I have no choice but to bring it up.'

Luke shrugged. 'Well, I do remember that particular get-together and, yes, we did talk about what should happen to the farmhouse. But it's been a regular topic of conversation in the bar for weeks and I've heard lots of people say it should be destroyed. I swear I didn't do it, though, and I have no idea who did.'

James asked a few more questions, including what kind of car he drove.

'It's a black Ford Fiesta – it's parked out back in the yard.'

James left it at that because his gut told him that Luke Grooms was telling the truth.

'If you do get wind of who might have done it then give me a call,' James said.

'That's something I'll have to give careful thought to,' Luke said. 'You see, whoever did it has done us all a favour. And as long as nobody has been hurt, then I don't see what the problem is.'

James went to Kenneth O'Connor's house next. The former farmhand to the Batemans was at home and claimed he had only just got out of bed. He said he hadn't heard about the fire.

After James told him it was believed to be an arson attack, he added: 'I thought something like that would happen sooner or later. To be honest, I wish I'd done it myself, but I just didn't have the guts. As far as I'm concerned the person who did it is a hero not a villain.'

He went onto say that he did not know who was responsible and vehemently denied it had anything to with him.

James didn't bother to ask him about his car because he knew he owned a dark blue Vauxhall Corsa and that it was parked in front of the property.

As he climbed back into his own vehicle, James started to think he was wasting his time and that this wasn't the best way to approach the investigation. After all, it wasn't necessarily the case that the arsonist lived in Kirkby Abbey.

He called DC Abbott and told her he'd soon be returning to the crime scene to discuss with her a better way forward.

But first he decided to pay a visit to one more of the individuals who took part in the pub discussion he overheard.

And he was glad he did because as soon as he pulled up outside the man's house, he suddenly felt sure he had a prime suspect.

Giles Keegan was busy hosing down his car which was parked on the driveway. It was the ageing Mini Cooper that James was already familiar with – small and white – and matching the description of the vehicle seen leaving Oaktree Farm that morning.

James's first thought was that Keegan could be washing it to get rid of any bits of ash that had blown onto the bodywork from the fire.

When the retired police officer saw James climbing out of his car, he released his grip on the hose's spray gun.

'Hi there, Giles,' James said. 'How are things?'

It took Keegan a moment to find his voice. 'All good, thanks. Thought it was time I gave the old girl a clean.'

Keegan clearly looked uncomfortable, and this made James all the more certain that he was right to suspect Giles.

He didn't want the guy to be the arsonist, but gut instinct and years of experience on the force were pointing him in that direction. He knew that what had happened at Oaktree Farm twenty-four years ago still haunted Giles, in particular his failure to solve the case of missing Megan Roth. It would surely make him happy to see the place reduced to rubble.

'When I heard you pull up, I thought you were Lisa Doyle,'

Keegan said as James approached him. 'She's on her way over after calling to say she had something important to tell me.'

At first James couldn't place the name, but then he recalled that she was the psychic who held a séance for Mary Bateman and claimed she had a vision of a baby.

'I'll try not to keep you long then,' James said. 'But I need to talk to you about Oaktree Farm.'

Keegan pursed his lips and put the hose down.

'I heard about the fire from a neighbour who drove past it and saw all the commotion. Any idea how it started?'

'It was arson,' James said. 'Fortunately, we have a witness who saw someone driving away from the scene. Funnily enough, the car he described was small and white – just like this one.'

Keegan frowned. 'And is that why you're here? Because you think it might be me?'

'Well, was it?' James said.

Keegan raised his brow. 'That's not funny and you know it detective.'

'I was actually being serious, Giles. In fact, I've already put the same question to two of the drinking pals you had a conversation with recently about burning the place down.'

'You've lost me there, James. I don't know what you're talking about.'

'Then let's go inside and I'll elaborate.'

But as they approached the house, James caught sight of another piece of incriminating evidence and his heart dropped. The garage door was open and just inside it on the floor was a petrol can.

* * *

'So, here's the thing, James,' Keegan said, ten minutes later when they were sitting at the kitchen table. 'What you have here is some circumstantial evidence at best. It doesn't prove I started that fire. I've told you I didn't and I'm asking you to take my word for it.'

James was finding the conversation increasingly awkward. Keegan was a friend, and they were relatively close neighbours. And even if he was guilty of the crime, he was going to be a tough nut to crack.

'I'm not the only person in Cumbria who owns a small white car and a petrol can,' Keegan said. 'I'll admit it's enough to give rise to an element of suspicion, but if you've got any sense you won't take it any further. You'll just be wasting your time and will probably make yourself very unpopular. I wouldn't want that because I like and respect you.'

'But a crime's been committed, Giles,' James said. 'And I wouldn't be doing my job if I didn't pursue every lead.'

'I completely understand that, but you will never secure enough evidence to pin this on me and I'll never admit to something I didn't do. It'd be different if someone had been killed or seriously injured, but that's not the case.'

'How can you be so sure?'

'Because I'm certain that whoever did it would have made sure the buildings were empty before setting light to them.'

James heaved a sigh. 'You were in the force long enough to know that however much damage has been caused, the forensic teams will probably turn up plenty of evidence to secure a conviction.'

Keegan smiled. 'But in this case, I suspect they won't really want to. You see, some crimes are in the public interest, James, and to my mind this is one of them. If I were you, I'd accept that.'

James was about to respond when the doorbell rang.

'That'll be Lisa,' Keegan said. 'Do you mind if I let her in?'

James got to his feet. 'Go ahead. I think that's all for now anyway. I need to think this through before deciding what to do next.'

He followed Keegan into the hall and had every intention of leaving right away. But he didn't because when the door was opened and Lisa Doyle saw him standing there her jaw dropped and she said, 'Oh my goodness. Hello, Detective Walker. This is really weird because I came to Kirkby Abbey to seek Giles's advice on whether to approach you about something. And here you are. I just hope this isn't a bad omen.'

'What exactly do you mean, Miss Doyle?' James asked her.

The woman appeared flustered and had to search for words.

'Well, it's difficult to explain, especially since I know from our recent conversations that when it comes to matters of the supernatural you are very much a sceptic.'

Keegan jumped in at this point. 'Look, come inside Lisa and tell us both what it is that's got you so concerned.'

When James finally got to leave the house half an hour later his head was spinning.

Lisa Doyle had told him about a vision she'd had in which he was standing over someone's blood-covered body.

'There was a voice too that wanted me to know that you and your colleagues will soon be having to confront another tidal wave of death and destruction,' she said. 'It was both vivid and disturbing, and I came to ask Giles if I should mention it to you.'

The conversation with Keegan had been strange enough, but the psychic's words reached another level of absurdity. At least that's what James told himself.

Hours later he learned that no bodies had been discovered in the wreckage of the farm, which came as an immense relief.

He chose not to tell anyone about his encounter with Keegan and kept his suspicions to himself. He was glad when no evidence turned up at the crime scene to incriminate him.

The investigation into the fire plodded on for weeks and got nowhere, partly because there were so many suspects and partly because no one in the Cumbria Constabulary was particularly interested in solving the case

James felt torn because he was convinced of Keegan's guilt, but decided that pursuing him would serve no useful purpose. But he refused to let it play on his mind or destroy his relationship with the man.

He also pushed what Lisa Doyle had told him to the back of his mind because he regarded it as total nonsense.

It wasn't until months later that her words resurfaced, as another bout of bloodshed descended of Cumbria.

And the county found itself once again at the mercy of a dark and calculated killer …